Praise for *The Quaker*:

'Pacy, inventive, assured – and authentic . . . a story of brilliantly crafted shifts of plot and pace . . . McIlvanney is a writer with unfolding, developing and substantial gifts'   *Glasgow Herald*

'Skilfully dovetailed . . . this is an atmospheric portrait of a dreich and seedy place in the throes of slum clearance, as well as a satisfying detective story'   *Guardian*

'An absolute master of Tartan noir . . . the corruption of the late Sixties is splendidly evoked, as is DI Duncan McCormack'   *Daily Mail*

'Atmospheric and arresting, *The Quaker* reveals 1960s Glasgow in all its lurid shades'   Val McDermid

'This is a terrific novel, dark, powerful and beautifully written. I finished it a while ago, but I'm still haunted by the characters and the place'   Ann Cleeves

'*The Quaker* is one of my favourite reads of the year. A power-house of a book with Liam McIlvanney's full lyrical powers on display. Loved it'   Steve Cavanagh

'Another atmospheric, scary and utterly brilliant book from Liam McIlvanney. Superb'   Adrian McKinty

Praise for Liam McIlvanney:

'There's nothing like a thriller done really well and *All the Colours of the Town* is a perfect example of why talented writers ought not to shy away from tackling genre novels. Noir doesn't need to be pap; this is a smart and engrossing crime novel'
Observer

'Gripping, unflinching . . . McIlvanney has flair and assurance and executes a powerful tale with all the dexterous sensitivity and ballsy swagger the subject is due'   *Scotland on Sunday*

'This is a bold, impressive debut'   *Daily Telegraph*

'McIlvanney evokes the city's dark underbelly with razor-like accuracy, and the novel roars off the page like a wild beast on the loose . . . superb storytelling, a wonderful eye for character, and a passion for dialogue; it announces the arrival of a Scots poet of the thriller'   *Daily Mail*

'McIlvanney tells the story with clarity, terrific dialogue and convincing characters'   *The Times*

'A terrific, ultra-modern crime novel . . . delivered in lyrical, emotive and often piercing prose, it's an assured and classy addition to the ranks of Scotland's crime-writing scene'
Independent on Sunday

'A distinctive and striking debut. One quality that makes the novel stand out is Liam McIlvanney's portrait of the deep-rooted tribal tensions in Glasgow and Belfast'
Times Literary Supplement

THE QUAKER

Liam McIlvanney was born in Scotland and studied at the universities of Glasgow and Oxford. He has written for numerous publications, including the *London Review of Books*, the *Times Literary Supplement* and the *Guardian*. His debut, *Burns the Radical*, won the Saltire First Book Award, and his most recent book, *Where the Dead Men Go*, won the Ngaio Marsh Award for Best Crime Novel.

He is Stuart Professor of Scottish Studies at the University of Otago, New Zealand. He lives in Dunedin with his wife and four sons.

🐦 @LiamMcIlvanney
www.liammcilvanney.com

Also by Liam McIlvanney

Burns the Radical
All the Colours of the Town
Where the Dead Men Go

LIAM McILVANNEY THE QUAKER

HarperCollins*Publishers*

HarperCollins*Publishers*
1 London Bridge Street
London, SE1 9GF

www.harpercollins.co.uk

This paperback edition 2019

1

First published in Great Britain by HarperCollins*Publishers* 2018

A catalogue record for this book
is available from the British Library

ISBN: 978-0-00-825994-5 (PB)

Set in Minion by Palimpsest Book Production Limited,
Falkirk, Stirlingshire

Printed and bound in Great Britain by
CPI Group (UK) Ltd, Croydon, CR0 4YY

MIX
Paper from
responsible sources
FSC **FSC™ C007454**
www.fsc.org

For Caleb

Surely, he walks among us unrecognized:
Some barber, store clerk, delivery man . . .

Charles Simic, 'Master of Disguises'

The houses are all gone under the sea.
The dancers are all gone under the hill.

T. S. Eliot, 'East Coker'

I
MEN AND BITS OF PAPER

'We are suffering from a plethora of surmise, conjecture, and hypothesis.'

Arthur Conan Doyle, 'Silver Blaze'

PROLOGUE

That winter, posters of a smart, fair-haired young man smirked out from bus stops and newsagents' doors across the city. The same face looked down from the corkboards of doctors' waiting rooms and the glass display cases in the public libraries. Everyone had their own ideas about the owner of the face. Rumours buzzed like static. The Quaker worked as a storeman at Bilsland's Bakery. He was a fitter with the Gas Board, a welder at Fairfield's. The Quaker waited tables at the old Bay Horse.

Some said he was a Yank from the submarines at the Holy Loch. Others said he was a Russian from off the Klondykers. He was a city councillor. The leader-aff of the Milton Tongs. A parish priest. He had worked with multiple murderer Peter Manuel on the railways. He was Manuel's half-brother, Manuel's cellmate, he'd helped Manuel abscond from Borstal in Coventry or Southport or Beverley or Hull. There were Quaker jokes, told in low voices in work-break card-schools and the snugs of pubs. The word was magic-markered on bus shelters, sprayed on the walls of derelict tenements. It rippled through the swaying crowds on the slopes of Ibrox and Celtic Park. QUAKER 3, POLIS 0. His name crept into the street-rhymes of children, the chanted stanzas of lassies skipping ropes or bouncing tennis balls on tenement gables.

And always there was the poster: IF YOU SEE HIM PHONE THE POLICE. The poster looked like someone you knew, like a word on the tip of your tongue. If you looked long enough, if you half-closed your eyes, then the artist's impression with the slick side-parting would resolve itself into the face of your milkman, your sister's ex-boyfriend, the man who wrapped your fish supper in the Blue Bird Café.

The face was clean-cut, the features delicate, almost pretty. To some of the city's older residents he looked like a throwback to a stricter, more disciplined age. A well-turned-out young man. Not like the layabouts and cornerboys who lounged on the back seats of buses, flicking their hair like daft lassies, tugging at their goatee beards.

Jacquilyn Keevins, the first victim, was killed on 13 May 1968. Strangled with her tights. Left in a back lane in Battlefield.

The Ballroom Butcher. The Dance Hall Don Juan with a Taste for Murder. The Quaker was something to talk about when you got tired of talking about football or the weather. That year of 1968, the worst winter in memory set in just after Halloween. On the first day of November a storm battered the city, shouldering down through the banks of tenements, scattering slates and smacking down chimney stacks.

On 2 November, Ann Ogilvie went out to the dancing at the Barrowland Ballroom and failed to come home. She was found two days later in a derelict tenement in Bridgeton.

On through Bonfire Night and St Andrew's Day the weather stayed bad. The football card was clogged with postponements, unplayed fixtures piling up. The posters on gable ends, where the Quaker's face had been pasted in threes as though he were a candidate for office, were pulped and defaced by the pelting sleet.

4

All winter, people wrote to DCI George Cochrane and the Quaker Squad at the Marine Police Station in Anderson Street. The letters waited on Cochrane's desk each morning. People wrote to denounce their friends and neighbours, relatives, enemies. The Quaker's names were Highland, Lowland, Irish, Italian. Sometimes the writer was anonymous, sometimes the letters were signed. As December wore on, the missives came in the form of Christmas cards, festive scenes of horse-drawn carriages and starlit stables bearing the names of evildoers in righteous capitals. A team of detectives followed these up, chasing the names across the map of the city.

The city itself was changing, its map revised by the wrecking balls. Slum clearance. Redevelopment. Whole neighbourhoods lost as the buildings came down. Streets cleared. Families dispersed. Some went to the big new schemes on the edge of the city but most of them left. They lit out for the coastal new towns or further afield, to Canada, the States, they took ship as Ten Pound Poms for Adelaide and Wellington. New lives in sunny elsewheres, the grime of the tenements left behind.

For those who stayed, it was the winter of the Quaker. There was no escape from the blond side-parting and the crooked smile. Like a slew of frozen mirrors, the posters threw back to the city its half-familiar face. Men with short fair hair, men with overlapping teeth, men with the thin slightly sensuous lips of the artist's impression would find themselves scrutinized in pubs and restaurants, underground carriages. Glancing up from the *Evening Times* as the bus took a bump they'd catch the fierce, unguarded stares of their fellow citizens. Whispers rasped around them, neighbours monitored their movements. Cards were issued by the Chief Constable to men who matched the wanted man's description: *The holder of this card is certified as not being the Quaker.*

Another big storm hit the city on 25 January. Burns Night.

The morning after the storm was when number three was found, torn and sprawled in a Scotstoun backcourt, like something ransacked by the wind. Marion Mercer's unwitting smile joined those of Jacquilyn Keevins and Ann Ogilvie on the splashes of the *Record*, the *Tribune*, the *Daily Express*.

Jacquilyn Keevins. Ann Ogilvie. Marion Mercer.

And then, in the weeks since Marion Mercer, nothing. The murders that had gripped a city stopped. The days ticked past, the weeks turned into months. With the warmer weather it was hard to keep the killings in mind, that wintry horror. The frenzy ebbed. The air began to clear. Suddenly it was six months since the Quaker's last killing. The prospect that he might strike again was like the memory of last year's snow: you couldn't picture it. There were queues once more outside the dance halls. Bouncers rocked on their heels outside the Plaza and the Albert. Women stood in line for the coat-check in the Barrowland and the Majestic. Blue-tuxedo'd band-leaders cracked jokes about the Quaker before leaning in to the mic for the next slow ballad. The university cancelled its night-bus service for female students. The city was moving on, looking out. News items from the wider world – riots in Belfast, the Kennedy bother at Chappaquiddick, One Small Step for Man – displaced the local stories in the *Tribune* and the *Record*. A new decade was coming, new money, new buildings going up along the central streets, citadels of glass and steel. Dead, imprisoned for another crime, or living somewhere else, the Quaker was fading from the city's sense of itself, dwindling to a whisper, a half-forgotten melody.

Only the shirtsleeved men in the Murder Room at the Marine Police Station in Partick kept at their task. In a fourteen-by-ten upstairs room, they stalked the Quaker through box files of witness statements. For months these men had been trying to piece it together, searching for motive and meaning in rubbled

6

backcourts. Three endings. Three bodies. Crumpled and sprawled, dumped like rubbish. *I thought it was a mannequin, a tailor's dummy. It looked like a bundle of rags. An old coat or blanket.* No one ever thinks that it's a body. A woman. Someone with a book half-read, a favourite song, bitter secrets, a patch of eczema behind her ear.

Then the newspapers started to turn. Detectives who had been the subject of reverent profiles – George Cochrane pictured in his mackintosh and trilby, gripping his pipe like a Clydeside Sherlock; Chief Constable Arthur Lennox in his pristine blues, flanked by a portrait of the queen – found themselves discussed with scoffing brusqueness. An element of black humour crept into the coverage. The papers had fun with the notion of CID men brushing up their dance moves as they mingled with the punters at the Barrowland Ballroom. In July, the *Tribune* ran an old photo of the Quaker Squad detectives at the scene of Jacquilyn Keevins's murder, walking three-abreast down Carmichael Lane, looking for clues. The picture had a caption: *Romeo, Foxtrot, Tango: The Marine Formation Dance Team.*

JACQUILYN KEEVINS

Everyone thinks that I changed my mind and that was what got me killed. Shaking their heads at my folly or at the capriciousness of fate. As though changing your mind was so terrible. As though I should have known better. But I didn't change my mind. I told Mum and Dad that I was going to the Majestic – they were right about that – but that was never the plan. I was going to the Barrowland all along.

I was going to the Barrowland because I was meeting a man.

The shoes that I'd bought in Frasers the previous Saturday were pinching my toes as I walked down the hill to the bus. I was wearing an emerald green crepe dress I'd just re-hemmed. The dress was sleeveless and my arms felt cool against the satin lining of my coat. I was conscious of my perfume – Rive Gauche – filling the lower deck of the bus and I remember noticing that the conductress had a ladder in her tights, all the way down the inside of her left leg, and thinking that she ought to have a spare pair in her bag.

Why did I lie to my parents? I'm not sure. I think it was to make it more complete. The secret, I mean. The man I was meeting was called William. He was tall, with good hair he was forever running a hand through, and strong slim forearms under folded sleeves. I hadn't known him long. There was something distant about him, something reserved. I wondered if maybe he'd turn out to be married but I didn't care. It had been a long time since someone had asked me out. The boy was the problem. Wee Alasdair. Just turned six. It puts them off, a kid does.

I got off the bus at Glasgow Cross and walked up the Gallowgate to the Barrowland and joined the queue under the green-and-red neon. Once I'd checked my coat in the foyer I climbed the stairs to the ballroom. That's the bit I loved, climbing towards everything, the music suddenly loud and the dancers whirling into view. I hurried the last few steps and the ballroom gulped me in. I felt safe there, secret, in the darkness and the lights.

I bought a bitter lemon at the bar and took a seat at a table so that people knew I was waiting for someone.

I lit a cigarette and looked at my watch. William was already fifteen minutes late. Benny Hamlin and the Hi-Hats played 'Boom Bang-a-Bang' and I was cross because I always liked to dance to that. I lit another cigarette, watched the smoke drift up towards the shooting stars on the ceiling.

By half-past nine I knew he wasn't coming. My bitter lemon was finished and I'd smoked all but two of my cigarettes. I remember how angry I felt, close to tears, not because he'd stood me up but because everything was spoiled, the night and the dress and the music and everything. I was sorting my lipstick and getting ready to leave when a shadow fell on my handbag and stayed there. When I turned and looked up, there he was. The lights from the stage were behind him and I couldn't really see his face. I'd forgotten how tall he was, how well-spoken.

'I'm so sorry I'm late,' he said. 'May I still join you?'

That's how he spoke. He offered me a cigarette and lit it with a nice gold lighter but he didn't take one himself. He didn't smoke, just carried a pack for occasions like this.

He bought me another bitter lemon and got another pack of Embassy Filter from the vending machine and draped his raincoat over a vacant chair. He had a nice woollen scarf that he folded and placed on the chair beside him. He was really good looking with his sharp jaw and his straight nose and his short fair hair in a neat side shed. He wore a regimental tie and a brown chalkstripe suit. Stylish. I couldn't stop grinning, leaning in to get my cigarette lit, resting my hand on his hand as he held the flame.

The music was loud so it was a struggle to talk but he asked me about my day and he spoke about his job. I wasn't really listening so much as just enjoying his voice, Glasgow but sort of refined, not like your typical city neds, whining out of the sides of their mouths like someone letting air out of a balloon. He was different altogether. A lot of the guys you'd see in the Barrowland were hard men, or thought they were, always spoiling for a fight. I'd see them in the Vickie on my night shift, carting their sore faces into A&E. I want to say that they didn't look so clever right then, with their faces gaping open, but the truth is they looked every bit as clever – or every bit as dumb – sitting there with their shirts drenched in blood, pleased as punch, already working out how they'd tell it to their mates. William was different, he seemed older, more sophisticated, somebody who knew things. Good dancer, too.

We left at half-eleven and walked down the Gallowgate to where he'd parked his car. Outside in the streetlights he looked younger than he had in the ballroom. He was twenty-five, maybe twenty-six, though he acted a little older than he was. Even so, I was older by five or six years and I liked it, it made me feel more in control.

His car was a sleek white affair, quite new-looking. He held the passenger door for me while I settled myself in the red leather seat, then he closed the door before walking round to the driver's side. I leaned against him when the car turned a corner and looked up into his face but he stared straight ahead and kept his hands to himself. He was talking away about decimalization with this earnest look on his face and when the car stopped at a red light I started poking him in the ribs, trying to get him to laugh if nothing else. It was nice he was such a gentleman but he needed to relax a bit. Nothing was going to happen anyway – it was my time of the month – but you'd want some fun from a night at the jiggin.

We got out of the car and he walked me to the close-mouth. And now, when we stepped into the darkened close, it all seemed to change, like a switch had flicked. He caught me by the shoulders and pressed his mouth against mine, hard, so that my head bumped against the wall of the close. About time, I thought. Then his hands were busy and his breathing got loud.

'Not here,' I told him. 'Come on.'

I took him down the hill to the lane behind Carmichael Place. I was laughing to myself, because it was like I was fifteen again. This was where you would come with boys, after the pictures or church socials, this is the place you'd winch a little before you went home. I hadn't been down here in fifteen years, but it was still just the same, the garages and the garden gates.

It was dark in the lane, away from the lights. The ground

is all grassy with stones jutting out – not cobbles but ordinary stones, sharp and uneven, and my heel caught on one of the stones and I clutched at his arm, fell against him, really, and I remember I was laughing, I couldn't stop laughing, it all seemed so funny and my mouth was locked open in this soundless laugh and that's when he hit me in the mouth.

At first I didn't know what happened. I thought maybe I'd slipped and bumped his shoulder or maybe someone had come running out of the lane and burst right between us and knocked me out of the way. I staggered backwards and clattered into the double doors of a garage, they rattled and shook. I raised my fingers to my mouth and took them away with something dark and glistening on them. That's when I looked up and saw him stumping across the lane with his fist raised high. I screamed then but I needed to swallow first and the scream was kind of thin and half-hearted and he stopped it with another punch and there was a kind of judder like you were bumping downstairs and then the ground was scraping my face and I looked up with the eye that could still open and he was standing over me, tugging loose his tie and sawing his head back and forth as he did it.

That was all. Now my father looks like he will never smile again, like he's forgotten the language of smiling and he's suddenly old, old, old, he's a wee small leprechaun, The Incredible Shrinking Man, his collars gaping, his jacket sleeves hanging down past his knuckles, and my mother walks around in a Valium trance. They try to put on happiness for Alasdair's sake but you can't fake it, a child isn't fooled. The boy knows that something's wrong and of course he thinks it's his fault.

They worried, when I was out in Germany, Mum and

Dad. Anything could happen in a country like that. They were so pleased when I came home, back to the flat in Langside Place, to the numbered buses and the local shops, the streets where nothing bad could happen. It's hard for them to face the truth: I would have been safer in Germany, in that cramped Army house in Bad Godesberg, tramping through the rain to the NAAFI store.

There are things we need to remember. I tell them to Alasdair, lying weightlessly beside him on the narrow single bed, wishing I could smell his skin. I pour them into his ears while he sleeps and I tell myself that when his eyelids flicker – his transparent eyelids with the red veins down them and the long blond lashes – then the words are getting through. I tell my boy about himself. How he used to be scared of the coalman with his leather apron and his grimy face. How, when I leaned over to say goodnight, he would play with my hair, twist it in his fingers. He did that whenever he was tired. Sitting on my lap, leaning back against my chest, he would throw his wee arm up and clutch at my hair. Now he'll forget. There'll be no one to remind him that he did that. Or that he liked the Monkees. Or that he shouted 'Lollo!' when a lorry went past or called a helicopter 'Uppatuptup'. My folks won't remember. They love him, but they won't remember those things and it seems hard to think that they'll be lost.

What could matter more than this? Not revenge, certainly; not catching the man. People think the murdered dead are chewed up by hatred, lusting for vengeance, we can't rest till our killer is caught. I couldn't care less. If a man is hanged in Barlinnie Gaol or locked up in Peterhead for the next fifteen years will that help Alasdair sleep at night? Will it give me back my sense of smell?

For a while I thought I was different from the others.

14

Better. Less to blame. I was the first. I had no way of knowing that he even existed. But the others, the second girl and the third: when they walked up those stairs to the noise and the lights and the shooting stars, they knew. They knew a man had picked up a woman on that dance floor and taken her home and killed her. But they went anyway.

And then I saw I was wrong, I was kidding myself. I knew he was out there too. I knew it all along. We all do.

1

DI Duncan McCormack sat at a desk in the empty Murder Room. It was the dead time between shifts. The night shift had knocked off at seven; the day shift wouldn't start till eight.

McCormack was early, on a point of principle. You're planning to sit in judgement on a group of your colleagues, you better be early. You better show them all the respect you can.

He lit a cigarette. This early, the Murder Room had a churchly peace. He hadn't turned on the lights, and the morning sun threw a soft gloss on the hooded typewriters and the glass ashtrays and the grey metal bellies of the wastepaper baskets. It was the usual shabby office, with its jumble of scuffed desks and unmatched chairs and olive drab filing cabinets, but for McCormack such rooms could be magical places. Mysteries were solved here. Murders redeemed. Lives that had been turned upside down could sometimes – with work and skill and the needful visitation of luck – be righted.

Luck, though. Luck wasn't a word you associated with the Quaker case. Nothing about this case had been lucky.

He rose and crossed to the one long wall that was free of shelving. There were maps here with coloured push-pins marking the murder scenes. There were photographs of three women, the familiar before-and-after shots. You couldn't look from the oblivious smiles to the sprawled bodies without your stomach dropping. Without feeling personally guilty.

He stopped in front of one of the smiles to acknowledge his own share of guilt. He had worked this one, the first one. Jacquilyn Keevins. Down on the South Side. In the spring of last year. A botch job, a case that was jiggered from the first. Mistakes. Dud intel. Sloppy direction. They'd wound the thing up after only two weeks. Then came Ann Ogilvie over in Bridgeton, and Marion Mercer out west in Scotstoun. That's when they knew for sure they were dealing with a multiple. That's when the legend started to form, the dark tales and rumours – a whole city in thrall to the arrogant, Bible-quoting strangler that the papers dubbed the Quaker.

And that's when the Quaker Squad set up shop in the old Marine, the nearest station to the Mercer locus. And this is where they'd been ever since, as the weeks turned into months and the man from the Barrowland Ballroom refused to be caught.

And now, just to add to the fun and games, they had Detective Inspector Duncan McCormack on their backs. On secondment from the Flying Squad, McCormack was tasked with reviewing the Quaker investigation, learning lessons, making recommendations. Everyone knew what this meant. Scale the thing down. Scale it down before we squander more money. Get us all out of the mess we've made.

McCormack was turning from the photos on the wall when the telephone rang. A shrill, tinny jangle in the silent room. He looked at the door as though someone might burst in to answer the phone and then gingerly, frowningly, reached for the receiver.

'Murder Room. McCormack.'

He felt like a butler in a play. Someone playing a part. There was a soft rasping sound, a kind of shadow-laughter, then the moist, masticating clicks of a man preparing to speak. 'No nearer, are you?'

'Say it again?'

'You're no nearer catching him. After all this time.'

The voice was local, Glasgow. Nicely spoken. Fifties, McCormack decided. Possibly older.

'Can you tell me your name, sir?'

'A year you've had. More than a year. Some people might view that as careless. Wasteful, even.'

'Sir, do you have information you'd like to impart?'

'Impart?' The soft laugh. 'I'll impart all right, son. I'll impart the name of the man who did it. How's that?'

'On you go, then.'

'Michael Ferris. Michael Ferris is the bastard you want. F-E-R-R-I-S, 12 Dollar Terrace, Maryhill. Are you writing this down?'

'Thank you for your help.'

McCormack put the phone down and turned to see a shape in the doorway, broad shoulders blocking the light. Big shaggy head of blond hair. Goldie was the detective's name. McCormack had pegged him early as a loudmouth. Blowhard. Also, he thought he knew the guy from somewhere.

'Christ, mate. I never heard you come in.'

Goldie rocked on his heels. 'Michael Ferris?'

'How did you know?'

Goldie shrugged. 'It's the same nutjob. Phones every three or four days.'

'Right.' McCormack nodded. He smiled his crooked smile. 'Look, I don't think we've met properly. I'm Duncan McCormack.'

'You think we don't know your name?' Goldie didn't

appear to see the proffered hand. 'You think we don't know who you are?'

'Should I take that as a compliment?'

'Well, it's the closest you're gonnae get in this room, buddy.'

'Fair enough. It's fucked up, this whole situation. I get it. But look, mate. We all want the same thing here.'

'Really?' Goldie chewed his lip. His fists were plunged in the pockets of his raincoat and he spread his arms. 'You want to get on with catching bad guys? Like, you know, proper police work? Because I thought you wanted something else.'

You could rise to it, McCormack thought. Or you could take a breath, see the job through, write your report and be done with this shit. File this fucker's face for future reference. Make sure he gets what's coming at some point down the line.

'I want what we all want.'

'Right. My mistake,' Goldie was saying. 'I thought you were here to grass us up. Do your wee spy number.'

McCormack smiled tightly. Do you know James Kane? he wanted to ask. James Arthur Kane, the man who ran Dennistoun for John McGlashan? The man who just landed a twelve-stretch at Peterhead? That James Kane? I put him away. I did the police work that nailed him. He's the fourth of McGlashan's boys that I've nailed in the past year, while you've been shuffling your lardy arse in this shitty room. Filing papers. Sticking pins in a corkboard.

But he said nothing and now Goldie was smiling. 'You don't even know, do you?'

McCormack tried to keep the tightness out of his voice. 'Don't know what, Detective?'

'Where you know me from? Jesus Christ. We worked the first one together. Jacquilyn Keevins.'

'Right. Right. Of course.'

It was true. That's where he'd seen him. How had he missed

it? McCormack cursed his own stupidity. It was as if one lapse of memory proved Goldie's point – there was only one detective present.

Goldie jabbed himself in the chest with a stubby finger. 'And I'm still working it. Me and the others. What are you doing?'

'I'm doing my job, Detective. Police work. Same as you are.'

'Naw, Inspector. Naw.' Goldie's teeth were bared in a sneer, eyes bright with scorn above the bunched cheeks. 'Naw. See, you cannae be the brass's nark and do good police work. Know why? Because good police work doesnae get done on its own. You need your neighbours to help you. And who's gonnae help you after this?'

He was using 'neighbours' in the special polis sense, meaning your partners, the guys you shared a station with. McCormack watched as Goldie tugged his cigarettes and lighter from his raincoat pocket, tossed them on the desk. Goldie was whistling under his breath and fuck this, McCormack decided, enough was enough.

'You know a guy called James Kane?' he asked.

'Yeah, yeah.' Goldie was hanging his raincoat on the hat-rack. 'You put one of Glash's soldiers away. And that gets you a pass? Maybe in your book. In mine, you need to turn up every day. Be a polis. Earn it all again.'

McCormack shook his head. Be a polis. The fuck would you know about that? McCormack had his finger raised to jab it at Goldie when he heard the smart rap of heels in the corridor.

'What's the score here?' The boss, DCI George Cochrane, was on the threshold, tall and thin and oddly boyish in his belted gabardine. He read the battle stance of Goldie and McCormack. 'The hell's going on, DS Goldie?'

'Friendly discussion, sir.' Goldie smiled, still looking at McCormack. 'We're all friends here.'

'Fine. Let's keep it that way.' Cochrane bustled through to

his own office, spreading the cherry scent of pipe tobacco. At the ribbed glass door he paused. 'And Goldie? We'll be doing some parades with Nancy Scullion over the coming week. Drop by her flat this evening, would you? Check what times she'll be free.'

'Sir.'

Goldie took his seat. McCormack crossed to one of the big sash windows, unsnibbed it, hooked his fingers in the metal lifts and tugged it open. The smell of the river came in on the breeze; the Clyde met the Kelvin just south of the office. He thought about Nancy Scullion. He'd heard the name a lot around the office. If the Murder Room was a cult, its High Priestess, the Delphic Oracle of the Marine Police Station, was Nancy Scullion. Sister of the third victim, she had spent the evening of 25 January in Barrowland Ballroom with her sister and the killer. He sat between them in the taxi on the way back to Scotstoun, where the sisters lived just a few streets apart. Nancy was drunk, blootered, smashed on gin and Babycham, but she'd heard him banging on about caravan holidays in Irvine, growing up in a foster home, getting verses of the Bible off by heart.

Nancy's description was holy writ. It was the tablets of the law for the men at these desks. They parsed it and probed it, took apart its description of a well-dressed modern man, with his short fair hair and his neat raincoat, his gallantry and his hair-trigger temper. Good manners. Nice diction. A cut above the common ruck of East End hoodlums and toughs. A golfer, no less, whose cousin had recently scored a hole in one. Polite but masterful, a man of strong views, who called for the manager when the cigarette machine malfunctioned and forced him to refund Nancy's money. A man who spoke darkly about sinful women in the taxi back to Scotstoun. Who professed to spend his New Year's Eves in prayer while the rest of the world gave itself over to drink and hilarity.

McCormack knew it all. After barely a week he knew the details about as well as if he'd been here all along.

Brown chalkstripe suit, regimental tie. Thick watchstrap. Embassy Filter. Overlapping two front teeth. Suede boots. Dens of iniquity. Woman taken in adultery. Hole in one.

This was the litany and these men blitzed it. Every man on the squad had criss-crossed the city, chasing these leads. In a hundred barber-shops these detectives had traded nods in the mirror with gowned customers as the barber slipped his scissors into a breast pocket and took the artist's impression in both hands. At specially convened meetings of city golf clubs they watched the blazer-buttons wink like coins as the members passed a laminated image along the rows. They took the picture to all the tailors on Renfield Street and Hope Street. They went to the churches, chapels, gospel halls of all denominations, spoke to priests, lay preachers, ministers. They visited dentists' surgeries, asked permission to sift their records.

And nothing worked.

The man with the short hair and overlapping teeth, the smartly dressed dancer in the desert boots whose cousin scored a hole in one, the zealot who quoted scripture in the back seat of a taxi, the man who raped and killed Jacquilyn Keevins and Ann Ogilvie and Marion Mercer; that man remained a ghost.

Now, as the day shift straggled in, hooking their fedoras on the hat-rack, shucking out of their blue raincoats, McCormack felt something like pity. This was the prime gig, the career-making case, and it had all turned sour.

There was a smell in the room, a brassy tang beneath the sweat and cigarettes. The smell was embarrassment, McCormack decided. They're sore at having their shortcomings and befuddlement exposed to an outsider, the brass's nark from

St Andrew's Street. But it was more than that, too. They were flat out affronted. With the details they had. All the specifics. That litany of ties and teeth and Old Testament imprecations.

Every man in that squad had made arrests on not a tenth of what they had to go on here. So what had gone wrong this time? How had they failed so badly? These were the questions that hung in the air and DCI Cochrane seemed to sense them as he stubbed his Rothmans out in an ashtray and slapped his hand on the side of a filing cabinet to bring the room to order.

We haven't been thorough enough, he told them. We haven't been systematic. We missed something the first time round and we need to put it right.

There was a pile of buff folders on top of the filing cabinet, maybe twenty-five or thirty. Cochrane turned and gathered them awkwardly in his arms and leaned over to drop them on the nearest desk.

'These are men we spoke to after one and two. After Keevins and Ogilvie. Men with records. Sexuals. We may have been too hasty to rule them out. I want you to roust out these individuals, bring them in. We'll see what Nancy Scullion makes of them.'

McCormack looked along the line and caught Goldie's eye. Goldie shook his head and looked away.

Cochrane clapped twice, chafed his hands together. 'Right. Now let's divvy these up and get cracking.'

The men shuffled forward and each lifted three or four folders, carried them back to their desks.

Ten minutes later Goldie went out for a piss and McCormack sidled over to his desk, started leafing through the folders. He pulled one out. A sorry-looking soul called Robert Kilgour, forty-two years of age, whose vulpine face seemed faintly familiar. Kilgour had been released from Peterhead in '67 after serving two years for a sexual assault carried out in Mill Street

24

in the East End of Glasgow, about a mile south-east of the Barrowland Ballroom. He'd been interviewed after the first killing, and it was McCormack himself – he remembered it now, and here was the sheet, rattled out on his own trusty Underwood – who'd grilled him in his Cowcaddens flat. Kilgour had a solid alibi – he'd been visiting friends in Ayrshire on the night of the killing and stayed overnight in Kilmarnock – and they'd ruled him out pretty quickly. There was nothing much more in the file, just a record of Kilgour's flittings. He'd moved around a lot in the past eighteen months. His current address was in Shettleston – a tenement scheduled for demolition.

Goldie was back, standing by the desk, hands on his hips. McCormack looked up. 'When you get round to this guy here' – he tapped the Kilgour file – 'let me know. I want to come along.'

Goldie glanced down at the file, back at McCormack. He dragged his chair out with a scrape, thudded down into it, jockeyed it closer to the desk. 'Your funeral,' he said.

2

The sky-blue Vauxhall Velox came nosing round the corner into the empty street. In the closemouth of a gutted tenement, Robert Kilgour watched it pass, gravel crackling under the tyres, the two men hunched on the front bench-seat, the slim passenger, heavyset driver.

Kilgour moved from the shadows towards the open air. He stood in the doorway, watched the pink taillights floating in the dusk. He pinched the bridge of his nose and his fingers came away wet, dripping, he shook the sweat from them. Framed in the back windscreen he could see the two heads in silhouette, twisting to look. They would know he couldn't have got far. Another fifty yards, another hundred they would stop, turn and come back. He had to move now.

He tried to remember the layout of these streets. His own flat was only three or four streets away but he had run blindly when he spotted the parked Velox as he crossed to his building. As he ran he'd been aware of nothing but the sound of the car's engine and now he was lost. It was barely three weeks since he'd moved to this district. They kept knocking bits of it down. Every time you went out there was another gap-site, another missing street, you never knew where you were.

Across the street was a block of empty tenements. It struck Kilgour that there was another dead street beyond this and then maybe the main road. Buses, bars, shops. People. Places to hide.

He took a breath, closed his eyes for a second, tugged his sweat-soaked shirt away from his chest. Then he left the close-mouth at a sprint, running low with his hands up around his head, as though fearful of falling debris. Without looking he knew the car had stopped. There was a hollow crunch as the driver found reverse and a veering screech as the car swung round. Kilgour made it into the building across the street, feet slapping through the echoey close and he heard the engine's angry rasp as the driver found first and ramped up through the gears.

Emerging into the dark backcourt Kilgour heard the car suddenly louder, the engine's whine stretching as the car took the corner and gunned down the straight.

He'd been heading straight across the backcourt but now he sheered off to the left, nearly slamming into a metal clothes-pole. The hard-packed earth was strewn with bricks and rubble and his ankles flexed and buckled as he ran. He ran with his hands out in front of him, feeling for clotheslines and other impediments in the gathering dark and soon a black wall reared up in front of him. He scrambled on to the roof of a midden, hauled himself on to the wall and dropped down into the next backcourt.

He kept running, weaving from side to side like a man dodging bullets. He couldn't hear the car, the only sound now was Kilgour's own breathing and then his running foot kicked something, a tin can that sparked and rattled over the broken ground, splitting the night like a burst of gunfire. When he reached the next wall and struggled on to the midden he was losing heart, his legs were heavy, the fight was draining out of him.

Before him was a big patch of waste ground: bricks and rubble, puddles catching the last of the light. He raised his eyes and saw the squat low outline, a building shaped like a shoebox.

Kilgour slipped over the wall. He drew his sleeve across his brow and picked his way through the rubble. His knees almost gave way as he pushed through the double doors.

'Did you win?' The barman was smiling as he passed him his change.

Kilgour stared at the red stupid face.

'What?'

'The race you were in, did you win it?'

Sweat was dripping from Kilgour's brow on to the bar-top, spotting a beermat. McEwan's Export: the Laughing Cavalier, with his foaming tankard of ale. Kilgour shook his head and slipped the change into his pocket and tried to still the tremor in his leg.

He was sick of running. He'd been running – one way or another – for over two years, since he'd walked out of Peterhead on a wet spring morning with his worldly goods in a black BOAC flight bag. He was sick of moving, changing flat every couple of months. But what could you do? It followed a pattern. For a while things would go well in a new flat. Then someone would place him, make the connection. And then it would start. Dogshit through the letter box. Catcalls from the local kids. Crude words scrawled on his door. Rocks through the windows. Getting jostled in the street. That's when he'd look for another place.

You could change your name, but why give them the satisfaction if you hadn't done anything wrong?

He heard the pub doors rattle. He didn't look round. He stared down at the bar-top and in the vertical black groove of a cigarette burn he saw the gable end of a building, a dark street. He saw a woman on the pavement, sitting up now, clutching her throat, choking, retching, her torn blouse hanging open, her skirt shucked up around her waist. Her face was pink and gorged, her eyes bulging and bloodshot, swimming in tears. A rope of snot and saliva swung from her upper lip. He remembered the burst of pain in his head and the ground swinging up to smack him, and a dead weight on his back, a man sitting astride him, forcing his arm up his back. He'd lain there, oddly placid, with his face pressed to the gritty street and the weight on his back until the siren drew closer and gulped to a stop and a pair of black boots filled his line of vision.

Now he watched in the whisky mirror as the burly man shooed the barman away and the thin man shook his head.

Kilgour wiped a hand down his face. The same hand reached for the whisky and then pulled back. He reached into his jacket pocket for his smokes and then changed his mind. The cops watched him. He could see his own face in the gantry mirror, sick and scared, the features obscured by the 'FIN' of 'FINEST SCOTCH WHISKY'. He looked bad, he was sweating, the hair at his temples in damp little spikes.

Then his leg started again, his right leg shaking, the knee joint flexing. He reached out for a drink and his hand knocked the glass, whisky pooling on the sticky bar-top. When he bolted to the Gents he could sense them coming after.

'Robert Kilgour?'

Piss and carbolic. The bare lightbulb flaring in the scuffed steel of the trough.

'Kilgour,' he said. The cop had pronounced it to rhyme with 'power': Kilgour rhymed it with 'poor'.

'Why did you run?'

The fat cop had backed him up to the trough.

'Why did you run, Kilgour?'

Kilgour glanced at the other cop, the tall one. He was still looking at the tall one when the fat one kicked his legs from under him and Kilgour slammed on to the dark concrete, his elbow cracking on the floor, the back of his head catching the lip of the trough. Then the fat one reached down and hauled him up like a bag of chaff and dumped him into the trough. Kilgour waggled his arms for balance, his hands paddling in the piss and running water, he felt the cold wet soaking into the arse of his trousers. He struggled to his feet, wiping his hands on the front of his jacket.

'How did you know it was you we were looking for?' The tall one had a different voice, softer, not a city accent. Kilgour felt the old injustice welling up again and fought to keep the tremor from his voice.

'It's always me. Ever since that lassie on the south side. The Keevins lassie. It's always me you're looking for.'

Kilgour's hand was in his pocket again. The fat one leaned forward and Kilgour flinched but the man gripped Kilgour's wrist and yanked his hand from his pocket. The cigarette packet flipped out and landed on the tiled floor. The two-tone red stripe: Embassy Filter. The cops exchanged a look.

'Smile.'

Kilgour looked up, uncertain. His eyes slid to the tall one, *Who is this lunatic?* and the fat one stepped forward and gripped Kilgour's jaw in the V of his right hand, thumb and fingers compressing the flesh. 'I told you to smile. You fucking nonce. Don't you know how to smile?'

He released his grip. Kilgour's lips drew back, exposing his teeth in a queasy sneer. They were ordinary teeth, nicotine-brown, averagely crooked.

'Good enough.' The fat one tugged the cuffs from his jacket pocket. 'Turn round.'

The cuffs went on. As they frogmarched Kilgour through the pub they passed a table of four men, near the door. Dominoes. Boiler-makers. Metal ashtray needing emptied.

'Hey!' One of the men was on his feet, a stocky man in a grey suit jacket. Pocked face. Rangers scarf. 'Hey! What's the score here? Ah'm talking to you. Hi! Fuckin' Zed Cars.'

The cops stopped. The fat one nodded for the other to take charge of Kilgour and rocked unhurriedly up to the table. He had two or three inches on the man with the scarf.

'You've got something to say?'

'The boy done nothin',' the man was saying. 'Mindin' his own fuckin' business. You think we didnae see that?'

'Just like you, eh? Mindin' your business.'

The man snorted. 'Fuckin' police state youse are runnin'.'

The cop stepped back and pointed at Kilgour. 'You know this guy? Is he a friend of yours?'

Rangers scarf kept his eyes locked on the cop's. 'I know he was minding his own fuckin' business. Till you cunts started.'

'Uh-huh. OK. The missus kick you out or something? Is that what this is about? You needing a bed for the night?'

The man glowered, said nothing.

There was a whisky and a half-pint of heavy on the table in front of the man with the scarf. The cop leaned forward and tipped the half-pint over, just pushed it with three fingers in an oddly camp gesture. 'Tsk, would you look at that.' The liquid spread across the tabletop, spilled over the edge in three ropy columns, spattering the lino. 'I've gone and spilled your drink. That was clumsy.'

'Bud, leave it.' The man's friends were grabbing his sleeves, pulling him back down into his chair. 'Leave it, Bud. It's not worth it.'

The cop took up the whisky glass and poured it on to the floor, raising the glass smartly as he poured so that the whisky formed a long golden string that hissed on the lino. He replaced the glass on the table, upside down, his fingertip resting on the base.

'My advice? And I say this in a spirit of reconciliation and public service. Be like your friend over here. Mind your own fucking business.'

Outside on the pavement, Kilgour found his courage. 'Youse huckled me for the last one. No remember? You've done me already. I'm in the clear.'

The night air was cool on their forehead and cheeks.

'This time's different.' A big hand pushed Kilgour towards the car, the Velox parked on the waste ground. When the hand gripped his shoulder, Kilgour tried to shrug it loose.

'How's it different?'

The thin one had the door open and the heavy one bundled him into the car.

'This time there's a witness.'

3

'Sandy's what she said.' DCI George Cochrane dragged a chair from a vacant desk and straddled it, crotch splayed. He rubbed two hands up and down his face. 'Sandy. Fair. Light-coloured. I don't know how else to say it.'

They were in the Murder Room at the Marine, maps on the wall, boxed statements on the shelves, the sun already burning in the high sash windows. Photos pinned to the board behind Cochrane's head. The victims' smiling faces. The victims' naked bodies.

Jacquilyn Keevins. Ann Ogilvie. Marion Mercer.

'Flaxen.' Goldie couldn't help himself. 'Straw-coloured, sir. Pale blond.'

Cochrane twisted a finger into the corner of his eye. He gave no indication of having heard Goldie. 'Jokes you can do.' He nodded heavily. 'Acting the clown. Catching killers? That's the tricky part for you boys, right? The fucking hotshots.' He stood up sharply and the chair scraped on the floor. 'Scottish Crime Squad. Fucking Flying Squad. What's the matter, they don't teach you how to read witness statements?' Goldie said nothing. Cochrane tugged his shirt away from his chest, blew down its front. 'Sandy, she said.'

Goldie shifted in his chair. '*She* said.'

'Meaning what?'

'The doormen tell it different, sir. The manager, too. Mid-brown, maybe darker. And the boy and girl, the couple, who came forward after the first one; they had him mid-brown, too.'

'We've been through this, Detective. She's the witness.'

'Plus the height. The doormen call it five-eight, nine. Not six foot.'

'She's the one shared the taxi with him. She's the one was in his company for most of the night.'

Goldie cleared his throat. 'She's the one too pissed to know her own name. Her *own* colour of hair.'

Cochrane turned his back, stared at the wall, the map of the city. 'He says you punched him,' he said.

'What's that, sir?'

Cochrane kept his back to them. 'Kilgour. Your suspect. The nonce. He says you assaulted him.' Cochrane turned. 'What's Boy Wonder going to say about that, hmm? How's that gonnae look in his report?'

Goldie shrugged. The question was put to Goldie but it was McCormack who had to answer it.

'DS Goldie behaved professionally throughout the arrest.'

'It's not going into your wee report? When you tell the brass how we're doing it wrong?'

McCormack said nothing. He figured Cochrane had a right to be aggrieved. He had watched his biggest case, the case that would define him, become a slow-motion nightmare. Three women murdered and still no one charged. Months slipping past, the task getting bigger, not smaller. There were thousands of fair-haired men in this city, tens of thousands, men between twenty-five and thirty-five, men with overlapping teeth. Men who matched the photofit, the artist's impression. Men who smoked Embassy Filter. But the papers didn't get any kinder as time went on and the pressure from the brass didn't slacken. If Cochrane was sore he had every excuse.

The suspect, Kilgour, had been held in the cells overnight. There was a magistrate's court attached to the Marine and the cells were often busy. They'd given Kilgour a mate, put him in with a fairy they'd lifted on Kelvin Way. Cold white tiles. A shitter with no seat.

They'd arranged a parade for the morning. Nancy Scullion, sister of the third victim, Marion Mercer. At 10 a.m. a squad car picked Nancy up from her work – she was a secretary at Harland and Wolff's – and took her to the Marine. Ten minutes later she was being driven back to Govan. She'd walked down the line of men, looked at Cochrane and shaken her head. In the foyer, she told Cochrane, 'You think it's number four, don't you? It's not really like him.' Kilgour was number four. Kilgour went home. Kilgour was a waste of everyone's time.

Now Cochrane had his hands behind his head, fingers laced, his teeth bared in a bitter grin. 'You know what they're calling us? The fucking papers?'

The two men knew. Everyone knew. But Cochrane told them anyway.

'The Marine Formation Dance Team.' Cochrane smiled. 'Cute, eh? Fucking clever.'

The Quaker Squad had been haunting the city's dance halls for the past year, brushing up their dance skills, mingling with the punters, looking for the man with the overlapping teeth and the regimental tie, the short fair hair and the desert boots. It was easy to spot the cops: they were the ones watching the men, not the women.

'I'd say we've never seen anything like it, but even that's not true.'

35

The two detectives nodded. They knew what Cochrane was talking about. It was Manuel all over again. Another dapper killer. Peter Manuel. Another stain on the city's name. Ten years back. Cochrane had worked it. Goldie too. McCormack was too young.

'Happening again, sir, isn't it?' Goldie grimaced.

McCormack remembered. He'd been too young to work it but not too young to remember. The crowds outside the High Court during the trial, men and women in their good clothes, wee boys climbing on the High Court railings. He was working in C Div at the time, lodging with Granny Beag in Partick. Manuel was convicted of seven murders, confessed to eight more. They hanged him on 11 July. McCormack's birthday. Waking up in Granny's flat, coming through for breakfast, the present on the kitchen table, the radio on, Granny Beag sitting in her quilted dressing-gown and fur-lined slippers, a lit cigarette in the ashtray, they announced it on the radio. *Sentence of execution was carried out on Peter Manuel in Barlinnie Prison at one minute past eight this morning.* McCormack unwrapping the parcel. *His body was buried in an unmarked grave in the prison grounds.* A watch, a Rolex Tudor with a leather strap, the watch he still wore.

Cochrane stood up, dragged the chair over to the other desk, rested his hands on its back. 'Sometimes I think it never stopped.' He sighed out some smoke. 'Him down in Manchester. Brady. He's one of ours, too, God help us. Pollok boy. You got a minute, McCormack?'

'Sir.'

McCormack followed Cochrane into the narrow office next to the Murder Room. He closed the door behind him.

'Did he hit him?'

'Like I said, sir, DS Goldie behaved professionally.'

'Ah fuck it. Guy's a nonce. Who gives a shit. Had your boss

on the phone.' Cochrane was stubbing his Rothmans in the ashtray, jabbing it into the scuffed red metal.

'You're my boss.'

'Your real boss. DCI Flett. Wants to know how long we're planning to keep you. When we might be able to spare you.' McCormack rode the little punch of irony on the last two words. Cochrane had stopped jabbing the cigarette butt and now he folded it over on itself, pressing down hard with the ball of his thumb. 'Told him you're playing it close to your chest. Any thoughts, though? How long this might take?'

'Few more days. Another week, maybe.'

'Then we learn our fate.'

Cochrane moved round the desk to stand beside McCormack. McCormack could smell something carious under the older man's tobacco breath, a rottenness that made him breathe in shallow sips. Above the height of four feet, the wall of Cochrane's office was frosted glass through which the torsos of the day-shift detectives floated like clouds.

'No slackers here.' Cochrane nodded through the glass. 'No shirkers, Detective.'

McCormack took this to mean that there were no Roman Catholics in the Murder Room. Thinks I'm a Prod, McCormack realized. Probably thinks all Highlanders are Wee Frees.

'Busy bees.' McCormack nodded. 'Work rate's not a problem, clearly.'

The word 'problem' tilted the atmosphere in Cochrane's office. He felt Cochrane giving him the stare.

'What do you suppose it might be then, Detective? The "problem"?'

'You'd know that better than I would, sir.'

'Uh-huh. Right. Well. You find out what it is, you let me know. First cab. Understood?'

McCormack watched the white shapes, avoided Cochrane's

37

gaze. 'You'll see the report, sir. It'll come to you. In the normal course of things.'

'Normal course of things?' Cochrane kicked a wastepaper basket as he stepped right up close to McCormack. The clouds drifted in the Murder Room. 'This isn't the normal course of things. This is you parachuting into my station to stitch me fucking up. Me and those boys out there. Tell the CC how we fucked it up. How you'd have done it better.'

'We're all on the same side here, sir. We all want him caught.'

'Is that right? You've been a polis how long, McCormack? How long you been on the force?'

'Thirteen years, sir.'

'Twenty-seven.' Cochrane slapped his own chest. 'Twenty-seven years. You make a lot of friends in that time.'

'This a threat, sir?'

'It's a statement of fact, Detective. I've got three years to go. Three years till I've done my thirty and I'm out. You're not gonnae fuck that up for me, son.'

Back in the Murder Room, McCormack tried to focus on the report he'd been reading, a press statement in Cochrane's lurid prose: *The man we are seeking is a man of dark urges and lawless drives. He may keep irregular hours. Anyone with inform—*

'That for my benefit?'

Goldie had appeared beside his desk.

'What?'

'The wee performance back there. Backing up a fellow officer. Look at me: I'm a good guy after all. One of the lads. That what that was about?'

McCormack shook his head. The whole Kilgour thing had been a stunt, he realized. It was Goldie declaring that McCormack and McCormack's review could take a fuck to themselves. It was also a test. Goldie had known that Kilgour

38

would complain. He'd known that Cochrane would want to know what happened. If McCormack backed up Kilgour, well, what do you want from a rat? If he backed up Goldie he was weak as piss.

'Got one or two things on my plate just now, Detective. One or two concerns. Am I on Detective Sergeant Goldie's Christmas card list? That's not one of them.'

'Well, that's handy.'

Goldie had a smoke in his mouth, fumbling in his pockets for a light. The cigarette bobbed up and down under Goldie's muffled curses. McCormack watched him for a few seconds then produced his Dunhill lighter, sparked it angrily.

'Here.'

He lit Goldie's then he lit one of his own. They stood smoking, watching the river, not talking. A minute ticked past.

'Fucking cheek on him, but.' Goldie was studying the end of his cigarette. 'Moaning about the press.'

'They're not on his case?'

'They're on his case, aye. But maybe he should stop holding press conferences every five minutes.'

McCormack said nothing. Goldie was right. Cochrane had run to the media with every development, however slight. His line was that they should use it to their advantage, the media interest. Keep feeding the papers little tidbits. The *Record* and the *Express* were like a daily door-to-door to every household in the city.

But the papers needed something to write about between killings. They needed an excuse to put the artist's impression on the front page, the half-smiling clean-cut killer, limned in pencil. They needed 'QUAKER' in a forty-point Tempo, stark black print on the off-white pulp. And when there was nothing else, when there were no 'developments', they wrote about the Murder Squad. Their failings, their wasted efforts.

39

How Long Must We Live in Fear? Will the Dance Hall Butcher Never Be Caught?

'Think we'll get him?'

'We?'

'You. Us. Whatever.'

'Will we fuck. We were beat from the start. The first one did it. The Magic Stick. That's what screwed us. Should have got him then.'

McCormack felt the rebuke. Jacqui Keevins was the first victim. She'd been at the dancing, the Majestic Ballroom on Hope Street. The Magic Stick, everyone called it. The cops went there the following night, team-handed, put her photo up on a screen, asked for patrons who'd been there the night before to come out and talk to them in the foyer. A bloke recognized her, said he'd danced with her at the start of night but lost track of her later on.

The cops were stoked. This was the early break you always look for, the sign that you're on the right track. Too bad the guy was making it up. Too bad he was a bullshit-merchant, attention-seeker. By the time he came clean it was too late. When the truth emerged – Jacqui Keevins had been at the Barrowland, not the Majestic – two weeks had passed. The trail was cold.

'So. What you planning to do?'

McCormack flicked his cigarette end out of the open window. 'I'm planning to keep my eyes open. I'm planning to review the evidence. Write an honest report.'

'Right. Shut us down, you mean. Put us out of our misery.'

'Not my decision, Detective.'

'At least look us in the eyes when you shaft us, eh? Give us that much.'

4

McCormack woke with a weight on his chest, the blankets damp and tangled. He struggled up, the headboard clacking against the bedroom wall. His hand scrabbled in the drawer of his bedside cabinet, found the inhaler. Two deep puffs and the panic subsided. His hand reached blindly out, dropped the inhaler back in the drawer.

He banked the pillows behind him and lay back, tugging the covers away from his sweating legs. The sound of his breathing, normally no sound at all, rasped in his ears as though he was snorkelling. It's OK, he told himself: the bad part is over. He craned round to see the luminous green hands on Granny Beag's alarm clock: nearly ten past four.

The night air felt cold on his shins. He stripped his T-shirt, mopped his armpits and the hollow at his breastbone, balled the damp garment and tossed it into a corner.

With the panic over, a sense of shame rose in its place. There was no need for these theatrics, though he knew well enough where his panic came from. It came from the nights in Ballachulish, nights when he'd wake to the clamour in his parents' bedroom, his father choking and hacking and the calm

41

yellow tone of his mother's voice talking his father through it. The sounds his father made were like those of a suffering beast – wild, rending cries and heaving snuffles that shuddered through the darkened house. Then McCormack would hear the bedsprings creak as his mother got up to come downstairs and boil the kettle. She would fill a bowl with hot water and Vicks, and McCormack's father would hobble down to sit at the kitchen table with a tea-towel over his head, inhaling the vapours he hoped would flare his passages, bring some air to his crusted lungs.

McCormack's own asthma was inherited, but from his mother, not his father. What destroyed his dad's lungs and brought him to a hard, slow death with a basin on his lap was working at the British Aluminium Company's plant in Kinlochleven. Willie McCormack worked in the furnace room, one of the big men – six-footers all of them – who spent their days crust-breaking, tapping, changing the anodes. You couldn't see a yard in front of your face, the air soupy with dust and fumes, and a noise like Hades. They learned later that the fumes contained sulphur dioxide and something called 'polyaromatic hydrocarbons', but no one at the time had heard of such words. When his father died the cause of death was listed as 'pulmonary obstruction', but what really killed him was British Aluminium.

McCormack found a fresh T-shirt in the dresser. He filled a glass of water at the kitchen sink and then stood at the living-room window. Some folk thought being a policeman was dangerous work. The choice in Balla was the plant at Kinlochleven or the Balla quarries. McCormack's grandfather – his *seanair* – worked in the slate quarries all his days. It was hard, dirty work – not as hazardous as the aluminium plant, and not a patch on the mines – but it was dangerous too. Dynamited rock could shoot out crowbars like javelins if they

42

were carelessly left in. A guy standing next to McCormack's *seanair* was killed that way.

The last quarry closed in 1955 but McCormack had already left for the city. Coming south to join the City of Glasgow Police was like coming up for air. McCormack left the Highlands to escape the dust and smog and grime, the sound of the hooter four times a day. Glasgow was the Dear Green Place, a city of parks and boating ponds, the Botanic Gardens, the bowling greens of Kelvingrove.

It was a city he knew fairly well, his mother's city and – even more – his granny's city. Granny Beag had grown up in Ballachulish, but she married a lowlander called Thomas Beggs, a welder in the shipyards, and flitted down to Glasgow, where McCormack's mother grew up, meeting McCormack's father at a dance at the Highlanders' Institute. Granny Beag was a short woman, not much over five feet tall, though her sharp tongue and guardsman's carriage gave her the presence her stature belied. When McCormack was young he misheard 'Granny Beggs' as 'Granny Beag' – that is, 'little granny' – and the name stuck. For Granny Beag, Glasgow was like the Highlands without the kirk ministers and the stink of fish. You could meet people from all over the Gaeltacht, not just from your own village, and you could hear the language spoken whenever you fancied, in the Highlanders' Institute or the Park Bar. And you needn't see a minister or a kirk elder from one year's end to the next unless you sought them out.

When her daughter married a Ballachulish man and moved back to the village, Granny Beag was dismayed. The real Highlands – or as much as you wanted of them – were right here in Glasgow, in the tenements of Partick and Maryhill. She took her revenge by encouraging her grandson to come down to the city whenever he liked. McCormack spent whole summers at the flat in Caird Drive. The old woman was lonely – the welder had died shortly after the war – and it pleased her to have a young man in the house, a boy she could pamper and feed. She taught him Gaelic songs and told him stories of the village in the days of her youth and showed him off to the shopkeepers on Dumbarton Road. When his mother remarried and moved down to London with her new husband, McCormack spent more and more time at the flat.

Towards the end, when Granny Beag was dying of lung cancer, she told McCormack she was leaving the flat to him. Her daughter was well provided for, thanks to her new husband, and she wanted the place to go to McCormack. 'It'll be a base for you when you're down in the city, and maybe you'll end up working here. And it'll be a place,' she said, avoiding his eye, 'a place where you can bring people back.' *People*, she said, as if she'd known all along, as if she'd worked it out.

McCormack moved in straight away. When he finished training and started as a constable in C Div, he bussed it to work from the Caird Drive flat. He changed nothing, kept all of Granny Beag's furniture, her old-fashioned copper pots and the cream-coloured crockery with the green trim. He drank in the Park Bar, went to concerts at the Institute, played shinty for Glasgow Mid-Argyll. He was becoming what she'd wanted him to be all along, the choicest specimen of Caledonian manhood, an urban Highlander.

Now, as he stood looking out at the city, he wondered if he'd come far enough. Maybe he should have followed his mother to London, a real city, a world city, where nobody bothered if you were a teuchter or a taig or anything else. Maybe there was still time. Maybe if he did a good job here he could think about getting away, apply to the Met, get off down to London or further afield. Half the population of

Glasgow seemed to be clearing out; another Highlander more or less would never be missed. He rinsed his glass under the tap, turned it upside down on the draining board and padded back to bed.

5

The train rocked to a halt. Alex Paton looked up from his paper and wiped a little porthole in the window's condensation. There was an advert painted on a gable at the far side of the platform – UNCLE JOE'S MINT BALLS KEEP YOU ALL AGLOW – and he knew at once where they were. This was Wigan. This was properly north, where you started to feel you were nearly home. He put aside his paper and leaned back against the headrest, closing his eyes. The station announcer's voice was muffled by the glass. It was now, Paton reckoned, 1963 or 64. No man on the moon. His father still alive in the single end on Hopehill Road. Bloody England hadn't yet won the World Cup. The doors slammed, the whistle blew, and the train hauled off on its journey north. By the time they rolled into Glasgow Central in three hours' time it would be 1959.

It was always 1959 in Glasgow and Paton was always nineteen. The ten years since he'd left for London fell away and the old life came back. He was Swifty from the Fleet, even the way he walked came back. The train from Euston was a time machine. You knew, of course, that life carried on in your absence but it was hard somehow to credit it. Glasgow would always be Glasgow, the sooty city where time stood still. Although, three hours later, as he shook himself awake with the train approaching Central, it was clear that this was no longer true. They were passing the Gorbals. Or where the Gorbals once stood. Now the Gorbals was a great bald prairie of mud. A single gas-lamp stood like a stunted tree and behind it rose the high flats, storey on storey, towers crowding each other with their broad square shoulders. They seemed to block out the light. He had to press his cheek against the window and crane right up to see the hard flat top of the nearest tower.

He checked his watch: plenty of time. He was back in Glasgow to look at a job. He lived in London now and he did jobs mainly in commuter towns in the stockbroker belt. Kent. Essex. He was good at what he did and seldom short on offers. You had to be selective, though. Paton never worked with the same crew more than twice, and he never did more than three jobs a year. He preferred a small number of big jobs to a large number of small ones. He also preferred not to work in Glasgow. In fact, you could call that a rule – in so far as rules applied to his line of work. But big jobs had been thin on the ground just of late and this Glasgow thing had seemed worth a look.

Now, as he folded his paper he wasn't so sure. They said the ones who lasted longest were those who kept their work and home life separate. Don't shit in your own nest. But was it still your nest if you'd flown it ten years back? Maybe in that case what mattered was the length of people's memories, whether or not they still remembered you.

In the compartment, passengers were pulling on raincoats and gathering their bags. Paton liked to travel by train. When he came back to Glasgow – which wasn't often – he took the slow train, not the express. He liked the rhythm of the journey, the carriages filling and draining and filling once more as local people made their short commutes and the train climbed up through the accents of England, through Oxford and the Midlands, up through Lancashire and Cumbria. Then over the border, Dumfries and then home.

Home? Paton pulled his holdall from the overhead rack as the carriage clanked across the Clyde and shunted under the great glass canopy of Central.

They remembered him all right. When his phone rang last week it took less than a second to place the voice. Dazzle from Hopehill Road. Stephen Dalziel. They'd known each other since they were six years old. They lived in the same street, went through St Roch's together, ran in the Fleet, tanned a few sub-post offices, shared their hundred days of borstal. 'Hoosey,' Paton remembered with a smile; that was what you called it; *Daein' hoosey*. They got tattooed on the same day at Terry's: a lion rampant on the shoulder for Dazzle; a wee swallow on the back of each hand for Paton. They hadn't spoken in ten years but Paton could picture the dark-brown eyes, the yellow shine of Dazzle's buzzcut, the purple acne scarring round the mouth. A job had come up, Dazzle told him. A job requiring particular skills.

Before the train had properly stopped, Paton had his arm through the pull-down window of the door, wrenching the handle.

He walked out briskly, the holdall tight to his side. The concourse was quiet. He left the station by the Hope Street exit and walked up Waterloo Street. At the junction with Pitt Street he flagged a cab and gave the driver the address of a small hotel on Argyle Street.

The sun was out for once, and the men on Bothwell Street had their jackets slung over their shoulders, hooked on one finger. It didn't look too shabby, the old place, not when the sun was shining.

The desk clerk at the Parkside Hotel was a fat, pale youth with thinning Brylcreemed hair. Paton paid in advance, letting the clerk glimpse the crisp English banknotes in his wallet. A radio was playing in the back office and a vaguely cabbagey smell was coming from somewhere.

'Up from London?' the clerk said. The flesh of his neck bulged over the tightly buttoned collar. Paton wanted to reach over and flip the top button with his finger and thumb, let the pressure off those veins.

Paton nodded.

'Long journey, sir.' The clerk pursed his plump lips. 'You'll be tired.'

Paton nodded. He scooped his key from the desk and turned to go.

'Could I arrange for something in the way of relaxation?'

Paton stopped. He bounced the key in his hand a couple of times. 'What did you have in mind?'

The clerk saw that he'd made a mistake. His eyebrows dropped. A pink sliver of tongue came out and wetted his lips. 'Something from the bar, perhaps. A wee reviver? Small whisky?'

Paton held the clerk's wavering gaze. 'I'll take a rain check on that.'

His room was on the second floor. A bed, a desk, a spindly chair. A tiny etching on the wall showed the spire of the university through the trees of Kelvingrove Park. He crossed to close the curtains. He opened the wardrobe to the silvery jangle of coat-hangers and hung up his jacket and trousers and shirt and lay on the bed in his Y-fronts and vest. There were still two hours before Dazzle's driver was due to pick him up. A walk in the park? A swift half in one of the teuchter pubs on Argyle Street? In the end, he dozed on the candlewick bedspread and studied the cornicing.

*   *   *

'You'll see changes, all right.' They were driving through Anderston, heading west. The pillars of the new motorway bridge loomed up in the darkness. The driver had introduced himself as Bobby Stokes.

'How do you know Dazzle, then, Bobby?'

Stokes frowned. 'I don't. Not really. I know him through Cursiter. Cursiter's the muscle. You'll meet him.'

They passed the Kelvin Hall on the left-hand side, the Art Gallery looming on the right.

'So what's the job?'

Stokes took his time overtaking a bus. Paton thought he hadn't heard. Eventually Stokes said, 'Better let Dazzle fill you in on that.'

'I get it.' Paton wound down the window to flick his cigarette-end. 'You're the driver.'

The driver took him to a tenement block in Scotstoun. Two flights up. Dazzle answered the door and showed them through to the living room where a great bear of a man in a brown leather jacket was squeezed into a chair at a round Formica-topped table. Paton and Stokes joined him. It looked like a card game without any cards.

'You've met Bobby,' Dazzle said to Paton. 'This is Brian Cursiter.'

The big man put his hand out as if for an arm-wrestle. Paton shook it. There was a bottle of White Horse on the table and a stack of upturned tumblers. Paton reached for the bottle and filled out a measure of whisky.

Dazzle rose and went through to the kitchen, returning with a four pack of tinnies, McEwan's Export. He passed them out.

Paton sipped his whisky, set his glass on the table.

'OK,' he said. 'Fill me in. What's the mark?'

'Glendinnings.' Dazzle pulled the ring on his beer-can and

the contents fizzed over: he clamped his mouth to the opening and slurped.

'The auctioneer's? They still on the go?'

'What, you think the world stops because you've fucked off to London?'

The others laughed. Paton sipped his whisky and waited. Dazzle wiped his mouth with the back of his hand and started to explain the job. Glendinnings was an old-school auction house in the city centre. It was also, according to Dazzle, the agent for a forthcoming contents sale. Big house in Perthshire, one of the shooting estates. The owners had died; now the son in London was selling it off, lock, stock and barrel. There were some paintings that had the valuers excited – a Raeburn and an early Peploe – but the good stuff was the jewels. Diamonds, mainly. Pearls. Bit of gold. They had an insider, a girl in the office. Cursiter knew her. (At this point the big bloke tipped two fingers in a mock salute.) The plan was to hit the place a week from now, just after midnight on the night before the sale. The nightwatchman was sixty-something, ex-army, bad hip, walked with a limp. Sometimes the firm gave him a short-term deputy in the run-up to a big sale. The stones would be in the safe in the MD's office.

'What about access?'

Dazzle smiled and jerked his head towards Cursiter, who was slouching down in his seat and working his fingers into the ticket pocket of his jeans. In a minute he was holding up a Yale key between his thumb and forefinger. It looked like a pin in his massive hand. He snapped it down on the desk.

'Basement door,' he said, grinning. 'We just walk in at midnight. No fuss. No drama. The night before the auction.'

Paton sipped his whisky.

'Bath Street, right?'

'Aye.'

51

'So it's central. Good chance of being spotted. Some busybody clocks a light.'

'It's all commercial, though,' Dazzle said. 'Round there. There's nothing residential for five or six blocks.'

'And the security's just the two bodies – we're sure about this?'

They all turned to Cursiter 'That's max. Could be just the old fella on his own.'

'Do we have a plan of the building? Do we know the layout?'

'Jenny'll get one.'

Paton nodded. The others said nothing, they were waiting for the verdict. He twisted his whisky glass on the tabletop, turned back to Cursiter. 'This your girlfriend?'

'Who?'

'Your insider. The secretary.'

'She's the cashier. No, she's not my girlfriend.'

'You've fucked her, though, right?'

'Yeah. I mean, twice. Three times.'

Paton was nodding. 'So they can link to you from her.'

'Naw, that's—'

'And they can link to us from you.'

'No! Look. It's not like that. Nobody knows.'

'Nobody knows what – that you fucked her?'

'That's what I'm saying.'

'Explain it to me. What's your name – Brian? Explain it to me, Brian. How did you meet her?'

Cursiter looked at Dazzle; Dazzle nodded. Cursiter planted his elbows on the table. 'Jenny McIndoe she's called. Nice lassie. She does the day-job at Glendinnings but works nights in a hotel out near Drymen. Used to have lock-ins. I took her upstairs a couple of times.'

'When the bar was empty?'

'What?'

'You said nobody saw you. You took her upstairs when the bar was empty?'

'Not empty. But nobody knew who I was. It was just mugs. Old guys from the village. Some hikers maybe. They didn't know me from Adam.'

'And you never met her outside the hotel?'

'Never.'

'Who said romance was dead? And how did she know you were in the market for information, Brian? Information about jewellery auctions. Since nobody knew who you were.'

Cursiter shrugged. 'We got talking.'

'Yeah.' Paton drained his whisky. 'That's what I figured.'

The others were quiet. There was a scratching at the inner door, the high tragic whine of a lonely dog.

Paton smoked his cigarette. 'She know what kind it is?'

'What kind what is?'

'The safe. What make.'

'I don't know. Does it matter?'

Paton looked round the table. 'Well, you boys certainly know your business.'

'Fuck you then.' Cursiter reared back, one arm swinging loose behind his chair. 'Mister Bigtime fucking London. You don't want in? There's the door.'

'Hey, now. Come on.' Dazzle was on his feet. Paton was grinning at the floor and shaking his head, stubbing his smoke out in the ashtray. He stood up, lifted his jacket.

'Well, come on, Dazzle.' Cursiter was pouring himself another shot. 'We need this kind of attitude? We need this kind of shit?'

'Nice meeting you fellows. Mr Dalziel: I'll see you again.'

Paton was ruing it all. The trip from London, the hotel room, wasting time with these losers. Ice heist at an auctioneer's? A sub-post office was more in their line. Screwing meters. Fucking bubble-gum machines. He shrugged into his jacket.

53

'Hold on, Alex. Brian.' Dazzle was pointing at Cursiter. 'Number one: shut the fuck up. You're not running this job: I am. Number two—' he pointed at Paton – 'Alex: hear the man out. You've come this far.'

Paton picked at something on the shoulder of his jacket. He shrugged, took his seat, reached for his smokes. 'What's the take, then?'

'Big.' Cursiter was still rankled, touchy. 'Big. Don't worry about that.'

'They might be different things, friend. Your idea of big. My idea of big. You got a figure?'

'Hundred grand. Minimum.'

They all looked at Paton.

Paton smoked.

'We'd need another man.'

Dazzle frowned, looked around the others in turn. 'It's a four-man job, Alex. It's all worked out.'

'Is it?' All the glasses were empty now and Paton stood up and moved them into the centre of the table. 'Stokes is in the car, right?' He moved one of the glasses to the edge of the table. 'The rest of us go in through the basement door. We need a man on the door. In case someone decides to stick their nose in.' He lifted another glass and smacked it down in the centre of the table. 'We move down the corridor and deal with the watchman. Lover Boy here' – Cursiter was the whisky bottle, and Paton slid it along the table a foot or so – 'stays with the watchman. Or watchmen. That leaves Dazzle and me.' Paton pinched the final two glasses between his finger and thumb and lifted them with a trilling click and placed them down at his side of the table. 'We go on to the office. I do the safe. Dazzle's spare, in case something comes up. Troubleshooter. But we need another man on the door.'

Dazzle looked at the other two with his eyebrows raised and

Cursiter pouted and Stokes shrugged and Dazzle spread his arms. 'Fine, Alex. Good. We get another man. Anything else?'

'Aye.' Paton moved the glasses back to their original positions. He sat down and reached for the bottle and filled his own glass. He pushed the bottle into the centre of the table. 'The timing's wrong.'

'Timing's not – there's no leeway, Alex. Stuff only gets there the day before. It has to be the tenth.'

'I don't mean the date. I mean the time. We don't go in at midnight. We do it in the morning. Before anyone arrives.'

Cursiter reached for the bottle and filled the glasses and waited for Paton to explain.

'You don't need all night to do a safe. Do it in half an hour if you can do it at all. We're wearing boiler suits, toolbelts, we're a crew of sparkies, plumbers, whatever. When it's over we walk out the front door, to the van parked down the street. This way, we're only over the railings on the way in, not the way out. Cuts down the risk.'

Stokes was playing with the zipper on his Harrington jacket, running it up and down. 'So, you're saying we wear masks? Is that the idea?'

'No masks. We don't need masks. We're a crew of workies. We're four guys in boiler suits. We're invisible. We're not trying to hide, we're not skulking about looking dodgy, so no one's paying attention. It's like four cops: you remember the uniform, you don't remember the faces or the hair or anything else.'

At this point the door handle clanged and the kitchen door swung open. The dog came skidding triumphantly into the room and stopped, its head raised, abruptly self-conscious, like a bull entering the bull-ring. It looked at the faces and trotted straight over to Paton and plumped its chin down on his thigh, twitching its brows. Paton drew his hand across the animal's head, feeling the smooth curved cap of the skull under the fur, and flattened the ears. Then he scratched the loose skin under the dog's jaw and the tail whacked against the carpet.

'Looks like we've found the fifth man,' Dazzle said.

Paton stroked the dog as he talked.

'We need a van. We need walkie-talkies. We need boiler suits, workboots, toolbelts. Balaclavas. We need some sort of decal or paint job on the side of the van, Such-and-such Electricians or Plumbers.'

Dazzle was writing it down. He finished with a flourish and tossed the pen down on the table.

'Right. Fine. We'll get to it.'

'Van's the priority.'

'Fine. We lift one on the night before the job. Easy.'

Stokes shook his head. 'I like to know what I'm driving, Daz. How it handles. You don't want surprises.'

'So drive it around on the night. Get the feel of it. A van's a van.'

Paton was still clapping the dog. He rubbed its belly and the creature emitted a high voluptuous whine. 'Stokes is right,' Paton said. 'You don't steal a van on the night before a job. Use your head, Daz. The owner gets up for a piss at 2 a.m., opens the curtains to check on his van. The van's gone. He reports it stolen. Patrol car clocks it parked in Bath Street at six in the morning. We're fucked before we start. You don't do a job in a stolen van.'

'What, then?'

'We buy one. Now. Tomorrow. Give Stokes time to drive it, break it in.'

'We *buy* it. *We* buy it?' Cursiter was incredulous. 'You're that keen to go about buying vans, it comes out of your end.'

Paton looked at Dazzle. Dazzle shrugged.

'You planning to walk home, are you?' Paton turned to Cursiter. 'After the job. Take a bus? Maybe wait for a taxi? We buy a van, it comes out of everyone's slice. If the payoff's what you say it is, it won't make any difference.'

'Aye but there's other outlays, overheads.'

Paton waited. The other three exchanged a look. Dazzle spoke.

'He means McGlashan.'

Paton had moved to London before John McGlashan took over from Eddie Lumsden. He knew who McGlashan was. He just didn't see the relevance.

'You've got your own arrangement there. That's your business, you do what you like with your share. Dazzle: you call another meet in three days when you've got the gear ready, the plan of the building. Not here, though. We meet someplace else.'

Paton scooped his cigarettes from the table and stowed them in his jacket pocket.

'Actually, hold on here.' Cursiter's big hand was raised. 'We all kick in for the van but you don't kick up to Glash?'

'The van's a necessity. It's part of the job.'

'McGlashan's a necessity, mate. McGlashan's a fucking necessity. Round here.'

'I don't live round here, Brian.' Paton buttoned his jacket. 'I live in London. Mr McGlashan will have to visit London if he wants to collect.'

'He might do that,' Cursiter said. 'He might just do that. Everyone kicks up to McGlashan, fella. Sooner or later. Some way or other.'

Paton shrugged. The dog got up and trotted across the floor and lay down in front of the dead electric fire.

'So you're in?' Dazzle's chin lifted in challenge. Everyone looked at Paton.

Paton frowned. He'd been looking for a reason to say no and he couldn't find one.

'Kinda looks that way, doesn't it?'

'He-e-ey!' Dazzle snatched up the whisky and twirled off the cap, but Paton clamped his palm across his glass.

'One thing.' He looked at each face in turn and then back to Dazzle. 'Why's McGlashan not moving on this himself? Why's he leaving it to you boys?'

For a moment nobody spoke. Paton had the feeling they had discussed this question before he came, worked out how much to tell him.

'He's not been himself.' It was Dazzle who spoke. 'He thinks the polis are watching him. He's been cagey. For months now. Everyone's frightened to move. Do anything. Till this gets sorted out. This Jack the Ripper shit.'

'But they're not watching you?'

'They're not watching him, probably. He's just paranoid. Anyway, who'd watch us, Swifty? We're not a big enough deal. We're the waifs and strays, mate. Slip through the cracks.'

Stokes turned to Paton. 'The Quaker, they're calling him.'

'London, Bobby,' Paton said. 'I live in London. Not the moon. We get the papers down there.'

He removed his hand and Dazzle poured the shots and they all clinked glasses and drank.

Ten minutes later, he sat in the passenger seat of Stokes's Zodiac, thinking it through. He liked to hole up after a job was done, get off the streets fast and go to ground for three or four days. The hotel was no good.

'I'll need a place,' Paton said. 'Somewhere quiet.'

Stokes nodded. 'For afterwards, like? I know a guy can probably help. Want me to set it up?'

There was a black market in houses. Everyone knew this. Glasgow never had enough houses and the clearing of the slums had only made things worse. There was an underground trade in vacant flats in buildings slated for demolition. Families would scrape together a couple of hundred quid for the keys to a room-and-kitchen in a condemned tenement. They'd get a few months' breathing space before the wrecking crews arrived, give them time to get something else sorted. That would be fine. A flat in a condemned block would be just the ticket.

He took Stokes's number when they pulled up outside the hotel. 'Set it up then, Bobby. I'll be in touch.'

6

McCormack sat at his desk in the Murder Room, staring at a typewritten document. The document was two pages long, held together by a paper clip. It contained the witness statement of a man who had danced a single dance with Ann Ogilvie on the night of 2 November 1968, in the Barrowland Ballroom in the city's East End. Ann Ogilvie, victim number two. Later that night, at some point between midnight and 3 a.m., Ann Ogilvie was strangled with her own American tan tights, having been raped, beaten and bitten by the killer known as the Quaker.

Every twenty-five seconds the pages of the witness statement rippled in the breeze from a circular fan on McCormack's desk. But McCormack wasn't reading the words. He was basking in hatred. The tension in the stuffy room was like a palpable force, a malevolent beast that crouched invisibly on top of the cabinets, stalked between the legs of desks, breathed its rank breath on McCormack's neck. The tension amplified every sound. Typewriter keys sliced the air like cracking whips. A filing cabinet drawer rolled open with a rumble of thunder. People lunged at ringing telephones, desperate to silence their clamour.

He knew, of course, what was causing the problem. The problem was him. He was the rat. The tout. The grass. Resentment came at him in waves from the shirtsleeved ranks.

But what did you expect? It was Schrödinger's cat: the observer affects the experiment.

Ten days ago Duncan McCormack had been the man of the hour. Ten days ago he'd been sipping from a tinnie in the squad room at St Andrew's Street, watching his Flying Squad colleagues ineptly gyrating with a couple of more or less uniformed WPCs and some of the younger typists from Admin. It wasn't yet noon but the party was hotting up. There were muffled whoops as someone upped the volume on the Dansette. All three shifts of detectives were present. Guys had left the golf course or the pub, or wherever they went on their days off. Brothel, maybe. Everywhere he looked people perched on desks or gathered in grinning groups with their plastic cups of whisky and vodka.

Flett was edging towards him through the throng. DCI Angus Flett, commander of the Flying Squad. Chins were tipped in greeting, cigarettes raised in two-fingered benedictions. Flett gripped elbows, punched shoulders, clapped backs, threw mock punches, twisted his hips in that drying-your-backside-with-a-towel move when he passed a dancing typist.

The squad room looked like Christmas. Strings of paper bunting were pinned above their heads. Two desks had been pushed together to form a makeshift bar. Bottles of spirits clustered in the centre: Red Label, Gordon's, Smirnoff, Bacardi. Four-packs of beer in their plastic loops, green cans of Pale Ale, red cans of Export. Someone had gone out for fish suppers and the sharp tang of newsprint and vinegar and pickled onions mingled with the smoke and sweat and alcohol.

On an adjacent table stood a large birthday cake edged with blue piping, a '12' standing proud of the icing on blue plastic

61

numerals. Twelve was the tariff. Twelve years in Peterhead. They'd watched him cuffed and taken down to the cells, James Kane, one of McGlashan's lieutenants. It took them over a year to build the case and now they'd got him. Attempted murder. Serious assault. Conspiracy to pervert the course of justice. Guilty on all three counts. Au revoir, fuckface. Have a nice life.

McCormack raised his can of Sweetheart Stout to salute Angus Flett. He felt the beer sway inside the tinnie. He didn't like beer. He'd drunk just enough so the can wouldn't spill. He liked whisky well enough but he was playing shinty tomorrow, a grudge match against Glasgow Skye, and he wanted to stay fresh.

'The hard stuff, Duncan?'

McCormack worked his shoulders, straightened up. 'Got a game tomorrow, boss.'

'A game? I'd say war would be nearer the mark. I watched a match once, up in Oban. Jesus. Tough game. They say ice hockey's based on it.'

McCormack shrugged, sipped his tinnie.

'Anyroads, need to talk to you, son. Won't take long.'

In Flett's office, McCormack closed the door behind him, muffling the noise of the party. Flett got straight to business.

'Job's come up, son. I'm putting you forward.'

McCormack nodded slowly. When Flett sat down with the sun at his back, McCormack noticed that he hadn't shaved; little filaments of stubble caught the light.

'What's the job, sir?'

'It involves a change of scene. You'll be based in Partick. The old Marine.'

'That's the Quaker inquiry. They've got Crawford, already. They need another Squad guy?'

Flett held his hand out flat, palm down, swivelled his wrist.

'It's not a straightforward job, Detective. It's not the

operational side of things. I had Levein on earlier' – he nodded at the phone on his desk. 'The feeling is, it's gone on too long, the whole circus. Guts is, he wants us to review the investigation. See where things went wrong. What can be learned. Make recommendations.'

Peter Levein. Head of Glasgow CID. Bad bastard. Due to retire at the end of the year, to no one's regret.

'Recommend what? What's Cochrane saying about this?'

'Nothing he can say. They haven't caught him, have they? He's not going to like it, but he'll cooperate.'

McCormack was still frowning. 'Make recommendations as in shut it down?'

Flett leaned forward. 'Do you need it spelled out, son? This job? It's not a popularity contest.' Flett nodded at the door. 'You think those fuckers out there like me? Think I want them to?'

'It's not that, sir.'

'What, then?'

'I'm a thief-taker, boss. That's what I know.'

'This still McGlashan? You're still on about McGlashan?'

'We're close, sir. We're gonnae get him.' He jabbed his thumb at the door, at the sounds of beery triumph. 'See that, sir? That's nothing. That's just the start. We're building the case. We'll bring it all down, the whole rotten empire.'

'All right, McCormack.'

'What – you think I'm making it up?'

'No, Duncan.' Flett spread his hands. 'No, I'm sure you are close. Thing is. Nobody knows who McGlashan is. *We* know who he is. The poor bastards in Springboig and Barlanark and Cranhill: they know. But the punters out there? The ratepayers? They've no idea. They know about the Quaker, though. Jesus.' He tapped the folded *Tribune* on his desk. 'They know about him.'

'So we tell them.' McCormack shifted in his chair. 'We've got people who deal with the papers, haven't we? We fill them in. Give them the goods. Glasgow crime lord, reign of terror. Fear on the streets.'

'Give them what, exactly? If we had solid on McGlashan we wouldn't need the bloody papers, we'd just arrest him. It's more complicated, son. They've got a hold of this Quaker thing and they're not letting go. They want answers. They want to know why we're still fannying about after all this time. It's not McGlashan that's making us look like— What: you got something to say, Detective?'

McCormack was shaking his head. 'Naw, it's just, I was under the impression that the guy who headed up the Flying Squad was the head of the Flying Squad. My mistake. Not the editor of the *Glasgow Tribune*.'

'Oh for fuck sake, Duncan, catch yourself on. It's always worked like this. Keep the papers off your back, you keep the councillors happy, the MPs. It buys you the space to do the real job.'

'This isn't the real job?'

Flett held his hands up. 'I know. I know. Look. You do a job on this Quaker thing we'll go after McGlashan. You head up the team. You pick your men. I'll give you everything you need. But first it's this. Son, you're either ready or you're not. I thought you were. Have I made a mistake?'

Had he? Maybe the whole thing was a mistake, McCormack thought. Maybe joining the police was a mistake. Leaving Ballachulish.

'You want to be a fucking DI all your life. One of the lads—'

'I'm not one of the lads.'

'Good. I'm glad to hear it. I'll bell Levein. Start on Monday. Now get out there and enjoy yourself.'

So now he was sitting in the Murder Room at the Marine.

64

Enjoy yourself, indeed. *The feeling is, it's gone on too long?* Jesus, tell me about it, McCormack thought. He'd been here barely a week, listening in on the morning briefings – *eaves*dropping, it felt like. Days that dragged like months. Absorbing the hatred of his colleagues. A spectator at the daily taskings, a nodding auditor of tactical discussions. He listened to the detectives talking about the case – Earl Street, Mackeith Street, Carmichael Lane – and it bothered him. The men were so sure there was a meaning, some mystical link connecting the victims or the places where they were killed. As if the murders were a language, a code. A work of bloody art.

There had to be a link, they thought, but the men in this room couldn't find it. The three victims were unknown to each other, lived in different parts of the city. They had no mutual friends, no common bonds of church or political party. Two of them had husbands in the forces, but this fact – which seemed so promising at first – now looked like a coincidence. The worst kind of coincidence, the kind that costs you a couple of hundred man-hours before you realize it means nothing. But now it seemed clear. The women were bound by nothing more than luck or fate, whatever word you hit on for the actions of the Quaker.

But still there was the feeling that the map might hold the key, the six Ordnance Survey sheets tacked to the Murder Room wall. Each locus was within a hundred yards of the victim's house. The sites themselves formed no kind of pattern, so was it the Barrowland, then? Did the ballroom itself mean something to the killer?

McCormack knew there wasn't much history to the building. The original ballroom above the 'Barras' market had burned down in the late fifties – an insurance job, supposedly. The new Barrowland, with its sprung hexagonal floor and its ceiling of shooting stars, was opened in 1960. Time enough for the killer to make his own history with the place. But then, if the killer had been a regular, wouldn't somebody have known him? They'd have his name by now, he'd be in a remand cell at Barlinnie waiting for his trial.

Didn't the map mean anything? What about the wider area: the Gallowgate, Glasgow Cross? At one point Cochrane had invited a lecturer from Strathclyde Uni to address the squad, an expert on the development of the city. McCormack had read the lecturer's report. The Gallowgate was one of the oldest parts of Glasgow, Dr Mitchell told the Murder Room. The four streets forming Glasgow Cross – the Gallowgate, the Trongate, the High Street and the Saltmarket – were part of the original hamlet on the Clyde. But Glasgow was unusual: it grew up around two separate centres. There was the fishing village and trading settlement on the Clyde, but further up the hill was the religious community centred on the Cathedral and the Bishop's Castle. In medieval times there was open countryside, maybe some farmland, between the two settlements.

In time, the trading settlement on the river grew to eclipse the upper town. The Gallowgate, where the Barrowland was located, stood at the heart of the growing town. And maybe you could see the Quaker – with his puritanism and his biblical imprecations, his rants about adultery and 'dens of iniquity' – as representing in some sense the revenge of the upper town upon the godless lower city.

McCormack pictured the detectives shifting in their chairs. They would see no mileage in this, but Cochrane would have warmed to the idea of a righteous visitation, a historical reprisal, murders somehow plotted by the streets.

McCormack yawned and stretched, returned the witness statement to its folder. Across the way a detective sat at a desk opening letters with a paperknife. McCormack watched him slit an envelope, tug out the folded sheet, flatten it out on the desk. After a pause his hands paddled at the typewriter keys. Then he put the letter back in its envelope, dropped it in a tray, reached for the next one.

'More fan mail?' McCormack had drifted over. The man looked up, grunted, waved a hand at the out-tray: be my guest.

McCormack drew up a chair. The letter on the top of the pile was written in a tight, crabbed hand. It came in an airmail envelope, sky blue with chevron edges, though the postmark was local.

To whom it concerns. The man you want is Christopher Bell. He resides at 23 Kirklands Crescent in Bothwell and drives a van for Blantyre Carriers. He is out in his van at all times of the day and night and frequently burns 'rubbish' in the back garden of this property though it is against the rules of his tenancy to do so. On two occasions in recent months he has been seen with deep scratches on his face. He has reddish fair hair, goes into Glasgow for the dancing. Everyone round here has suspicions of this character and even the wee boys in the street call him the Quaker.

There was no signature and no address. The detective nodded at the pile of letters and told McCormack that six months ago they'd get twice as many. Three times. He seemed pained by the city's fickleness, its timewasters' dwindling stamina.

'Are you vetting them?' McCormack asked. 'Or do they all get checked out?'

The man looked up slowly, fixing McCormack in his gaze. 'Now that would be good, wouldn't it? Two years down the line he's killed another four women. Someone finds out we've had a letter all along, naming the killer in so many words. Of course we check them.'

It was the hard calculus of police work. If you got your man then all the effort, all the statements taken, the knocking on doors, the ID parades, the hours of surveillance, the sifting of dental records, it was all worthwhile. If you didn't get him then you might as well not have bothered. If you'd sat on your hands the result would be the same: the case still open, the killer still free.

You knew that was part of the deal. You knew that some crimes went unsolved, for all the hours and the sweat that got thrown at them. It was nobody's fault and no one was handing out blame. But it was hard not to take it personally. There were men in this room who had worked all three. Jacquilyn Keevins. Ann Ogilvie. Marion Mercer. Three women who'd gone to the dancing and never come home. Mothers of young children. You were failing them all.

McCormack went back to his desk, rolling his shirtsleeves to the elbow. As he watched the day shift go about their tasks there grew in him a kind of despair at the very diligence of these men. They were only undefeated because they kept trying. Day after day they sat at their desks beneath the high windows in the late summer heat and worked their leads. Dark patches bloomed at their armpits, down the backs of their shirts. The smell of sweat and cheap nylon was pushed about by the table-fans along with the blue clouds of cigarette smoke.

They worked the telephones ('Goldie, Marine Murder Room'), they typed up reports, collated statements, while McCormack sat at the end of the room like some kind of exam invigilator. He wanted to leave his chair and weave between the desks, placing his hands on the shoulders of these men, on their forearms, to calm their efforts, still their labour.

They were getting further away from it, he thought. Further away from the truth, not closer to it. They couldn't understand why the methods that had worked in the past weren't working now. They didn't change tack. They didn't try different things. They did the same things, only harder.

They needed some luck. No, McCormack thought: what they needed wasn't luck. What they needed was another death. To redeem their time, give them a fresh start, another crack at the Quaker.

He looked up to see Goldie standing at the map, lost in the grid, the dainty streets, the spidery contour lines, the sweeping arcs of train-tracks and rivers, the square white blanks of the public parks, the solid black geometry of the public buildings – the railway stations and churches, the hospitals and schools, the post offices, the army barracks.

Everyone did it. When someone sat down after a spell at the map, ten minutes would pass and a chair would scrape and another shirtsleeved figure would be stood there, hitching his trousers and leaning into the grid. It was a rota, an unscripted vigil. The detectives stood in turn before the Ordnance Survey sheets, waited for the map to yield its secrets.

He was losing it, McCormack thought. They all were. They had thrown so much at this inquiry. Talking to reporters, feeding the papers till the whole city, the whole country could think of nothing but the Quaker, the Quaker, that clean-cut face on the posters. It came down to numbers. Fifteen months of work. A hundred cops in teams of twelve working fourteen-hour days. They'd taken 50,000 statements. They'd interviewed 5,000 suspects, visited 700 dentists, 450 hairdressers, 240 tailors. Scores of churches and golf clubs. How many man-hours did it come to – a million? Two? How could all these numbers add up to zero?

And how could you let it go? How could you stop now, admit it was over, you'd done as much as you could? You couldn't. You couldn't let go. You kept on, placed your faith in police work. Placed your faith in procedures. Luck. Magic.

Santa Claus. Pieter Mertens. Mertens the clairvoyant. Mertens the paragnost. *I see a room in an apartment. A river is close. Also a factory. A crane can be seen from the window* . . .

McCormack watched the roll of fat bulging over Goldie's collar. He heard Goldie ask a sergeant called Ingram where Cochrane was.

'DCI Cochrane?' McCormack spoke up. 'I saw him half an hour ago in the car park. He was getting his wife a lift home in a squad car. What?'

The look between Goldie and Ingram; Goldie grinning at the floor.

'His wife.' Goldie snorted. 'Is that what they're calling it?'

'It's not his wife.' Ingram came over with two mugs of tea, set one down in front of McCormack. 'It's the witness, sir. Sister of Marion Mercer.'

'The third victim.'

'Yeah. Nancy Scullion. Shared a taxi with our man.'

They didn't like saying *The Quaker* in the station, it smacked of the tabloids. It was always 'our man', 'the killer', 'the perpetrator'. McCormack turned to Goldie.

'The schoolgirl smirk, Detective: is there some point you're trying to make here or is this how you normally look?'

Goldie's face darkened, the lower lip curling. 'It's called a joke, sir. The chief and the victim's sister. They're pretty close.'

'DCI Cochrane and Mrs Scullion, you mean?'

Goldie looked across at Ingram, back to McCormack. He opened his hand in a gesture of impatience. McCormack set his tea to one side, leaning his elbows on the desk. He felt an urge to let his head slide down to the desk, pillow it briefly in his folded arms.

'Sorry, can I get this clear, Detective? You're suggesting that DCI Cochrane is having improper sexual relations with a witness in a murder investigation? That's your insinuation?'

70

Goldie smiled slowly and shook his head, not meeting McCormack's eye. 'That's in your mind. You're the one who thought she was his wife.'

McCormack took a pull on his mug, grimaced. The tea was scalding but he swallowed it down, savoured the pain. He was vexed with himself. It was his own innocent error that had opened the door for Goldie. He thought back to the scene in the car park, Cochrane helping a woman into the passenger seat of a squad car, closing the door solicitously and tapping the roof for the car to move off. It was the air of intimacy, the gentlemanly stoop of Cochrane's shoulders. He ought to have known that she wasn't his wife.

McCormack looked round the office. The heads were all bent to their work but he felt that they were silently chalking this up, another facer for the turncoat, another round to Derek Goldie. He sat at his desk, spotting the files with sweat and watching the men ignore him, lean in close to mutter to one another. They were like a surly class with a strap-happy teacher.

The canteen was worse. Even the uniforms knew to avoid him. When he took his tray to a table the others would finish up, drain their glasses, scrape to their feet. Three days of this and McCormack gave up. He took to lunching out, up Dumbarton Road to a small Italian place popular with university lecturers and doctors from the Western. On the third day of this he sat in his window seat and thought: I'm becoming a ghost. I'm fading away. The best I can hope is that they ignore me altogether, start acting as if I'm not there. They're never going to connect with me unless I force them to.

That was why he'd gone out on a tasking with Derek Goldie. It was time to act, try to break down the squad's reserve. He'd seen enough of the Murder Room operations; now he needed to come out on a job. He chose Goldie, the malcontent, the troublemaker. Big, sneering, blond, cocksure Derek Goldie.

The roster told him Goldie was on late shift, 6 p.m. till 2 a.m., tasked with chasing up known sex offenders, bringing them in for identity parades.

And then Goldie had spent the whole shift winding him up, driving too fast, abusing suspects. It ended up with the beating he handed to the poor sap in the toilets of that shithole pub in Shettleston.

McCormack winced at the memory. He'd made his choice, lied for Goldie, covered his back. He wasn't stupid enough to think that this would make him Goldie's best pal but shouldn't it buy him a bit of goodwill? Fat chance. If anything, Goldie's hostility rose. Goldie had taken his backing as a personal affront, as if McCormack lacked the courage to stand his ground, couldn't even scab with proper conviction.

7

'It's Jeff Arnold, Rider of the Range!'

'Fuck off.' Dazzle was laughing, he couldn't keep the pistol straight. He dropped his arm and composed himself and raised it again, fired.

Nothing. The others jeered.

'It's too low!' Dazzle gestured with the gun. 'You'd never target somebody at that height. What are you aiming for, his knackers?'

Five big bottles of Bass, empty, stood in a line on top of a rock, thirty feet off, under a stand of silver birch.

'Give us it here.' Cursiter took the gun from Dazzle. He broke it open, dug a fistful of rounds from his jacket pocket and thumbed them home. He snapped the cylinder shut, planted his feet and sighted down his straight right arm and squeezed off six shots in quick succession.

The bottles shone guilelessly in the dappled light. The men's laughter rang round the clearing. Cursiter ran his tongue along his upper gum, shaking his head.

Now it was Campbell's turn, the new guy, the fifth man. Cursiter reloaded the pistol and held it out by the barrel.

Campbell took the gun in both hands, turning it over as though it was an object whose precise purpose eluded him. He was younger than the others, early twenties, with long straight hair and bell-bottom cords that whispered when he walked. He shuffled over to where Cursiter had stood and squinted at the bottles. Holding the gun tight against his waist like a quick-draw artist he pulled the trigger.

The middle of the five bottles burst with a bright *pock*, the glass dissolving in a silvery fizz. They all cheered and Campbell turned smiling, his hands spread in benediction, pistol dangling from his index finger.

'House,' Paton said. 'Thank fuck.' He was on his feet, dusting the seat of his jeans. He hadn't been keen on this shooting lark to begin with. 'Can we get some work done now?'

Cursiter took the pistol and stowed it in his jacket and they moved off in a ragged group, five men, stretching and yawning, down towards the cottage at the lochside.

Dazzle had booked it in a false name, collecting the key from the hotel in Rowardennan. They were supposed to be a party of hikers. They'd done a solid two hours' planning in the cottage that morning before breaking for lunch and a spot of extempore target practice. Jenny McIndoe, Cursiter's contact in the auctioneer's, would be joining them that evening with the floor-plans of Glendinnings.

The path narrowed for the final stretch and they marched in Indian file out of the trees. The white block of the cottage had swung into view when Dazzle, at the head of the file, gave a backhanded slap to Paton's chest. They all bumped to a stop.

'Is it Jenny? Is Jenny early?'

A dark blue Rover 2000 was parked beside Stokes's Zodiac on the apron of gravel in front of the cottage.

'It's not hers.' Cursiter was frowning. 'That's not Jenny's car.'

They stared at the scene and a stout, bald-headed man in an

orange cardigan came round the side of the cottage He stopped in his tracks when he saw the five men framed by the trees.

They started forward, awkward, bumping each other, trying to look normal. Normal hikers. The man stepped out across the grass to meet them.

'George Brodie,' he said. 'Landlord. You'll be Mr Maxwell's party.'

'I'm Maxwell.' Dazzle had his hand out. The landlord shook it. He took the others' hands in turn. No one else ventured a name.

'Right. Well. You've brought the weather anyway.' Brodie had his hands on his hips, like a fitness instructor. 'I just wanted to make sure you were settled all right. Had everything you need.'

Dazzle nodded. 'We're fine, thanks.'

'The shop in the village.' Brodie jabbed a thumb over his shoulder. 'It shuts early. Catches people out. Anyway,' he was moving towards the car, 'I got some provisions.' He hauled on the Rover's passenger door, lifted two carrier bags from the footwell. 'Just milk, bread. What have you.'

Dazzle took the bags. 'That's very kind of you. Appreciate it.'

Brodie shrugged, hands in his trouser pockets, thumbs out. 'You'll be off up the loch the morrow, then?'

He was looking at their feet, Paton noticed. Dazzle was the only one wearing hiking boots. Three of them wore trainers; Stokes in bloody winkle-pickers.

'That's the plan.' Dazzle was nodding again. 'Up to Crianlarich. Take it from there.'

'Right. Well, the weather should hold. If you believe the radio.' Brodie scowled up, shading his eyes with the fat blade of his hand. They all stood around looking at the sky as if something was about to drop out of it.

'So.' Dazzle hoisted one of the bags. 'Thanks again, Mr Brodie. Much obliged.'

'Righto.' Brodie gripped the roof of the Rover as he eased himself into the driver's seat. He reached for the door-handle. 'Just post the key through the letter box when you're leaving.'

'Will do.'

They watched him three-point-turn beside Stokes's Zodiac, spraying gravel, nosing past Dazzle's Triumph. Too many cars: they should have thought of that. The Rover gave a double toot of its horn as it wobbled up the track.

Inside, Stokes went straight to the fridge and hauled out more bottles of Bass, two at a time, set them up on the table. He went down the line of bottles with his bottle-opener, his elbow jerking. The bottle-tops skittered on to the table. Each man reached wordlessly for his bottle, tilted it in a spread palm.

The fun and games among the trees seemed a long time ago. Paton took a matchstick and scraped some mud from the sole of his training shoe. There was an odd smell in the room, he'd noticed it earlier. Cinnamon, maybe. Something sweet and spicy.

'You think he . . .?' Stokes jerked his head at the window, the path leading up to the trees.

'You mean is the landlord deaf?' Paton carried his bottle over to an armchair in the corner and flopped down. 'I don't think so. Nor, unfortunately, is he blind.' Paton waggled his bottle at the table, where a street map of Glasgow was spread out.

'It's a map,' Dazzle said. 'So what?'

There was a pencil line tracing the getaway route from Bath Street to the Gorbals but you probably couldn't have seen it from the window.

'Five guys with Glasgow accents,' Paton said. 'A map of the city of Glasgow.'

'A map doesn't mean anything.'

'Not yet it doesn't.'

Dazzle shrugged. There wasn't much point in taking this further. The guy was suspicious or he wasn't. He'd heard them shooting in the woods. So what? What did that prove? Plenty of people went shooting in the woods.

'Hey, there's peaches and corned beef here and everything.' Campbell had been unpacking the carrier bags. He turned to face the others, hoisting a tin of peaches in each hand, grinning.

'Highland hospitality.' Dazzle stood, yawned. 'Are we working here or what?'

They all sat at the table. Stokes reported on the van. It was handling well. He'd driven it round Govan a few times. He was planning to stow a can of petrol in the back ('That's a little Dillinger trick') in case they got involved in a prolonged chase. The van was off the road for the moment, getting a decal at one of McGlashan's garages.

'He know about it?' Paton said.

'McGlashan? Does he know about the job? No.' Stokes spread his hands. 'He knows there *is* a job, aye. But he doesn't know what it is.'

'He's expecting his taste, though,' Cursiter said.

This was why London was better, Paton thought. Nobody ran London. It was too big to run. You had the freedom to work how you liked. You were your own man.

'Yeah. Well. We've been through that.'

They worked on the game-plan. They finalized times. They'd go in at 5.30, long before the staff started to arrive, before the buses started running on Bath Street.

They broke it into pieces, little blocks of narrative. The entry. The watchman. The safe. They went over each piece. The time before, the time after. They went over it again. Leaving the building. The getaway. The idea was that Paton would take the goods – the jewels and any cash – in a toolbox and stow them in the safe house. Only Stokes knew the address of Paton's safe house; the others just knew it was in Bridgeton.

Paton's plan was that the string would make off in the van while he strolled down the hill to Central Station and caught a low-level train to Bridgeton.

'Or you could just use your time-machine,' Dazzle said.

'How's that?'

'They shut the station at Bridgeton,' Stokes explained. 'Few years back. You can't get a train.'

Paton looked round the faces, nodded. 'Buses still run?'

'Last time I looked.'

'I'll take the bus, then.'

Cursiter set his bottle down with a thump. 'You just walk down Hope Street with the gear in your hand and jump on a bus? Quite the thing?'

'We've covered this,' Paton said. 'The best getaway is the one that isn't. The one no one clocks as a getaway. I'm just a guy on his way to work.'

In another half-hour they had done all they could do until Jenny arrived with the plans. Dazzle produced a bottle of Grouse. The others started talking about stuff they would buy. Cars. John Stephen suits. Trips to New York. High-class hoors. Paton thought about time. How much time his share would buy him. How much time before he would have to do another job. Or the time he'd spend inside if they got caught.

Then they heard the hiss of wheels, a car door slam, high-heels mashing through gravel.

Dazzle opened the door.

The first thought Paton had was how far out of Cursiter's league this woman was. You knew, as soon as you clapped eyes on her, that she had fucked Cursiter as a purely instrumental act, a means of getting her hands on a share of a hundred thousand pounds. She was wearing a red woollen coat, cinched at the waist, belted, black high-heels. Her hair was black, glossy, bobbed.

She stood there enjoying the impression she was making.

'The age of chivalry is past,' she said. No one knew what to say to that. Her shoulders slumped theatrically. 'What's a girl got to do to get a drink around here?'

'Sorry!' Dazzle was on his feet, scuttling over to the cupboard for another glass.

'Did you bring the plans?' Paton was put out by the woman's appearance. He'd expected someone nervous and fretting, a dolly from the typing pool, out of her depth. The woman's poise and beauty changed the balance in the room. Her beauty seemed to put her in charge.

'I was about to ask who's the gaffer here.' She took the glass from Dazzle and held it high, in front of her face. Her nails were lacquered a vivid red. 'Think we've answered that question.'

'Our friend here put it together,' Paton said, nodding at Dazzle. He didn't know if it was a names thing, if she was supposed to know their names.

'But now you're in charge.'

'I've had some experience.'

'I'll bet.'

She set her drink down on the table and started working the buttons on her red coat. Cursiter rose and went to stand behind her. As he drew the unbuttoned coat from her shoulders, he leaned in to kiss her on the neck. She flinched away, clapped a palm to her neck as if slapping a mosquito, wiped the fingers down the skin. 'I think we've had enough of that, darling, haven't we?' She was wearing a short shift dress in a clingy black fabric.

Cursiter turned away. He tossed her coat on the back of a kitchen chair.

What she drew from her bag, rolled up in a tube and tied with string, were the blueprints from when the building was remodelled as an auctioneer's. Previously the address had been a private house. The architect had partitioned some of the rooms for offices and knocked others together to form the showroom.

Paton spread the blueprints out on the kitchen table, on top of the map, and the others gathered round.

'Somebody's not going to miss these?' Campbell asked.

'What's to miss? They go back where they came from tomorrow.'

The blueprints showed the basement door, the point of entry. The basement floor held storerooms and the night-watchman's cubbyhole, down a corridor on the right-hand side. On the ground floor were offices, toilets, a small staff tearoom. The first floor held the big showroom and the manager's office, where the safe was housed.

'This comes off,' Paton said. 'Even if it doesn't come off, they're going to come for you. You know that. They'll know it's an inside job.'

She was looking out the window and she raised her arms now in a long, slow stretch, fingers interlaced, her shoulder blades lifting in the clingy fabric. The window was turning glossy in the dusk. Paton could see the glass clouding where she blew out a sigh. She twisted her head to look coolly at Paton. 'You think I'll fall apart, break under questioning, blurt it all out?'

'I think you should be prepared. I think these people can be very persistent.'

'There's seventeen people know about this sale. I imagine at least some of them have more interesting backgrounds than mine. Anyway,' she flashed a smile at Paton; 'if it comes off, there's other things we need to decide. Like who's getting what?'

'Nothing to decide,' Paton said brusquely. 'Six-way split. Equal shares. End of discussion.' Paton stood up. He could have argued for a larger share of the take – he was the skilled tradesman, after all; the rest were just manual labour – but he knew from experience the trouble this caused. An equal split was clean and straightforward. If the take was big enough you didn't worry about trying to leverage a bigger share. Make the split, move on, everyone's happy.

'You'll be taken care of,' Dazzle told her. 'Same as everyone else. No one's stiffing anybody.'

She looked at Paton through her fringe. 'Well, I hope that's not the case.'

They drove back separately, leaving ten minutes between each car. Paton went last, in Dazzle's Triumph, the smell of dog, dog hairs on the upholstery, he thought of the dog resting its chin on his thigh, the mobile eyebrows, the sad, wet, intelligent eyes.

'That Jennifer,' Dazzle said, shaking his head. He looked across at Paton then back to the road.

Paton cracked the window an inch, kept it open while they drove, the smells of the night mingling with his cigarette smoke.

'I handle gelly for a living,' Paton said. 'Not for fun.'

8

'That's four bob, bud.'

McCormack put a ten-shilling note on the bar and took a pull at his pint, the brown sourness cutting through the milky head. *After Work You Need a Guinness*. The Smiddy was quiet, a trio of pensioners nursing their halves at one end of the bar, two guys in suits and ties playing pool. He thought he'd missed the rest of the day shift but then one of the pool players bent into the light to play a shot. It was Goldie, his features puffy and harsh in the overhead glare.

McCormack scooped his change from the bar and took his pint across to a table, opened the *Evening Times* at the sports section. He could see the TV, hear the click of the pool balls behind him. *Ask the Family* was finishing up and then it was the opening credits of *Z-Cars*, the patrol car's flashing headlights and a dotted line across a map of the city. He thought of the maps in the Murder Room and the boxes above them, boxes that ran on shelves covering three sides of the room.

At first he'd thought it was some kind of storeroom. They'd set up their Murder Room in the station's storage area and these boxes held the archives of all the old cases. Then it came to him that the boxes were current, the boxes were the Quaker files.

On his first afternoon he took down the first two boxes and leafed through them. Witness statements. He took a box from the middle and one from the end of the twenty-odd yards of shelving. Each was filled with the same buff folders of typed statements, the verbatim accounts of those who had some connection – however tenuous – with one of the victims. He tallied the boxes and made his calculation. There were fifty thousand witness statements on the Murder Room shelves.

He thought again about the madness of that number. You had fifty thousand statements and no suspect.

A shadow fell on his *Evening Times*. McCormack looked up. The angry one, Goldie, was stood there in front of him, pool cue in hand. He shook the cue like a spear. McCormack thought for a moment that he was being challenged to fight but it was only a game that the burly man wanted.

'Ten bob a throw?'

'Fine.' McCormack eased out from behind the table, followed Goldie to the lighted baize. 'Last of the big spenders.' McCormack meant this as a joke but Goldie wheeled round.

'Fine then, nicker a game.' He tossed his cue on the table. 'Rack them up, I'm away for a pish.'

McCormack took the plastic triangle down from the lampshade. He swept the balls together, lifted and dropped the stripes and spots until the pattern was right, the black nestling in the centre.

When Goldie came back McCormack broke off. They played the frame in silence. McCormack won, dropped the black with Goldie stuck on three. They racked up again and Goldie broke off viciously, the balls spreading in slow motion and something clunked home in a middle pocket and rumbled down.

'Stripes?' Goldie said. McCormack bent to check the ball as it slotted home, nodded. Goldie surveyed the table.

'You know what bothers me about you?' Goldie kept his eyes on the table, chalking his cue. 'Don't take this personal, but you know what gets me?'

'My clearance rate? My impeccable taste in clothes?'

'You sit there every day like you're one of us. You listen to our conversations. You drink our coffee. And all the time you're taking notes for your wee report, what we're doing wrong. I've worked this inquiry fifteen months.' He was watching the tip of his cue, tiny blue clouds rising as the chalk-cube scuffed it. 'Fifteen months. You're gonnae take a fortnight to tell me how I should've done it different.'

'You think I should take fifteen months to write my report?'

'Aye, very good. But that's not even it.' Goldie waited till McCormack had played his shot, a long five that rattled the mouth of the left baulk pocket, failed to drop. 'You know what it is? You sit there – day in, day out – the fucking boy genius of the Flying Squad, the man with the answers. And have you made one suggestion? Have you made a single positive contribution to what we're trying to do here?'

'I'm writing the report, mate. That's my brief. If I get involved in the investigation it just muddies the waters.'

'Aye. Fair enough.' Goldie lifted his pint from the windowsill and took a pull. 'Or maybe you're just as fucking lost as we are. Could that have something to do with it?'

'Ah come on, now. Don't sell yourself short. I've got some catching up to do to be as lost as you are.'

Goldie's laugh was soft, he was nodding to himself. 'We're getting it now, are we? The big insight. This should be fucking good. How lost are we, DI McCormack? Where did we go wrong?'

It occurred to McCormack as he straightened up that a pool

cue was a useful object, its fat end nicely weighted for connecting with someone's mouth. He held the cue at arm's length and leant it gingerly against the wall. He planted his palms on the pool-table's edge and leaned down into the light.

'All right then, DS Goldie. Listen to yourself. *I've worked this inquiry fifteen months.* You're boasting about that? You should be embarrassed. Fifteen months and you've never had a sniff. What does that tell you?'

Goldie's face was in shadow. He didn't say anything. He was bouncing his cue on the floor, you could hear the rubberized end bumping on the lino. McCormack leaned down further into the light. 'No thoughts? What about this then. How many parades have you held?'

'How many what?'

'ID parades. How many have you held? Do you even know?'

'This is how you spend your time? Doing sums in your wee book?'

'Three hundred and twelve, Detective. Three hundred and twelve. That's a number, don't you think?' McCormack frowned. 'What's the plan, you bring the entire male population of Glasgow to the Marine one by one? Get Nancy Scullion to check them out?' He spread his arms. 'She's seen three hundred guys, mate. She's no idea what the Quaker looks like any more. Assuming she ever did. I could be the fucking Quaker. You could, for all she knows.'

'Spent an evening with him,' Goldie said. 'She was in his company. Shared a taxi.'

'Poured into the taxi. Pished, by all accounts. Hers included. You said it yourself, for fuck sake. You said it to Cochrane.'

'She was there!' Goldie threw an arm up and his cue caught the lampshade, sent it swinging. His face danced in and out of the yellow glare. 'She saw him. She spoke to him. What – we just fucking ignore her?'

85

McCormack reached out to steady the shade. 'I don't think she's feeling ignored, exactly. Anyway, at this stage it hardly matters.'

'Because you're shutting us down.'

'Cause you're not fucking catching him.'

'And why's that?'

'Because he's dead, Detective.' McCormack swirled the last of the black in his glass, skulled it. 'He's dead or else he's gone, he's left the city. It's seven months since the last one. You think he's biding his time? It's finished. You had your window, you never took it. We playing pool here or what?'

They finished the frame. It was scrappy play, with fluffed shots and fluked cannons, both of them potting the white. McCormack won again. Goldie paid out his two quid with an air of resignation, as if defeat was a foregone conclusion, as if people like McCormack always won. When McCormack looked back from the double doors, Goldie had his elbows on the bar, staring down at another pint.

It was time to head home, time to put the whole affair to bed for another day, but McCormack walked on past the Gardner Street junction and shaped his course for the West End. He was heading for Kelvin Way, the avenue that bisects the park. A wind had arisen. A big branch flapped against a yellow streetlight. He was sick of it all, sick of the Marine and its fruitless labours. He was sick of chasing shadows. There were places you could go. There were people who wanted to be caught.

9

His father sang Merle Travis numbers in the bath. 'Sixteen Tons'. 'Nine Pound Hammer': *You can make my tombstone / Outta number nine coal.* It always made him think of the tombstones in St John's churchyard in Ballachulish, out there on the lochside. They were beautiful things. Not the chunky upright slabs you saw in other kirkyards, but dark, slim wafers carved with elegant cursive script, all loops and spirals. Like everything else in Balla, they were made of slate. The men worked them during slack times at the quarry. That's what you did when you found a free half-hour: you worked your own headstone, cutting the cross or the crown at the top, and then carving your name and birthdate under 'Sacred to the Memory of' and a bas-relief opened book, leaving only the final date to be carved by another hand.

McCormack used to walk there on Saturday mornings, out the loch road to St John's. He liked to ramble on the lumpy turf, tramping down the bones of MacInneses and Stewarts and MacColls, tracing with his fingers the chiselled lines, the extravagant pattern of curves, the word 'Sacred' hedged about in scrolls and folderols.

They were works of art, he thought. This is what they had instead of an art gallery, these hard black portraits signed with laboured care by each artist. The slate didn't weather like the other stones did. While the sandstone crumbled and blurred, the slate – even on the oldest stones – kept its edge. The morning sun above the Pap of Glencoe filled the chisel-strokes with shadow that was black and fresh as ink.

Now he stood in a different graveyard in the dark southern city with the slate roofs of tenements all around him and looked at the poor bare words on another stone:

MARION MERCER

BELOVED WIFE OF HENRY MERCER

DIED 25 JANUARY 1969

AGED 31 YEARS

'IN MY FATHER'S HOUSE ARE MANY MANSIONS:
IF IT WERE NOT SO, I WOULD HAVE TOLD YOU.'

He lifted his eyes to the rooftops, where the slates shone and smoked in the wake of a sunshower. This was his third of the day. He'd been to two gravesides that morning – Jacquilyn Keevins's and Ann Ogilvie's – and now he'd completed the set. He wasn't sure why. Paying his respects didn't cover it. He hadn't known these women in life. He had worked Jacqui Keevins's murder, but not the other two. And he wasn't Pieter Mertens, he wasn't a 'paragnost': he didn't expect to garner psychic data from his nearness to their rotting bones. It was more by way of introducing himself, he figured. Getting his bearings, in some basic way. They were his concern now, these three women. They were his responsibility, even if his task was to bring the investigation to a close.

The light in the Necropolis was failing.

He rubbed his thumb along the top of Marion Mercer's

stone. The face of the stone was polished and smooth – you could see your blurred face in the pink marbled shine – but the top edge was rough and grainy. Would he end up here himself, in a Glasgow cemetery, when his own time came? Or back in Ballachulish, in the lochside plot amid the slim dark stones? But the quarry had closed, there would be no black slate for him, wherever he wound up, just a stone like this one, thick as a doorstep, with his Sunday name in fat capitals.

He turned from the grave. Marion Mercer had been buried towards the northern end of the Necropolis and he climbed the little hill into the old section where the mausoleums of the merchants and tobacco lords studded the turf. Further up, near the crest of the brae, John Knox stood on top of his Doric column, wagging his fist at the city.

McCormack thought about the men at the Marine, the fatalistic gloom in which they laboured. Cops were superstitious. They believed a case could be hexed, jinxed, the guilty man uncatchable. Sometimes it was hard to disagree. The Quaker case had been dogged by ill luck. The third victim, Marion Mercer, was murdered on 25 January. Burns Night: a Saturday. On the Sunday morning, when Marion's partially clothed body was discovered in a backcourt in Scotstoun, the city was gripped by a terrible storm. The rain drove down and the wind stripped slates from the rooftops. The gable end came off a tenement in Bowman Street, Govanhill. Chimneys collapsed in Abercromby Street in Bridgeton. The Levern flooded and the Cart burst its banks. Streets in different quarters of the city under three feet of water. Cars stranded, abandoned in the highway. Families evacuated to higher ground.

Just at the moment when the cops should have descended on Scotstoun, blitzing the tenements of Earl Street with the door-to-door, they were wanted elsewhere. By the time they got back to Earl Street they were playing catch-up. Another trail gone cold.

He had reached the Knox memorial now and he stopped for a breather, lit up a smoke. It was hard not to feel for the Quaker Squad, but the truth of the matter was simple. The brass had lost their heads. They'd thrown so much money at this, poured so many man-hours into a holey bucket, that they didn't know how to stop. You stir the papers into a frenzy, keep the public in a lather with constant updates, appeals and public info posters. You couldn't just turn the tap off now that you'd run out of ideas. You couldn't scale it down and hope no one would notice. You needed a process, you needed a mechanism. You needed someone to do your dirty work for you.

You needed a sucker.

McCormack flicked his cigarette end into the dank grass. Turning to go, he looked up at the statue of Knox and saw to his surprise that he'd been wrong. It wasn't a clenched fist at all: the great Reformer was holding out a book. He wasn't damning the city to hell; he was preaching, though possibly it came to the same thing.

Streetlights were flicking on as McCormack came down the gravel paths. At one point he thought he saw movement in the gloom ahead of him, a flitting shape, someone ducking behind a stone.

The sky over the Infirmary had a cast of electric blue but the shadows were massing in the low ground and there were pockets of midnight round the headstones.

The warmth of the day still hung in the air. McCormack plunged his hands in the pockets of his jerkin, walking on the grass now, not the path. He was aware of the pink tip of a cigarette, then a man stepped out of the shadows ten yards ahead, his white jeans vivid in the gloaming.

McCormack slowed, let his hands slip from his pockets and hang loose by his sides, ready for whatever measure of tenderness or strife he might be offered.

A man with dark urges. Lawless drives.

'Got a light, mate?'

The man had an unlit cigarette between two fingers, jiggling back and forth. As McCormack held his lighter the man cupped his hands around McCormack's hands, held them there once the cigarette's tip was glowing. In the light from the flame McCormack studied the eyes, the cheekbones, he was younger than McCormack, twenty, twenty-one.

McCormack drew his hand down the man's sharp jaw, felt the boyish stubble catching on his palm. The man's fist closed on McCormack's wrist and pulled the hand away.

'Not here,' the man said. 'This way.'

The man strode off without looking back. McCormack followed the white jeans up the slope. One of the old mausoleums had its iron door ajar. The man slipped into the stripe of black shadow, McCormack at his heels.

ANN OGILVIE

The funny thing is, I remember the posters. Not the posters of him – those came later. The posters of her: 'MURDER: DID YOU SEE HER?', with the Daily Record*'s logo at the top and a smiling photo of Jacquilyn Keevins and the telephone numbers to call the police. She looked so happy and oblivious in the photo. On the plain side, too, God forgive me. Not a looker.*

I remember thinking that she'd gotten herself into something she couldn't get out of. And when it came out that she had a husband and a kid, your first thought was, Well, what is she doing at the dancing? Even though they were separated and the husband was living in Germany. That's what you thought. If she hadn't been out gallivanting in the first place, none of this would have happened. As if she was to blame. Not the man who raped and killed her, but the mum who went out for a dance.

So why did you go back? That's the question, isn't it? Why did you go to the Barrowland? Did you never think about the woman who died? Well, here's the thing. You knew she'd been dancing at the Barrowland, you knew that she'd met her killer there. But the Barrowland was local. It was 'our' dance hall. It was where – don't laugh – we felt safe. We weren't about to trek all the way into town for the Albert or the Locarno. And we even felt that the Barrowland was safer now that this had happened. Well, he won't try that again in the Barrowland, was the feeling. Like lightning wouldn't strike twice.

Plus, if I'm honest, it gave a little thrill to the proceedings. We'd joke about it in the Ladies', pretend that we'd spotted the Quaker, that the bloke who asked us up for the slow dance had a look of the poster about him, overlapping teeth, a stripy tie.

We'd even josh the blokes we danced with: Your grip's a bit tight there, Jim, watch your hands, are you sure you're not the Quaker? You'll never know, they'd fire back with a flash of their teeth. You'll never know until it's too late . . .

I lay there all the next day, all the next night, a hundred yards from my kids, from my sister Deirdre. It was Deirdre who finally found me.

I heard her heels on the bare wood boards, footsteps coming towards me in fits and starts, as if she couldn't make up her mind, knock . . . knock-knock-knock . . . knock knock. Then the gasp as she saw my legs and how she tiptoed over the last patch of floor and her scared face peeping into my dead eyes like someone peering into a well. The white plume of her breath in the cold room.

Thirty-six hours earlier I'd been getting ready to go out. The boys across the landing at Deirdre's and Louise sitting on the bed, watching me put my face on.

'Will there be shows?' Louise was saying. 'Down in Irvine.'

I could hear the kids playing in the backcourt, lassies at their skipping games:

Eight o'clock is striking,
Mother may I go out?
My young man is waiting
To take me round about.

'I suppose so,' I said to Louise. 'In the summertime, anyway.' She always loved the shows. Her mouth a wide pink blur as the waltzer whipped her round; her high laugh rising past the blue electric crackle as the dodgems jolted her shoulders back. Candy floss. Toffee apples. A goldfish twitching in its plump clear bag. I think she associated the shows with her dad. Her dad used to take her, before he left. Day-trips to the Ayrshire coast. Fish and chips and double nougats and the sea breeze through open windows on the train home. Louise went and stood with her back to me, looking out the window:

He will buy me apples,
He will buy me pears.
He will buy me everything
And kiss me on the stairs.

'What's the uniform like? I bet it's brown and yellow or something. I bet it's boggin.' Her new school was to be Irvine Royal Academy. It sounded posh, like some fee-paying high school in Edinburgh, but it was just the local academy. The boys would be starting at the primary in the scheme. Ravenspark.

'What will you miss, Mum?'

She looked at me over her shoulder. I smiled at her in the mirror, raised my elbows and gave a little shimmy with my hips.

'The dancing,' I told her.

I would miss the Barrowland. I'd miss the dancing.

I loved the dancing. I loved the whole thing about it. The music and the lights. The silvery crash of cymbals and the clean hard snap of the snare. I loved the men in their shiny suits, the light catching their tie-clips and cufflinks, glinting on their polished toecaps. The whole dance floor getting into the rhythm, working so hard but enjoying it too.

My click that night was a good mover. Not a talker, a bit aloof, but smart as paint in his lightweight suit, navy with a sky-blue check. I'd known him for a few weeks but we'd never been to the Barrowland before. The band segued from 'Time is Tight' straight into 'Street Fighting Man' and the crowd surged a bit and started jiving like mad and I spun away from him with my arms crossed over my chest, spun like a top and finished my spin with the glitterball right overhead and the dancers whirling around me, the music whirling and the swirl of stars overhead, I was the still centre of everything, poised between movements, everything balanced within me, the past and the future, and it seemed in that instant I had everything still before me, I was young and alive and anything might happen.

Then he stepped from the shadows and gripped my wrist and yanked me back into the dark.

We'd been scheduled to flit the following week. I'd been down to the Housing Department in Clive House to see pictures of the scheme, a new-build on the outskirts of Irvine New Town. Pebbledash semis. Indoor toilets. Private gardens with privet hedges. Five minutes' walk to the shore. I pictured Louise and the boys running wild on the beach, chasing each other up through the dunes to the path that wound back to our scheme. A rim of sand round the plughole when I washed the boys' hair at the sink.

In a drawer of the sideboard I had the new rent book with my name printed on the first page, from a time when my name was still my name, Ann Ogilvie, a name like anyone else's, not the name on a poster, not the name in a news report, not the name beneath a smiling, tragic photo.

He wanted to get us a taxi. No need, I told him; we can walk it. He waited while I queued for my coat in the cloakroom, helped me on with it. Soft hands. Hands that rested on my shoulders for a second as I fastened my coat.

The kids still come to the derelict flat. They file down the darkened close with their hands on each other's backs and dare each other to cross the threshold. They stand on the bare boards with their eyes squeezed almost shut and their arms and legs held rigid until one of them finally breaks and runs and the lot of them scatter, charging and whooping out to the backcourt.

They will keep coming back till the building comes down. The bare room exerts a pull, a dark fascination. This is the hub of it all, the heart of the crumbling city. The place where the lady lay naked and dead. The place where a story ended.

10

'The story, son. Start it again.' Greg Hislop was cutting up his Scotch pie, two vertical strokes of the knife, two horizontal. The smell of spiced mutton gusted up from the table. 'This bible basher, this – what do they call him? – "demon of the dance halls". Talk us through it. What does he do?'

McCormack shuffled back in his chair. He leaned forward, focusing on the tabletop, sliding the ashtray out of his line of vision. 'He kills women. He rapes them and chokes them. Hacks their hair off with a knife. He leaves them in a place where they'll be found – not right out in the open but not hidden. And he's careful. He takes their clothes with him and he doesn't leave prints.'

'OK.' Greg held his hand up, chewing down a mouthful of food. 'That's from your end. That's what you see as a polis.' He jabbed the table with his finger. 'What's it mean to him, though? What does *he* think he's doing?'

McCormack pictured the glossies on the Murder Room wall, the sprawled white limbs, the close-ups of bruises and bite-marks. The blood. 'Punishing women. Women who would go off for sex with a man they've just met, when they've got kids and maybe a husband at home.'

Greg speared a chunk of pie, used his knife to smear some beans on to the fork. 'OK. Good. He's a zealot. An instrument of vengeance. A wee Glasgow John Knox. Punishing how? What is the punishment he gives them?'

'He kills them.' McCormack shrugged, his hands jumped off his lap. 'Death sentence. The ultimate punishment.'

'Tsk, Dochie. No, no, no.' Greg set his knife and fork down on his plate, spread like the legs of a compass. He wiped the sauce from his lips with a paper napkin, took a sip from his half-pint of heavy. He was a retired chief inspector with the CID and the boss manner never left him. 'You're all off there, Dochie. Killing's incidental. Killing's a by-product. He humiliates them. He exposes them.'

McCormack was feeling stupid. The long day in the hot room, thumbing through files, the ache in his left bicep from hauling open the filing-cabinet drawers and lugging box files, the throb in his head from the fluorescent lights. They were sitting in the Park Bar, at the corner table, and the buzz of post-work conversation and the evening sun streaming through the window and warming his scalp were making him sleepy. 'Their nakedness? Their sex?'

'Their *blood*, Detective.' Greg tapped four fingers on the varnished tabletop. 'Their menstrual blood. He takes the thing that every woman hides, that you can't even speak about except in code-words and euphemisms and he brings it into the open. He puts it in the public street.'

'You're saying it's not just coincidence? All three on the rag?'

Greg shook his head. 'Blood, Duncan. Blood is the key. Temptation here is to think you're dealing with an animal, a tabloid maniac. Crazed sex-killer. He's planning to rape these

98

women and even when he sees they've got their rag on it doesn't stop him, he just ploughs on. That's all wrong. It's not that he keeps going in spite of the blood. Blood's the whole point.'

Greg finished his meal, mopping up the tomato sauce with the last shard of pie-crust. '*Glè mhath*. That filled a hole.'

McCormack lit a Regal. The old man sitting across from him, rolling a handmade cigarette in his huge gnarled hands, the skinny old guy with the fleshy big ears, had fought crime on the streets of Glasgow for three decades. He was a Ballachulish man, like McCormack. Brought up in West Laroch, a Son of the Manse. Though he hadn't lived there for forty-odd years, he was famous in the village, not for his police work but his wartime adventures. He was one of four Argyll and Sutherland Highlanders – all Balla boys – who'd been stranded at Dunkirk, left behind by the British flotilla. They decided to set off down occupied France, aiming for neutral Spain. All four spoke Gaelic and they passed themselves off as Russians on the long trek south. They made it across the Pyrenees and into legendary status back in Balla. Drank out on the tale for the rest of their days.

The others settled back in the village but Hislop returned to his pre-war job with the City of Glasgow Police. McCormack worked under him briefly, as a rookie constable in C Div on Tobago Street, but it wasn't till later, drinking in the Park Bar and the Highlanders Institute, that McCormack got to know the older man, started to meet him for after-work drinks on a Friday. Hislop had played shinty with McCormack's old man back home and he treated McCormack like a slightly wayward son. It was on Hislop's recommendation that McCormack applied for the Flying Squad.

Everywhere he went, Greg Hislop was feted for his great escape, pints and whiskies landing in front of him. The stories of his journey through France were legion. Usually they involved dastardly Nazis and nubile blond Resistance fighters. People loved the fact that it was the language that had saved the Balla men, the Gaelic they'd passed off as Russian, bamboozling the Nazis. The stories were all derring-do and hairsbreadth feats. But sometimes, too, you'd hear a rumour, a whispered tale that had a darker edge. At some point on their journey south the Ballachulish men were supposed to have killed a man, a priest they suspected was planning to betray them. Sometimes you'd hear that it was Sandy 'Blood' MacDonald who'd done the killing. Sometimes it was 'Ginger' Wilson. Sometimes it was Peter Kemp, who strangled the priest with his bare hands. But sometimes, in the story, it was Gregor Hislop who'd dispatched the padre, plunging him with a knife.

McCormack looked at him now, an old man wiping tomato sauce from his lips with a folded napkin, nursing his dram and his pony of beer, glancing up at the clock above the bar. You couldn't tell from looking at a man what he'd done, whether he'd killed another man, what he might be capable of. Thirteen years on the Force taught you that if nothing else. McCormack noticed the old man's lips working as he balled the napkin. Greg was asking him something.

'I'm saying who did you piss off this time? Getting sent to work this Quaker gig.'

'No, Greg. I'm not working it. They've got me doing a "review". I've to write a report for Levein. What it is, they need an excuse to wind it down. My job's to come up with the excuse.'

'But you think there's something more?'

'You think I'm wrong?'

Greg smiled. 'Not at all, son. There's always something more. They'll want it scaled down, aye. It's gone on too long, they're throwing good money after bad. But maybe they think you're the best shot at solving the thing. Last throw of the dice. If you solve it, dandy. If you don't, what have they lost?'

McCormack reached for his glass, found it empty. 'Great. They bring the psychic in. And Plan B is me.'

Hislop laughed. A few months back a Dutch clairvoyant had offered his services to the Quaker inquiry. Pieter Mertens, a 'paragnost', had apparently solved a couple of missing persons cases on the continent and had the testimonials from the gendarmerie to prove it. The *Daily Record* had stumped up the money to bring him across, in return for exclusive access to the venture. In a moment of desperation Cochrane had agreed and a smiling, sixty-year-old Rotterdamer with a gauzy cloud of Albert Einstein hair pitched up at the Marine with a *Record* hack and snapper at his side. They put him in a room with a scarf belonging to the third victim, Marion Mercer, and he closed his eyes for five minutes, fingering the scarf. Then he started to talk. He saw a room, he said, an empty room with a ripped-out fireplace. The river was close by and also a crane, he could see a tall crane against the sky. And that was it. It wasn't much to go on. Uniforms made a desultory search of derelict tenements in Govan and some of the waterfront warehouses. Nothing was found. Mertens was thanked and sent smilingly home with his paranormal hair and the Quaker inquiry was back to square one.

'Who put you up to it?' Hislop was asking now. 'Flett? Sell it as a big opportunity, your shot at the big time? Right? Well, who knows, son, maybe he's right.'

Greg downed his whisky, shook the last drops of it into his beer. The sauce-streaks on his plate had stiffened into ridges. McCormack twisted his empty glass on the tabletop. A woman at a nearby table had started singing in Gaelic, a high slow air: *Gura mise tha fo éislean, / Moch sa mhadainn is mi 'g éirigh* . . .

'Some opportunity,' McCormack said. 'Opportunity to go

down with a sinking ship. Ach, fuck it. I'm on a hiding to nothing here, Greg. I'll get the report done, move on. Quaker's gone anyway. Dead or fucked off.'

Hislop's silence had the weight of reproof. They listned to the Gaelic song, the smatter of claps when it finished. Finally Hislop leaned forward, planted his elbows on the table. 'Why you doing the job, Dochie? Is it just to get you out the house, put some siller in your pocket? Because there's easier ways. What age are you, son?'

'Thirty-five.'

'Christ, you feel like this at thirty-five you're as well jacking it. Do something else while you've still got the time. It's not like other jobs, son. If you're not making a difference, you're just in the road. Write your report. But give it a go at least, give it a shot. You find a new angle, follow it up. All right?'

'All right.'

McCormack got to his feet. 'Same?' He pointed at the empty whisky glass. The old man nodded. The barman was wiping the taps as McCormack approached, holding up two fingers.

'*Té bheag?*'

McCormack nodded. As he watched the barman, McCormack told himself he kept up these meetings with Greg out of respect for the old man and the Ballachulish connection, but now he wondered if there wasn't a different reason. Maybe he met Greg to remind himself what a real cop looked like and how far he was from being one.

They had a good night, listening to the music and drinking. It wasn't till they were standing outside at closing time with the usual Argyllshire crowd that Hislop brought it up again.

'What are they like anyway?' he said. 'Cochrane's boys.'

'*Meadhanach math.* About what you'd expect.'

From what he could tell, the Marine guys were all right. For cops. McCormack had never warmed to his colleagues on the

Force. The older ones all had that regimental air – if you weren't ex-service then you weren't quite up to scratch. The young ones were all about shinning up the pole. The lot at the Marine seemed OK. It was hard to get an accurate picture when most of them hated you on sight.

McCormack didn't blame them. You could see their point of view. But even the ones who did give you the time of day could be a pain in the neck with their cracks about sheep-dip and single-track roads.

The city cops thought the whole of the Highlands was Brigadoon. You couldn't tell them that growing up in Ballachulish was like living in a pit village. The men worked in the slate quarries, clocked on and off like factory bodies. The hooter sounding four times a day, men coming home as black as pitmen. Tin baths in front of the fire.

'You not a Brother yet?' Hislop asked him. 'That couldn't hurt.'

McCormack shook his head. He'd been approached more than once, but decided against it. There was the Catholic angle – the Church frowned on it – but mainly it was a question of taste. He didn't like clubs. He didn't like the kind of men who joined clubs. And he saw quite enough of his colleagues on the job without jogging their elbows in the Lodge.

They lit their cigarettes. The moon was full and McCormack glanced up at the tenements opposite, the neat slate roofs in the moonshine. Glasgow people knew that their water came from Loch Katrine. They didn't know that what kept the rain out was Ballachulish slate. Every roof in this city was covered with slates from the Balla quarries, slates McCormack's *seanair* and his muckers had blasted, cut and dressed.

'Can't expect them to like you,' Hislop was saying. 'But do a good job of work and they've got to respect you. There's

103

still some good men on the Force, despite everything. You know Seamus MacInnes?'

McCormack nodded. James MacInnes was the Detective Superintendent, second-in-command to Peter Levein in the Glasgow CID. Rumour was that MacInnes should have got the top job but his religion – he was Roman Catholic – kept him out.

'You know he's Argyll? Dunbeg boy. James of the Glen, we used to call him. I did a couple of favours for him.'

'Aye?'

'If Cochrane gets on your case, give Seamus a shout. Tell him I sent you.'

'I'll do that, Greg. Thanks.'

The singing had started again, party songs this time, football chants, Celtic and Rangers. The Oban lot were Rangers fans and the Balla boys were Celtic. Time to go.

'*Oidhche mhath*, Greg.'

'Don't be a stranger.'

The next evening, in the Mitchell Library, McCormack read books on primitive cultures, the taboo surrounding menstruation. He read of the 'deeply ingrained dread which primitive man universally entertains of menstruous blood'. How women were isolated from the tribe during their confinement, set apart in outlying huts. It was forbidden to cross their path. The pots and vessels they used during their 'unclean' time had to be smashed and discarded. The touch of a menstruating woman could wither crops, turn milk, spoil beer. She would rust metal, render milk-cows barren, make livestock miscarry. Trees would drop their fruit. Boys who caught sight of menstrual blood would find their hair turning grey. A menstruating woman could not go near water, for fear of fouling the fishermen's luck. Wherever she walked, the plants would die under her feet.

In certain tribal societies, garments touched by a menstruating woman would be taken off and burnt. He thought of the naked limbs on the Murder Room photos. The missing clothes of all three victims. He read the words from Leviticus: *And if a woman have an issue, and her issue in her flesh be blood, she shall be put apart seven days: and whoever toucheth her shall be unclean until the even. And every thing that she lieth upon on her separation shall be unclean.* These were the bits of the Bible you never heard at St Muns or St Peter's, the crazy, superstitious bits with their frothing anathemas and interdictions, wild-eyed, random, weirdly specific. *And if any man lie with her at all, and her flowers be upon him, he shall be unclean seven days; and all the bed whereon he lieth shall be unclean.*

McCormack stacked the books and took them over to the desk. On the walk home along Dumbarton Road he watched the taxis swish past and thought it all out. Greg Hislop was just an old guy in a pub who liked to watch the horses and drink Bowmore. He also had thirty years on the job. He'd worked the Peter Manuel case with Cochrane, you had to figure he knew a few things. But this wasn't biblical Palestine or some lost African tribe. This was Scotland's biggest city in 1969. This was Battlefield and Scotstoun and Bridgeton, the names on the front of buses and trams. What did tribal superstitions have to do with these murders? The man who placed soiled sanitary towels beside his victims wasn't enacting a primitive ritual. He was laughing at them all, the victim, the cops, or he was showing his disgust at the world and all its works. They'd had over a year to find the Quaker. They'd come up with nothing. And now Duncan McCormack, the Boy from Ballachulish, would set them right, do what the longest, most expensive investigation in the history of Scottish policing couldn't? Aye. That would be right.

11

The next day McCormack was back at the Mitchell, reading the files on the three killings. *The body of a 31-year-old Glasgow nurse was found yesterday in a quiet lane a hundred yards from her home. She had been strangled. The dead woman was identified last night as Jacquilyn Keevins, who lived with her parents and six-year-old son at 29 Langside Place, Glasgow.* McCormack read the report to the end and found nothing that he didn't already know. Chief Superintendent Peter Levein, head of the Glasgow CID, appealed for anyone who'd been at the Majestic Ballroom on the previous evening to come forward. There was mention of the cars, the white Ford Consul 375 that picked up a woman on Langside Avenue at 11.15 p.m., the Morris 1000 Traveller that slowed down on Overdale Road, backed up to the entrance to Carmichael Lane and then roared off when a car came up behind.

They never found the cars and the Majestic was the wrong ballroom. McCormack studied the smiling face of Jacquilyn Keevins. A 'Late News' sidebar next to the Keevins piece reported that Sir Laurence Olivier had undergone a successful operation for appendicitis in a London hospital after an emergency flight from Scotland. He had been taken ill while playing the role of Edgar in Strindberg's *Dance of Death* at the King's Theatre in Edinburgh.

McCormack flicked on through the pages. *Vietcong Keep Up Offensive Despite Losses. Warhol Shot in His New York Loft.* Reports on the Keevins murder petered out after a couple of weeks. He let his eyes play over the headlines. *Princess Margaret in Hospital for Tonsils Op.* He read the local news and the international. Edinburgh Presbytery was urging the university authorities to ensure that the contraceptive pill would not be provided to unmarried students through the university health service. A fire in a nursing home killed nine elderly residents in Limoges, France. A seventeen-year-old Barrhead youth got two years in a young offenders institution for resetting 17,440 stolen cigarettes and striking a Paisley man with a pick shaft. Richard Nixon announced his candidature for the US Presidency. A twenty-four-year-old woman in the Calton was referred for alcohol counselling and had her four kids (five years down to seven months) taken into care after leaving them in a 'squalid condition, without adequate clothing or bedding, and exposed to the danger of an open fire'.

It was hot in the newspaper room of the Mitchell Library and McCormack took his jacket off and slung it on the back of his chair. An old guy on the other side of the room was wearing a heavy overcoat in a herringbone tweed. His nose was around four or five inches from the desk: he was either reading the *Tribune* short-sightedly or had fallen asleep.

The big ledger made a satisfying soft detonation when McCormack closed it. He hefted it back to the shelf, slotting it into the gap between April and June 1968. Then he sidestepped through the late summer and autumn of 1968 and hooked November and December with his forefingers and drew both

107

ledgers out together in his splayed hand and carried them over to the desk. He went back for January and February 1969.

A wintry breeze came off the pages as they turned. All the stories seemed to hinge on terrible weather. Three trawlers were lost off the coast of Iceland in a squall. Three naval apprentices were airlifted from the Cairngorms by a helicopter from RAF Leuchars after being trapped in a blizzard during a survival course. The football card was decimated, pitches unplayable. In the midst of all this wind and ice and snow Ann Ogilvie was raped and murdered on the streets of Bridgeton and Marion Mercer was raped and murdered on the streets of Scotstoun.

There was a story by Edgar Allan Poe that McCormack remembered reading on the train back from Oban High School to Ballachulish on the Christmas holidays one year. Auguste Dupin, Poe's detective, is investigating the murder of a young woman called Marie Rogêt whose body has been dumped in the River Seine. All he has to go on are the reports carried in the press. He solves the crime not by narrowing his focus but by broadening it to encompass the unrelated incidents recorded elsewhere in these papers: *experience has shown that a vast, perhaps the larger portion of truth, arises from the seemingly irrelevant.* The report of an attack by a gang of 'blackguards' on a young girl in the country outside Paris is, Dupin realizes, what has sent the gendarmes off on a false trail. They assume that Marie Rogêt has been the victim of a criminal gang. Dupin, for his part, uses the newspaper report of an abandoned boat found drifting down the Seine to identify the killer in the person of a sailor.

But that was books. In real life, papers told you nothing. All you found in these yellowing *Tribs* was the whirling jetsam of events: celebrities cutting the ribbons on new supermarkets, ten-year-old boys drowning in canals, bombs dropping on

Vietnam. He slotted the ledgers back in place and wickedly bumped the chair of the old loafer in the overcoat on his way out.

McCormack walked home through Anderston. There were kids playing in the street, lassies chanting their songs and rhymes, he remembered them from the Ballachulish playground:

> Not last night but the night before,
> Twenty-four robbers came to the door.
> I went doon the stair to let them in,
> They hit me on the head with a rolling pin.

It was kids who'd found the second one, Ann Ogilvie, in Mackeith Street. The papers said it was the victim's sister who discovered the body – they liked the symmetry of that, the element of family drama – but it was local kids who found her. All that Sunday they'd been playing in and out of a derelict tenement, daring each other to run up the stairs and hide in the rooms. They found the woman in a bed-recess. Word of their find had filtered up to the adult world but no one paid any attention. A body in a building? It was just a game, the kind of stupid thing kids dreamed up. Or maybe a jakey was dossing in a vacant block, sleeping it off. Ann's sister heard the rumours, but it wasn't till Monday morning, spare with worry, that she crossed the street to number 27.

She picked her way through the empty rooms. On the first-floor landing she turned into a room and saw her sister's white legs, the blackened soles of her feet. Ann Ogilvie was lying in the bed-recess with her tights around her throat and a sanitary napkin on the floorboards at her side.

Maybe they should be listening to the kids, McCormack thought, as he started up the long steep slope of Gardner Street.

Maybe the weans held the secret. These killings betrayed a kind of fairytale horror, the logic of children's skipping games. Playground rhymes encoding historical trauma. *Mary Queen of Scots got her head chopped off on the fourteenth of No-VEM-ber*. It wasn't the newspaper reports that held the key. They didn't need the Forensic Science Department and the Identification Bureau. They needed to think like kids, inhabit that world of poetry and violence: *Down in the valley where the green grass grows / There sat Marion as sweet as a rose . . .*

That night, McCormack watched the city, softened in the blue and yellow dusk, the high flats like strips of shadow. Down at the river the shipyard cranes looked oddly elegant against a yellow sky. He stood at the window till the sky deepened and the glass threw back his image, a shivery ghost with a tumbler of malt. He had a gammon steak cooking under the grill, tatties rattling in their pot.

Behind him on the table was his Underwood and a metal ashtray filched from a pub. His report was proving hard to write, though he wasn't sure why. He'd had ten days at the Marine, long enough to get a handle on things, read the runes of the Murder Room. It shouldn't take long to describe what he'd seen. A murder case that was busy going nowhere. Detectives doing what they'd done for the past six months, working their lists, eliminating the fighting-age population of Glasgow, man by fair-haired man.

Goldie, at least, was different. McCormack sat down at the table, set the whisky at his elbow. Goldie at least had a spark, a sense of where they were going wrong. It was frustration that made Goldie act as he had. He wasn't a thug. He was a good cop turned reckless by a bad investigation. But it wasn't McCormack's job to rescue Derek Goldie.

When the food was ready he turned the telly on to catch the end of the news. He sat on the couch with a tray on his lap.

A diamond tiara appeared on the screen, resting on a red velvet cushion. After a few seconds the image gave way to a brooch studded with red and green stones, then a solitaire diamond ring. A measured voice described each item as it appeared, pausing for a beat before the image gave way to the next. It had the feel of a memory game, like they'd be asking questions at the end of the show.

He cubed his gammon steak and watched the succession of jewels. It was the haul from an auction-house robbery. Thieves had broken into the premises of Glendinnings in Bath Street in the early hours of Tuesday morning. *If you recognize any of these items, please call the number at the bottom of the screen.*

The bulletin ended. *The Kenneth McKellar Show* was on next. McCormack took his plate through to the kitchenette. He filled the basin and squirted the liquid, waggling his hand to bring up the suds. He thought about the robbery. You'd need a London connection, obviously. You couldn't fence a haul like that in Glasgow. He rinsed the plate and stacked it in the rack. Maybe the peterman, the one who moved down south a few years back. What did they call him? Prentice? Provan?

When McCormack got back to the sofa, Kenneth McKellar was singing 'The Northern Lights of Old Aberdeen'. He was wearing a lounge suit instead of his normal Highland outfit. McCormack lit a Regal. Glendinnings was on Bath Street. That was A Div – Bertie King's boys. Who'd be working it? Halliday, probably. Adam Halliday as CIO. John Drennan and maybe the new DC, Yuill. And King would have been on the phone to Flett: Can we borrow your boy, can we borrow McCormack?

Or maybe not. Maybe Bertie King had no especial need of a back-stabbing Highland thief-taker.

McCormack stood and stretched. He moved across to the table and sat down in front of his Underwood. The sooner he finished his report the sooner he'd get back to St Andrew's

Street, back to catching thieves, back to McGlashan. He kept the television on, half-listening to Kenneth McKellar, as he turned the platen knob of the Underwood and aligned the sheet of triplicate. He would recommend that the investigation be wound down. That's what the brass wanted anyway, what the whole charade had been about. They just needed someone to pull the plug.

He worked on the report and for an hour he was aware of nothing but the words snapping on to the page, shaping themselves into sentences. When he looked up from the keys the screen was showing the demolition of a sooty tenement. There was a long shot of the building, its chimneys black against the sky, and then the boom of an explosion as the building slumped in a spreading cloud of dust.

A city of a million souls, said the voiceover, *is shrinking. Today Glasgow's population stands at eight hundred and fifty thousand. Another hundred thousand Glaswegians are expected to leave in the next five years. The Glasgow of 1975 will be a very different city, with fewer people enjoying greater space. More parks and more green spaces.*

The screen showed a gull wheeling away above a vista of high-rise blocks, with verdant parkland behind them. He thought of the men in the Murder Room, men in shirtsleeves, bent to their work. He understood what it was now, the fear that he'd smelled as the days wore on. It was the fear that they'd already missed him, that the Quaker was gone, part of the overspill, starting afresh in a seaside New Town or waving from the deck to the Broomielaw crowds.

They didn't want him gone. They wanted him caught. They needed a name, a conviction, a man in cuffs with a blanket over his head, a vengeful crowd on the High Court steps. They needed a line drawn, a page turned. Otherwise he would always be there. Every time a woman was killed, or a girl went missing, the artist's impression would be smirking out from the *Record*'s front page. Is he back? Is this another? Has the Quaker struck again?

The screen showed more half-demolished buildings, disfigured streets. It looked like the footage from Europe after the war. Bombed cities. Smoking ruins. Sometimes it felt like they were fighting a war. The enemy was one man but he could have been anyone. He struck at various points in the city and left his dead for some civilian to discover. You responded by flooding a district with uniforms, knocking a thousand doors, but you never got close.

When the programme finished, McCormack turned back to his report. He worked for another half-hour. Then he stopped to lift the cigarette smoking in the ashtray and caught his reflection in the window and the name of the peterman came to him: Paton.

12

Paton watched from the kitchen window, standing well back, high up on the fourth floor. Down in the backcourt the boy picked his way through the bricks and rubble, a slight figure, ten, eleven, aeroplaning his arms to keep his balance. Something in the boy's demeanour told you he was a loner, off in a world of his own, lost in a dreamscape of rubbled dunnies and fever puddles. Paton felt a gush of sympathy, a kinship with this skinny kid. He'd been holed up in this flat for a matter of hours but already it felt like being back in the Digger at Polmont, the striplight slicking the greasy walls.

The noise of a jet plane filled the sky. The boy craned up, shielding his eyes, and Paton stepped back from the window. He reached his arms up in a stretch and fought the urge to light another smoke. With no carpets and not much furniture, the room seemed to sing with potential echoes, as if a single footstep might set it ringing like a plucked guitar string.

There was a flimsy-looking wooden chair in the corner. It had a circular seat and no arms, like something from a Greek Street bistro. Paton placed one hand on the back of the chair and another on the rim of the seat, as though preparing for some feat of acrobatics. He moved his shoulders: there was give in the legs but not too much: it would hold. He lifted the chair and set it down beneath the hatch in the ceiling and he climbed on to the seat with his arms out for balance. Then he stretched up and unhooked the latch and used both palms to lift the hatch lid and jiggle it free.

He still couldn't see into the loft so he paddled his fingers lightly round the rim of the hatch, feeling for splinters. He lodged his fingertips on the faraway lip of the hatch and hauled himself up till his head was clear. The light inside was dim. He could see the lines of the rafters, long beams running in parallel, and a dark blockish shape. He let himself down to the wobbly chair.

He looked around the room. Aside from the bed and the chair the only other item of furniture was an old square-shouldered wardrobe. The wardrobe was empty. There was a key in the wardrobe door and Paton turned it. He canted the wardrobe on to its side and slid it across the floor to the hatch. He put the torch in the back pocket of his jeans and lifted the toolbox and stepped up on to the chair and then on to the wardrobe. He set the toolbox down on the loft floor and heaved himself up.

When the beam clicked into life something scraped and skittered in the shadows. Rats. *Rats, lice and Scotsmen*, that was the old saying: you'd find them everywhere. In Glasgow tenements they came as a package. The cone of light bounced around the attic and picked up droppings, dust-balls, a dead bird – biggish, a starling, maybe a thrush. The dark shape he'd seen was the chimney. He made his way towards it, keeping to the wooden beams, bent over, arms out once more, the torch in one hand, toolbox in the other. On the far side of the chimney he found a small space between the brickwork and the sloping roof and he slid the toolbox into it. Back at the hatch he played the torch over the bricks of the chimney and the beams of the roof. You couldn't see the toolbox, just an angled patch of shadow. When he got the hatch lid jiggled back in place he hooked the latch and jumped down from the chair. He righted the wardrobe and slid it back to its original position. Then he took a T-shirt from his holdall and drew it across the floorboards to wipe off the trail that he'd left in the dust.

He fished the roll of banknotes from his jacket and sat on the bed and counted it out. He divvied the notes into four equal piles. One pile he folded and wedged in his shoe. Another he slipped down his sock. The third he stowed in the lining of his jacket and the last one he put in his wallet. Then he lay on the bed and smoked a cigarette. Clouds drifted past the window. He doused the cigarette in a soup can that stood on the floor by the bed. A bluebottle wobbled noisily into his vision and droned up to the ceiling, looping a figure-of-eight around the frayed cord of the light-fitting. He followed its arc for a moment before swinging up from the bed and snatching the folded *Tribune*. It took him four swipes – great shoulder-wrenching lunges – but he felt the hard ping that knocked the flight from the fly. It lay on the dirty floor, legs working. Paton flopped down on the bed.

He looked around the room: Stokes had done well. Mouse-shit by the skirting-board and dampness on the walls, a fur of mould on the mattress, but so what? He remembered the stewed-apple smell of the old box-bed in Hopehill Road. This was better. It was only four nights. You could thole anything for four nights.

He yawned and turned on his side. He was tired. He was always tired after a job. Tired, too, from the early start. At a quarter to five that morning they'd stood in the dark outside Dazzle's building, waiting for the van. Mild chill in the air. No one said much on the drive into town, Stokes at the wheel, Dazzle and Cursiter side by side on the passenger seat. Paton and Campbell on a bench-seat in the back. He was going into himself, getting prepared. The others sensed it, spoke softly among themselves. Wordlessly he took a cigarette when the pack was passed round.

When they parked in Bath Street it was almost dawn. They crossed to Glendinnings in a bluish swimming-pool light. They took off their donkey jackets and laid them on the spikes and eased themselves over the railings and dropped down on to the dank stone flags. The bars on the basement windows looked rusty and cold. Stokes passed down the metal toolbox to Paton, a heavy holdall to Cursiter, and a lighter one to Dazzle. Then Stokes crossed back to the van.

The basement door stood in the shadow cast by the steps. If you hadn't known the door was there, you'd never have spotted it. When Dazzle took out the key that Jen McIndoe had provided he had to run his gloved fingers down the panels to find the raised disc of the Yale-lock. He let his forefinger rest in the slot, then fed the key in. It slotted home with a crisp slither. He turned the key and the door opened half an inch then stopped. Dazzle took out his torch: it played on the shaft of a bolt. Dazzle extracted a pair of tweezers from an inside pocket and started to ease the bolt along, moving it a fraction of an inch with every flick of his wrist. An incongruous gulp of birdsong sounded from somewhere close by and then the bolt slid free and they were filing through in their rubber-soled boots. Campbell took up his post by the basement door and the rest of them trooped down the corridor in the weak yellow glow of the night lights.

The nightwatchman's cubbyhole was a converted storeroom at the end of the corridor. You could see the wedge of yellow light from the open door. Ten yards from the door they stopped

117

and used their free hands to tug their balaclavas down over their faces. Dazzle produced a .38 Webley and they all moved forward again. Paton was at Dazzle's shoulder when he stepped round the edge of the door with his gun-arm extended.

The room was empty. A calendar pinned to the wall. A desk standing crosswise to the room. A folded *Evening Times* and a paperback book beside a glass ashtray, a Golden Virginia tobacco tin, a plain white mug. A roll-up was smouldering in the ashtray and suddenly the watchman reared up from under the desk, his face flushed from bending down. When he saw the hooded figures and the pointed gun he rocked back in his seat and flailed his arms to keep from toppling over. One of his hands struck the white mug and it bounced on to the floor, throwing a dark stain on to the carpet.

The watchman was still trying to form a word when Cursiter stepped smartly across and hit him backhanded in the mouth. The watchman put the back of his own hand to his mouth and drew it away and looked at the blood.

Cursiter worked quickly. He knelt beside the watchman and unzipped the holdall. He seized the watchman's wrist and removed a wristwatch with a brown leather strap. He laid the watch on the table. He lashed the man's hands together behind his back, passing the rope between the metal struts of the chair-back and tugging it tight. Then he gagged him with a roll of silver gaffer-tape and taped the man's ankles to the front legs of the chair. He pulled a canvas money-bag out of the holdall and tugged it down over the watchman's head. He cut the telephone cable with pliers and unplugged the two-bar electric heater that the man had been adjusting when they all walked in. Then he stood and cleared the desk with a sweep of his arm and sat on the desk with a shotgun laid across his knees.

No one had uttered a word.

There was a clock the size of a dinner-plate mounted on one of the walls. Paton stood on a chair and lifted it down, dropping it to the floor where he smashed the face with the heel of his boot. Then he took the watchman's wristwatch from the desk placed it on the carpet and ground the face under his heel.

Paton lifted Cursiter's holdall and followed Dazzle into the corridor. On the first floor they found the main office. There was a push-button security lock on the door. They had the combination from Jenny MacIndoe but Dazzle used the sledge on it.

A desk. A green filing cabinet. An armchair in red buttoned leather. A bag of golf clubs propped in a corner. The safe, as Jen had said, was under the desk. They laid the framed photographs of the boss's kids face down on the desktop, then they each took an end of the desk and carried it free. No security cameras, but Paton kept his balaclava in place as he knelt down before the safe. He dug in the toolbox for the headlamp with the elasticated strap, got to work.

Twenty minutes later they were back in the nightwatchman's cubbyhole. Paton wondered fleetingly if the sharp, smoky smell was cordite; then he noticed the stain on the watchman's trousers. Dazzle dumped the heavy holdall on the desk and the man jumped at the sound, wrenching at the ropes and bucking his torso so that he rocked forward on the chair. Cursiter held the shotgun like a kayaker's paddle and jerked the butt-end and cracked the man on the temple and the chair keeled over and they left him slumped on the floor.

On the way out they stopped at the basement door. This was the risky part. Dazzle took the sledgehammer from the holdall and stepped outside. Campbell closed and bolted the door and stood well back. They heard the splinter and crack as Dazzle used the sledge. When the door burst open and Dazzle stumbled through they climbed the stairs to the front door.

They were grinning now, they couldn't stop grinning as they rolled their balaclavas back into beanies. Nobody notices a squad of workies but they might notice a squad of workies in balaclavas. It was daylight now, you could hear the early traffic on Bath Street. They opened the front door and walked out between the Doric columns, down the front steps at an easy pace, joking and laughing, making plenty of noise. They crossed the street and climbed into the van and Stokes released the handbrake and pulled out from the kerb.

And that was that: as easy as you like. Paton walked down to Argyle Street and caught a bus to Bridgeton Cross. The others were heading south, planning to torch the van on a patch of waste ground in the Gorbals before switching to Dazzle's Triumph, parked three streets away beside the Southern Necropolis. At Queen Mary Street, Paton climbed the stairs and used his key to the top-floor flat where he'd already stashed provisions to last him a week.

Not quite the Central Hotel but so what? A Primus stove and a saucepan. A jawbox sink to piss in. Beneath the sink was a stack of tins and chocolate bars, cans of ginger. In the bedroom there was a plastic bucket into which Paton had emptied a bottle of Dettol. Beside it a twin pack of toilet rolls, two bottles of water, a cube of carbolic soap and a small hand-towel.

On the mantelpiece above the torn-out fireplace was a loosely folded yellow rag. Inside the rag was a short-barrelled Browning.

Paton went back to the window and moved the net curtain an inch. The grassless backcourt. Banks of dark windows. It looked like anywhere in the city. He had to think for a moment where he was. The East End. Bridgeton. It was perfect. You didn't want to hole up too close to the job; the cops might get lucky. But you didn't want to leave the city either: maybe someone's already stumbled on the scene. Cops could be watching the stations, throwing up blocks on the roads out of town. Best to get clear of the locus, get off the streets as fast as you can, hole up for four or five days, let the shitstorm blow over.

He'd followed this drill after every big job. He'd refined it to a point where he'd cut out everything that wasn't needed. On previous jobs he'd taken a transistor radio for this part. Follow the news, get a jump on the cops. Lately, though, he'd stopped even that. You worried less with no connection to the outside world. Better not to know if Stokes or Dazzle or Cursiter had been picked up. If the nightwatchman had succumbed to his injuries.

He lit another cigarette – there was a whole carton in his holdall – and ran through his plan. On ice for four days and nights. Up sharp on the morning of day five, fetch the gear from the attic. Across Glasgow Green to the city centre. Down to Jamaica Street, catch the service bus to Kilmarnock. Train from Killie to Carlisle, then change for Oxford. Bus from Oxford to Reading, train into Paddington, one tube stop to Bayswater. He'd be in the back room of the Duke of Clarence by Friday closing-time, fencing the gear with Johnny Matrenza.

He nodded to himself. Down in the backcourt the boy was still messing around. He'd found an old plank of wood and propped it against the ruined wall of a midden to make a kind of ramp. He was climbing the ramp with his arms out like a tightrope-walker. Paton had the odd sensation that the boy was somehow him, that he was watching a movie of himself as a ten-year-old boy in the old Hopehill Road backcourt. But if the boy was him then Dazzle would have been somewhere in the vicinity and if this was Hopehill Road then the window he stood at would have been – what? – the Donnellys' kitchen window, Mr Donnelly with the old black bicycle he carried up and down four flights of stairs and the black-haired fanciable teenage daughter who practised her majorettes moves in the backcourt, marching on the spot and tossing her baton up in the air, the sunlight flashing off its bright chrome shaft. As he watched the boy balancing on the ruined wall Paton leaned against the window frame and started working his way through the flats in his Hopehill Road close, the families on each landing, the surnames, the pets, the father's job, the names of the kids. It would take some time, but time was not a problem.

13

In the showers, one of the Skyemen – a great, freckled walrus of a full back with a tuneless, honking voice – was murdering a ballad amidst the anguished hooting of his teammates. McCormack finished towelling his hair. He forced the wet towel into a plastic bag containing his shinty kit and pushed the whole damp wodge into his sports bag. The taped end of his caman poked out from the bag.

He carried his dirty boots to the door of the clubhouse and whacked them together. The gravel around the clubhouse steps was dotted with little rosettes of mud, each with a perfect stud-hole at its centre. As he turned to go back inside, Tearlach Mor was coming out.

'Heading over the road, Dochie?' Tearlach jerked his head in the direction of Pollokshaws Road; a few of them were meeting for a pint in Heraghty's Bar.

'I'll see you there,' McCormack said, but when he shouldered his bag and clattered down the clubhouse steps, something struck him. They were in Queen's Park on the city's south side. Just over the hill, up there in Battlefield, was Carmichael Lane. It was five minutes' walk: he should see it again.

Carmichael Lane. One of the three green pins on the Murder Room map. Where it all started. Scene of the first Quaker killing. Jacqui Keevins, the local girl who worked as a nurse at the Victoria Infirmary. '*Angel Slain by Dance Hall Demon*' was the *Record*'s headline.

It wasn't a happy memory for McCormack. The mix-up over the dance halls had wrong-footed the case from the start. It was wound up after two weeks. No leads, no suspect in the frame.

At the cross McCormack turned left and started to climb Langside Avenue. At the top of the hill he dodged between cars to the big roundabout where the monument to the Battle of Langside rose into the sky. At the other side of the roundabout he crossed again and cut down a side street into Langside Place. It was just before noon. Langside Place was a short, quiet street of low, well-kept tenements. The pink stone glowed in the midday sun. The street had a short parade of shops on one side and the Keevins's two-bedroom flat was above the baker's, next to the chemist and the newsagent. He thought about ringing the bell, but what could he bring them but more bad news? *I'm winding down the Quaker investigation. Your daughter's killer will never be found.*

He walked down Millbrae Road and turned into Overdale Street. A narrow lane opened out on the right, twenty yards down. It was cobbled with sharp irregular stones and the grass grew up in the gaps. He walked a little distance into the lane, between the garden walls of Cathkin Road and Carmichael Place, and stopped in a recess beside a garage door.

This was where Jacquilyn Keevins was found, naked and stiff on a morning in May. The man who found her – the garage owner, a local joiner – was so shaken that he didn't stop to make sure if it was a man or a woman. He stumbled off and phoned the police and told them a man was lying dead in Carmichael Lane.

McCormack hitched his sports bag and stood there for a minute on the jagged stones, not sure what he'd expected to find. A woman with shopping bags was labouring up the lane from the other direction and she gave a start when she spotted McCormack. She met his cheery 'Fine day' with a tight smile. He watched her go and then he walked back up the hill. He rested for a spell on the roundabout, sitting on the base of the Langside Monument. He looked down on the low homely tenements and neat sandstone villas of Battlefield.

Since she'd come back from Germany, Jacqui Keevins had stayed local. Six or seven streets marked the limits of her world. Her whole life had shrunk to this tiny corner of the South Side. Her parents' flat in Langside Place, where her mum was always happy to babysit the boy. The hospital where she worked as an auxiliary nurse. The park where she took the wee fella on Saturday mornings.

It was perfect, her parents told the investigating officers. Ideal. Everything she needed right there on her doorstep. McCormack wasn't so sure. What did you do when you got a lumber at the dancing and wanted to bring him home? McCormack remembered the file, the witness statements from Jacqui's mum and dad. They were adamant that Jacqui and wee Alasdair were staying with them permanently, or at least long-term until Jacqui got back on her feet.

There was a friend, though, wasn't there? McCormack remembered, a girl who worked beside Jacqui at the Victoria. She thought that Jacqui was planning to leave, she said Jacqui spoke about getting a flat for herself and the boy.

Would that have saved her? Would a place of her own have made any difference? Maybe it would. Maybe the killer would have thought twice about killing her in a flat. He might have worried about leaving prints, about waking the boy, about the neighbours hearing a scream. Jacqui's parents had thought they were keeping her safe, wrapping her up in a tight wee corner of their tight wee world, but maybe that's what helped kill her.

Anyway. He'd expected nothing to come of this and nothing had. McCormack slapped the base of the monument and was turning to go when the lettering caught his eye. He had passed this monument a dozen times but had never properly seen it. Now he craned back to take in the great fluted pillar and the foreshortened lion squatting on top before focusing on the plaque:

THE BATTLE OF LANGSIDE WAS FOUGHT ON THIS GROUND ON 13 MAY 1568 BETWEEN THE FORCES OF MARY QUEEN OF SCOTS AND THE REGENT MORAY, AND MARKED THE QUEEN'S FINAL DEFEAT IN SCOTLAND. THIS MONUMENT WAS ERECTED IN 1887.

Above the plaque, the date of the battle was carved into the soiled yellow stone in letters half a foot high: 13 MAY 1568. Something seemed to shift position in McCormack's mind, like the arm of the jukebox slowly slapping a disc down on to the turntable.

He scribbled in his notebook and set off down Langside Avenue. The phone booth near Shawlands Cross was empty. He told the desk sergeant to put him through to Goldie.

'Derek. It's McCormack. Do us a favour. Can you get the Keevins file out? I need to check something.'

'What you looking for?'

'I want the date of Jacqui Keevins's murder. Get the file, would you?'

'Don't need to get the file. It was my wedding anniversary. Believe that? The thirteenth of May. We'd booked a table at Etrusco's. Took me a week to get out the dog-house.'

The thirteenth of May. McCormack wedged the handset under his chin, flicked the pages of his notebook: 13 May 1568. A girl from Langside Place, murdered in Battlefield on the 400th anniversary of the Battle of Langside. The young queen's final defeat in Scotland.

'Still with us?'

'I'm here.'

'What's the score? What is it you've found?'

A woman had appeared outside the phone box – elderly, prim, in a purplish coat and hat despite the heat, handbag hooked on a rigid forearm. McCormack grimaced and shrugged, caught the handset as it slipped from its berth between his chin and shoulder.

'I don't know, Derek. Possibly nothing. I'll talk to you later.'

He used two fingers to hook the unused coins from the steel dish and pushed against the heavy door. The old woman leaned forward from the waist to peer into the interior of the box, as if inspecting it for damage, before stepping forward and ducking smartly under McCormack's outstretched arm as he held the door. He let the door swing shut, stooped to retrieve his sports bag from the pavement and turned to go. The old woman's perfume stayed in his nose as he crossed the road to the bus stop.

Did it mean anything, he wondered, as he waited for a bus; was the date anything more than a coincidence? What could the murder of a young Glaswegian mother possibly have to do with a 400-year-old battle? Still, it was something. It was a line to pursue. It was worth a punt. You owed them that, at the very least. Jacquilyn Keevins. Ann Ogilvie. Marion Mercer. You owed it to the three of them.

MARION MERCER

'I wouldn't bet on it,' he says to me. He's standing at the window, a dishcloth over his shoulder. This is where it always starts, this is what I always come back to. I replay it all, from this point forward. Henry shakes his head. 'If anything, it's getting worse. Look at the puddles.'

I come and stand behind him. I put my arm round his waist and hook my chin over his right shoulder. It's kind of sore and comfortable at the same time.

'They're like tiny seas.' My voice sounds a little thick, coming up through my stretched throat.

They are like tiny seas. The wind is making these furrows and waves on all the puddles down on Earl Street. The big branches of the trees are wagging up and down and the television aerials on the tenements opposite are shuddering. The wind is making whooshing sounds in the chimney. I feel like Dorothy at the start of The Wizard of Oz.

'It'll clear,' I tell him. 'Anyway, the tatties are ready.'

Henry likes to mash the potatoes. We're having haggis, neeps and tatties (it's Burns Night). I got the last haggis from MacSorley's and it's boiling away on the hob.

'There'll be slates down,' Henry says, turning from the window. 'Chimney stacks maybe.'

Last winter there was a big storm and the slates came down like purple guillotines, exploding on the roadway or embedding themselves in the narrow front lawn. In the morning the front lawn looked like a fairy cemetery, all these tiny headstones sticking up out of the grass.

The whole building is falling to bits. We've talked about moving away, out to one the New Towns or maybe the high flats on the Kingsway. But who'd want to be up there on a night like this, on the eighteenth or nineteenth floor, the whole tower tilting in the wind, bending like a reed?

Henry drains the tatties and clatters the pot back on to the hob. He takes the butter dish and slices off a corner of the block and draws the knife across the rim of the pot, so that the butter drops into the tatties. He takes a full pint of milk from the fridge, shakes it to disperse the cream, thumbs the silver top and tips a little into the pot with the earnest, comical concentration of a man watering whisky. Then he gets to work with the masher.

I go through to put on my face in the hallstand mirror and I hear the regular strokes of the masher – thump, thump, thump – and every few strokes the clang of metal on metal as he bangs the masher on the edge of the pot, clearing the tines and starting again.

There's something in the rhythm that reminds me of sex, of Henry's steady, dogged pace and the laughter starts bubbling up. I'm doing my lippy and I can't keep it straight, I have to stop and lean on the hallstand.

The clanging stops. 'What the hell are you laughing at?' he calls through.

I can't speak for laughing.

'Nothing,' I say. 'Don't stop now. You're doing great!'

I blot my lippy and leave the square of tissue with my Peach Frost kiss on the hallstand, a square of tissue that Henry will keep in a cigarette case in the top drawer of his bedside table.

I take the haggis off the boil and set it on the oval dish. It sits there, tight in its skin, fit to burst, a compact wee bomb. I shout the boy through from the front room where he's playing with the dominoes, setting them up in a snaky line along the tiled hearth.

Henry has carried the plates to the table, each with its orange splodge of neep and its white splodge of tattie.

'Will we have the poem?' Henry asks, though he always recites it. It's his favourite part, when we're having haggis.

'Go on, then.'

Calum grinds his wee backside into the chair, grinning, he loves it when Dad does the poem.

I take my seat and Henry stands at the head of the table, arms spread wide. The big knife is on the table in front of him, a checkered dishcloth beside it.

When he gets to the bit about 'His knife see Rustic-labour dight', he snatches up the breadknife and wipes it with the dishcloth – 'An' cut you up wi' ready slight' – and plunges it into the haggis, drawing a line down the middle of the skin.

The insides seethe up, spilling out over the cut – 'warm, reekin, rich' – like freshly ploughed soil. It's a good haggis, spicy and moist, with the pinhead oatmeal through it.

I'm hungrier than I thought, watching Henry scoop the haggis out and dollop it on to the plates beside the dollops of mashed tattie and bashed neep.

The boy attacks it, packing it away in urgent forkfuls, till Henry tells him to take his time.

The windows rattle as we eat. The wind whoo-whoos in the chimney. When Calum's fork is clacking on the china Henry clears the plates. He comes back through with two mugs of tea, an empire biscuit for the boy.

Calum picks the jelly tot from the top of his biscuit and sets it to the side for later. Then he takes a bite from the biscuit and sets it down on his plate. You can see the wee teeth marks in the white fondant icing.

'Can you do the ring, Dad?' he says, his mouth full of biscuit. 'Dad, do the ring.'

'Ah, Jeez,' Henry says. 'I'd need to soap it to get it off, son. I'm no as slim as I used to be.'

But he tugs the wedding band off and sets it on the table, balanced on its end. He's been doing this for years, his little trick, ever since Calum was a baby in his high chair. He grips the ring between the forefinger of his left hand and the thumb of his right and springs them sharply apart.

Suddenly the ring is a gold translucent ball, spinning in the centre of the table with a kind of wet rasping hum. Calum is mesmerized, as he always was, and he watches as the tiny potter's hole at the very top of the ball gets wider and the noise gets raspier and the ring starts to materialize in the golden globe, wobbling through its drunken figures-of-eight until it clatters to a stop with a kind of snappish trill.

'When you were wee,' Henry says.

'I know. You used to do it on my high chair and you'd have to watch that I didn't snatch it up and put it in my mouth.'

Henry picks up the ring and works it back on to his finger. The panes rattle fiercely as he does this and he looks up sharply, catches my eye.

131

'You sure this is a good idea? It's getting worse out there.'

He's not jealous, there isn't a jealous bone in his body. He's not trying to stop me going to the dancing. He's away a lot, he knows I like to go dancing with Nancy. I shouldn't drop Nancy just because he's home. Where's the harm in a night at the jiggin?

'She'll be disappointed,' I say. 'You know what she's like.'

Nancy goes dancing three nights a week. She'd go seven nights if she could.

'OK, but here . . .' Henry's digging into his pocket, holds up a note. 'Take a taxi. There and back. Don't mess around with buses. And stick together. Be careful.'

He doesn't say it, but we both know what he means: The Quaker.

'OK.' I lean over to pluck the note from his hand and he grabs me round the waist, topples me on to his lap.

'Who's good to you?'

'You are.'

'You behave yourself.'

'Always.'

He kisses my neck. Calum eats his biscuit.

At half-past nine we're in the Trader's Tavern. Nancy's in full flight, accepting drinks from a gaggle of suits at the bar, flirting like a champion. The storm's getting wilder, which only makes the pub brighter and warmer, the lights and the smoke and the flickering fire, the thick weave of voices, glasses clinking.

Nancy's more outgoing than me. She always knows what to say, always has a smart bit of backchat for the fly men, the chancers. It comes from her job. She spent nine years on the buses before she got the secretary job in Harland and Wolff's.

It's getting close to ten o'clock, and the men at the bar are throwing back whiskies. They're not interested in us now – only in getting as much booze down their necks as they can before chucking-out time – and we gather our things and hurry over to the dance hall, coats wrapped tight, heels clacking smartly on the pavement, through the swirling rain to the big bright neon sign.

The queue isn't long and we're soon climbing the stairs arm in arm towards the muffled beat and suddenly we're in, we're part of it, the whirling lights and the crowds, the chest-thumping bass and the slashing guitar, we're on the dance floor, light bouncing off the thighs and shoulders of the sharkskin suits, the lassies in their short frocks, spoor of sweat and smoke and perfume, the sprung floor bouncing under three or four hundred feet. In front of us a lassie in a Paisley-pattern minidress is thrusting and pumping, all blond hair and legs, little triangle of white flashing up beneath her hem. Nancy elbows me and points and we're clutching each other's arms and pushing through the crowds to the bar.

Within five minutes Nancy's got a click, a tall, sharp-featured bloke, black hair, blue suit. Good dancer. I'm watching them on the floor when I hear the low voice in my ear – 'May I have the pleasure of this pleasure?' – and I smile and turn. William's wearing this beautiful brown three-button suit with the thinnest scarlet pinstripe. Tan brogues. Slim regimental tie. Glint of gold in his smile.

We move out on to the floor. I haven't told Nancy about William. We're pretending we've just met, though in fact I've known him for three or four weeks. As the dancers move I catch sight of Nancy. Over her partner's shoulder she hoists her eyebrows and pouts, as much as to say, Not bad!, and I laugh and do the same. It's a slow number and I hook my hands round William's shoulders and close my eyes. He smells excitingly of eau de cologne – something piney and green-smelling – and the noise of all the conversations around us, all the shouted remarks beneath the snap of the snare, is like the buzz of friendly bees.

Nancy's click is called John (no doubt his surname would turn out to be 'Smith'). He's the quiet type, just sips his drinks between dances, smiles, doesn't say much. I whisper to Nancy that he might be the Quaker and she grins into her drink. We've got a table for four behind one of the pillars near the bar but we spend most of the night on the dance floor.

At one point we're dancing right at the centre of the hexagon. William makes a funny remark and I throw my head back to laugh and there's the glitterball overhead, throwing off light, and I think of Henry's wedding ring, spinning on the kitchen table, spinning on the high-chair, spinning back through the years to when Calum was a baby.

'What's the matter?' William's standing over me now, frowning, touching my elbow.

'Nothing. I feel a bit iffy. Let's get a seat.'

He lights my cigarette and watches my face. It might never happen, he tells me. I force a smile. I tell myself I'm doing it for us. For Henry and Calum and me. William can help us. You can't get ahead on your own in this city. You need to know someone. Someone who knows someone. And now I do.

Nancy and her click come back to the table. William stands up until Nancy takes her seat. Nancy finds this hilarious. 'Where did you find him?' she asks. William just stands stoically until she settles herself and then sits himself down, smoothing his tie with the flat of his hand.

*　*　*

134

At the end of the night we've collected our coats from the cloakroom when Nancy decides that she needs cigarettes. She feeds her money into the machine in the foyer but the drawer sticks. She can't get her fags and now the money's stuck too. Nancy just shrugs – it's late and we all want to hit the road – but William won't leave it. He's like a man possessed, summoning the manager, demanding satisfaction. When the manager arrives he's a rough-looking ticket in a rumpled tux. William looks like a schoolteacher in his belted raincoat, scarf tucked neatly into the collar. All he needs is a rolled umbrella. He starts berating this man, what an outrage it is, stealing patrons' hard-earned money, running defective machines. You can see the manager doesn't know whether to placate William or chuck him down the stairs. Finally he stumps up the missing money and we march off in triumph, William muttering loudly about 'dens of iniquity'.

It's nearly midnight when we leave the dance hall. Nancy's click goes off for the night bus at George Square and will never be seen again; despite repeated pleas from the police, he will never come forward to assist the investigation. The three of us walk down the Gallowgate. I've got my arm linked through William's. On the way to Glasgow Cross we pass a group of wee neds. One of them's pointing at William's boots. He says something to the others and they erupt in nasty laughter. William just looks through them, strides on as if they don't exist.

In the taxi I sit between William and Nancy. Nancy is drunk. She's still laughing at William and she thinks he doesn't notice. When he offers me a cigarette, Nancy demands one too, and plucks three or four when he offers the packet. William's off on a rant about something or other. Real bible-thumping stuff. Odd phrases stick out over Nancy's drunken giggles. *Wages of Sin. Taken in adultery.* Nancy finds it hysterical.

Nancy lives out in Yoker, but William insists that we drop her first. There's an air of gallantry to this manoeuvre, but of course he wants me to himself. Three's a crowd.

Nancy gets out at the foot of Kelso Street. The last I see of her, she is standing at the kerb, still doubled up with laughter and then suddenly the laughter stops and she straightens up. She raises her hand as we pull away. It's an odd gesture, as if she's hailing the cab she's just gotten out of.

I stop the cab in Earl Street, a block before my own. And everything from this point onward seems like it's a rerun, even the first time round. William seems to know that we can't go to my place. As if we've agreed it in advance we walk up the path of another tenement and walk through to the back close. William is whistling quite loudly, a kind of folksy tune that I know but can't place. It seems important that I find out the name of the tune but instead I shush him. In the back close he starts to kiss me, roughly but without urgency, as if he's just passing the time.

I hear a noise. There's something stirring further back in the close and this, I realize, with a rush of belated insight, a backwash of regret: this is a mistake. Henry's words come back to me: *You sure this is a good idea?*

William is pressing into me, his hands braced on the wall beside my head, and he takes his mouth off mine for a moment and cocks his head, as if he's heard something or maybe he expects to hear something, and I take my chance. I rake my shoe down his shin and duck under his arm and set off at a run. Nervous laughter bubbles up as I charge through the close but it dies out when I see my mistake. Instead of running up the stairwell, shouting and banging on doors I'm running out into the backcourt, into the darkness and emptiness with nobody there.

There's a grass banking on the far side and I set off for that, stumbling across the broken ground.

I've lost a shoe. I kick the other one off and set off up the banking but my stockings are slippy on the grass and I land on one knee and scramble back up and fall again and this time there's no scrambling back up because a hand has grasped one ankle and yanked hard and I'm clawing at the banking but there's nothing to grip and my fingers are gouging down into the mud and I'm sliding right down and he flips me over now and he's blocking the light and the scream that pours out of my throat is cut short by the punch that explodes behind my eyes and my head is bumping and bumping on the low retaining wall at the foot of the banking and I want to scream but the blood from my broken nose is slipping thick down my throat and it's all I can do just to lie there and breathe.

The man who finds me next morning in the bluish first light is the proverbial dog-walker. I've been strangled with my own tights, like Victim Number One and Victim Number Two. A sanitary towel tucked under my armpit. The city rousing itself for another day, like nothing has changed.

From now on my name will be yoked with those of two strangers in a sequence that will never be broken, three names forever linked, like the Ronettes or the crew of Apollo 11. Jacquilyn Keevins. Ann Ogilvie. Marion Mercer.

In the flat, Henry is worried. He hasn't slept well. He looks out over the early morning street. He has given Calum his breakfast. He's waiting until it's late enough to phone Nancy. Maybe I got caught in the storm and stayed over with friends in town. Maybe Nancy got sick and I spent the night at hers.

Maybe I'll come padding up the stairs with my heels in my hand any minute, and he'll hear my key in the lock.

He's standing at the window, dishcloth over his shoulder. 'I wouldn't bet on it,' he tells me.

14

A hearse passed McCormack on Dumbarton Road and he drew the hat from his head and held it against his chest, it was useful for that if nothing else, Cochrane's bombastic insistence on hats. The family came next, glooming out of the gorgeous black car like moping royals, like a dynasty heading into exile. An adolescent boy – the son? the sibling? – watching McCormack as he passed. Flashiest ride of his life, McCormack thought, the black Daimler. That was probably true of the principal, too, the corpse. Of his death.

He was going to meet a tout called Billy Thomson. He sometimes wondered if Billy Thomson was a pseudonym, it seemed suspiciously apt as the name of a police informer: forgettable, bland, it blended right in. Thomson was a short, fat man with a drinker's face. Forties, balding, he worked as a painter and decorator and hung around the East End pubs. His brother-in-law owned a betting shop in Shettleston.

McCormack was meeting him on a bench in Kelvingrove Park. They figured Kelvingrove Park was far enough from the East End. But then they'd chosen a sunny day at lunchtime and the bench they'd planned to meet at was taken. An old man in shirtsleeves and broad blue braces was tilting his face to the sun, his hands folded primly in his lap, a folded *Tribune* on the bench beside him. At the other end of the bench a young mother with an open Tupperware box was feeding segments of apple to a rowdy-looking toddler.

He climbed a little further up the hill to a vacant bench in the shade and lit a Regal. In a while he caught sight of Thomson in his painter's overalls, picking his way between the sunbathers. He saw Thomson pause in mid-stride as he noticed that the bench was taken, and then come on more slowly, scanning the grassy hillside. When Thomson's face was pointed in his direction McCormack lifted his hat and set it back on his head and Thomson came on now with more purpose, his paint-spattered knees working as he laboured up the hill.

'You in training, Billy? Looking trim.'

Billy had his hands on his knees, bent double, gasping for breath. He held a finger up and in due course was able to say 'Fuck you', twice, wheezily. He tugged a hankie from his overall pocket and dragged it across his face.

'So what do you hear, Billy?' McCormack offered the pack of Regals. 'You hear any names?'

Billy Thomson shrugged, leaned in to McCormack's lighter.

'Gangsters stopped dancing, have they?'

'Oh, they still dance.' Thomson exhaled deeply, mopped the back of his neck. 'They just don't dance in the Barrowland, in my experience.'

'Naw?'

'Naw. Too much chance of getting a sore face off one of the young teams. All these mental young guys wanting to make a name for theirselves. Chibs smuggled in in their birds' knickers. The top boys prefer the Albert. Different crowd. More upmarket.'

'That's valuable information, Billy. That's a nugget. Which

140

Glasgow dance hall's got a classier crowd than the next one. That's a dollar's worth all on its own.'

'Well, what are you looking for?' A wounded whine had entered Billy's voice. 'What can I tell you? They know fuck all. You don't think they want him caught too? They want him caught more'n you do. Then maybe we could all go back to work.'

'"We?" Who's "we", Billy?'

'They. Whatever. Have you asked Walter Maitland?'

Maitland was McGlashan's chief enforcer, reputed once to have offed a defaulter by forcing a joiner's rasp down his throat.

'Glash's muscle? Why would I ask him, Billy?'

Thomson's eyes narrowed. 'Maitland? Well, he only fucking works there.'

'Where?'

'The Barrowland, for Chrissake! He works the door.' Thomson frowned. 'I figured you knew.'

McCormack took a folded banknote, stabbed it into the tout's top pocket. 'Do us a favour, Billy. Figure fuck all. Assume I know nothing. All right? Jesus. Less than nothing. Go buy yourself some Lanny, Billy. Bottle of El D. Have yourself a party.'

Billy patted his top pocket. 'You want to get onside with Maitland you'll need to go higher than that. Glen Grant's what he drinks. Nothing but the best.'

Cranhill was a fifties scheme of roughcast tenements and porridge-coloured tower blocks hemmed in by the new motorway. It was the kind of glorious future that the city's slum-dwellers had been promised, back in the thirties. Nowadays the only futuristic feature was the big square water tower on Bellrock Street. McCormack parked beside it. He left his hat in the car. If you needed a hat to tell he was a cop then what were you doing in Cranhill?

The address in Bellrock Street was a three-storey tenement. Washing was draped over brown-brick balconies. A dog rooted around in the uncut grass behind the front railings. The hollow ticking sound was a stick being dragged along the railings by a blond-haired boy. Two more boys had their heads pressed to the windows of a red Ford Zephyr, hands clamped on to their foreheads like twin salutes to kill the glass's reflective glare. McCormack climbed to the second floor, flipped the letter box of the left-hand apartment.

A boy of maybe four or five opened the door and looked glumly up at him. He was dressed in a grubby pullover and rumpled grey shorts, black sandshoes with elasticated tops. At the far end of the narrow hallway a big man was shrugging into a dinner jacket and watching McCormack in the mirror of a hall-stand. He smoothed down the jacket's satin collar and turned and came striding towards the door.

'I'm on my way out, copper. Some of us have jobs to go to.' He rested his palm on the boy's head. 'Go on through and see your mammy, wee man.'

The boy toddled off. McCormack nodded. His hands were plunged in the pockets of his raincoat.

'You might be a wee bit late tonight,' he said. 'I'm sure your boss will make allowances.'

The two ends of a bow-tie were hanging down on the man's white shirt-front and he grasped them in his big fingers and started to fold.

'Let's see it, then.'

McCormack found his warrant card, flipped it open. The man studied the card as he finished with the bow-tie, tugging on the ends and craning his neck.

'McCormack. You one of Flett's boys?'

'I'm Flying Squad, aye. Do I get to come in?'

142

The door swung free and McCormack followed the man's broad back down the short hallway and into the kitchen.

A half net curtain on the window. Dishes in the sink. A smell of lavender from somewhere. A bottle of Glen Grant on the dresser and on the fold-away table, nestled in soft cloth, two lovely fearsome objects: a chisel, with its bluish blade and a bright stripe of light along its bevelled edge; and, yes, here was the fabled rasp – a varnished handle of orangey wood and the long flat slab of a blade with its rows of tiny teeth.

The man followed his gaze, said nothing.

'Tools of the trade?' McCormack offered.

'I'm building something.'

'Aye? What are you building?'

'A hutch. For a rabbit. The boy wants a rabbit.'

They both knew that these tools were destined for less innocent tasks than the construction of a rabbit-hutch, but McCormack nodded. He fished into his pocket for his notebook just as the man reached into his hip pocket. McCormack flinched and bumped back into the doorframe, knocking a picture from the wall.

'Easy, tiger.' The man snorted. A metal comb glinted in his fingers and he stepped to the wall-clock and started fixing his hair in its glassy convex face.

McCormack set his notebook on the table. He bent to retrieve the flimsy wooden frame and fixed the picture back on to its nail: King Billy on his white charger, crossing the Boyne, his sword held aloft in a straight-armed salute.

'You're Walter James Maitland?'

The comb paused in mid-air. 'Sunday names, is it? Yes, I'm Walter Maitland.'

'You work as a bouncer at the Barrowland Ballroom, Mr Maitland. Is that correct?'

'Nope.' Maitland kept combing his hair.

'You're not a bouncer?'

'I'm a ballroom supervisor,' Maitland said.

'Right. Forgive me. You're a ballroom supervisor. You were working as a ballroom supervisor on the night of twenty-fifth January. The night Marion Mercer was killed.'

'This is the Quaker stuff? We've been through all that. I gave my statement at the time.'

A blast of noise from the living room, the nasal *whang* of caroming bullets from a TV western. A door closed and the sound died. Was it his imagination or did Maitland look positively relieved? As if he thought McCormack was here on some other errand.

'So you can give it again. You were working that night?'

'If you say so.'

'Did you speak with Marion Mercer?'

'I was working till one in the morning. I've got one or two people can confirm that. Like maybe three or four hundred. I think they call that an alibi.'

'That's not what I asked you.'

Maitland frowned. 'Did I speak to her? There's twelve of us on the door. Four hundred punters. Did I speak to one particular woman? Who's gonnae remember that?'

The comb had been stowed and Maitland was buttoning the dinner jacket. He looked both incongruous and entirely at home in the shabby little kitchen.

'The manager's statement,' McCormack said. 'The manager said there was a fracas at the payphone, an altercation that night. You sorted it out. Is that true?'

'A guy wouldnae get off the payphone. Somebody in the queue was getting shirty. Yeah, I sorted it out.'

'He also said, your manager, that this was the only disturbance of the evening. It was a very quiet night for the bouncers.

144

Excuse me, the ballroom supervisors. You had nothing to do. Plenty of time to check out the talent, study the punters. So take your time. Think back. It was a company of four. Two men, two women at a table. One of the men wore a woollen scarf, a regimental tie. Might have been a soldier.'

'I don't get into their life stories, pal. I chuck them out when they start fights.'

'Right. And hit on the women? Do that too?'

'What you on about?'

'Perk of the job. Get your pick of the birds at chucking-out time. Is that not how it works?'

'I'm a married man, copper. You want to look to your own. That's where most of the trouble starts, if you want to know the truth. Off-duty polis, throwing their weight around. Hitting on folks' birds.'

'So you don't remember Marion Mercer. What about the other ones? Jacquilyn Keevins? Ann Ogilvie? Were you working those nights?'

'You've seen the rosters, copper. You know I was working. There a point to all this?'

McCormack looked again at the painting on the wall, the foppish royal in his floppy, feathered hat, the white horse with one daintily raised hoof. Was there a point to all this? Yes, you fucker. The point is to piss you off. The point is to put you out. Put down a marker. Remember this face. I'm coming for the lot of you. Once this Quaker shit's finished, you're my special project. You and your boss and all your scummy underlings, all your toy soldiers.

'Three women are dead, Mr Maitland. That's the point.'

The door at McCormack's back clicked open and the boy stood there. He was in his pyjamas now, uncertain whether to go to his father, glancing at the strange man standing by the sink. Maitland tugged the knees of his trousers and dropped

145

to his haunches, arms wide. When the boy slammed into his father's chest, Maitland hoisted him high, the slippered feet kicking, and lodged him in the crook of his elbow. Secure in his father's grip, he looked down boldly at the man in the raincoat, big-eyed, unblinking.

'So how come you're back to see me? Why am I getting it?'

'Well, we didn't know we were dealing with a celebrity.'

Maitland said nothing.

'How long have you worked for John McGlashan?'

'Who?'

'Uh-huh. OK, Mr Maitland. You live in Cranhill. You work the door at the Barrowland. But you don't know who John McGlashan is.'

Maitland lowered the boy to the floor. The boy skipped back through to the living room.

'I know who John McGlashan is. I just don't know why you're bringing him up. You gonnae let me out of my house now, copper?'

'You don't work for McGlashan?'

'I'm *trying* to work. If you'd fucking let me.'

Maitland bounced on his toes just then, and the boyishness of the gesture somehow offended McCormack. It was all just a game to this guy. All the collecting and the hurting, all the threats and pleas and beatings, it was just a way of keeping score. Well, some games had forfeits. McCormack stowed his notebook in his pocket.

'You seen Jimmy Kane lately? Give him my regards.'

Maitland was lighting a cigarette and he paused, the tiny bud of flame on his gold lighter. He took the unlit ciggie from his mouth. 'I fucking knew I knew you. You're the teuchter. It was you that put Kane away.'

'Aye. That's me. Well, we'll know each other next time, Mr Maitland.'

They left together, walking in silence, McCormack crossing to the Velox. The kids who'd been lounging around the railings straightened up as Maitland came down the path. A boy in a Harrington jacket and a Rangers scarf stepped out from the little crowd. Hands in his jacket pockets, he spread his arms, displaying the tartan lining.

'Good as new, Mr Maitland. Naebody's been near it.'

Maitland dug a hand into his trouser pocket and spread his fingers as he brought it free. A clutch of coins spread glinting in the failing light and fell to earth. The boys were crouching and scrabbling in the gutter before the coins hit the tarmac.

The red Zephyr's engine turned and Maitland roared off, flashing a grin. *The teuchter*. It could have been worse, McCormack thought: I could have been the Fenian. McCormack watched the car climb west, heading for the lights of the city. Actually, it could have been worse than that. He repeated the registration to himself, fishing in his pocket for his notebook.

15

When McCormack got back to the Marine the Quaker Squad were discussing the Glendinnings job.

'Some stones,' Adam Farren was saying. 'Walk out the front door, broad daylight, a hundred grand in the tail.'

'Be a shame to catch them, almost,' Doug Gemmell said. 'Make them give it all back.'

'Stones?' McCormack slung his jacket on the back of his chair. He had spoken with more force than he intended. The rest of them looked up at him.

'Balls, my friend,' Farren said. 'Audacity. Ro*mance*, for fuck's sake. Four blokes in overalls. Hundred times your annual salary.'

McCormack sat down, jockeyed the chair a little closer to the desk and flipped open the folder he'd been reading before lunch. 'Five,' he said.

'What?'

'Minimum. You're forgetting the driver. It's five, not four. Six, if there's an insider. And what you'd admire is technique. The timing. The execution. The intel and planning that made it come good. It's a job of work, Detective. Fuck all to do with romance.'

He kept his eyes on the witness statement but you could tell they were grinning among themselves, waiting to see who would run with the ball, make the next move.

'Anyway.' Doug Gemmell spoke up. 'Mibbe it's only fifty times your annual salary. You Flying Squad boys. High fliers.'

McCormack said nothing.

'You earn it, though. No doubt about it. I mean us fucking plodders, we just see what's in front of our faces. But *you*, you've got the bird's-eye view, you see the whole story. Just like that. Like it's a job of work.'

Could you be bothered? Was it worth the effort to engage with this shit? McCormack sighed.

'I see it's a robbery, if that's what you mean. I see it's a bunch of gangsters. I see that. Scumbags.'

'You're saying it's the same, though?' Farren was frowning. 'What this guy does and what these guys did? They're all just crims?'

'You mean these pricks are Robin Hood?'

'Compared to him they're Robin Hood. Compared to him they're Florence Nightingale.'

Somewhere out there, somewhere in the dirty city, people were doing actual police work. They were chasing down this Glendinnings crew, rousting McGlashan's soldiers, grilling the nightwatchman, lifting prints from the railings and the safe, trying to trace the gelignite, trying to trace the van, leaning on the employees till they found the insider. He could have been helping them, instead of listening to this dipshit.

'Fine then.' McCormack leaned back in his chair, pushed the folder away from him. 'Who do you think these guys are, actually? As a matter of interest. I mean, who do they work for?'

They were all grinning now, big ignorant smiles pasted on their faces.

'Why don't you tell us, Professor.'

'Well, I think you already know, Detective. Unless you're thicker than you look. Which seems unlikely. Probably they're with McGlashan or they want to be with McGlashan. Let's say they kick up to McGlashan. Ten, fifteen grand. He puts some of it out on the street, at six hundred per cent interest. To sorry fuckers who can't pay him back. He spends five grand on heroin from his Liverpool connection. Another five boosting his stable of whores. Maybe some of it finds its way into the pockets of the City of Glasgow's finest – present company excepted – and the next time there's a raid on his big hoose in Pollokshields, well, fuck me, it's clean as the pure driven. No guns, no drugs. He's free to keep spreading his poison.' McCormack tapped the desk. 'That twenty grand ruins more lives than the Quaker could dream about. Do I think it's the same? These guys and the Quaker? I think these guys are a lot fucking worse than the Quaker.'

The door banged open and Cochrane's head appeared. 'Right, gents. Let's be having you.' No one bothered with Cochrane, everyone still clocking McCormack.

Cochrane looked around the faces.

'The fuck's happened here? Somebody died?' The heads craned round. Cochrane was grinning. 'Look lively, lads. Boy in the lobby needing handers.'

They all piled out of the Murder Room and clattered down the stairs. At the back of the group, McCormack could hear the ruckus echoing up the stairwell. High hooting shouts. He emerged into the lobby to see two detectives grappling with a youngish man in denims. The man was cuffed but kicking out and twisting, hollering, flexing his shoulders as the two cops gripped his elbows. A sort of rumbling cheer went up from the Quaker Squad and they surged forward. Hands grabbed the man's legs and arms and the detectives bore him through to the cells like the captain of a cup-winning team.

In the gloom of a white-tiled cell they uncuffed him, tossed him down on the concrete floor. He sprang up and faced them in a battle stance, his skinny legs planted apart, arms flexed, fists flashing open and shut. The cops sidled in and spread out along the wall on either side of the door.

It could have been anything – domestic, drunk and disorderly, breach of the peace – but McCormack knew already what it was. Something in the defiant shine of his eyes, the torn neck of his navy-blue polo shirt.

'Met this upstanding young man on the Way,' one of the detectives was saying. 'Friendly bloke. I'll give him that.'

The grins spread along the line of cops. They looked down at the floor, shaking their heads. This was going to be good.

'Wanted to know the time, for some reason.'

'That's original.'

'Maybe his own watch had stopped.'

'Time for what, sweetie-pie? Time for a quickie?'

McCormack felt sick. He couldn't be here. He couldn't be part of this. Whatever this turned out to be. He looked down the line of cops, teeth bared like dogs in their sick grins.

A black leather wallet lay on the floor. It had slipped from the man's hip-pocket as he twisted and writhed. Now Farren stepped forward and stooped to pick it up.

The man stood there, catching his breath. He swept his hair from his face and lifted his chin, half-defiant, half-afraid.

'Hey! Hey!' Farren had a driving licence between finger and thumb, wagging it in the air like a referee showing a card. He could hardly speak for laughing. 'It's the cunt's birthday! It's his fucking birthday!'

The cops cracking up.

'Give him his dumps!'

'This calls for a toast.'

McCormack turned to see one of the detectives – Doug Gemmell, it looked like – slipping out of the cell. Farren tossed the wallet on to the concrete pallet that served as a bed.

'Now the rest of it,' he said. 'Turn out your pockets.'

The man drew a comb from his back pocket and threw it to the floor. A biro from his left-front pocket, folded handkerchief from the right.

'And the ticket pocket.'

The man worked two fingers into the ticket pocket and drew out a square cellophane wrapper. The cops jeered. The Durex landed on the floor with the rest of his stuff.

'Just the one? Selling yourself short, boy.'

'Fuck you! Fuck the lot of youse!'

A delighted chorus of high-pitched, outraged squeals.

'Don't get him angry.'

'So butch.'

Gemmell was back in the doorway, brandishing a stack of plastic cups. Farren seized it and plucked a cup from the top and the stack made its way down the line.

McCormack glanced at the doorway. Cochrane was gone. The stack of cups was thrust at him and he took one, his neighbour snatching the others from his hand.

McCormack was frowning. He didn't see what the joke was. Then Farren had his flies undone and was pissing into a cup. It overran and spattered on the floor and he fumbled his cock back in with one hand. He stepped forward with the brimming liquid held high. 'The queen!' he cried. 'And all who sail in her!' Then he jerked his wrist and the urine lashed on to the man's face and neck. He staggered back, sputtering, retching.

Then the others were busy, laughter bubbling up as they hurried to fill their cups, and they stepped out in ones and twos, shouting their toasts, ragged arcs of piss hanging in the air, plastic cups tumbling after one another and bouncing on the floor. The man was hunkered down now, arms clasped on the back of his head, making himself small as the urine lashed his back in darkish stripes.

McCormack's empty cup was crunched in his fist. He let it drop and turned to leave and his eye caught Goldie's. The gaze held for a second or two. Whatever Goldie saw there made him grimace and drop his eyes and when McCormack stepped into the corridor he heard Goldie's voice, matey, cajoling. 'OK, fellas. He's had enough. Show's over. Let's get back to work.'

That night, back in the flat, McCormack looked out over the river and the cranes, sloshing the malt in lazy circles round his tumbler. He thought about the man in the polo shirt with the stripes of piss on his back. He thought about the look in Goldie's eyes. He thought about Flett. *Not a popularity contest, son.* Was it an *un*popularity contest, though? Was that what it was? If so, close the book. We have a winner.

16

Paton woke to the sound of screaming. Muffled shouts and cries were ringing through the stairwell. For a second it crossed his mind that they were knocking down the building, that the cranes and the wrecking ball had swung into place while he was sleeping and the old condemned walls were being levelled where he lay.

Then he struggled up on his elbows and glanced at the window: daylight. Whatever was going on, he couldn't be found here, he had to get out. He sprang to his feet, the sleeping bag bunching round his ankles. He was fully dressed – for the last four nights he had slept in his clothes – and he stooped to snatch his jacket from the floor, then grabbed the Browning from the top of the mantel. He pulled the door behind him as he left.

He clattered down the stairs, wrestling into his jerkin and wedging the pistol into the waistband of his jeans. As he rounded the final banister and daylight flooded the stairwell the clamour got louder.

A boy stood in the back close, framed in the doorway, a scrawny silhouette. Ten years old, eleven, a primary kid. The skinny kid from the backcourt. He was crying in a harsh rhythm, his cries bouncing off the whitewashed walls. For a reason he couldn't explain, Paton knew that whatever was causing these cries was in the room that faced him now. He stopped on the threshold; his palms braced on the doorjamb, and leaned into the room.

In the light from a half-boarded window he saw the body on the floor, half-in and half-out of the bed recess. He saw the pulped smudge of the face, the black flow oozing from between the white legs, he saw the utter, stark deadness. He pushed himself off from the doorjamb and plunged towards the back close. The boy straightened up as Paton passed him, his wide white eyes locking on to Paton's, holding the gaze till Paton wrenched away and scanned the backcourt.

A white sheet fluttered from a washing line. Wagging clumps of weeds. The ribbed, overturned drum of a dustbin, a dented tin can. A man coming towards him in a waddling rush across the rubble, a heavyset man in an undershirt and trousers, rolling his shoulders as he pulled on his braces. There were heads poking out of second- and third-storey windows. The rubble crunched as Paton turned on his heel, back through the close, the boy flinching as he passed, down the steps and into Queen Mary Street.

He turned south and set off at a sprint, turning into Hozier Street. Sunday silence, the blank, blind windows of the tenements. Slow down, man, he told himself: walk, look like someone walking to buy the Sunday paper. But his legs wouldn't be told.

The barrel of the pistol jarred against his body as he ran and he reached back to check it wasn't working loose.

At Old Dalmarnock Road he turned down Muslin Street and on to Tullis Street. The Green was just ahead and a last frantic spurt took him through the gates.

*   *   *

It was Sunday lunchtime when the phone rang. McCormack was fixing breakfast. Two eggs, three rashers and a mottled tattie scone were spitting in the pan; crisping under the grill was a disc of black pudding, one of fruit pudding and a slice of Lorne sausage. He had the radio tuned to *Round the Horne*: 'Here are the answers to last week's questions . . .' It took him a moment to place the voice.

'I hope to fuck you said your prayers at ten o'clock Mass, son.'

Cochrane.

Jesus, that was quick, McCormack thought: *he's seen it already*. On Friday afternoon McCormack had finished his report, sent it in triplicate to St Andrew's Street. Reading it over before he sealed the envelope he winced at the schoolmasterish tone, the idiom of the end-of-term report. He had praised the Marine detectives for their diligence and application, their attention to detail. The black marks were more specific. Too much store had been set on Nancy Scullion's testimony. Other potential avenues of inquiry were neglected. The very perseverance of the Quaker Squad was in some ways counterproductive: faced with a brick wall, they kept on pushing.

The report ended as everyone knew it would, with a recommendation that the investigation be wound down, particularly in view of the significant lapse of time since the last killing. 'On the balance of probabilities,' McCormack wrote, 'it would be logical to assume that the perpetrator is no longer at large in the Glasgow area.'

It was a fair report. Cochrane wouldn't like it but he couldn't paint it as a stitch-up. Still, you couldn't grudge him a right of reply and here it came. McCormack wedged the phone under his chin and scooped his smokes from the kitchen table. He turned off the radio. Cochrane was saying something about a pen.

'A pen?'

'To take things down, Detective. A writing implement. Pen or pencil. That class of thing.'

McCormack scanned round the room. He didn't have a pen. 'I've got a pen,' he said.

'Forty-eight Queen Mary Street.' Cochrane spoke with pedantic clarity, like the speaking clock. 'That's in Bridgeton, Detective.' McCormack could see smoke curling out from under the grill. 'Bridgeton's in the East End of Glasgow.'

There was something under the heavy edge of Cochrane's irony, a wrinkle of hilarity that McCormack couldn't work out.

'Sir, sorry: why are you telling me this?'

Somehow he could hear Cochrane smiling.

'He's back,' Cochrane said. 'The Quaker. He's killed another woman. On the balance of probabilities, son, I'd say your report is a bag of shite.'

II
THE BLOODY FLESH

'God's refuted but the devil's not.'

Charles Simic, 'The Scarecrow'

17

McCormack sat in the Velox behind the dark green scene-of-crime trailer. He turned off the engine. The tick of cooling metal gave way to silence and then to the sound of his own breathing. He hadn't eaten breakfast: he was grateful at least for that, the fry-up went straight in the bin. As always when he was nervous, tiredness seemed to flood him like adrenaline. He leaned his head against the head-rest.

Queen Mary Street: the Quaker was spelling it out for them now.

The trailer looked like a horse-box. Nothing snuffled and stamped its feet on dirty straw in there, though. Instead, as McCormack had learned on the sergeant's course at Tulliallan and confirmed on a dozen investigations, the trailer contained a sinister assemblage of functional implements: Klieg lights, a folding ladder, a spade, a yardstick, a crowbar, wire-cutters, a hatchet, a saw, tarpaulins, two flashlights, four pairs of Wellington boots. More than anything else it was the boots; the boots were what got you. He took a quick puff of his inhaler, lifted his hat from the passenger seat and hauled himself out of the car.

Crossing the road he could feel the grit and stones through his shoes' thin soles. His whole body felt preternaturally sensitive. He felt like he did when he walked out on to the shinty pitch at Balla, with the sun on his back and the green-brown bulk of Meall Mor lifting its peak to the heavens. He parted the sparse crowd with his warrant card and nodded to the constable at the closemouth.

'Second on the left, sir.'

Another cop was stationed outside the flat, guarding the space where the door should have been.

The flat had two rooms. There was nothing at all in the first one and not much more in the second.

The fireplace had been removed. What was left was just a naked hole, a black slot at the foot of the wall. In the far corner some of the floorboards had been torn up for firewood. Tidemarks of damp lapped the walls. The room smelled strongly of piss and burnt rubber. In the centre of the room was a dirty mattress and the body of a woman. She lay sprawled there, head on the mattress, feet on the floor. The light from a partly boarded-up window splashed across her upper body. She wore a blindfold, some kind of scarf round her neck. A soiled, bloodstained slip was ruched, bunched above her waist. A tacky black pool spread over the boards to where the two detectives stood.

McCormack crossed to the body. As he squatted down beside it he noticed the dead woman's feet. She had painted her nails a glittery green. The little toe on her right foot had the merest fleck of glitter on its tiny nail. He shuffled back, tugging the hem of his raincoat away from the blood.

She was naked, apart from the blindfold, the scarf and the cream-coloured slip. She lay on her back, the face purple and swollen, features bloated and squashed. The face looked like a balloon full of water. The body was boyish and thin, breasts almost flat above prominent ribs. There were purplish bruises on her upper chest and left shoulder. What looked like a smiling mouth had been carved into the flesh of her left breast. Like the others, she had been menstruating. The black pool on the floor had seeped from her vagina, whose black tuft stirred in the draught from the glassless window.

'It's our boy, all right.' Goldie's voice was dry and papery, as if from lack of use.

The woman's hair had been hacked off and lay in clumps around her head. McCormack thought of the bulletins from Ulster, women with their heads clipped and shaved, chained to railings in Belfast or Derry.

He leaned closer. The blindfold was not a blindfold. The blindfold was a sanitary napkin. The scarf was not a scarf but a stocking. Its twin was gone, along with the shoes, the bra and pants, whatever dress she was wearing. She had been stripped and pillaged, like this flat, this building.

McCormack walked round to the other side of the mattress where the light was better. The woman's left arm hung over the mattress, knuckles touching the floor. The fingernails were painted, same green as the toes, but two of them were chipped and split and the nails of the middle and index fingers held a crescent of black that might have been dirt but most likely was blood. She had fought her killer, raked his face. Left a mark. On the ring finger of her pale left hand was a still paler strip, the ghost of a wedding band.

'Footprints.' Goldie was over by the door now. He gestured at the floor, clicked his tongue. 'Careless. Not like him.'

There were two separate prints on the bare wooden boards. A small ribbed sole that suggested a child's sandshoe and the thick ridges of a man's workboot.

A bluebottle swayed in the air, fat as a bee. McCormack felt it bump the back of his hand as he swatted it away.

There were footsteps in the close, the familiar booming tones of Cochrane's voice. He strode into the room with Farren and Gemmell at his back. With his fedora tipped back on his head he looked tipsy, there was a Bank Holiday swagger to him. He smiled grimly at the body on the floor and then looked at McCormack, shaking his head as though McCormack was to blame.

'"No longer at large in the Glasgow area".' He shook his head. McCormack shrugged.

Cochrane had his hands on his hips, surveying the room. 'Who found her then?' he said.

'Wee boy playing in the backcourt,' said Goldie. 'He wandered in through the back close then ran out screaming blue murder and a neighbour came out to see what was happening. The neighbour phoned it in from a box on London Road.'

Cochrane nodded, breathed out slowly through his nose. He swung abruptly round and strode out. They could hear him giving orders in the close, his footsteps diminishing towards the backcourt.

Seawright came in, the police pathologist. The police photographer was right behind him. Seawright kneeled in front of his black case and sprung the fasteners and lifted the lid. The police photographer was already moving round the body, crouching and bending, the flashbulb detonations searing the shadows with bursts of white light. Seawright said something to the snapper and he squatted down to get close-ups of the face, the knife marks on the breast.

While the photographer was finishing up, Seawright scribbled in his notebook. McCormack turned to the snapper.

'Get the wall.'

The snapper was fiddling with his gear, dismantling the big lens. He looked up. McCormack was pointing at the back wall, the mess of overlapping letters, the blizzard of slogans and acronyms. The snapper followed his finger.

'You want me to take a picture of the wall?'

'That's the idea.'

The snapper's lips tightened. He was all briskness and business now, rattling off the shots, winding on the film with flicks of his thumb.

'Get some close-ups,' McCormack said. The snapper nodded, didn't turn round.

Seawright was fitting transparent plastic bags over the hands of the victim, tying them in place. He placed one over the victim's head and secured it at the neck. Then he and his assistant unfolded a large plastic sheet and laid it on the floor. They lifted the body on to the sheet and wrapped the sheet around the body before zipping it into a body bag. The last thing McCormack saw was the short blond hair, some of it black with blood as if the roots were showing through.

Cochrane would be riding down to the Saltmarket with Seawright to watch the post-mortem. McCormack had seen enough. He swung through the back close and out into the sunlight, gulping lungfuls of air. A uniformed constable was stationed at the tenement's back door. He refused McCormack's offer of a cigarette with a quick shake of his head.

McCormack had seen his share of dissections. He'd stood at Seawright's shoulder with the dab of Vicks on his upper lip, trying to fight the flutter in his stomach, taking it all in. The harsh mortuary light. The big crude 'Y' that they drew on the body: incisions running from behind each ear to meet at the breastbone and drop down together to the pubis. The skin peeled back like an orange. Internal organs scooped in double handfuls, weighed and bagged. The contents of the stomach spread like a divination on a brushed steel tray.

Seawright reading the entrails, giving a running commentary in that flat keelie voice.

McCormack closed his eyes, felt the sun on his lids, let the smell of death, of that damp, bloody room, dissipate in the clear air, drew the clean harsh smoke deep into his lungs.

'Detective.' He turned to see Cochrane in the doorway. 'Take him home, would you? Take the boy home. Talk to him there. Do some proper police work for a change.'

McCormack stepped on his smoke. 'Sir.'

18

The door to the neighbour's flat was ajar. He could hear the murmur of low voices, a clink of crockery. He knocked on the door, pushed it open.

Down the hall to the kitchen. There was an old woman in a tatty armchair and a boy on a kitchen chair with a WPC beside him at the table.

'This is Detective Inspector McCormack, Andrew. He's a policeman. He's going to take you home.'

McCormack squatted down in front of the boy. He was nine or ten, slumped in the kitchen chair with his hands in the pockets of his grey school shorts. The toes of his sandshoes kept catching with a squeak on the scuffed white lino. There were marks on the lino, black streaks from the blood on his shoes.

'You doing OK, wee man?'

The boy looked up at McCormack then back at the floor, nodded. His dark hair hung in lank strands.

'What's your name, son?'

The boy shrugged.

'You're not in trouble, all right? What's your name?'

'Andrew Gilmour.'

'Where do you live, Andrew?'

'Birgidale Road.'

McCormack knew Bridgeton fairly well. He'd worked a payroll robbery here in '67 and knocked a lot of doors. But he didn't remember Birgidale Road.

He clapped a hand on the boy's shoulder. 'Think you can show me where that is, pal?'

The boy looked up. He nodded. 'Aye, mister. It's in Castlemilk.'

McCormack looked at the WPC. 'Caste*milk*! You live in Castlemilk, Andrew?' He was almost shouting. The boy flinched. He said it quieter, starting again: 'You're from Castlemilk?'

The boy's fringe juddered.

'Then what were you doing here?'

The boy looked at the floor. 'Nothin'.' Defensive, sullen. The shoulders lifted and fell. 'Wasnae doin' nothin'.'

Castlemilk was, what, five, six miles away, out on the edge of the city. The boy was clearly alone. No jacket. Just a brown V-neck pullover and the grey shorts. Castlemilk was another orbit, it might as well be Mars.

'Who brought you here, Andrew?' McCormack asked him. 'How did you get here?'

'Took the bus.' The boy's fringe screened his eyes. The toes of both sandshoes were touching the floor now, like a ballet dancer on points.

They drove to Castlemilk in silence, the boy only talking to give directions. Birgidale Road was like the coast of Britain approached from the south. Along one side a colossal row of white-harled four-storey tenements dropped the whole length of the street, a dirty-white unbroken cliff. They stopped halfway down it.

McCormack followed the boy's sclaffing sandshoes up to the

third-floor landing. The boy rattled the flap of the letter box. Nothing.

McCormack was crouching down to peer through the flap when the door yanked open.

'Again?' The woman was wearing slacks and a sleeveless blouse and an expression of tight-lipped belligerence.

'Mrs Gilmour.' McCormack had his warrant card in his hand. The hard eyes dropped to scan the card and two discs of green eyeshadow bulged out like second eyes. McCormack put his card away. 'Your son is the witness to a very serious crime, Mrs Gilmour. He's had a severe shock. I think it might be best if we all went inside.'

'He's been warned. He steals from the mantel for the bus fare. He's been tellt. What "serious crime"?'

'Let's go inside.'

The house smelled of paint and dampness and the sour brown smell of neglected pet – a rabbit or guinea pig.

'Mrs Gilmour. Why was your son in the vicinity of Queen Mary Street in Bridgeton this morning?'

The woman laughed. 'Cause he's soft in the head. He thinks if his da comes back he'll go to Queen Mary Street. He won't know to come here.' She snorted. 'He thinks his da's coming back.'

McCormack took out his notebook. 'You clearly don't share his optimism.'

'What's that?'

McCormack looked up. 'I said you don't think Andrew's father is coming back.'

'He'll be in Timbuktu by now, if he knows what's good for him. Outer Mongolia.'

The boy looked across at her then, a look of narrow-eyed loathing, and then back to the floor.

'We moved here when Eric left us,' the woman said. 'He

169

doesnae have our address and I don't want his. We're well shot of him.'

The boy continued scowling.

'A woman was killed, Mrs Gilmour. Last night or early this morning. Andrew found the body.'

Something gleamed in the hard green eyes. 'A woman? Is it the Quaker?'

'At this stage we can't say for definite what—'

'It's the Quaker, isn't it?'

'Mrs Gilmour: we don't know. Andrew disturbed the man we think may have killed the woman.'

'He saw the Quaker?' She turned to the boy. 'You saw the Quaker?'

The boy said something then. McCormack had been focusing on the mother and had missed what the boy said. 'Say it again, son?'

The boy cleared his throat. 'He had birds on his hands.'

McCormack looked at the mother and the mother shrugged. 'What do you mean, son, he had birds on his hands?'

'There,' the boy said, tapping the back of his right hand, where the thumb and forefinger joined, then tapping the same place on his left.

'Tattoos? You mean his hands were tattooed?'

The boy nodded. McCormack knew what he meant. He'd seen it before, little swifts or swallows in the fleshy part between finger and thumb.

None of the other witnesses had mentioned tattoos. Not the boy and girl who gave the descriptions after the first murder. Not Nancy Scullion, who spent a whole evening in the Quaker's company. The man Andrew Gilmour had seen wasn't the Quaker. Unless the tats were new, unless he'd had them done precisely to muddy the trail, then the man he had witnessed was somebody else.

* * *

170

That afternoon, back at the Marine, McCormack was typing up his interview with the boy when Adam Farren and Doug Gemmell breezed in. Only Goldie and McCormack were in the Murder Room; everyone else was doing door-to-door in Bridgeton. Farren tossed his keys on to his desk and slung his jacket on the back of his chair. He didn't sit down. He stretched and gave a false noisy yawn and when he spoke it was to no one in particular.

'This is cosy. All boys together. Part of the squad now, is he? One of the gang. Quick as you like.'

McCormack kept his eyes on his work. Sour reek of beer. He could smell the beer from where he sat. Another murder, a world of fresh leads to be chased, and here were these pricks sinking buckshee pints.

'Doesn't let the grass grow under his feet, this boy. Gotta give him that.'

'I was doing my job, Detective.'

'Right. The excuse of rats and wankers through the ages. Doing my job.'

McCormack was reading over what he'd written so far. He kept his tone light, distracted. 'Hm. That's right. You might want to try it sometime.'

'How's that?'

McCormack gave the platen a couple of twists. 'Doing your job. If you'd done your job properly I wouldn't have to be here. Could've stayed doing what I'm good at. Putting thieves away. Stead of wiping your backsides.'

'Hey hey hey.' Gemmell was on his feet now, hitching his trousers. Farren moved clumsily, bumping his way through the empty chairs. McCormack stood abruptly, turned.

'What, you're going to start on me now? Run out of suspects. No human punchbag in the dunny? Tell you a secret, lads. There's more to being a detective than a Slater's suit and acting the hard man. Or nicking over to The Smiddy for a pint. You're working a murder; start acting like it.'

Gemmell had Farren by the arm now, holding him back. Farren's fringe had fallen across his eyes. Breathing seemed to be a problem.

'Two weeks.' Rage had compressed Farren's voice to a bated rasp. 'I'll give you two weeks before someone fucking sorts you out.'

McCormack's eyebrows climbed. 'Two weeks? Well, if it's gonnae be you, you better get into shape, fella. Start doing sit-ups or something. Because you couldnae beat a fat man to the bus.' He grinned. 'Look at the fucking cut of you. Even talking a fight's got you knackered. You want to settle it now?' He jerked his thumb at the doorway. 'Plenty empty cells down there. I'm sure Angelo Dundee here would hold your jacket.'

There was a spell of thirty seconds when the only sounds were Farren's troubled breathing and the whir of the fan on the desk. Then McCormack turned his back and sat down. He started typing. The keys snapped home in savage bursts, rattling the platen. He worked for twenty minutes. When he stood up to file the report, Goldie was watching him in silence.

'What?' he said.

19

'Detective!'

The men around the front door swarmed him, tugging note-books from their raincoat pockets. He pulled the fedora brim down another half-inch and braced his arms in front of him, breaking his way through the crowd.

'Is this number four, Detective? Is this the Quaker? Will you catch him this time? Can you name the victim?'

In the light drizzle their upturned faces had a look of tragic intensity, of holy supplication.

McCormack shouldered through to the bright yellow glow of the station lobby.

The Murder Room was packed. Men were perched on desks, lining the walls, standing two deep at the back. Cochrane had his hands in the air, calling for order. McCormack found a space beneath the wall-clock, took off his hat, held it at his chest like someone standing for the national anthem.

Cochrane was standing on a chair now, clapping his hands. The voices subsided, the hubbub dropping an octave, then another, rumbling to a halt.

'OK. All leave is cancelled as of now.' Cochrane climbed

173

down from the chair. 'That's the first thing. Those of you with wives and weans, I hope you spent some time with them at the weekend. Maybe leave a photograph out on the mantelpiece, cause they're going to forget what you look like. This is seven-day weeks till further notice.'

The photos were up on the pinboard already. He slapped the board with the back of his hand. 'This, gentlemen, is why we're here. Body of a female, as yet unidentified, found in the ground-floor flat of a derelict tenement block at forty-eight Queen Mary Street, Bridgeton. The PM report will come in tomorrow but the circumstances tally with those of Jacquilyn Keevins, Ann Ogilvie and Marion Mercer. Victim was bludgeoned, raped, strangled with her tights. These are the details that will be made public.

'The details that will *not* be made public also tally with the earlier murders. Victim was menstruating at the time of her death. A sanitary napkin was placed on the body – in this case across the eyes, as you can see. There are knife marks on her chest and the face has been beaten beyond recognition. Let me remind you, gentlemen, once and for all: these details do not leak. If they do leak, I will find the leak and I will personally ensure that his career with the City of Glasgow Police ends that same day. Fuck traffic duties: you're out. Finished. Am I understood?

'Let's be clear then. This is our man. This is number four. He has killed again but he's been careless. He was seen leaving the locus yesterday morning. He left a footprint. He may have left fingerprints. We have two tasks. Number one: find this man. Number two: identify the victim. Uniforms will be tasked from the incident caravan at the locus. DI McCormack will now be part of the investigating team. You will make him welcome. And now' – Cochrane glanced to his left as the door opened and a dark-suited figure blocked the doorway. 'And now, gentlemen, we have a visitor.'

Detective Chief Superintendent Peter Levein, head of Glasgow CID, strode to the front of the room and turned to face the men. You didn't see him too often in the normal run of things and the men straightened a bit in their seats. He stood for a moment, enjoying the scrutiny, leading with his big clean-shaven chin. He wore a bright white shirt whose thick twill was visible to the first three rows of men, red and gold diagonal stripes on his tie, a dark blue suit of the kind you might keep good for a wedding or a funeral.

'Gentlemen.' He liked the sound of his voice, its deep, chesty reverberation, and he said the word again. 'Gentlemen. We will find this man.' He looked round the room, meeting all the eyes he could. 'Until we do, life will not be fun. Life will bear remarkably little resemblance to a bowl of fucking cherries. Having me on your back is the least of it. You'll have Chief Constable Lennox. The *Daily Express* and the *Daily* fucking *Record*. It will get political. The Secretary of State will take an interest; there may be questions in the House. You want this shit to finish, you want to go back to your cosy wee lives, there's a simple solution. We find this man.'

Then he turned to confabulate with Cochrane and the meeting broke up, the detectives rising in a buzz of talk with Levein's words hanging in the air. *We find this man.*

But what they found first of all was the locket. A broken chain, glinting in a clump of weeds. One of the uniforms spotted it in the backcourt at Queen Mary Street. Next to the chain a fancy golden locket edged in pearls. There was no picture in the locket but it looked distinctive enough for a detective to be detailed to take it round the city's jewellers.

Next day the City of Glasgow Police issued a new likeness of the Quaker. The artist – the same as for the first drawing, a teacher at the city's School of Art – had spoken to the boy. He'd spent time with the other witnesses, the ones who watched the man flee the scene. The result was a harsher, more human face with distinctive, believable features: a long pinched nose; a sullen mouth with a deep hollow over the top lip; hazelnut eyes under hooded lids. The vacant expanses of the original sketch – those smooth beardless cheeks and the unlined brow – had been filled in with stubble and creases. The first drawing might have been anyone; the new one was a man you might recognize if you saw him at the bookies or passed him on a subway escalator.

The posters were everywhere. Shop windows, taxis, barbershops, bus stops: the new face proliferated across the city. McCormack felt menaced by the updated posters, he sensed a shift in the balance of power. It had to do with the eyes, where the artist had captured an expression of hostile scrutiny. To McCormack it felt like the tables had turned. The cops had been seeking the Quaker. Now the Quaker was watching them.

20

Close up, it looked like a piece of abstract art. Purples and browns, navies and reds: deep tones laid on in splotchy blocks. Dirty streaks of yellow. Only when you stepped back a couple of feet and narrowed your eyes did the image resolve itself into a face. There were eyes amid those purples, a mouth without its teeth. Swollen and crushed, the face had lost its contours, become a child's crayoned outline of a face.

McCormack turned from the headshots on the Murder Room wall and snatched his burning Regal from the ashtray. The victim's face told them nothing. It was like one of those buildings out there, half-demolished. No way to reconstruct it. No way to tell how it used to look.

The other photos were useless too. The snapper's close-ups of the wall had come back. McCormack had hoped for some dark revelation in the nest of graffiti but it was just the usual palimpsest of gang slogans, sexual boasting and sectarian slurs.

Their best hope now was the locket. Photos of the locket would appear on tomorrow's front pages and the TV bulletins. Someone would point at the screen, punch their partner on the shoulder, reach for the phone.

McCormack was halfway through a pudding supper when Goldie came in with the pathologist's report.

McCormack kept eating. He looked up and nodded at Goldie and turned his attention back to the pocked and cratered batter and the fat white chips. He knew what the pathologist's report would say. The blood was menstrual blood. The victim had been choked by the ligature round her neck. Cause of death: strangulation.

'No surprises?'

'Surprises?' Goldie tossed the report on the desk. 'How's this for surprises? She wasnae menstruating.'

McCormack looked up. 'What you talking about? The blood—'

Goldie leaned over to steal a chip. 'She'd been stabbed.'

'Oh Jesus, naw.' McCormack stayed a chip on its way to his mouth. 'Stabbed? Fuck.' He dropped the chip back in the wrapper.

Goldie shrugged out of his jacket. 'Short serrated blade. Probably a chopping knife. Jeez, that smells good.' He nabbed another chip. 'Internal lacerations but no damage to internal organs.'

The others were gathering round now, eager to hear.

'Cause of death?' McCormack said.

Goldie chewed down his food, pointing at his mouth. 'Aye. Get this: cerebral haemorrhage.'

'What? Fuck off.'

McCormack wiped his fingers on the newspaper wrappings and fished the report from Goldie's desk, started leafing through it. The medical terminology jumped out in Latinate gouts. Left parietal bone. Depressed fracture of the vault. Extensive abrasions. Ragged lacerations. The victim had been bludgeoned repeatedly with a blunt object, fracturing the skull in four places, shattering the orbit of the left eye, breaking

178

the jaw and dislodging nine teeth. There was no evidence of strangulation. The internal organs showed no signs of asphyxia, the larynx was undamaged, no petechial haemorrhages in the eyes.

The ligature had left no mark around the neck. It had probably been applied posthumously. It played no part in the victim's death. Cause of death was cerebral haemorrhage induced by multiple blows to the head.

'For fuck sake.' McCormack closed the report. 'Is it even him?'

He felt his stomach heave. The half-digested supper rose in his gullet, burning. He swallowed it down. He looked for the limeade but the neck of the bottle was clouded with greasy fingerprints and the sharp stink of vinegar-sodden newsprint was suddenly overpowering.

McCormack clenched his hands on the arms of his chair. He closed his eyes. Please don't be sick. Just don't be sick. He opened his eyes. Something not right. 'The sanitary towel. There was a sanitary towel on the body, over her eyes.'

'I know.'

'But she wasn't menstruating.'

'No.'

'You mean he brought the thing with him?'

Goldie shrugged. 'Tools of the trade. You going to finish that?'

McCormack looked at the remains of his pudding supper, the chips limp and shrivelled, the pudding like a severed dick, black bloodcrumb sheathed in yellow batter.

'Be my guest.'

Goldie settled down in his chair, pulled the food towards him. McCormack drifted over to the map. He heard the voices behind him.

'Bridgeton again.'

'Uhuh.'

'Eastern'll want it.'

'Eastern can want.'

He pulled a drawing-pin from the corner of a poster on the corkboard and ran his finger over the East End till he found Queen Mary Street. He stuck the pin on to the map and stood back to see how the pattern had changed. Now there were two close together – Mackeith Street and Queen Mary Street, barely an inch of Bridgeton between them – and another two further apart. Did the pattern make more or less sense than before? Who said it was a pattern?

21

Queen Mary Street. Some of the locals had gathered near number 48, backing into the tenement walls to evade the whirling drizzle. They looked like a bus queue, McCormack thought, as a man turned the collar on his thin brown suit.

'Monday morning,' Goldie said. 'These people don't have jobs to go to?'

'Can't get to their jobs,' McCormack said. 'They've forgotten where the bus stop is.'

They were here to help with the door-to-door. Donkeywork. Climbing tenement stairs. Flapping letter boxes. There were uniforms for this but sometimes it was better to do it yourself, get whatever dope was going before they garbled it into witness statements. Plus they had the new artist's impression, whatever that was worth.

The drizzle spritzed their cheeks as they wrestled into their mackintoshes, tamped the ludicrous CID fedoras into place and split up to knock on doors. For the next hour and a half McCormack held up his warrant card and said the same words, showed the picture, gave the same smile to the string of women and the odd workless man who answered his knock.

Apart from the two or three witnesses who'd already helped with the artist's impression, no one had seen anything. You could see the faces harden when they saw it was the polis. You mentioned the Quaker and the faces lit up briefly but then the shutters crashed back down. Fuck the polis. Tell them nothing. A few old women had seen a man crossing the back-court. A man in a dark suit. What kind of suit? What colour? What did he look like? A tall man, would you say? Taller than me? Was he fair-haired? How old was he? A dark suit, son, that's all I know.

He was getting depressed. Again that morning he'd had to elbow through a shouting pack of reporters on the pavement outside the Marine. It was fever pitch all over again, the press screaming for results, the Secretary of State on the blower to Levein. Someone had sprayed graffiti on a wall across the street. QUAKER SCORES AGAIN. QUAKER ROOLZ YA TOOLZ. For weeks McCormack had gone into work to judge other men; now he went into work to be judged. By the press, by the boss, by the shirtsleeved men at the desks.

He caught up with Goldie outside number 48.

'Any joy?'

'Fuck all.'

'Me neither. In here a minute.'

They flashed their cards to the constable at the closemouth. McCormack led the way down the hall and another uniform stood aside to let them into the flat. McCormack was briefly thrown by the room's sunlit innocence. It crossed his mind that they had entered the wrong flat but the boards had been crowbarred off the window and the sun was flooding in. Here was the stain on the floor. A woman had been murdered here. You expected to find the place altered, charged, whatever the opposite of 'hallowed' was. But the walls stood stiffly erect and a rhombus of sunlight lay on the far wall and the black mess on the bare floor might have been oil or treacle. Profaned.

The mattress had gone, and with it some of the atmosphere of the previous day when the cops had stood round the body and the snapper took his shots. It was as if the flashbulbs had bleached the room of menace. There was nothing here to see.

Back in the hallway McCormack had a thought.

'Constable. The woman across the hall – she's the last remaining resident?'

'That's right, sir. Building's condemned, she's holding out to the end. A Mrs Lindsay. Building's coming down next month.'

'Not any more it's not.'

Goldie had the details in his notebook. Sixty-five. Widow. Former cashier at a hosiery in Dennistoun. The push-bell sounded with a dull thunk and Goldie rapped on the door. Nothing. He dug a coin out of his trouser pocket and clacked its edge on the door's glass panel.

They heard a heavy scraping sound, then the *shunk* of the mortice, the twist of the Yale. The door slid open on its chain.

'Mrs Lindsay?' Goldie had his card at the ready. 'We're the police, Mrs Lindsay. I'm DS Goldie, this is DI McCormack. Do you think we could come in?'

'I told it all yesterday.' You could see a glint of spectacles in the gloom, a coil of white hair. The line of the door-chain obscured her mouth. 'You people don't speak to each other?'

McCormack gave it his best smile, stretched his Highland vowels. 'Well, I do apologize, Mrs Lindsay, for the inconvenience. I was here yesterday, if you remember. To talk to the boy. Do you think you could tell us again?'

The hallway smelled of wet dog and urine. She was the kind of old woman who would be found six weeks after her death, rotting among the knick-knacks and geegaws, fused to her own mattress.

In the living room they took their seats on a spongy sofa while Mrs Lindsay shifted her paper from the armchair. Immediately she leaned forward. McCormack looked down at the bony fingers that had clamped his knee.

'There's somebody here.'

'Sorry?'

'There's someone *here*.' She hissed this with such vehemence, baring a trim line of dentures, that McCormack flinched. The skin prickled on the backs of his arms. An intruder in the flat? Was the killer here now? The thought stunned McCormack and it was Goldie who spoke, in the suave, rational tone of a man talking somebody down from a ledge.

'Where, Mrs Lindsay? There's somebody where?'

She raised an index finger. McCormack waited for her to speak but then she nodded significantly and he saw that she was pointing at the ceiling.

'You mean there's someone in the building? Someone upstairs?'

That was all she meant. McCormack relaxed. There would be kids in and out of the flats all the time. Playing house in the empty rooms. She'd heard them clattering up and down the stairs. He gave what he hoped was a reassuring smile.

'When did you hear them?'

She shook her head. 'Don't need to hear him. He makes no noise but he's not fooling me.'

McCormack exchanged a glance with Goldie. 'But if you haven't heard him, Mrs Lindsay, how do you know he's there?'

Mrs Lindsay shook her head, her teeth clicking with impatience. 'I'm the last one, officer. Everyone else has gone. I've lived alone in this block for the past nine months. Do you think I don't know when there's someone else here? You think I can't sense it?'

In the end they agreed to check it out. The briefing had said that Mrs Lindsay was the last inhabitant of the building, and the uniform on duty had confirmed it, but there was no harm in making sure.

Of the six flats on the first and second floors, four had no front door and the doors of the other two were lying open. All of the flats were empty. There were three flats on the top floor. The single-end in the middle was doorless and empty but the flats on either side had doors with knockers and Brasso'd name-plates. And someone had tried to clean off the 'FLEET RULES' sprayed beside one of the doors: you could see the halo round the letters where turps had clouded the pale green paint.

They took a door each: both locked. Banging and calling and rapping the door-knockers brought nothing but echoes in the stone stairwell. Goldie flapped a letter box. They looked at each other from opposite sides of the landing.

It was McCormack's call. They had plenty of doors to be getting on with. Of the tenement blocks that shared a backcourt with this one most were still inhabited. Stop making a fuss, Goldie's pursed mouth seemed to say. Let's get on with the job in hand, let's get back to chapping doors.

This was three flights up from Mrs Lindsay. She couldn't have heard a thing from down there. A waste of time and resources to call this in. Still, there was the green door in front of him, flush to the jamb. He rested his fingertips on the wood, gave it a gentle press. If it wasn't hiding something, why was it locked?

'Fuck it. Call it in,' he said. 'Sledgehammer. The heavy mob.'

Goldie nodded, tight-lipped, went down to use the car radio. McCormack stepped down half a flight of stairs and stood at the landing window. The rain blew in sheets through the empty backcourt. Packed earth. Clumps of nettles and dockens in the ruined walls of the wash-house and middens. Clothes-poles dotted like crazy goalposts.

You're in the game now, Dochie. That's what Tearlach Mor used to say when he subbed you on at the shinty games, on the Jubilee pitch back in Balla.

He was in the game all right. With a killer to catch and a partner that hated his guts.

He sparked up a Regal and sucked in the smoke, felt it buffet his lungs. Up until now his brief had been clear: find a way to wind this down, bring a botched inquiry to a close. Now the brief was still clear but a little more daunting. Find the Quaker. Stop the Quaker before he kills again.

For a while it seemed that the Quaker *had* stopped. McCormack had never worked a multiple before, but he knew this much: the space between killings got shorter. That was the pattern. The Quaker had followed it till now: six months between the first and second murder; two between the second and the third. And now this. Seven months after Marion Mercer. It made no sense. The pattern was wrong.

The rasping steps of Goldie ruptured his train of thought and ten minutes later a patrol car from C Division pulled up in the street. Two uniforms clattered up the stairs. One of them held a sledgehammer crosswise on his chest. A crowbar swung from the other one's grip.

The first flat held nothing. Stale air. Bare white walls looking blue in the gloom.

They crossed the landing in a group. The three of them formed a kind of huddle behind the taller cop as he hefted the sledge and swung it sideways. The door bounced and slammed back as if someone were pressing against it from the other side. The uniform staggered a little and flexed his shoulders and set his feet for the second shot. He grinned back at the watchers when a loud cracking sound met his second blow. Then the grin dropped and he set his shoulders once more. Another swing. The fourth one popped it.

They all craned in to look, Goldie's gabardine back blocking McCormack's line of vision. He knew, though. Even before Goldie stepped back, even before the uniforms exchanged a glance, he knew that this was good.

22

First thing was the smell. Cooking smells. The heavy fug of meat. Fresh. And a human warmth in the air that had McCormack and Goldie drawing their truncheons. The taller constable clasped the sledge across his chest, fingers flexing on the shaft. The short one stepped smartly in with his own truncheon drawn and recce'd the room, ducked his head into the kitchen. He nodded all clear and the three of them stepped forward.

McCormack crossed to open the curtains. Everyone blinked a little in the light and then McCormack did his clockwise thing, working his way round the room, itemizing the objects. A milk crate filled with tin cans: Irish stew, Campbell's cream of mushroom, Ambrosia creamed rice, Armour's corned beef. A Primus stove. Six slabs of Bournville chocolate, eight cans of shandy. A tin-opener, knife and spoon set out on a hand-kerchief beside a packet of paper tissues. An opened tin of spaghetti hoops with a spoon or a fork poking out of it. A sleeping bag in the bed-recess. A short stack of paperbacks – Ambler, Greene, a Josephine Tey – on top of a pornographic magazine. A blue-and-white striped ceramic mug filled with cigarette butts. A bottle of Johnnie Walker Red Label, two thirds gone. A *Glasgow Tribune* folded to the crossword, with the clues half-completed and a blue bookie's biro lying slantwise on top. A carton of Rothmans King Size. An army kit-bag whose gaping neck – when McCormack peered into it – disclosed a stack of folded white T-shirts. Beside the kit-bag was a boxy torch with a head the size of a saucer. On the mantelpiece above a ripped-out fireplace was a candle held in place by its own melted grease and a soft-looking square of cloth scored with black oily marks.

Through an archway was the tiny kitchen with a view on to the backcourt. A wooden jawbox-sink held empty tins, their serrated lids jutting up like metal sunflowers. There were sodden cigarette ends. Crushed cans of shandy. Under the jawbox were two blue buckets, an empty bottle of disinfectant and a four-pack of Andrex toilet tissue with two rolls gone. The smell of the disinfectant failed to mask the other smells. Against the back wall was a plastic bag with Younger's Tartan Special on the side. McCormack took a pen from his inside pocket and held the bag open: he saw striped cotton boxer shorts, a ribbed black sock.

This time McCormack went down to call it in. Within half an hour the room was thick with bodies. The uniforms had gone back to Tobago Street but the techs from the Identification Bureau were squatting and dusting and another snapper was busy. Someone had brought a surveyor's wheel from the incident trailer and was measuring the distance between the various objects. Later all the movable objects would be placed in brown paper evidence bags and taken off to be stored. McCormack and Goldie were getting ready to leave when a shape blocked the doorway.

'What did I tell you?' Cochrane was all teeth, a leering victor's grin. 'I knew it was right putting you boys together. Look at this place, would you?'

They looked round once more at the lab boys bending to their tasks, dusting the surfaces – cans, cutlery, buckets, books – where a man might leave his prints.

Cochrane's hands rested lightly on his hips. The shoulders of his light-coloured jacket were spattered with rain. He was hatless, too, McCormack noticed, his brown hair plastered to his head. 'If this boy's got a record, he's already bagged.'

It was lunchtime when Goldie and McCormack left the flat. At Bridgeton Cross they turned down Main Street to the Blue Bird Café.

The waitress brought all-day breakfasts, side plates of buttered bread, mugs of tea.

'You know, you'll feel a lot better if you just say it.'

Goldie was salting his food. He scanned the table and then leaned back on tipped chair legs to snatch the ketchup bottle from the vacant table behind them. He smacked the base of the bottle till the sauce glugged out in a scarlet bolus. He screwed the top back on to the bottle and lifted his cutlery.

'If I just say what?'

'Get it off your chest, mate. Way to go, McCormack. Nice work. You won a watch.'

Goldie stopped chewing for a second. 'Way to go, McCormack,' he said, through a mouthful of black pudding.

They ate in silence, plugging their mouths with food, sluicing it down with sweet tea. Donovan's 'Season of the Witch' was on the radio.

'Way to go for what, by the way?'

McCormack smiled. 'Well maybe you should ask Cochrane about that. He seemed pretty made up.'

'Not the toughest crowd, though, is he? He's going down in history as the guy who couldnae catch the Quaker. He'll clutch at any straw you throw him.' Goldie folded his last triangle of white bread and mopped up the red and yellow streaks on his plate. 'You're sure the guy on the top floor's the killer?'

'You think it's a coincidence? Is that what you're saying?'

'See, that's not an answer, is it?'

'OK. Look. Derek. Can we put aside the fact that you hate my guts? That I was here to fuck you all over and drag your names through the shit and make myself look good in the process. I get all that. OK? You've worked more of these than I have: I get that too. Still. It's not possible that we're on to something here?'

'No, you're right.' Goldie drained his tea, signalled the waitress for another pot. 'Fair play. That was a good call. I was all in favour of letting it go and getting started on the door-to-door – which, by the way, we still haven't done. But tell me this, Detective: if this is the Quaker, why'd he kill a woman in the same building where he's holing up? You want one of these?'

Goldie was lighting a Mayfair. McCormack took one from the packet, shared the match.

'Maybe that's how he does it. He picks a location, recce's it for a few days, watches the lay of the land. When he thinks it's safe, he makes his move.'

'And then, what, forgets to leave? He's a criminal mastermind for murders one to three and he's shit-for-brains at number four?'

He was right. McCormack flicked ash on to the ruins of his breakfast. Goldie was right. There was no supposition by which this made sense. Why would the Quaker kill a woman on the doorstep of his own bolthole? Why was he hanging around on the following morning, waiting to be spotted in broad daylight? And why leave the sleeping bag and stove and all his other bits and pieces for the Quaker Squad to find?

'Maybe he was planning to leave but something stopped

him.' McCormack smoked to give himself time. 'Maybe . . . maybe he was injured and had to treat himself. Maybe he fell asleep. Had a blackout.'

'Aye.' Goldie doused his cigarette in the yolk of a fried egg. 'Or maybe he had nothing to do with it. Maybe he came down to see what the fuss was about and panicked when he saw the body.'

Back at the Marine the forensic reports had come in. As McCormack anticipated, the oily rag had held a firearm. The man in the top-floor flat had taken it with him. McCormack sat at his desk and thought about this. A blast of wind swept the rain against the window and the frame juddered. He's out there now, McCormack thought. With a handgun. Skulking through the rubble like some jungle fighter, some apocalypse survivor.

23

Paton found the blade that served as a tin-opener and punched it into the top of the can. Then he shifted his grip and pumped his elbow, working the blade round the lid. The blade made a pleasant gnashing sound as it tore through the metal. Carefully he tipped the serrated lid back and held the tin over the saucepan. The contents slithered out in a solid, glistening tube. They would break up – it was chunky Irish stew – under the heat from the Primus.

He stirred the stew with a metal spoon and looked out over the darkening loch. He could see the wooded bulk of Inchcailloch and some of the smaller islands. As boys, they had paddled to Inchcailloch in a home-made canoe belonging to one of Dazzle's uncles. Paton rose to his feet and a low ache ran down his thighs. He could feel the rhythm of the day's walk in his legs, a tightness in the calves and hamstrings. He rose to his tiptoes in his stocking soles and stretched up with interlaced fingers. His heels chafed from walking in the new boots – the chunky Red Wings that stood side by side outside the tent – but his feet were free from blisters.

The walk that tired him had freshened him too. He wondered

if he would fall asleep quickly, or maybe not at all. He remembered waking that morning, somewhere in the city, and not knowing for a moment where he was. He had opened his eyes and looked at the black slot where the door should have been. He'd put out his hand and felt bare, gritty floorboards. There was the heavy, clogging reek of urine, and the draught from a boarded window on his shin: he was in another tenement. South of the river. The Gorbals, probably. Indian country to a boy from Maryhill.

The bare floor was hard beneath the thin suit trousers and he shifted position, rolling his shoulders against the hard wall. His neck ached. The Browning lay on the floor within easy reach, a darker stain on the dark ground. Paton closed his fingers over the flat reliable shape. The cold metal felt like the one true fact in a world of supposition.

He'd snatched the gun up when he fled from the safe house, the flat in Bridgeton, when the boy's screams had brought him clattering down the stairs, and the girl's body had sent him out into the morning, running for his life. Before he knew it, he was sprinting through the gates of Glasgow Green. Dog walkers. Two boys on bikes. Distant shouts from a football match on one of the downhill pitches. The faces of people he passed were stretched in fear and alarm. He forced himself to walk. The effort it took not to break into a sprint made his limbs quiver.

The Green was bright and sharp in the sunlight. Everything new and strange. Templeton's carpet factory was an exotic hallucination, rising in Venetian splendour with its battlements and towers, its glazed and coloured bricks. He passed the People's Palace, the Doulton Fountain. At the far side of the Green he crossed the river by the Albert Bridge, the looming slabs of the Hutchie C blocks almost blotting the horizon.

He found himself in a district of shabby tenements, shutting out the sun with their high black walls. He walked in their shadows and his mind kept cutting back to the same frame: his palms on the jamb of a doorway, the splayed and naked form, the dark patch at the crotch, the pulped and bloody face.

As if to escape that face he dodged up a darkened close, mounted the sagging stairs. A doorless flat, a hallway. In the main room three figures, sitting cross-legged round a burning brazier, one of them reaching a bottle to his neighbour. The faces turned in the ruddy light. He saw mad eyes, a scurf of white around a chin, the glint of gold from a tooth. One of them putting his palm on to the floor to help him get up.

Paton turned. Back down the stairs, along the street, up another close. Straight to the top this time, another doorless flat, a cave, nothing inside it but walls and floors. Not even floors – the boards had been torn up in the centre of the room. Paton skirted the hole and leant against the far wall, sliding down till he sat on the floor. At some point he took out the Browning and laid it beside him.

He sat there all day. Twice he heard sounds in the close-mouth, kids' voices and running feet, and he gripped the gun but no one climbed the stairs. He waited for darkness, watched the comforting black absence of the doorway. Were the cops on his trail? They would have his prints. He'd touched the doorjamb at Queen Mary Street. Pretty soon they would find his hideout, if they hadn't already. He'd pulled the door until the Yale lock engaged but they would find the flat, they would break down the door. More prints. His holdall and clothes.

The floor beside him was thick with dust. He traced his name with his finger and then smudged it with his sleeve. Once they matched his prints they would know his name but the photo would be ten years old. He had never let himself be photographed since that mugshot in '59. But what did photographs matter? The boy had seen his face. So had those people in the Green. They would do an artist's impression, an identikit maybe. His face would spring up all over the city. And his hands, those fucking swifts on his hands: they wouldn't need a photo if they knew about those.

The thing to do was get out of the city. He thought of the toolbox wedged in the roofspace. They would find it or they wouldn't, there was no point in fretting. He would come back and get it when it all died down.

He shifted his position and settled down to wait it out. It was between midnight and dawn, when time seeps imperceptibly, like a gas. At one point a bottle broke softly in the next street or the next again and then there was nothing, just the hard floor and the luminous paint on his watch showing how slowly a night could pass.

As the dawn brought the contours of the room into view he thought of the snooker hall on the Garscube Road. His father used to take him there when Paton was twelve or thirteen. Away from the planes of bright green baize beneath the curtained oblong lights, the hall was a valley of shadows. *You haven't a prayer, son.* The words his father spoke when the reds split nicely at the Imperial and he started on a clearance came back to him now. You haven't a prayer. For the first time he felt their literal sense. There was no one he could turn to now. Nobody would help him. Everyone's hands would be raised against the Quaker.

In the morning he pissed in the corner of the room and stole down the sagging stairs. He walked into town along the Trongate. He felt his head glow, his tell-tale fair hair flaring like a torch, a struck match. Here's the culprit, folks, the man you've all been waiting for, the poster boy for multiple murder. Call a polis, get him huckled.

He moved quickly, not running, keeping close to the wall, head down, lighting a smoke.

At Black's on St Vincent Street he bought a 'Safari' frame tent and a Primus stove and a quilted canvas sleeping bag and a rucksack to put them all in. He bought moleskin trousers and a blue cagoule and a bobble hat and hiking boots. Two pairs of socks. In the gents toilet at Queen Street Station he rolled up his suit and squashed it into a plastic bag along with his shoes. When he stepped out on to Buchanan Street he was a hiker striking out for the hills. At the corner of Hope Street and Bothwell Street he wedged the plastic bag into a litter bin.

At a grocer's on St Vincent Street he bought packets and tins. Biscuits. Oatcakes. Bars of chocolate. Sardines and crackers. A Melton Mowbray pork pie. Two big bottles of oatmeal stout. He stowed it all in the rucksack. He bought a pair of sunglasses in Boots the Chemist and caught the bus for Maryhill. On Maryhill Road he changed buses. He worried that someone he knew, one of the old Maryhill crew, might spot him, but the reflection he caught in a butcher's window – hat, glasses, week-old beard – was like no one he'd ever seen. The bus took him to Milngavie and he walked out on the Drymen road, heading for the far blue hump of Dumgoyne.

It was after four when Paton reached Balmaha, on the shores of Loch Lomond. He crunched across the shingle, the sun warming his scalp. His shadow, broad as a tombstone with the pack on his back, slid over the blue-grey stones. His eyes picked out the flat thin stones, the skimmers, and filed them away for future use, another and then another until his head filled up with stones and he shrugged out of his pack, let it fall where he stood, and dropped to his haunches to gather them up, flat and round-edged and smooth and dry. He filled his pockets. At the water's edge he hooked his index

197

finger round a stone, drew back his arm and whipped it smartly at the loch. It hit the water and kicked up once, twice, little spurts of foam, before the hits speeded up and petered out. He chose another stone. A few more skimmed stones and the city and the cops, the corpse, the Quaker, the toolbox in the roofspace, all of it fell away. As if you could leave it all behind, wish it all away.

A sharp mashing sound behind him: Paton turned his head. A man was making towards him down the shingle beach. Paton watched him come.

'Fine day.' The man was fiftyish, fat. He stood with his hands on his hips, nodding. Paton glanced back at the rucksack, where his bobble hat was sticking out of a side pocket.

'Let's hope it lasts.' Paton's hands had found their way into his pockets.

'You'll be at the fishing?'

Paton hesitated. There was no rod in his rucksack but fishing was plausible, fishing was a pretext.

'Well, could be. Maybe.'

'Relax, son. It's perfectly legal. You'll get a permit at the hotel. Best to get one, though – it saves any confusion.'

'I'll do that. Thanks.'

The man nodded. He clicked his tongue and thrust out his hand as if he'd forgotten what he came for. 'Spencer Gilchrist. I run the shop in the village.'

His handshake was firm and dry. Paton didn't give a name. There was a folded newspaper sticking out of the man's pocket and he saw Paton notice it.

'D'you want a look at the paper? I've finished with it. Here—'

'No!' Paton smiled miserably. 'I mean: no, thanks. I try to avoid the news when I'm on holiday. Get away from it all.'

He had the feeling that if the man drew his paper from his

pocket they would both see Paton's face reproduced beneath a headline and the whole bright day would shudder to a halt.

The man shifted his feet, poking the stones with his stick.

'You'll be up from Glasgow?'

'Actually, London.'

Shit, Paton thought. Why add London to the mix? Keep it simple.

'London, now? Is that right?'

Paton caught the man's frown and his own mouth split in a gormless grin. 'I mean, Glasgow, yes. Originally. But I live down south now.'

'Just up for a wee break?'

'That's the idea.'

'Well,' the man whacked the ground twice with his stick. 'You've brought the weather. I'll leave you to it. The hotel's up yonder, past the kirk.'

The man tipped a finger to his forehead in a jaunty salute and crunched back up the beach. Paton let out a breath. He emptied his pockets, the stones spattering on to the beach and bent to pull his beanie from the rucksack.

Now he sat outside his tent in the shadow of Conic Hill, watching the stew bubble and sputter. He could hear a guitar from down at the lochside, laughter, a girl's high pure voice, singing. He had gotten away with it, he thought, the encounter with the busybody, Gilchrist, but he wished that he'd been wearing the hat. He would wear it at all times, now. He thought of the gun at the bottom of his pack, folded into a pair of woollen socks. The food was ready and he ate it straight from the pot.

The *Tribune* lay beside him on a rock. He'd bought a copy in the village shop, nervous in case Gilchrist came in and caught him. There were copies of the *Record*, the *Express* and the

199

Scotsman on the counter and he would have bought these too if it hadn't seemed suspicious.

Though the headline – QUAKER KILLS ANOTHER – was huge, the report in the *Trib* was frustratingly short. The victim was unidentified. A man seen leaving the scene on Sunday morning was described as six feet tall, red-haired, weighing around twelve stone, dressed in a dark suit that was either blue or black. Paton himself was five feet ten, blond, and ten stone two. The suit he'd left in the Glasgow litter-bin was charcoal grey. It ought to have cheered him but the inaccuracy troubled him, as though it was some kind of trap. The report also mentioned the suspect's 'light beard'. Maybe the village shop sold disposable razors.

The paper also carried the new artist's impression of the Quaker, though the officer in charge of the investigation – Detective Chief Inspector George Cochrane – had declined as yet to confirm this as a Quaker killing.

Paton put the pot aside and lit a cigarette. The sick feeling, the hard tight ball in his chest, had nothing to do with Gilchrist's paper. It had nothing to do with the violence he had seen, the viciousness inflicted on the poor woman. What troubled him now was just the coincidence. There were all these derelict tenements in the city, a city of a million people. And the Quaker kills someone in the building where Paton is hiding? It couldn't be a coincidence. But how could it be anything else?

Paton lifted the pot and walked over to kneel beside the burn. He sloshed out the pot, scouring it with a sprig of heather and filled it with water. When the tea was brewed he looked through the paper again – maybe he'd missed something on the Glendinnings job – but nothing jumped out. The tea in the new steel mug had a harsh salty taste. He was reaching over to slosh it out on the bracken when a thought stayed his hand. The shock brought him to his feet and made him stand in his socks with the half-filled mug in his hand. He'd missed the meet! He'd been due to meet with Dazzle and the others at exactly – he looked at his watch, twisting his wrist to catch the last of the light and spilling some of the tea on his socks – two hours ago in the lounge bar of the Lord Darnley. They'd be sitting there now, gathered round the table, getting drunk and nasty. Cursing him out. Maybe Dazzle would speak up for him, give him the benefit of the doubt. Cursiter, he knew, would be bitter against him, urging them to hunt him down. McGlashan would get involved. McGlashan's crew would be after him now, as well as the cops.

He paced around on the spot. He could phone Dazzle tomorrow. There was a payphone in the bar of the hotel. He would explain about the body, how he'd left the flat in a panic. Maybe they'd seen it in the paper, the murder, put two and two together. Maybe he could get Dazzle to speak to McGlashan. Maybe – actually, fuck maybe. He tossed the dregs of the tea and bumped back down on to the ground, flopped right back with his hands behind his head. Why phone at all? Why not keep it all for himself? He laughed out loud, staring up at the nameless stars. It was he who'd busted the jewels out of the Glendinnings safe. It was he who'd stashed them, he who'd have to get them back. Even if they got their hands on their share, Dazzle and the others would only waste it, kicking upstairs to a wanker like Glash. Fuck them all. They want to come after him? Let them come.

The light breeze had dropped and suddenly there was an indoors feeling on the hillside. Looking down on the loch in the failing light he felt for a moment that he was back in the Gorbals flat. The packed earth was the wooden boards and the hole in the floor was the darkened loch. Something was missing, though, and he rooted in the rucksack till he found the balled woollen socks and fumbled them till a dark object thudded on to the ground. He closed his fingers on the gun. The whole thing – the grip and the snub-nosed barrel – almost fitted into one splayed hand. He hefted the Browning and pointed it downhill towards the yellow lights of the village. He made a soft explosion with his lips and let the barrel kick up in his fist.

24

And after all the bad blood and suspicion and the near-miss of a stand-up fight in the Murder Room, it was Goldie – out of all of them – who came to McCormack's aid. It was Goldie who told Cochrane he was happy to go on partnering McCormack and who took McCormack's part with the squad in the Marine. McCormack was as baffled as anyone by Goldie's change of heart. Maybe it was belated gratitude for McCormack's support during the Kilgour episode. Or maybe Goldie figured that McCormack was their best shot at cracking the case now that a new death had thrown them a lifeline. McCormack never asked and Goldie never told. They just got on with working the case.

Tuesday evening. McCormack and Goldie strolling down the sunny side of Buccleuch Street, looking at the numbers.

The locket had appeared on that morning's front pages and calls had begun to come in. There was the usual number of cranks. Some of the callers wanted to claim it as their own. It was explained to them that, by doing so, they were placing themselves at a murder scene. At that point their interest tended to flag.

Two calls, however, seemed worth the legwork, and this was one of them. Denise Redburn, thirty-three, cocktail waitress at a riverside casino. She'd called in to say that she recognized the locket. Her colleague, Helen Thaney, had worn one exactly like it for the past few weeks – a gift, apparently, from a new boyfriend. Helen had missed her last three shifts at the casino and no one had seen her since early last week.

The detective who took the call asked about distinguishing marks. No marks, said Denise Redburn, but a few weeks back Helen had dyed her hair. Blond.

'Here we are.'

One-four-five was a well-kept four-storey tenement. Little railed garden out front. Flight of steps up to a bright red door. White-tiled hallway. Redburn's flat was on the top floor. Of course it was. Goldie flapped the letter box, mopping the back of his neck, and McCormack held his warrant card ready.

Denise Redburn was dressed for her shift. Black waistcoat, white blouse, floppy black riverboat gambler's tie, black pencil skirt over sheer stockings. The fluffy pink slippers, McCormack surmised, were not regulation.

She invited them through to a living room that smelled of incense sticks and menthol cigarettes.

'Yep. That's it.'

Goldie had produced a laminated photo of the locket.

'She got it last month,' Denise said. 'Wore it every day since.'

She held the photograph in both hands, shaking her head. She sat down, still gripping the photo. 'I knew something wasn't right. I had a bad feeling. But the Quaker? Jesus.' She shook her head again.

McCormack fished his notebook from his inside pocket. 'But you didn't call the police, report her missing?'

'She'd missed shifts before. Actually, she'd been doing it a lot lately. Maybe not three in a row but, I don't know. I figured it's the new boyfriend. Maybe they're getting married, she doesn't need the job any more.'

'Married? They were serious, then?'

'Well, she was getting on, wasn't she? I mean it was now or never.'

McCormack's glance strayed to Denise's own hand. She shook her head. 'Oh, that ship's sailed, Inspector. Anyway, when I saw her last Monday she said she was going to the dancing at the weekend. Saturday night. Wanted me to come. She was giving the boyfriend the night off.'

'She went dancing on Saturday? Whereabouts?'

'The Barrowland,' Denise said. 'At least, that was the plan. I told her I'd let her know. Turns out I had a date on Saturday. I was planning to tell her on Friday but she never turned up for her shift.'

'And you never went?'

Denise pouted, a sad little moue. 'Maybe if I'd gone she'd still be here. But then, maybe I'd have got it instead. Maybe he'd have taken me.'

McCormack finished what he was writing, pointed the pen at Denise. 'What was his name, then?'

'The boyfriend? That would be a state secret. She kept it all very hush-hush.'

'Maybe he was married already.'

She smiled. 'Oh now. Let's not always think the worst of people.'

'And you never met him?'

A little flicker of the lids before she sparked up the menthol ciggie. 'No.'

'How about you tell me the truth, Denise?'

The pink lips pursed in a smile. 'Or what? Youse'll take me down the station? I am telling the truth. I never met him. Not met, not properly.'

'Not properly. What does that mean?'

She shifted in the chair, tucked her legs up underneath her, tugged her skirt down. 'It means I was in Helen's flat once and he was there. But I never met him. He was in the bedroom. Sleeping it off, I suppose.'

'This was when?'

She blew smoke at the ceiling. 'Three weeks ago? Four? I'm not sure.'

'Was this a social call? You'd arranged to meet?'

'No.' Denise tapped her cigarette on the standing ashtray. She looked up, met McCormack's eyes, the full glare. 'I was borrowing money, OK? That's what I was doing. If you're short before payday you can generally get by on, you know, tips. But I'd had a cold that week, I'd missed a couple of shifts. Helen was cool about it, I'd done the same for her often enough.'

'You ring the buzzer,' Goldie said. 'Helen answers.'

Denise looked at him for a beat, shook her head. Then she sighed, clamped her hand on her ankle, tugged her legs further under her. 'Helen answers. I thought it wasn't her at first, cause she'd dyed her hair. Bottle blond. Anyway. We go in. Well: at *first*, she doesnae want to let me in. I tell her I'm not telling the whole fucking close my business, so she lets me in. But she's nervous, telling me to keep my voice down.'

'She doesn't want Lover Boy waking up?'

'But I'd never met him, remember. She wouldn't even tell me his name. Nobody's even seen him. So I threatened to march into the bedroom and introduce myself.'

'That would do it.'

'Aye. Well. She couldn't get me out of there fast enough. How much did I need? She was practically crying with nerves at this stage. So fuck it: I said a fiver. I thought she'd tell me to chase myself but she goes to his jacket – his jacket's hanging

206

on the back of a chair – and she gets the money. Pound notes, counts them out. Then she's practically throwing me out the door.'

'She took it out his wallet?'

'Yeah.'

'Did you see a photograph when she opened the wallet? A card? Anything with a name on it?'

'No, but when she was getting the wallet from his pocket something else came out along with it. Like a booklet or something. She nearly ripped the jacket stuffing it back in the pocket and she sort of looked round to see if I'd seen it.'

'What kind of booklet?'

Denise frowned. 'Like a passport maybe? I don't know. But not ours. Something foreign.'

'Foreign how?'

'The colour. Kind of a purply blue. Indigo you'd call it.'

Denise dropped the smouldering butt in the ashtray as if she didn't want to risk her nails. McCormack leaned forward and folded it over, extinguished it under his thumb.

'What did you need the money for?'

'None of your business. Food. Ciggies. The usual.'

'What about friends? Among the girls at the casino?'

'You mean apart from me? We're not that friendly. As a rule. They're mostly bitches, to be honest, the girls at the Claremont. We don't get too close. Helen was close to one girl, though.' Denise tilted her head, sighted along her outstretched arm to her lacquered fingernails, red as petals. 'Until they fell out.'

'What happened?'

'I don't know. She said Helen— Well. She told her she'd end up in Black Street.'

McCormack turned to Goldie. You could live in a city for fifteen years and still know nothing.

'It's where the VD clinic is.'

'Right. She was friendly with the clients, then?'

'Well, you're not short of offers. It's a perk of the job.' She leant a little on 'perk', gave it a sarcastic stress.

'Tell me about the job, Denise. What's it consist of? What do you do?'

'Smile.' She gave a big fake grin. 'Smile, smile, smile. Keep the punters drunk and happy so they keep spending their money. Ply them with drink. Flirt a bit.'

'What about the clientele? Who's your typical punter?'

'All sorts come in. Gangsters. Bigshot lawyers. Business types. Yanks. Chinks. *Cops.*' She said this last word in a stage whisper. 'They all think you're dying to spend some time with them.'

'It's all that smiling,' McCormack said. 'Creates the wrong impression. She didn't talk about the boyfriend, though, give you any clues? Come on, Denise. She's your best pal; what else you gonnae talk about?'

'You'd like that, wouldn't you? That's all we've got to talk about. Anyway, who said we were best pals? And Helen talk about her boyfriend? She'd talk about anything but. Change the subject when you brought him up. It was actually weird how she avoided it. I think she was involved in something.' Denise nodded significantly. 'I think something was preying on her mind.'

'What makes you say that?'

'Different things. Like recently she'd get nervous when certain people were in. Once she dropped a tray of drinks. Another time she said she had a headache and left in the middle of a shift. She'd been right as rain ten minutes before.'

'Who's certain people?'

'Oh, *I* don't know. Must have been people she knew.'

At this, Denise swung her legs down, stood up and stretched. She tugged on the points of her waistcoat and smoothed her skirt at the back. 'Well, this has been fun, chaps, but it's not paying the rent. I need to get ready.'

'Hold on.' McCormack stood up too. 'What about the jacket? The boyfriend's jacket?'

'What about it?'

'Big? Small?'

'It was hanging on the back of a chair. How would I know what size it was?'

'Colour, then.

'Grey, I think. Sort of tartan but not really tartan. A kind of check. Stylish.'

Houndstooth, McCormack thought. No: Prince of Wales. 'Anything else you can think of, Denise? Anything at all that might help us?'

Denise stepped out to the hall and came back with a short white wet-look coat on. She'd also stepped into her heels and now everything was braced and taut, she was all business and breeze, looked at them with a practised hauteur.

'There is one thing.' She flicked her hair out over her collar with a graceful turn of her wrists. 'We were going into town one day after work. We were walking up Hope Street and these two nuns were coming towards us in the distance and Helen, well it was mad, she just sort of flipped. You could feel her go stiff and she starts cursing these nuns under her breath, calling them all the bitches and whores of the day. Then, when we come alongside them, she leans over and spits on the pavement, right in front of them. Spits at their feet. She was shaking with rage.'

'Did she say what was wrong?'

'Naw. She just kept walking. I thought it was funny. It was like she was Orange or something but she comes from Ireland, doesn't she, so she's Catholic herself. By the way, isn't there, like, a reward? For information?'

McCormack stowed his notebook. 'This is a murder inquiry, Denise. Your pal's dead. You want a handout for helping us catch the killer?'

Denise didn't flinch. 'No harm in asking.'

'By the way,' McCormack was inspecting a photo on the mantelpiece, Denise in a summer dress, the Blackpool Tower in the background. 'Who was the friend?'

'Sorry?'

'You said she was close to someone at work. Before they fell out. What was the name?'

'Carol Strachan.'

'She still work at the casino?'

'Last time I looked.'

McCormack put the photograph back. 'Do you have one of Helen, by any chance?'

'A photo? Yeah, I think so. Out here.' They followed her out to the hall. She dug around in a drawer of the hallstand and produced a strip of photobooth images – herself and Helen Thaney, heads together, eyes wide, pouting, mugging for the camera.

'Thanks.' McCormack held up the strip. 'We'll bring this back.'

McCormack visited the toilet on the way out and caught up with Goldie in the closemouth. They started back up the hill.

'Thought you were in there, mate.' Goldie made a clicking noise with his tongue. 'Planning a follow-up visit on your own?'

'Absolutely. As long as you're providing the penicillin.'

Goldie stopped. 'You think she's on the game?'

'Unless she's got a sideline in family planning. She's got a box of condoms in her bathroom cabinet that would last the Scots Guards for a fortnight.'

They walked along Renfrew Street. Goldie was catching a bus on Hope Street. McCormack carried on into town. On

St Vincent Street he pushed through the big brass-plated door of John Smith & Son, Booksellers, and climbed the stairs to the History Department on the fourth floor. He browsed the new arrivals table for a couple of minutes.

A sales clerk kneeling beside a pile of new stock said, 'Mary Queen of Scots?' and rose smoothly to his feet. 'We do. Just a minute, sir.'

He came back holding a book face out between his palms, like someone displaying a religious icon. A new biography had been published earlier that year, he told McCormack. It had sold well and this was the shop's last copy.

McCormack walked back out on to St Vincent Street with a package under his arm, heading west. He was passing a newsagent's when the 'Q' of 'QUAKER' caught his eye. He stopped in front of a poster in a latticed frame: LAIR OF THE QUAKER.

So Cochrane had fed it to the *Evening Times*. He bought a paper. He stood on the pavement with the book wedged under his arm and leafed through the pages. The cover carried a photo of the sleeping bag in the bed recess: a whisky bottle in the foreground and the army kit-bag at the edge of the shot. More pics on an inside spread, the stacked cans and the paperback books.

How sordid it looked in the newspaper photo. Like the Führerbunker. How furtive and squalid and overexposed. How sinister and ordinary.

25

He watched them nudge each other, speaking out of the sides of their mouths, glancing in his direction. Finally the redhead strode over, earrings flashing, she was the looker of the two, tall and hippy in a grey sheath dress.

She stopped close to McCormack. Beneath the fizz of perfume was a meaty musk. The hair at her temples was damp. She looked as though she'd just had sex. The dark-haired friend drifted across.

McCormack held out the laminated picture, the blown-up passport photo.

'You recognize her?'

'Oh yeah.' The redhead nodded. 'That's her. The bitch. That's her all right' They were standing in the foyer of the Barrowland, near the cloakroom. Detectives with clipboards were stationed at the entrance to the ballroom and in front of the stairs down to the outside doors. Fifteen minutes earlier McCormack had led a team of six officers – four men, two women – into the dance hall. The band had been stopped and McCormack mounted the stage in his CID raincoat and stood too close to the singer's microphone. Screech of feedback. Heat from the lights. He was aware of the band behind him, gripping their instruments. The singer stood off to one side, head bowed and hands clasped over his groin, the pallbearer's stance.

Behind him, projected on to a large white screen, was the photobooth snap of Helen Thaney, pouting next to the grinning head of Denise Redburn. Under the photo was the telephone number of the Marine Police Station. McCormack shielded his eyes from the spotlight's glare and leaned into the mic. The dancers were in shadow. Some had moved back to their tables, but others stood on the dance floor, waiting for him to speak. They looked curiously vulnerable, standing there with their arms at their sides, their blank white faces turned up to the stage.

The woman on the right, he told the crowd, the woman with dyed blond hair, was Helen Thaney. Twenty-nine years old, of Alexandra Parade in Dennistoun. She spoke with a soft, southern Irish accent. She was found murdered in a derelict tenement at 48 Queen Mary Street in Bridgeton in the early hours of Sunday morning. She spent last Saturday night in the Barrowland Ballroom and may well have met her killer in the dance hall. Anyone who recognizes Helen, or who has any information that may help police identify her killer, should speak to one of the officers stationed in the foyer or else telephone the number on the screen. The domestic situation of all patrons would be respected.

McCormack then left the stage and took his place in the foyer. Behind him the singer announced the next number and the drummer clacked his sticks together four times.

The red-haired girl was called Barbara Bell. She looked like trouble. She had reached that stage of drunkenness where she had decided that she was forcefully and mysteriously alluring. McCormack avoided her eyes as he put his questions.

'And you're sure you recognize her?'

'Uh-huh. Oh yes.'

'Why are you so certain?'

'She tried to get off with my boyfriend Frank. Kinda sticks in your mind.'

McCormack could see a wall-mounted payphone over Barbara's shoulder, a queue of patrons waiting to use it. He could also see the door of the gents toilet. As Barbara spoke, a man in a midnight blue three-button mohair suit came out of the gents, slipping a comb into his inside pocket, moving smartly. He moved with a touch less snap when his eyes locked on to McCormack's. He drifted over and came to a stop beside the girl.

'Evening, sir. And your name is?'

'Francis Gibney. Officer.'

Regimental tie and brown brogues. Three fingers wedged in the ticket pocket of his suit jacket. When McCormack asked him for ID he produced a driver's licence that gave his address as Deanston Drive in Shawlands.

'Barbara here's been telling me about last week. You were present too, I understand. Can you tell me what happened?'

Gibney looked at Barbara and then, as if he'd been caught copying someone else's work, he stared off into a high corner and frowned in earnest recollection. 'Well. I really don't know what to tell you. It was all over in a flash. It was nothing really. I was buying Barbara a ginger and this lassie, this woman appeared beside me at the bar. She said something about the heat – she was fanning herself with a beermat – and how it was thirsty work. Dancing, she meant.'

McCormack waited.

'So I bought her a drink.' Gibney's eyes slid towards Barbara as he said this, then jerked away from the tight flat line of her mouth. 'Just to be polite. Then the band started up and she sort of grabbed my arm and said that she loved this song and then we were out on the dance floor. Dancing.'

'Just to be polite,' Barbara said.

'Then what?'

'Then I put a stop to it.' Barbara leaned in with her chin thrust out, her finger in McCormack's face. 'I saw what she was doing. Pressing into him. In that dress. I marched right over and sorted her out. Bitch did this to me.' She moved the collar of her blouse to reveal twin scratches, three inches long, scabbed roughly over in purple and green. 'But I got my own back.' Her smile showed little white teeth. 'Pulled a clump from the crown of her head. Blond? Some blond. Her roots were black as the Earl of Hell's waistcoat.'

A group of teenage top boys moved in loose formation through the foyer in their Reid and Taylor threads, just the top button of their jackets fastened. They passed McCormack. One of them said something in an undertone. The others laughed. McCormack watched them out of sight.

'Last Saturday night,' he said to Gibney. 'What were your movements last Saturday night, Mr Gibney? Once you left the dance hall.'

Gibney shuffled his feet, frowned a bit to show he was thinking. 'We left here at maybe half-eleven, twelve. Got a cab at the Cross, out to Barbara's place on Victoria Road?'

'And you stayed there all night?'

'Well, no.' He glanced at the girl. 'No. I stayed for maybe an hour. Then I went home.'

'Shawlands?'

'That's right. Deanston Drive. Number eighty-seven.'

'Another cab?'

'No. I walked it. Through the park.' He nodded firmly, as if this might bring the proceedings to a close.

McCormack was writing in his notebook. He looked up.

215

'How long did it take you to walk through the park, Mr Gibney?'

'I don't know. Ten minutes. Fifteen max.'

'Right. So you got home at, what, 2 a.m.?'

'That's right. There or thereabouts.'

There was a slice of jangly guitar as someone pushed through the doors from the dance hall, then the doors swung back and muffled it.

'And you live alone, do you, at Deanston Drive?'

A sickly grin split Gibney's face. McCormack deadpanned him. Gibney's fingers were scrabbling again in his ticket pocket. 'Officer. Look. This is a wee bit embarrassing.' He turned his back on the girl. From his ticket pocket he brought out something shiny, showed it to McCormack on his palm before slipping it back in his pocket. *The domestic situation of patrons.*

'And your wife,' McCormack said. 'She'll vouch for you? She'll confirm that you came home at . . .?'

A patron pushed between them, stumbling, drunk, heading for the toilets.

Gibney watched the drunk with something like envy. 'Yes,' he said morosely. 'I suppose so. I mean, she didn't hear me come in. I didn't want to wake her so I slept on the couch.'

'That was very considerate of you.'

He left them arguing in vehement whispers beside the cigarette machine and jogged downstairs to meet up with the others.

Back at the Marine they talked it out. The canvass at the Barrowland had been something of a mixed bag. Barbara Bell wasn't alone in having spotted Helen Thaney. Lots of people had seen her. But the picture that emerged was confusing. Helen Thaney had been dancing with a tall man in a light grey suit. She'd been sharing a table with a heavy, short man who looked like David Frost. Then it was a long-haired man with a Zapata moustache. No, it was a chib-marked top boy in a yellow shirt and a polka-dot tie.

You had the feeling that people were filing out to the foyer just to feel important, to play a part in the Quaker story, telling the police whatever rubbish came into their heads. But each separate version was confirmed by more than one witness and it soon became clear that they were all telling the truth. Helen Thaney – clearly making the most of the boyfriend's absence – had been seen with half a dozen different men by dozens of different witnesses.

Good-time girl. That was the phrase that they would use, the police, the papers. That was the code-word. *Slut* was what it stood for. *Hoor.*

A few people mentioned the fight between Barbara and Helen Thaney. There was some hair-tugging and scratching but the bouncers were on it in a flash. Fights between women were awkward. With men you just threw them out, tossed them in the Gallowgate gutter. With women, the bouncers generally settled for a warning, told them both to cool it.

McCormack sat at his desk in the Marine, piecing it together. Helen Thaney in a tight white dress. Helen Thaney dancing with five or six men. Helen Thaney in a catfight. It sounded like someone who'd lost control, but he saw now what Thaney was doing. She was in total control. She was registering her presence. She was making sure she'd be remembered.

26

'Right. Hands off cocks, gentlemen. Let's come to order. Thank you.'

Cochrane slamming in to the Murder Room, bringing the fresh air in on his clothes. The belt from his raincoat clanged against a filing cabinet as he threw it off and stood beside the maps with his feet planted a yard apart. He waited till the day shift settled down, turning their chairs to face him, or easing their backsides up on to the desks. He was holding a pile of Xerox'd sheets and running his tongue across his teeth to keep himself from grinning. He still had his hat on.

'OK. This is it, men. Gangbusters. We've got an ident for our man. Take one of these, pass them on. He's one Alexander Paton, P-A-T-O-N. DoB fourth December '39. Formerly of Burnhouse Street in this parish, last known address in Scylla Road, S-C-Y-L-L-A, Peckham, London. Believed still to be living in the London area.'

Cochrane had waited a long time to put a name to the Quaker. He'd spent a lot of mornings with nothing to give these men except more streets to pound, more shitwork to divvy up among them. He broke off now to write the name on the board behind him.

McCormack scanned the sheet. Alexander James Paton, known as Alex. Born Maryhill, 4 December '39. Father, also Alex, ex-serviceman (corporal in the Cameron Highlanders, MC at Monte Cassino), whose post-war career as a house-painter suffered a bit of a hiatus when he spent eight years in HMP Perth for the attempted murder of a part-time barman under the railway bridge beside the Laurieston Bar.

Alex Jnr attended St Roch's in Maryhill, left with no qualifications. Following a stint in juvie he left Glasgow. Living in the Peckham area of London since '64. The Met's touts had linked Paton to a string of robberies in London and the south-east over the past five years but nothing had come to court.

'Mr Paton's a petty crook, housebreaker. We have prints from a ninety-day juvie stint he did for housebreaking in '59. Met's been alerted but so far – sorry: DI McCormack, you've got something to say?'

'He's not a housebreaker.'

Cochrane expelled a long slow breath. He took his hat off and set it on top of the filing cabinet. 'OK. Yes. Well, we haven't mounted the largest criminal investigation in this country's history to find a guy who's screwing hooses. He's moved on to bigger things, Detective.'

Sniggers from the day shift.

'No, I mean I know him, sir. He's a peterman. Housebreaking's just the last thing we got him for. He blows safes. He did the British Linen Bank on Kilmarnock Road in '66 and probably the Clydesdale Bank out in Moodiesburn last year. He's good. Careful. That's why it's not on your sheet, sir – we've never caught him.'

'Well, OK then. Thank you for that bulletin, DI McCormack, that news update. Now. Whatever the precise extent of Mr Paton's accomplishments as a robber, we now have a name. We have a photo. On your sheets is a list of Known Associates, maybe DI McCormack can add to it. Also family members in the Glasgow area. We work that list till every name's been – what is it, Tam?'

DS Tam Ferguson held up the sheet. 'He'll have buggered off though, sir, won't he? How do we know he's still in Glasgow?'

'We don't. Met hit his last-known address this morning. Looks like he's not been there in days, possibly weeks. For now, we're assuming he's still in Glasgow. Or else someone in Glasgow knows where he is. And that someone's gonnae talk. Meantime we send a message to the neds and ne'er-do-weels of Maryhill. And anywhere else. Nobody gets a minute's fucking peace in this city until Alex Paton's in clink. This man is the Quaker. This man will be caught. Are we clear? DI McCormack: a minute.'

The sun was back out now, lighting the dirt and streaks on Cochrane's window. Cochrane tugged the blind down and sat behind his desk.

'You say you know this guy?'

'Know of him, sir.'

'So he's a peterman? What about it?'

McCormack sat in the hard plastic chair, shifted his hams. 'Supposed to be good. Reliable. He's the go-to guy for anything big.'

'Flying Squad take an interest?'

'Like I said, sir, he's careful. Got near him on the Linen Bank thing but, yeah, the witness had a change of heart.'

'It happens. He one of McGlashan's?'

'We don't think so. More of a lone operator. Picky. Just takes the jobs he fancies.'

'He fancied our ones all right.' Cochrane plucked his paper-knife from the wooden holder, tested the point. 'No gen on current associates, then? Where he might hang out?'

'Nah.' McCormack smoothed out a crease in his tie. 'Know where he was last Tuesday, though.'

Cochrane frowned. 'That Bath Street thing? The auctioneer's?'

'It wasn't him it was someone trying bloody hard to look like him.'

'You get this from your mates in St Andrew's Street?'

'Well. Common sense, sir. But yeah, I spoke to the CIO. Halliday. Nice clean job, he says. Traces of Polar Ammon. In and out within the hour. It's got Paton written all over it.'

'Right.' Cochrane nodded. 'So he rips off eighty thou from the auctioneer's on Tuesday. Beats, rapes, stabs and strangles a woman on the Saturday. Been a busy boy.'

McCormack frowned.

'What?'

'That's your explanation, sir? He's a busy boy?' McCormack drummed his fingers on the underside of the plastic chair. 'Paton's got no prior here. Sex crime. Murder. What makes you sure this is him?'

The paper-knife stood upright in Cochrane's desk, quivering. 'Well who knows, Detective? Based on the fact that his prints are on the doorjamb of the flat where the woman was killed. He's, what else, squatting in the same building. Identified leaving the scene. He's got a sheet. He fits the profile of the man I've been chasing for fifteen months. I don't know, Detective. I'd have him down as a person of interest. But that's just me.'

McCormack nodded. He rose to go. As he reached the door, Cochrane's voice stopped him, calmer now, the voice of reason.

'Don't make everything into a chess problem, son. Sometimes how it looks is how it is.'

'Sometimes,' McCormack said. 'Sometimes it is.'

*   *   *

221

Later, heading through Whiteinch on the way to the Clyde Tunnel, McCormack lit a Regal, offered the pack. Goldie shook his head, wound down his window.

'What?'

They were in the tunnel now, under the ribbed shell, fluorescent striplights ticking past overhead.

'Take a day off, would you? Once in a while.' Goldie reached out the window to adjust the wing mirror. 'From being a prick.'

'There's four women dead,' McCormack said. 'Jesus. I sound like you. There's four women dead. While we're breaking open the bubbly. Putting up the fucking bunting.'

'If they're happy it's be*cause* of those women. Because they've worked these murders for sixteen months. Fifteen more than you have. And they see an end in sight. They've got a collar. A man's going away for those killings. Might even hang. You'd grudge them that?'

The car emerged into daylight. McCormack closed his eyes. A man might hang. They'd suspended capital punishment in '65, for five years. Could Paton hang if they brought it back? Into his mind came the rough grey stone of the memorial on the hill above the bridge outside Ballachulish. Overgrown with trees and ferns but still commanding the highest spot above the crossing for the ferry. James Stewart hung there for eighteen months, James of the Glen; gibbeted, rotting, plucked at by crows, as punishment for murdering the king's factor, till the Livingstone brothers defied the interdiction and cut him down.

Was he innocent, Seamus a' Ghlinne? He'd been a captain in Charlie's army, he collected rents for the exiled chief of Ardsheal, he was a 'disaffected man', a Jacobite, a rebel. But he was blameless of the crime for which he hung. He never shot Colin Roy Campbell. He never killed the Red Fox.

Goldie was talking.

'What?'

'I said, what were you so excited about anyway? Over in Battlefield. What did you find?'

'Oh, nothing. I don't know. Probably nothing. Doesn't matter now anyway.'

But it did. That morning a call had come through to McCormack from one of the jewellers in Argyle Street. He recognized the locket on TV, Helen Thaney's locket. It wasn't one he stocked but he knew it because it was famous. It was a replica of a locket that was part of a set known as the Penicuik Jewels. The jewels were famous because of who they'd belonged to: Mary Queen of Scots.

The papers splashed with Paton for the next three days. Paton's face – in a decade-old photo that made him look like a boy – was on every front page. For the rest of the week the detectives of the Marine division made themselves unpopular in Maryhill. A loan-shark leaving the Kelvin Dock pub was bundled into a patrol car, spent a night in the Marine on a charge of D & D. Card schools were knocked over by masked men with police-issue weapons. Uniforms used 'the Powers' on random neds on Garioch Road and Maryhill Road – stop and search, spot of harassment. The door-knock came for the unlicensed bookies, the after-hours lock-in. A brothel in Garrioch Road was raided, the johns yanked into the street with their shirts wrongly buttoned.

When darkness fell the CID's short pocket truncheons were used on the headlights of cars registered to KAs of McGlashan's lieutenants.

At the end of the week McCormack met his tout at a bench on the towpath of the Forth and Clyde.

'It's a fucking war youse have declared. Why no send in the fucking Paras and have done with it?'

'Aye, well.' McCormack was dusting the bench with flicks of a handkerchief before sitting down. 'It's easy stopped.'

'How's it easy stopped? You think anyone round here knows where he is? Cunt's no lived here in eight or nine years. How we supposed to tell you where he is?'

'C'mon, Billy. Alex Paton's a local boy. Ran with the Fleet, didn't he? Somebody knows where he is.'

Thomson gave him the side-eye. 'I don't know where he is but I know what he's done. And it's not killing women.'

McCormack fished the note from his pocket; Thomson's fist closed around it.

'He done the Glendinnings job.'

'Who with?'

'I don't know. But he was the peterman. Aye. And I'll tell you something else. You'll walk a long way in the East End before you find someone who thinks he's the Quaker.'

'OK, Billy. You want more of that, you get me the names of the string. Who did Glendinnings with Alex Paton?'

McCormack left him on the bench, chucking pebbles at the ducks on the canal.

Paton wasn't the Quaker. You could keep saying that till the Jags won the league but who would listen? No one had time for doubts and misgivings. The thing they'd prayed for had happened. The Quaker had a name. The man who had flitted through the city like a ghost, who seemed to loom above the districts like a vast distended phantom, now had a name. He was a twenty-nine-year-old peterman, formerly of Burnhouse Street in Maryhill. His name was Alex Paton, thought to be living in the London area. It was finished. Even if it took them a month or two to catch him, he would never chill the city as he'd done these past two years. You might say that the myth of the Quaker was his final victim. The Quaker was dead. Killed by Alex Paton.

27

Paton left his clothes in a folded pile with his boots on top and stepped down to the water. He was conscious of his stark whiteness, the sun-struck glare of his limbs. The water was cold. It clenched his ankles and edged up his shins as if pulling him down. The bank shelved steeply. His heel slipped on crumbling mud and suddenly he was out of his depth with his arms spread out on the surface to keep himself from going under.

He looked down at his kicking legs, his knees flashing white in the gloom. It took him a second or two to get his breathing under control but then he kicked off for the far bank. The shearing crash of that first stroke seemed to shatter the peace of the whole forest but the water came slopping back and he hit a steady rhythm. The pool was broad. It took him seven strokes to reach the other side where he turned and pushed back with his ungainly breaststroke. He swam a few more breadths and felt his temperature climb. It was nice to feel safe and alone, hidden in the pond inside the wood, with the sun flashing on the brown water. Long-tailed blue dragonflies zipped around the pool. They hovered six inches from the surface, right in front of your nose, then they vanished in a flash.

Paton turned on his back and floated, his head tipped back, the comforting slurp of water at his ears. The sun was strong through the pink membranes of his eyelids. He could feel the steady current of the pool, the thrum that slid towards the far side where the water spilled out in a glossy curve into the next stretch of river. He remembered there was a bar of soap in the rucksack and he kicked off for the bank and stepped out on to the grass.

There was something luxurious about a new bar of soap, its squared-off edges and shiny, compact bulk. He ran his thumb over the sharp stamp of the maker's logo. The soap lathered up surprisingly well and Paton soaped his arms and torso while kicking to stay afloat. He worked up some suds and tossed the bar on to the bank and lathered his hair with both hands and ducked under to rinse it off. He reached for the bar once more and was feeling down to soap the sole of one foot when the bar squirted from his grasp. He watched it spin and dwindle out of sight. He dived a couple of times, scissoring down with his legs, but the pool was too deep and the water too murky.

Out on the bank he stood on a sun-warmed rock and let the sun dry his skin. He smoked a cigarette, holding it aloft between puffs so that the drops from his hair wouldn't spot it. A cloud passed over the sun and the gooseflesh rose on his ribs and he hurried into his clothes.

The water looked deeper and darker in the altered light and he wondered if there were fish down there, big drifting pike or spiky tench. He wished he'd brought a rod. Maybe he could get one at the shop in Balmaha, and a permit in a false name from the sandstone hotel. He imagined hooking a big trout and gutting it, shucking the innards into the water and cooking the flesh on his wee Primus stove.

He was hungry, he suddenly realized. As he walked back through the forest he thought about food. There were sardines and Ritz crackers and he might open another can of stew. Tinned pears to follow and a bar of chocolate.

The sun came back out as he walked. It made the trees on his left look as though they were moving, strobing past like the spokes of a wheel, and he was slow to spot the other movement, the jogging gait of a man climbing the hill but then he caught it again, a flash of red through the trees.

Paton dropped down on his haunches. He felt the rucksack's weight tugging him backwards and he silently eased himself free of the straps. He strained to see, parting a clump of green ferns. There it was: the red anorak: Gilchrist.

Without taking his eyes from the figure in red, Paton worked his right hand into the loosely tied mouth of the rucksack. He rummaged around for the bunched socks and drew them carefully out. Glancing swiftly down he worked the gun loose from the socks and snatched it up, flexing his fingers on the crosshatched grip.

Gilchrist was at the clearing now. He squatted down to study the remains of the fire and now he was crawling forward to inspect the inside of Paton's tent, his fat backside jutting comically from the tent flap. Then he was back on his feet, his head high as if sniffing the wind, scanning the horizon.

If he comes this way . . . Paton thought, and tightened his grip on the Browning. His palm was slick. He had never killed anyone, never fired a gun in anger, but he took the piece in both hands and held it in readiness. *If I aim for the belly I can't miss. Then one in the head when he's down.*

Paton's hamstrings were starting to ache but he didn't move. A twig might crack if he changed his position and the high bald head snap round. He lifted the gun to eye-level and sighted along the short barrel. He squeezed one eye shut and then flashed it open. Another figure had appeared in the clearing. He saw the dark blue tunic, a flash of checkered hatband.

The cop stood with his hands on his hips, getting his breath back after the climb. Gilchrist and the cop were talking. Gilchrist gestured towards the tent and the cop had a quick look inside. They stood around for a bit, nodding and pointing, then they started back down the hill. Paton watched them out of sight and then he toppled back till he lay on the ground with his back resting on the rucksack. He stretched his legs out in front of him. His arms flopped to his sides, the gun held loosely in his right hand.

He closed his eyes. The shadows of trees lay in bars across his eyelids. He felt he could sleep for the next twelve hours, right out in the open, but he forced himself to his feet and walked down to the clearing.

He had shifted camp the previous night, moving uphill a good way from his first night's pitch. But Gilchrist had found him. And the cop would come back, more cops, they would fan out on the hillside, cutting him off. He felt the unfairness of it but it was funny too. They all thought he was the Quaker. You couldn't tell them, *It's all right, boys, don't worry, I'm just a robber*. You couldn't explain that you were holed up in that flat after the heist at Glendinnings. And maybe the cops wouldn't find the flat. Maybe they'd miss his prints on the ground-floor jamb. There was no point in doing anything dramatic till he knew where he stood. The thing now was to keep on the move, keep yourself hidden.

It took him ten minutes to pack up his gear. He took time to snap a few branches and flatten the ferns on the path leading south-west out of the clearing, down to the village. Then he picked his way carefully north.

In a few minutes he was out of the trees. The sun was hot on his scalp and the nape of his neck. The bobble hat was no use. He wished he'd bought a cap, one of those French foreign legion affairs with the flap down the back. Finally he stopped.

The pack hit the ground. He took off his shirt and his T-shirt. He put the shirt back on and knotted the sleeves of the T-shirt and fitted it on like some kind of headdress and lifted the pack and set off once again.

The climb was getting steeper. The hillside was covered with bracken and the fronds brushed his thighs as he climbed. There was a nice pain in his thighs and his calves from yesterday's walk but he knew that he would work this off. He wasn't tired. The sun threw his shadow on the bracken ahead of him and it seemed as though the shadow was leading the way. As long as the shadow kept moving then Paton could follow.

He stopped at one point and looked back down the hill, surprised at how far he'd come. The bracken seemed to spring back into place as soon as you passed and his progress up the hillside had left no trace. It was waist-high, the bracken. If he sat down now he would disappear.

On the summit of Conic Hill he shrugged out of his rucksack. He finished the burn water, tipping the last drops over his head. The sky was a clear milky blue. To the south he could see the Campsies and the Kilpatrick Hills and the faint, grey tower-blocks of Glasgow. Westward was the loch and the islands, the low blue bulk of Arran. Further north the three peaks of the Cobbler and the purple shoulder of Ben Lomond.

He looked again at the islands on the loch. Could you steal a boat and hide out on one of these brown and green puddles of land? But the boat would be missed and the smoke of a fire might be seen from the shore. And an island would be a rat-trap if the polis landed on it. Better to keep pushing north, up the eastern shore of the loch. Hold to the high ground; avoid the busier shoreline road.

His knees juddered as he tramped downhill. The land lay all before him, half of Scotland it looked like, spread out like a map and he himself the only moving object. How could they catch him here? Even a plane or a helicopter would be useless if he simply lay down in the ferns. Unless they came with dogs. The thought stayed his leg and he paused for half a minute. They could track him with dogs. Scenes from a dozen convict movies sprang to mind. A pack of straining hounds slipping the leash and pelting into the distance; and a wide-eyed, leaden-legged convict scrambling hopelessly through a muddy forest. Paton hitched his pack and quickened his pace.

He was halfway down the hill when he heard a noise. He stopped. Was it someone at his heels? An odd whispered sound. He moved forward a few paces and stopped again. Then a pheasant rose up in front of him and he thrashed through the bracken. It was a burn. Shallow and barely broader than a road but big enough to mask his scent once he crossed it. He splashed into the burn and was making for the far bank when he pulled up short. If they tracked him to this point they would just need to cross the burn to pick up the trail on the other side. He should choose one direction, uphill or down, and walk in the water for a while to throw them off.

He turned uphill, splashing through the shallows, the stones shifting and sliding under his boots. His feet were wet but the cold water was pleasant in the heat. He could feel his socks squeaking when he flexed his toes. After another ten minutes he needed a rest. In the pack there were two bottles of stout that Paton had bought from the Balmaha shop. He stepped on to the far bank and found the bottles and wedged them in the water with four or five stones to hold them in place. The current split whitely round the curved brown glass and the canted necks of the bottles looked like the prows of tiny ships.

Sitting on the bank he picked the wet bootlaces loose and worked the boots off and set them on a rock in the sun with their laces spread loose and their tongues pulled out. He wrung out his socks and set them beside the boots and sat with his arms resting on bent knees and the breeze playing coolly on his feet.

He smoked a cigarette. After a while he reached down for one of the bottles and clamped his palm on its belly to check for coldness. Then he rooted in his rucksack for the knife and found the bottle-opener. When he prised off the cap the beer foamed up out of the bottle and spilled down over his fingers. He sucked the beer from his fingers and wiped them on the grass and took a long pull from the bottle.

The beer fizzed in his nose and he spluttered and then the splutter turned into a laugh. He was happy, he suddenly realized. Here, on a bare hillside with wet feet and sore legs, with the police forces of several counties on his tail, he was happier than he'd been in months. He could have burst into song. He drained the bottle and drank the other and stowed the empties in the bracken. He felt rejuvenated. He felt as if he could walk for miles.

The pack was lighter without the bottles. Traversing the flank of the hill with the lochside in view down to his left, he broke into a slow jog. Would he have shot him? Would he have shot that fat tub of lard, Spencer Gilchrist? He was glad it hadn't come to that. It might still happen, further down the line, but not now, not yet. Maybe it was like cracking safes. Sometimes you nudged and twirled and listened, it was a question of clicks and delicate adjustments. And sometimes you blew it to fuck. Gelignite was the clincher. Use it sparingly and only when needed. You got results but you lost some control. He needed to keep what control he still had. You did that by keeping out of sight.

He was above Ross Point by now, where the loch narrows and deepens. They said the loch was six hundred feet deep here. He thought about the darkness down there. The eels swirling in the black icy depths.

He took a shit in the trees and wiped himself with docken leaves and washed his hands in the burn, scouring his fingers with gravel.

It was getting too dark to walk without stumbling. Soon it would be too dark to find a proper camp. He moved along the ridge, found a space beneath an outcrop of rock, an oval clearing, broad enough to pitch the tent. He worked quickly, dragging the inside of his boot across the ground to smooth it down, howking out a couple of stones, spreading the tent, tamping the pegs with a tin of baked beans. He hung his pack on the branch of a tree.

He would risk a fire. It was almost pitch-dark now, the waters holding the last pale light from the gleam above the Arrochar Hills, but he gathered twigs and sticks from under nearby trees and used the saw-blade of his Swiss Army knife on the low-lying branches and soon a good-sized blaze was crackling and smoking near the entrance to the tent. He took the can of beans he'd used to tamp the pegs with and opened it and tipped it into the pot and crumbled some oatcakes into the pot and warmed it up on the open flame. It tasted good and before he knew it his spoon was clattering on the sides of the pot and he wished he'd had some bread to swab up the sauce. He picked his way over to the burn, holding the pot like a tomahawk.

When the pot was cleaned he stowed it in the pack and threw some damp grass on the dwindling fire and crawled into the tent. He wrestled out of his boots and shuffled into the sleeping bag. He was using a couple of folded shirts for a pillow. When he closed his eyes the face of Bobby Stokes came into his mind as if Stokes had poked his head inside the tent.

It was Stokes who'd set him up. Paton sat up in the tent and fumbled for his cigarettes. Stokes was the one. Stokes set him up with the safe house. Stokes knew where he would be. It had to be Stokes. Otherwise it was all just coincidence, magic, the Quaker choosing the building out of shitty bad luck. That kind of luck was never just luck. So what did it mean? Paton sucked on the cigarette. Did Stokes know the Quaker? Was *Stokes* the Quaker? It made him cold to think of Stokes – smiling, gormless, Bobby Stokes – stalking women through the dance halls, taking their elbows, walking them into the night.

He got out of the tent for a piss. He stood in his bare feet, his water spattering on the grass. Off in the distance was the sodium glow above Glasgow, the low, black, smouldering city. He'd have to find Bobby Stokes. Find Bobby Stokes and not get found himself. Tomorrow would be soon enough. Tomorrow he would make his way back.

28

'Thirteenth May.' Goldie kept repeating the date. 'So how the fuck did you come up with that?'

'It was staring me in the face. Literally. I was looking at the date in big stone letters on the side of the monument. It just struck me.'

They were in McCormack's flat, sinking some tinnies after another twelve-hour shift at the Marine. All day the Marine had been buzzing. The news broke that morning that Paton had been sighted. A shopkeeper in Balmaha had recognized him. He'd been camping on the shores of Loch Lomond. Half of the force was up there now. Dogs, frogmen, chopper, the works. Everyone at the Marine walking round with these quiet little smiles. The scent of imminent triumph in the air.

Meanwhile McCormack was explaining his theory to Goldie.

'So that's Victim One. Found in Carmichael Place in Battlefield on the four hundredth anniversary of the Battle of Langside.' McCormack tapped the map. He had a dog-eared street map of Glasgow spread open on his kitchen table, weighted at the edges with an ashtray, a sugar bowl and two cans of Pale Ale. 'That's the battle that gives its name to the district. Victim Two: Mackeith Street in Bridgeton.'

'What's Mackeith Street named after?' Goldie swigged from a third can of ale.

'You mean what's Bridgeton named after? After the battle, when everything's lost and Mary's getting chased for her life, she stops off at Bridgeton.'

McCormack had read it in the biography. Mary watched the Battle of Langside from a hill overlooking the field. When she saw her men routed by Moray's smaller force she spurred her horse and fled with an escort of loyal troops. She was heading south but stopped for some food and fresh water at Bridgeton before crossing the Clyde.

'She's a Catholic and she stops off at Bridgeton?' Goldie snorted. 'Not the sharpest knife in the drawer, was she?'

'It was just a fishing village then.' McCormack's tone had hardened, quashing Goldie's raillery. 'But the key thing it had was the bridge. She was heading south for England, so she crossed the Clyde at Bridgeton.'

He could picture it, the party clattering up to the crossing, the tall queen on the snorting horse, her rich silks and stuffs, the men casting backward glances, wary of pursuers. Later they would burn a bridge after they'd crossed it, down by Dumfries, to thwart the Regent's men. Here, though, they simply passed over, hooves drumming on the timber, heading pell-mell for England, for Elizabeth, the poor cell in Fotheringhay, the block, the blade, the head tumbling into a wicker basket.

'Hold on.' Goldie's raised index finger stopped the course of Scottish history. 'Hold on a jiffy. She's already on the south side. Langside's south of the river.'

'OK, Sherlock. She flees north from the battlefield to escape Moray's forces. But she's heading for England so she has to recross the river later on. Happy?'

'That's two,' Goldie said. 'What about three? What about Marion Mercer?'

McCormack nodded, conning the map like a field marshal. He slid a finger to the west. 'Earl Street, Scotstoun. Any number of earls come into the story. Darnley. Moray.'

Goldie frowned. 'Jesus, it's a bit thin, isn't it?' He crumpled his empty tinnie and pumped his fist when the tinnie landed in McCormack's bin, eight feet away on the other side of the room. The south-east corner of the map sprung back as Goldie lifted the second-last can of beer and cracked it open. The ring-pull lay on the map where he tossed it, a curling metal tongue.

'OK. I know. But then, this new one. Number four. It's as if he's spelling it out for us. You're too thick to spot it with the first three, so here it is in so many words.'

'Queen Mary Street. Right. But I still don't get what you're saying. What does this mean?'

'I'm not sure what it means. But for sixteen months we've been struggling to see a connection between the pins on the map. Maybe this is it.'

'But Mary Queen of Scots? The fuck do we do with that? There's choppers scanning the hillsides for a fugitive and we're having a history lesson?'

'There's choppers scanning the hillsides for a peterman. Not a killer. Not the fucking Quaker.'

'So where is the Quaker?'

'That's down to us. They're not even looking for the Quaker.' McCormack slapped the map. '*This* is what the fuck we do with it. This is how we find him.'

Goldie shook his head, frowning at the tattered map. 'And Helen Thaney, what about her? Did you find the friend, the one she fell out with? What's-her-face?'

236

'Carol Strachan. Yeah, I did. I saw her last night. Turns out she lives round the corner. Partickhill Road.'

'So what was the fight about?'

'Men.' McCormack drained his own can of beer, crumpled it between his palms, tossed the flattened disc on the table. 'She said she and Helen had a thing going. With the big spenders.'

'Whoring?'

McCormack made the seesaw gesture with his outstretched hand. 'Not exactly. More a kind of informal arrangement. If a punter was tipping you big enough, you'd maybe think about joining him when your shift finished. She said she and Helen were a team. Worked the same shifts, paired up to snare the high rollers.'

'So what happened?'

'She says Helen got greedy. Says she wanted what was hers and what was Carol's and everyone else's in between.'

Goldie snorted. 'You mean she was better looking than Carol and Carol couldnae compete.'

'Maybe. I don't know. I think Carol knew she was the consolation prize. I don't think it bothered her. It all worked out fine until Helen got carried away. She wanted all the good ones for herself. At least she did until the new boyfriend came on the scene.'

'Right. The bloke with the Prince of Wales jacket. Does Carol know who he was?'

'If she does, she's not saying.'

Not saying seemed to be the way of it, McCormack reflected, so far as Helen Thaney was concerned. The Quaker Squad had been digging into her background but there wasn't much background to dig. She had no family to speak of. She grew up in the Irish Republic, got into trouble with a boy in her teens.

She'd been taken into care, some kind of church-run institution in Waterford, and then came to Scotland to start a new life.

Goldie sipped his beer. He plucked a Mayfair from his packet and jabbed it at McCormack like a dart. 'If the boyfriend was so serious, what was she doing at the Barrowland?'

McCormack nodded. 'And why was she putting it about so bloody blatantly?'

'She was cutting loose for the night? Slipping back into her old routine?'

'I don't think so. It was more than that. She was making sure she was noticed. Dancing with five or six guys, scrapping with somebody's bird. It's too calculated. She wanted everyone to remember she'd been there that night.'

'Why, though?'

'That's the question.' McCormack reached for the last can of beer and the map curled back on itself. 'Did she maybe know she was in danger? Was she trying to send out some sort of signal?'

Goldie yawned, stretching extravagantly, and swept both hands through his shaggy blond hair. He studied the landscape of crumpled tinnies and heaped ashtrays on McCormack's kitchen table. 'Well, I know what signal that's sending. Get your arse home to bed, Goldie boy.'

He hauled to his feet and wrestled into his jacket. He stood nodding solemnly at McCormack for a minute, swaying under the kitchen's bare bulb. Then he drew McCormack clumsily to him and clapped him on the back with his big soft paw and headed off to find a taxi on Dumbarton Road.

29

Bobby Stokes caught the barman's eyes and signalled for another Grouse. When the whisky arrived he ordered a chaser of beer to go with it. The beer tasted sour and he tipped the whisky into it. Now it tasted worse. He drank it down in three convulsive gulps. His drinking was getting out of hand. Since the Glendinnings thing, he'd been putting it away like a man with hollow legs. Since Paton had missed the meet. Since Paton had gone AWOL. Dazzle was taking it badly but, Jesus, McGlashan was another thing again. You'd have thought Glash had done the job himself. He needed his taste, he'd told Dazzle. Fifteen grand. They had a week to front up. Find Paton or start paying.

Stokes signalled for another whisky and tried to wipe the memory of McGlashan's light blue eyes. Not half an hour before, McGlashan had swept into the pub with two lieutenants who took up their stance at the bar while the boss slid into a booth opposite Dazzle and Cursiter. Stokes took a stool at the end of the booth. Dazzle launched into his spiel, his hands dancing like puppets as he assured McGlashan that Paton would be found, the stones recovered, the money paid, the earth returned to its axis. McGlashan never spoke. He sat straight-backed, his slabbed hands loosely folded on the table, a thick gold wedding-band sunk in the flesh below one knuckle. His black hair was longish, carefully cut. Between his bulldog jowls a girlish lip, plump and pinkish, protruded in a slight frown. Blue eyes, pale and raw-looking, never strayed from Dazzle's face.

There was a tumbler of malt on the tabletop in front of him but he left it untouched. When Dazzle's excuses petered out, McGlashan leaned forward slightly, the light catching the nap on the shoulders of his lightweight suit, grey with a light blue check. His low, unhurried voice set out what would happen. One week. Fifteen grand. Then he turned with a lifted finger and one of his men crossed with the water jug. McGlashan tipped a splash of water into the whisky, swirled it for a minute and threw it back. Everyone stood as the boss slid out of the booth, buttoning his jacket as he made for the door.

Stokes finished his drink. McGlashan was bad enough. And now this: Paton's face on the front of the *Record*. Paton as the Quaker. It made no fucking sense.

No one knew what to believe. He looked down the bar to where Dazzle and Cursiter huddled in their booth, hunched like two witches over their brews.

He needed air. Outside it was mild, a fine August night. Pale yellow sky. Something hopeful in the breeze that rocked a dented tin can in the gutter. He strolled to the end of the block and turned the corner. He'd gone about ten yards when a man stepped out of a doorway as he passed.

'Jesus! Paton! You frightened the shit out of me. The fuck happened to you?'

'You've got a guilty conscience, Bobby.' Paton stepped back in the shadows. 'Anyone would think you weren't happy to see me.'

'What the fuck?' Stokes glanced back at the corner. 'You're all over the papers, man. They're saying you're the Quaker.'

'Oh really? That's what "they" are doing, is it? That's what "they" are saying?'

'It's not true, though, Alex, is it? Alex, tell me it's not true.'

'You fucking lying piece of shit.'

Paton looked different, thinner, with a full blond beard. He reminded Stokes of a junkie Jesus, sunken-eyed, far gone.

'Alex. You're fucking scaring me, pal. I mean, Jesus.' Stokes swallowed, seemed to think of something. 'How'd you even get here? Papers saying you're up Loch Lomond. Cops everywhere. Fucking manhunt.'

'Let's focus on the matter in hand, Bobby.'

In fact, getting back to Glasgow had been easier than Paton expected. He'd hidden out in the bracken above Ross Point for another day and then, in the late gloaming, he struck up the lochside, heading north. At Inversnaid he stole a rowing boat and slipped across to Inveruglas. Then he hiked across the Arrochar hills and came through the narrow glen to Arrochar in the blue dawn. He paid a scallop fisherman fifty quid to take him down Loch Long and up the Clyde in his Loch Fyne skiff. The fisherman dropped him just west of Dumbarton, and Paton caught the bus back to the city.

Now he stepped out of the doorway again. 'A woman gets murdered, Bobby. Murdered in the building where I'm on ice? Forty-eight Queen Mary Street. In the ground-floor flat.'

'Alex. Hold on a minute.'

'Out of all the empty buildings in the city. Out of all the condemned blocks, he picks the one I'm holed up in.' Paton had circled round so that he was on the outside of the pavement, edging Stokes towards the doorway. 'That's pretty shit luck, Bobby. Or wouldn't you say?'

241

Stokes had his hands up. 'Whoa, fuck, Alex. Hold on. You think I set you up?'

'Who else knew?'

'Alex. Come on.'

'Who knew, Bobby? You're the one who set it up. The safe house. So-called. Who else did you tell? Who knew I was staying there?'

'Mate. Alex. Catch yourself on. Listen to yourself. Jesus.'

Stokes was shaking his head. He zipped his jerkin as far as it would go, plunged his hands in the pockets. When Paton pushed him two-handed in the chest he stumbled back and slammed against the door. Paton had one hand locked on Stokes's throat, holding him stiff-armed against the door. With his other hand he mashed Stokes's pockets, feeling for a chib. There was a lock-knife in Stokes's back pocket and Paton tossed it behind him into the street.

'I need the name, Bobby. Who did you talk to? Who set the house up?'

'Mate. I don't know. I fucking swear.' Stokes had his hands on his head, rocking back and forward. 'I don't know anything any more. You're the fucking Quaker. McGlashan wants his fifteen grand. Have you got the gear at least?'

'What do you mean, he wants fifteen grand?'

'It's not a fucking joke, Paton. They think you've stiffed them. They're putting the word out, they're coming for you. You better hope the polis get you first. I told them you weren't like that, but, you know.'

'That was nice of you, Bobby. What's McGlashan got to do with it? You're fucking smiling now?'

'Alex. Jesus. What's Glash got to do with it? That's what you're asking? We rob an auction house on Glash's patch—'

'City centre's nobody's patch.'

'Whole fucking city belongs to Glash. Is it London or fucking Mars you live in?'

'He can't expect an outsider, an independent operator—'

'You're dictating terms? I could turn you in right now, you'd never see the light of day. McGlashan can expect whatever the fuck he wants. That's the point. His ball, his fucking rules. He wants his taste.'

Stokes had talked himself back on to the front foot. He rolled his shoulders, glaring at Paton.

Paton clicked his tongue. 'Thought I'd explained this. I'm not kicking up to anyone, Bobby. All right? Not to McGlashan or anyone else.'

'Well, good for you. Stick it to the man. Thing is, we live here. Glash is the fucking weather round here. OK? He's given us a week. We need fifteen grand. Where's the fucking money, Alex?'

Stokes glanced up the street, wiped a hand down over his mouth.

Paton stepped up to Stokes. In a single movement he brought his hand up and clamped it on Stokes's throat. 'It was McGlashan, wasn't it? You told him, didn't you? You told McGlashan?'

'What?'

'Did you do a deal? Cut the others out and share it between you. Get me out the way, tell the others I'd shot the crow, taken the gear with me.'

'Alex. I swear to God. I never told him, I never told Glash. He doesn't even know who I am.'

'He wants fifteen grand from you but he doesn't know who you are?'

'He knows I'm with Dazzle. Fuck. I've never fucking met the guy. I never told him.'

'You told someone, though.'

243

'No!'

A car was coming down the street and Paton leant into Stokes, close as a lover. He could smell the beer on Stokes's breath, the cheap stink of his aftershave.

'Thing is, Bobby. They think it's me. I was spotted leaving the building. Man in his late twenties. Shoulder-length fair hair, neatly trimmed beard. They found the flat. Call this number.'

Stokes tried to shake his head. Paton tightened his grip on Stokes's throat. 'This was your safe house. This was your baby.'

'It's the Quaker!' Stokes's voice cracked, straining through Paton's grip. 'Fuck's sake, Alex. You cannae blame me for the Quaker.'

'OK.' Paton let go of Stokes's throat and stepped back. 'It's bad luck. That's your line, is it? Fine. Well, I think there might be more of it around. That's just a hunch, like, but I think the bad luck might be getting shared around a bit. You might want to pass that on to your mate.'

'OK. Right. Alex. Now let's think about that.'

'Done thinking, Bobby. You see McGlashan, tell him to watch his back. He's not gonnae need to find me. I'm finding him.'

'Fuck!' Stokes had his hands clasped behind his neck, head bowed. 'Fuck! What about the gear?'

'The gear's safe.'

The rain was coming on. Stokes stooped down and picked up his knife where it shone in the gutter.

'What'll I tell the others?'

'I'll be in touch.'

Paton was walking away.

'Alex!' Stokes slipped the knife into his back pocket. 'How'll you find me?'

He looked abandoned, distraught.

Paton half-turned. The tight lips, the hard cold glint in the hooded eyes. His hands came out of his jerkin pockets and gestured at the street, the blackened buildings, the pub with its red neon sign. 'It's not that fucking hard, is it?'

30

McCormack sat in the squad room, swinging on the chair's back legs. The day was cooler after yesterday's fierce heat, but the fan on his desk still traced its lethargic arc. He liked the soft whirr of the blades. He liked the air on his cheeks, how it lifted his fringe.

He was trying not to think too hard. It was something he did. Not meditation, exactly – just holding the facts in his head, paying them out like a hand at cards, the elements of the case. Watching for a pattern.

Victim number four. Twenty-nine years old. Queen Mary Street. Vaginal lacerations. No kids. Ground-floor flat.

A drunk was passing in the street, singing or shouting, it was hard to tell which. McCormack closed his eyes.

Cocktail waitress. Blindfolded. Gold locket. Knife marks on both breasts. Fractured skull.

The cool air passed and repassed his face. The air felt wet on his eyelids. He sat in the shadows, dealing out cards.

Ground-floor flat. Bridgeton. Fractured skull. Tights used as a ligature. Tan slingbacks. Cocktail Waitress. Queen Mary Street.

He opened his eyes. He was getting nowhere. A change of scene might help.

He signed out an unmarked car and drove up the Saltmarket in the sparse mid-afternoon traffic. At Glasgow Cross he turned right up the Gallowgate and felt the change in pressure as he crossed the invisible boundary between the city centre and the East End. The shops were smaller and meaner now, fruiterers and butchers, a dark little baker's with the yellow cones of pineapple cakes glowing in the window. He passed the City Ham and Egg Stores, Top Form Shoes, Reets' Fashions.

Outside the Saracen Head pub, with its window-grilles and hanging sign, a man in a bunnet was sitting on the pavement, slumped against the wall, legs straight out in front of him. His charcoal overcoat enveloped him like a one-man tent. Across the road was the shuttered, unlit bulk of the Barrowland.

He drove on, past Sydney Street and Melbourne Street, past the Royal Bank of Scotland and the Gallowgate Post Office ('Robber's Corner', as the C Div boys called it), and hung a left up Bellgrove Street, crossing the junction with Duke Street and on up Westercraigs. The wind was westerly and he could smell the brown biscuity smell from the brewery.

The plan – so far as he had one – was to hit Alexandra Parade and make his way back down Castle Street in a big circuit of the Necropolis, but he craned up now to see a street sign and suddenly he was slowing as if the car had a puncture and his foot eased off the accelerator and he guided the car to the kerb. An angry blare of horn stretched past his window but already his eyes were closed and he was waiting for the memory to crystallize.

The street name he'd seen was Seton Terrace and now a vision of a fiddler's slim fingers gripping a bow flashed into his mind, and a long-haired woman singing with closed eyes, spotlights glossing her straight brown hair. It was the Park Bar, the ceilidh band, and one of the songs they sang on a Saturday night, a song Granny Beag used to sing, and he wondered now how he'd managed to miss it:

> *Yestreen the Queen had four Maries.*
> *This night she'll hae but three,*
> *There was Mary Beaton, and Mary Seton,*
> *And Mary Carmichael and me.*

Mary Carmichael. Carmichael Lane. The first victim: Jacquilyn Keevins. Four victims. The Queen's Four Maries. The young waiting-women who went to France with the infant queen.

His hands were shaking as he started the car and headed west, past the construction site for the new M8, the Neolithic pillars of the half-built Kingston Bridge. He parked on Berkeley Street. Through the revolving door of the Mitchell Library, up to the Literature Section on the second floor where the librarian brought him a book: *The English and Scottish Popular Ballads*, edited by Francis James Child. 'The Queen's Four Maries' was one of the ballads (Number 173), except it wasn't called 'The Queen's Four Maries', it was called 'Mary Hamilton'. And there were two different versions ('A' and 'B'), though neither was the one that Granny Beag used to sing. Never mind: that was the oral tradition, that's how it worked, a song kept changing with every singer.

There was a short introductory note to the song. It stated that 'This ballad purports to relate the tragic history of one of the Queen's Maries. In some of the versions her lover is said to be the King (Darnley).'

Both versions of the song told the same basic story. A serving girl, Mary Hamilton, is pregnant. Her lover is 'the hichest Stewart of a' – presumably, thought McCormack, the king – and

248

the scandal has broken: 'Word's gane to the kitchen, / And word's gane to the ha'. Panicked, the girl drowns her baby, tying it in her apron (or putting it in an earthen pot in one version) and throwing it in the sea. When the queen asks her what has become of the baby whose cries the whole palace has heard, the girl denies all knowledge. She's been ill, she tells the queen: the cries were her own cries of pain.

The queen, of course, sees through this story and Mary Hamilton is hanged in Edinburgh. On her way to the gallows she calls for wine, drinks a toast to the 'jolly sailors', and repents her own folly:

> *'Ye needna weep for me,' she says,*
> *'Ye needna weep for me;*
> *For had I not slain mine own sweet babe,*
> *This death I wadna dee.'*

In the 'A' version, the ballad ends with the verse that McCormack remembered Granny Beag singing, the verse about four Maries becoming three. He hadn't realized that the reason for this change (*'This night she'll hae but three'*) was that Mary Hamilton was hanged.

The librarian also brought him a copy of *Blackwood's Edinburgh Magazine* for 1895 containing an article by Andrew Lang on 'The Mystery of "The Queen's Marie"'. Lang argues that the ballad records an actual event from the reign of Queen Mary, but that the names have gotten confused. 'Carmichael' is wrong and so is 'Hamilton'. There were no Maries of that name among the queen's waiting-women. In the historical record, the queen's Four Maries were Beaton, Seton, Livingstone and Fleming. One version of the ballad gives three of the names correctly, but Mary Hamilton (the 'me' in the line about 'Mary Carmichael and me') remains wrong.

'Can I photocopy this, please?'

The librarian asked him to fill out a form and came back in five minutes with the Xerox'd sheets.

Driving back through the city centre the song ran through his head, sometimes in the voice of the long-haired woman from the Park Bar, sometimes in the harsher voice of Granny Beag. He thought of Helen Thaney coming over from Ireland to get herself murdered in a Bridgeton tenement:

> Oh little did my mother think,
> The day she cradled me,
> What lands I was to travel through.
> What death I was to dee.

He parked in Tobago Street, opposite C Div. Goldie was in the squad room, stabbing at his typewriter keys, a notebook propped open beside him when McCormack slapped the photocopied sheets on to his desk.

'Carmichael Lane,' McCormack said. 'I knew the name meant something.'

Goldie looked at the sheets and then up at McCormack. Without a word he lifted the sheets and began to read. He straightened up as he read and when he finished he waved the sheets gently at McCormack.

'You're saying this is the pattern? The four victims represent these . . . Maries? The Queen's Four Maries?'

'It joins the pins, doesn't it? Carmichael Lane, Mackeith Street, Earl Street, Queen Mary Street.'

'So who were they?' Goldie set the sheets on to the desk, tapped them with his fingers. 'The Four Maries.'

'They were the queen's attendants. Ladies-in-waiting sort of thing. They were picked out to keep her company. When she went over to France to be brought up at court, the Four Maries went with her.'

'And who's "me"?'

'Who's what?'

'In the poem.' Goldie took the sheets up again. '"There was Mary Beaton and Mary Seton and Mary Carmichael and me." Who's "me"?'

'It's Mary Hamilton. The woman in the title. The name's a mistake, apparently, there was no Mary Hamilton. But that doesn't matter. Did you read the last verse? Read the last verse.'

Goldie spun the sheets towards him, cleared his throat:

> 'Cast off, cast off my goun,' she said,
> 'But let my petticoat be,
> And tye a napkin on my face,
> For that gallows I downa see.'

He nodded at McCormack. They were both remembering the shabby room, Helen Thaney on her back on the soiled mattress, a white strip across her eyes, a sanitary napkin. *And tye a napkin on my face.*

'He was what, reenacting the ballad?'

'I don't know. It looks like it.'

'But what does it mean? If the victims are the Four Maries, what's the message? What's he trying to say?'

They were back to this, thought McCormack. Murder as a work of art. A species of code. Something needing construed. Like a reading comprehension. So what was the answer, smart-arse? What *did* it mean? McCormack ran his tongue across his lips. Dry mouth. Some lubrication was in order. Swift half.

'Let's get a pint,' he said to Goldie. 'Fancy it?'

They adjourned to the pub across the street, a deceptively

251

spacious lounge with booths along one wall and Glasgow Celtic paraphernalia pinned above the gantry. McCormack took a seat in a booth. Goldie walked towards him with two brimming pints.

They sipped the cold lager, enjoying the cool dark secrecy of the booth. They lit their cigarettes and smoked.

'Mary Hamilton,' McCormack said eventually. 'The woman in the song. She kills her bastard child. They hang her for it. What's that got to do with Helen Thaney?'

Goldie smoked. 'Maybe she did something similar. Back in Ireland. Had a wean. Couldnae look after it.'

'If she killed her kid, we'd know about it. What about the others?'

'You're the expert. What does the book say?'

'About the Four Maries? I don't know. As far as I remember they just get lumped in with the queen. They're like mini versions of the queen.'

'And the queen is . . .?'

'Frivolous. Adulterous. Bit of a tart.' He remembered the words of a pamphlet quoted in the biography: *Marie Stewarde late Quene of Scotland hath defiled her own body with many adulteries.*

'And our women are the same?'

McCormack finished his drink. 'Well. In his eyes, yeah, I think so. They're married. OK, two of them are separated but they're still married. They've got kids at home. They should be watching their weans, not out gallivanting at the jiggin.'

'He's punishing them, you mean? This Paton bloke's John Knox?'

'It's not Paton. But, yeah, something like that.'

'Are we any further forward, though?' Goldie said. 'Haven't we just confirmed what we already know? He's probably religious. He's educated, knows a bit about history. He's playing games, thinks he's smarter than us. Probably *is* smarter than us.'

'Speak for yourself.'

'He's spelling things out for us, mate. Your words. And there's something else, isn't there? I just thought of it.' Goldie had a pinched little smile on his face.

'What's that?'

'If it's the Four Maries, then he's finished. He's completed the pattern. His work here is done.'

McCormack caught the barman's eye, lifted two fingers in a victory sign. 'He'll never be done. He'll start a new pattern. It's not in his nature to stop now.'

He rose and crossed to pay for the drinks. While the barman worked the till, McCormack leaned his elbows on the bar. On a shelf beside the whisky bottles someone had propped a cardboard cutout of the European Cup, covered in tinfoil, the vase-shaped body, the jug-eared handles. He could picture Billy McNeill hoisting it in triumph, last year – no, the year before – at the Estádio Nacional in Lisbon. He'd watched the game in the rec room at St Andrew's Street, the whole shift – even the diehard bluenoses – dancing round the room with their hands on each other's shoulders when the final whistle blew. Champions of Europe.

It had seemed so incongruous. Eleven guys from Glasgow winning the biggest prize in football. Beating the tall, tanned aristocrats of Internazionale. And now the thought formed into words, the thought that had been nettling him for the past few days. It was too incongruous: what was a peterman, a petty crook from Maryhill doing with these allusions to Scottish history and Mary Queen of Scots? It can't be Paton. He's a peterman, for Christ's sake. He's not a historian. He's not John Prebble.

He took his change and carried the pints to the booth.

31

Paton stood at the broken landing window. Another dead building. Another gutted flat. He was a troglodyte, skulking through the caves of the abandoned tenements. He watched the pigeons down in the backcourt, creeping through the rubble, pausing with a lifted foot, heads cocked, light sliding like oil down their blue-green necks.

There was a cold spot in Paton's stomach and a warm one. The cold spot was the Quaker. People thought he was the Quaker. The police thought he was the Quaker. There was something irretrievable here. Something that couldn't be dodged, that would have to be faced. He thought about the villa in Peckham, with its wooden gate, its white rose-bushes overflowing the shallow front garden. You couldn't go back and pick up where you'd left off. Not after something like this.

The warm bit was the toolbox of jewels. Paton had gone back to Queen Mary Street the previous night. The flat had been secured; new door, new locks. But the single-end was still doorless, and Paton had wrestled a lidless dustbin up the stairs from the backcourt and stood on its upturned base to reach the hatch to the roofspace. The toolbox had been waiting there faithfully, in the shadow of the chimney, snug and patient and loyal with its scuffed tin sides, its sweat-blackened handle.

He toted it out to Moodiesburn on the bus. He broke into a garden shed and stole a shovel and buried the toolbox in a patch of forest south of Muirhead.

Then he walked back into Glasgow, wondering what to do.

Working it out.

What it all meant.

The Quaker. Was it a coincidence that the Quaker had murdered a woman in the building where you happened to be hiding?

Like fuck it was.

Was Bobby Stokes lying? Did Stokes set you up?

Unlikely.

Who then?

Whoever Stokes is working for. Whoever gave Stokes the keys.

Why aren't you lighting out for the territory, now that the gear is safe?

Why are you walking back to the city?

Why do you fucking think?

On the landing behind him was the door to the gutted flat. He'd slept there for three nights. The dark, bare, hard, cold rooms took him back to borstal, to the months in Polmont with Dazzle.

Polmont wasn't too bad, apart from the faceless crying. You heard it after Lights Out, the wailing boys, abandoned to their grief, abject on their narrow cots, shouting for their mammies. Paton never sank to that. He wasn't hard but he had the respect of the hard men, thanks mainly to his reckless readiness to defy the screws. He would flout orders, backchat, curse them out, spit in their eyes.

He spent a lot of time in the Digger.

The Digger was the punishment cell. Down a narrow staircase, down to the windowless dark and damp. Paton's secret was that the Digger never bothered him. There was a kindness in the dark. The dark could take you in, absorb you, make you part of it. What troubled the other boys – the absence of windows, the velvety black – never worried Paton. Through the black window of the Digger you could escape into a rich black nothingness. You could disappear.

It amused him to see the fear in the eyes of the screws who came thumping down the stairs to let him out. Paton would rise unhurried from the bare pallet, silent and serene, and climb up the stairs ahead of the screw like a child climbing upstairs to bed.

He climbed down the stairs now, his heels echoing in the empty building. He emerged from the back close, blinking, like a lag stepping out to the exercise yard. A clump of nettles, the wicked glint of a broken bottle. He walked a few yards, lit a cigarette.

A rat the size of his hand lay before him on the broken ground. He hadn't seen a rat since he was a boy in Hopehill Road and a ludicrous nostalgia buoyed him up. He had a vision of an older boy stumping towards him across the backcourt, grinning, the point of a tail pinched between finger and thumb, and Paton having to dodge away as the boy swung his burden towards him.

This one lay on its side, legs rigid. Poisoned, clearly. It looked oddly healthy, with tawny fur and a slick, ringed, thickish tail. Its hairless feet looked clean and human.

The flies were already getting busy. Paton hacked a little hollow in the mud with the heel of his shoe, tipped the rat into it with his toe and settled a rust-edged triangle of corrugated iron on top, held in place by a crumbling half-brick.

He would have to face the facts. There was no going back

to a world before his photo on the *Record*'s front page. There was no train that could carry you back to last week, never mind 1959. From here on out Alex Paton was either the Quaker or The Man They Wrongly Thought was the Quaker. If he wanted to be The Man They Wrongly Thought was the Quaker he had to be The Man Who Robbed Glendinnings. There was no other man to be.

32

The thing to do was to call it in. Even now, in this mess of ruined streets, there had to be a phone box. Call it in. Let Cochrane get the heavy mob together. Do the job properly. No heroics.

The thing to do was not to load a torch, a ball-peen hammer, a lock-knife and a truncheon into the pockets of an army surplus field jacket and drive east with the taste of fear in your mouth.

McCormack had taken the call at home, half-past ten, just as *Horizon*'s end-credits were running. The pips of a payphone, then Billy Thomson's nasal whine. Paton was back. He was here in the city. He'd been spotted in Bridgeton, skulking around the closemouth of a condemned tenement block. McCormack took down the address and ten minutes later he was driving down the Gallowgate.

Everything was quiet. The shops were shuttered and dark and the pub lights glowed feebly in the misty air. He turned south on Abercromby Street and on to the London Road. It wasn't raining now but the rain had slicked the streets with an oily sheen.

He was scared. This was a stupid thing to do, but the stupidity sat lightly with McCormack. It was stupid? Fine. It was also something. It was a contribution. You spent so long as an observer, an assessor, fiddling with your wee report. The spare prick, the wallflower. Even when they brought you on board as part of the squad, you couldn't shake that status. Fine. How's this for useless? Brace yourselves: I'm bringing him in. The man you think's the Quaker. The man I'm certain isn't.

It was wearing late when he parked in Baltic Street and started walking west. He dug his inhaler out of his pocket and took a couple of puffs. Ahead of him the tenements stood out blackly on a yellow sky; behind him all was shadowy and blue. Elsewhere in the city the streetlights would be flickering into life but here the only light was from the moon. It lit up the cracked pavements and the white painted slogans on the ground-floor walls.

He was in one of the Development Zones. The official talk – in the brochures and the public information films – was of progress, improvement, amenities, vistas. There were white balsa-wood models in the City Chambers showing how this district would look in five years' time. For now, it was like walking through a newsreel of Dresden.

The tenements on one side of the street had come down and brown humps of rubble ran down the roadway like the spine of some half-submerged Leviathan. On McCormack's right as he walked the windows rose in motley banks, boarded or gaping or smashed in jagged stars. Every few blocks the facade hung off a building and the moonlight splashed on a patch of wall-paper, a doll's-house interior.

Alex Paton was armed. Forensics had identified traces of Hoppe's gun-cleaning solvent on the rag that was left in the Queen Mary Street flat. So what, though? You don't kill polis.

Even the mentals knew that. Where's the percentage in offing a copper?

You don't kill polis, but a terracing chant was running in McCormack's head, to the tune of 'London Bridge Is Falling Down', something you'd hear on *Match of the Day*: 'Harry Roberts is our friend, is our friend, is our friend, Harry Roberts is our friend, he kills coppers.'

Two years back. Down south. Three plainclothes coppers in Shepherd's Bush got suspicious of a van near HMP Wormwood Scrubs. When they went to investigate, Harry Roberts – one of three armed robbers in the van – opened fire. All three coppers died at the scene. One of the killers was a Glasgow man: John Duddy. He fled back to Glasgow after the crime. Cochrane was part of the team that ran him down and brought him in.

You shoot polis if you have to. That was the truth of it. If a ten-stretch is stood there blocking your way with his fat belly in a bluebottle tunic you put a bullet in him. What else can you do?

McCormack gave the pockets of his army surplus jacket a pat, as though checking for his keys. In his khaki jacket and his black beanie hat he felt like a burglar, not a polis. There was nothing to hear but his own two feet. He hadn't thought to change his shoes and his heels clacked and echoed in the empty street. His shoulders prickled under the eyes that might be watching from behind the broken glass. He replayed Billy's phone-call in his head. It couldn't be a set-up. No one could anticipate that a cop would be so stupid. Turning up on his own, gunless in a howling wilderness, to bring in an armed desperado.

Something flickered up ahead, a kind of wrinkle in the darkness and McCormack slowed his pace. He saw long legs, shoulders working in a leather jacket, a smudge of white face.

The man was tall – you could see it as he passed one of the dead lamp-posts. Close to six feet. The thought struck McCormack that this could be the Quaker, sallying forth to repel the invader, and his fingers closed on the butt of the truncheon. As the two men came abreast they nodded hello as if they had been passing on a country lane.

What errand could have brought him out tonight, McCormack wondered; what shortcut led him through these shattered streets?

It was too dark now to read the numbers and McCormack thumbed the torch and the white beam danced up and down the walls. Could you still call this a street, when the houses were no longer houses? It was as if the ashlars and lintels had reverted to blocks of stone. He felt like he was skirting a coast, a black cliff screening an unknown interior.

And now he saw the tall man's errand. Standing on a corner with her foot propped on the wall behind her, a white knee poking into the night. A whole district could die, its pubs and its tobacconists, its wash-houses and bookies could fall silent, but this would go on – would flourish, even, in the darkness of the empty flats. He dropped his eyes as he passed the girl and moved on up the road.

Finally, 356 jumped into the beam and he turned up the path. The closemouth swallowed him. He climbed slowly, walking on the balls of his feet to keep his heels from knocking on the stairs. The torchbeam played on banisters that were more or less intact but he kept to the inside edge. Strips of blacker darkness on the first-floor landing showed where doors had been removed from all three flats.

He was on the second flight of stairs when something brushed against his ankle and he fumbled his step. A cat? he thought. Please: not a rat. But when he shone the beam it was a dark bundle of cloth. The torch picked out a collar, an epaulette

261

and the flash of a button: an old greatcoat. He kicked it to the side and rested a moment, leaning on the wall. He held his breath and strained to listen but he couldn't hear a thing above the thumping in his chest and the pulsing in his temples.

At the left-hand flat on the third floor the torch played not on a gaping hole but on a door. It seemed a homely thing to encounter in this wilderness, with its panels and its cheerful red paint, its brass letter box and china door-knob. It even had a nameplate – KESSON, on a see-through Perspex oblong. But it wasn't Mr or Mrs Kesson who waited beyond the ribbon of black that edged the door and showed where it stood ajar.

Again McCormack's thumb traced the switch on his torch. You'd almost prefer to take your chances with the darkness than march through there in a blaze of light.

On the balance of probabilities . . . The fatuous phrase from his report came back to him. On the balance of probabilities, what? Was Alex Paton crouched in the hallway, pointing his piece at the gap in the door? Had Billy Thomson tipped him off? Was the whole thing a set-up, a fool's errand? He felt the fear well up and he knew he had to act now or not act at all and he kicked the door and ducked back. Nothing. He shifted the torch to his left hand and eased the hammer from his inside pocket with his right. The dimpled grip was tacky in his fist. He clutched the hammer at the base of the shaft, feeling the head's dull weight in the tendons of his forearm. Do it. Do it now. He took a breath and plunged into the darkness, slashing the torch in front of him, hammer held high, whooping like an Apache, making noise enough for half a dozen men.

The flat was empty: the light bounced and zig-zagged off the walls. He leaned against the jawbox in the little kitchenette and caught his breath. Then he walked back through the flat slowly, dividing the floor into segments with the torch beam, taking stock. Newspapers. A sleeping bag and a rumpled blanket. A rucksack wedged in the corner. Paton had been here all right.

Back at the Marine he parked behind the cell block and lunged up the stairs to the Murder Room.

Cochrane and Goldie and Ferguson were standing round a table. Other detectives were sitting on their desks or lolling on their chairs. It was near midnight, during the two hours when the late shift and the night shift overlapped and the room got crowded. Everyone turned as McCormack burst in.

He stood in his army surplus jacket, catching his breath.

'Man on a mission there, Detective.' Cochrane was smirking. 'Where's the fire?'

There were tins of beer on one of the desks, glasses, a bottle of Red Label with the cap off.

'I know where he is.' McCormack jerked his thumb at the doorway. 'Where he's been, anyway. I've got the address. I went there but he'd gone.'

'Is that right?'

'Aye. Look, maybe forensics can get something. We need to get the tech boys on to this.'

One or two of them smiled and looked at the floor. Cochrane crossed to the open door, closed it gently. He turned round with a smile that McCormack couldn't read.

'That's good work, Detective. Thing is: we know where he is, too.' He jabbed his index finger at the floor. 'He's down there.'

For a second, McCormack thought he was saying that Paton was dead and had gone to hell. Then he realized: he was down the corridor. He was down in the cells.

McCormack tugged his beanie off and dropped it on a desk. There was a scrape as he dragged a chair out and settled slowly into it.

'Paton's in the cells?'

Goldie spoke. 'Turned himself in an hour ago. Just walked through the door and announced his name.'

Someone pressed a can of Export into McCormack's hand. He tugged on the ring-pull and took a slug. 'Has he confessed?'

'Aye, to the Glendinnings job. Not to anything else. Not yet.'

'Cheer up, fella.' Goldie's gums were bared in a fierce grin. He held his own beer can loosely between finger and thumb and swung it towards McCormack. 'It's finished, Dunc. We got him.'

McCormack reached up and bumped his can against Goldie's. He tipped his head back and drank.

III
THE SEA IS ALL ABOUT US

'Man is not truly one, but truly two.'

R. L. Stevenson,
The Strange Case of Dr Jekyll and Mr Hyde

33

Even now, with the suspect under lock and key, people feared the Quaker. As if bricks and mortar couldn't hold him. As if he might pour himself through the locks of Barlinnie and wreak his will on the stricken city. When they brought the boy Gilmour in from Castlemilk, the boy who'd seen Paton in the backcourt at Queen Mary Street, the kid could hardly stand for fear. His leg kept trembling as he waited in the corridor.

Cochrane gave him a pep talk outside the identification room. The boy kept his eyes on the floor. A WPC had been detailed to escort him and he kept very close to her side.

'The man's in there, son. He's one of the men in that room. Go on and pick him out for us like a good lad.'

'Will he come and get me?' The boy stood looking at the floor, gripping the policewoman's hand.

'We've caught him, son!' Cochrane was almost shouting but he modified his tone, squatted down to meet the boy at eye level. 'We've already caught him, Andrew. He's going straight back to his cell after we do this. He's not getting out.'

When he walked along the line of suspects, the boy flicked his glance at the faces, scared of what would happen if he caught the Quaker's eye. He stopped in front of Paton, eyes on the ground. He still held the policewoman's hand. He raised his free hand and pointed.

'You're sure?'

The boy nodded.

'Good lad.' The policewoman took the boy out. Paton was shaking his head. The other four men rolled their shoulders and craned their necks, filed out to collect their fee.

So Paton was safely banged up in Barlinnie. But he wouldn't confess, not to being the Quaker. The only way he could clear himself of being the Quaker was to implicate himself in the robbery. So he did it. He copped to the heist at the auctioneer's, but denied all knowledge of the Quaker and his works.

After three days Cochrane called a council of war with Goldie and McCormack. In Cochrane's office they set out what they had on Alex Paton. They had his fingerprints at the scene, but not in the room where the body was found. They had a bloody bootprint in the room to match the size of Paton's feet (nine and a half), but not the boots that Paton might have been wearing. And they had no convincing answers to a number of obvious questions. Why did Paton kill a woman in the very building where he was hiding? Why did he stick around till the following morning? The defence would waste no time in putting these questions. There was another troublesome fact: they couldn't place Paton in Glasgow on the dates of the earlier killings.

The papers never doubted that the Quaker had been caught – profiles of Paton, interviews with his neighbours, primary school teachers and childhood friends were running every day in the *Tribune* and *Record* – but a jury might be harder to convince.

They all took turns at talking to Paton in the interview room at Barlinnie. McCormack was among the last to try.

His heels rang out as he walked the stone corridor to the interview room. His mind was a blank. This was the time to be marshalling your facts, rehearsing your questions, working out how to catch him off-guard, trip him up, bluff a confession out of the man. Today he had nothing.

How did you interview a man you didn't catch? A man who just walked in off the street to save you the bother?

The screw outside the interview room stood up from his wooden chair and unlocked the door.

Maybe it came to you in the moment. Maybe it was like preaching, you mounted the pulpit and opened your mouth and the right words started to flow. The door swung open. The good old smell, cabbage-piss-carbolic.

First things first.

'Mr Paton, I'm Detective Inspector Duncan McCormack.'

'I know fine who you are.'

McCormack settled at the desk. He rested his hands on the scarred, varnished surface. Again he fought the urge to slide his hands forward and lay his head down on his arm. He had spent aeons, it seemed, whole eras of his life sitting across from men like Paton, trying to build a story out of shrugs and grunts. And this time was worse. This time he had to pretend he thought Paton was the Quaker.

Paton looked surprisingly stylish in his regulation striped shirt and corduroy jacket, as if he'd chosen these items himself. McCormack tugged his notebook from his pocket and slapped it on the desk, chucked his pen down after it.

'Mr Paton. A man fitting your description was seen running from the tenement block at forty-eight Queen Mary Street in Bridgeton on the morning of 10 August, the block in which Helen Thaney was found murdered. Were you that man?'

'You know I was.'

'You were? Good. Your fingerprints were found in the

269

top-floor flat of that building. You had been living in those premises?'

'I've already said that.'

'How long?'

'Four days. Five. Something like that.'

McCormack flicked through the pages of his notebook. 'Mr Paton, why did you kill Helen Thaney?'

'Next question.'

'Jacquilyn Keevins. Ann Ogilvie. Marion Mercer. Why did you kill those women?'

'It's not me. I'm not the Quaker.'

'Right. Can you explain then why you were living at that address and why you were seen running from the locus when Helen Thaney's body was found?'

Paton leaned forward. 'You know what I do, polis?'

'You're a peterman. You blow safes. You were here to do the Glendinnings job.'

'I'm giving you that. Are you with me? I'm confessing. And you're trying to put a murder on me?'

'Four murders.'

Paton laughed. McCormack fought the urge to join in.

'Four murders? You know where I live, right?'

McCormack nodded.

'OK. You're gonnae frame me for three murders when I wasnae in the city? In the same fucking country? When I live in London. This is gonnae be good. Let's hear it.'

'You can prove you weren't in Glasgow on those other dates?'

'The fuck do I know? I don't know the fucking dates.'

'That's a good start.'

'Can you prove I *was*? Can you prove I *was* here on those dates?'

'Ah, the burden of proof. Technically, yes, it rests with the prosecution. But in this case? With all the publicity?'

McCormack had a *Record* in his jacket pocket. He took it out now, unfolded it, placed it on the desk. Paton's photo and the artist's impression side by side on the front page.

'If it wasn't you, Alex, then what were you doing in Mackeith Street? Why didn't you go home to London? Why hang around Bridgeton for four or five days? It's not exactly the Riviera.'

Paton was twisting one of the buttons on his corduroy jerkin. 'It's all in the fucking notes, polis. I've been through all this.' Somebody passed in the corridor, whistling badly. Paton pushed up the sleeves of his jacket. 'Look. OK. In my line of work, there's a routine you follow. Right? You do a job, you need to get off the streets. That's the priority. You don't get out of the city, not right away, cause maybe they've got roadblocks on the motorway slip-roads. Maybe they're watching the train stations. You need a place you can get to quickly, but far enough away from the target. Hole up for a few days, let it all blow over.'

'That's very interesting, Alex.'

'So that's where I was. Holing up. Waiting it out till it was safe to move. Then, the day I'm planning to leave, I wake up with someone shouting blue murder. There's a woman lying dead in the ground-floor flat. What would you do?'

'I'd like to think I'd be home in bed, Alex, to be honest. Tell me whose flat it was.'

'It was no one's flat. It was empty – what do you call it, condemned.'

'How did you get the key to the flat?'

'Guy set me up with it.'

'Set you up's right. This guy got a name?'

'Can't remember.'

'Cos that's working out really well for you, Alex, isn't it? That code of honour bullshit.'

271

Paton shook his head. He folded his arms, recrossed his feet under the desk.

'You see my problem, Alex? Your alibi is that you were hiding in the building where the murder took place. It's not what you'd call cast-iron, is it?'

Paton shrugged. He was tracing patterns on the desk with his thumbnail. He didn't look up.

'You say you did the Glendinnings job.'

Paton nodded.

'Can you prove it? Can you prove you did the Glendinnings job?'

Paton looked at him for a long time. Finally he said, 'Aye, because there's a really long line of people who could do that. People who could blow that safe.'

'I've got a sceptical frame of mind,' McCormack said. 'Comes with the job. Humour me.'

'You mean describe the place? I can tell you what was taken, details of the pieces.'

'Yeah, I can read the papers too, Alex. You'll need to do better than that.'

Paton sat up and jerked his chin at McCormack. McCormack dug his smokes out of his jacket pocket and passed one to Paton and sparked his lighter. Paton took a couple of drags and started to talk. He described the décor of the building down to the colour of the curtains, the pistol-whipping of the watchman, the watchman pissing his pants, the spilled cup of coffee, the make of the safe, the contents of the safe.

'Where's the jewels, Alex? Where's the money?'

'Fuck you, copper.' He nicked the cigarette between his finger and thumb, stuck the dowt in the pocket of his shirt. 'You're getting greedy now. You've got me. That's enough.'

McCormack consulted his notes. 'You got away with jewels

and cash in the region of a hundred and twenty grand, Alex, but I'm the greedy one. OK. Did you know Helen Thaney?'

'Never seen her in my life. Not till that morning.'

McCormack loosened his tie, rolling his shoulders and working his neck. 'You walk under ladders, Alex? Go round smashing mirrors?'

Paton looked around the room, looked through McCormack, shaking his head.

'You must have a low opinion of the polis, Alex. Or maybe just of me. Maybe I'm a big stupid teuchter so you'll need to bear with me here, explain it to me again. It's a coincidence? That's your explanation? Out of all the vacant tenements in Glasgow, he picks your one. Kills a woman and leaves you to carry the can.'

Paton said nothing.

'We can place you at the scene, Alex. Known criminal. Someone who knows the city well but doesn't live here, which would explain why you were never interviewed until now. You fit the age range. Physical description. You want to keep up the Silent Sammy routine, be my guest. We'll see you down the Saltmarket at the next circuit.'

Paton was picking lint from the sleeve of his corduroy jacket. 'This is where I break down, is it? Spill my guts? Beg for mercy.'

'You do what you fucking want, Alex. I don't give a fuck. I'm driving home in five minutes. You're never going home again, probably.'

'But why would I do it, though?' There were white flecks of spittle on Paton's clenched teeth. 'Jesus Christ. You've said it yourself, there's hundreds of empty tenements in the city. I kill a woman in the one I'm fucking living in? My prints are all over the flat! Why would I hang around? I'm still there at ten in the morning when I've left a fucking body there for everyone to see?'

McCormack was nodding. 'Thing is, it's not me you need to convince. It's my boss. It's the jury. It's the public, the *Record*, the *Daily Express*.'

'It's you that needs to prove it.'

'We don't need to prove anything, Alex. The papers have done it for us. You could walk out of here right now, take a bus to Sauchiehall Street, and not find a single soul who doesn't think that you're the Quaker.'

'Is that right? I think I'm looking at one right now.'

McCormack laughed. 'Fairs dos, Alex. Hands up. You're right. You're spot on. I do believe you. But like I say, mine's a minority view. But let me ask you this: why did you hand yourself in?'

'Clear my name.' Paton shrugged. 'I'm a peterman. Not a beast. Not a fucking nonce.' He sat up in his seat, unfolded his arms. 'You can place me in the building. Fine. Can you place me in the room? Got my dabs in the room? I can see by your face that you havenae. But you don't need to tell me that? Know how? Cos I was never in the fucking room. You've got no prints. You've got no semen stains. You've got no blood or fibres on my clothes unless you planked them. You've got fuck all.'

McCormack stowed his notebook in his pocket, rubbed his palm along the bristles on his jaw.

'What size of shoe do you take, Alex?'

'Come again?'

'Shoe size, Alex. What size are your feet?'

'Nine and a half.'

'There was a footprint in the room. In the victim's blood. Workboot, an Irish Setter they reckon. Guess what size?'

Paton was nodding slowly. 'Right. Good. I left a footprint at the scene. Was that after I carved my initials on the lassie's stomach and dropped a monogrammed hanky?'

'Aye, jokes are good, Alex. Keep them coming. I'm sure the judge'll appreciate them. Gallows-humour. Laughing all the way to the rope.'

'They've suspended it, polis – did you no hear? Capital punishment's been suspended.'

'Till thirty-first December. You better hope your trial goes lickety fucking split, mate. Tick-tock, Alex. Tick-tock.'

Back at the Marine, McCormack packed up his stuff. There wasn't much to pack – a few papers and folders, they fitted into his briefcase with room to spare. Around the Murder Room clerical staff were toting cardboard boxes along the corridor. Box files were going into crates for storage. The pictures and maps had come down from the walls, leaving snowy white oblongs. In the car park McCormack was closing his boot when he saw Farren pulling away in his Rover 2000. The car stopped beside him, Farren rolling the window down.

'You're off, then, Duncan. Back to St Andrew's Street?'

'Looks like it. You?'

'Fucking C Div, again. Bandit country. Still, we got him, eh?'

McCormack shrugged.

'Listen.' Farren's hand was reaching out the window. 'We got off on the wrong foot back there. This whole thing. No hard feelings.'

McCormack grasped the hand. 'Break a leg,' he said. 'Just not your own.'

34

'I won't tell if you won't.'

DCI Flett had produced a bottle of Red Label from the brushed-steel cupboard beside the window. He set out two shot glasses and tipped the whisky, splashing it over the sides. Clutching his own glass he leaned across the desk, wheezing with the effort. McCormack lifted the other glass and clinked it against Flett's and set it back down on the desk. Flett drank.

'To a job well done. It's good to have you back, Dunc. And listen, I know why you're here. I know what you're going to say. And you're right. I gave you my word and I'll keep it. I just need time to set things up.'

It had been odd to come back. A hero's welcome, of sorts, as if he'd returned from a voyage. The backslaps and hand-shakes, the pints in the till at the Grapes. It was easier just to nod and grin than explain it anew to every person in the building. But Flett: you had to explain it to Flett.

'I'm not sure you do know, sir.' McCormack ran a hand down his tie. 'I don't think you do know what I'm going to say.'

'You want to go after McGlashan. I promised you a crack

at him and you'll get it. You pick the team, you play it how you want. But I'm short-handed, son, just this minute. I'll need a bit of time.'

McCormack stared at the bottle before him. The slanting label and the raised gold lettering, the jaunty striding figure with the monocle and cane. *Keep Walking*.

'I want to go after the Quaker. Sir.'

The words drained something from the room. Flett's whole face sagged and he grimaced at the desk as if his whisky had turned sour. There was no surprise in his eyes, which meant that he'd already spoken to Cochrane. McCormack watched as Flett poured himself another dram, slower now, setting down the bottle with exaggerated care.

'Can you help me out here, McCormack? Can you explain to me what the problem is? Because I can't see it. You fucking aced it. We sent you over there to shut the thing down and what do you do? You nail the fucking Quaker. No one gave you a prayer – me included – but you did it. They don't come often, son, moments like this. You savour it. Don't question it.'

'I didn't nail the Quaker.'

'Now come on.' Flett held up a hand. 'I've spoken to Cochrane. The breakthrough was the hideout. That was you. Everything followed from that. You did it. It's out of your hands now, it goes to trial. Let it lie.'

'What I mean, sir; Alex Paton's not the Quaker.'

'Well, let's see what the jury says about that, will we?'

'We know what the jury'll say. The jury'll find him guilty. Like the papers have. Like you have. But he's not the Quaker.'

'Sweet Jesus.' Flett squeezed his eyes shut and let out a pained exhalation. He might have been asleep. He opened his eyes. 'But you know better. Duncan McCormack knows better.'

'I know he's not the Quaker, sir. I know that much. I know it's not him.'

The grinding gears of a bus rose from the street to the open windows. McCormack shifted in his seat and started to make his case. He could sense Flett withdrawing as he spoke. The more he talked, the more Flett withdrew behind his flat grey eyes, pursing his lips and breathing through his nose. But McCormack couldn't stop.

'And then,' he was saying, 'why does he kill her in the same building where he's squatting? Why's he hanging around in broad daylight the following day? Why leave your prints all over the hideout? He gives us *nothing* for the first three murders and it's Christmas on the fourth? It makes no kind of sense.'

'It's sex murders, McCormack. It's not supposed to make sense. The man's deranged. You want consistency? He's a maniac. The normal rules don't apply.'

A dark flush had risen up Flett's neck, and his fists were fat round paperweights on the desktop. He seemed to notice them then, and unclenched them slowly, pressing his palms down flat like sheets of paper.

'You want a maniac?' McCormack spread his hands as if checking to make sure; he was a salesman now, he could provide a maniac – an assortment of maniacs – at the drop of a hat. 'Nancy Scullion,' he said. 'The sister? The man she sat with at the Barrowland, the man who shared her taxi: *he's* a maniac. *He's* a zealot. "Adultery, sinful women, dens of iniquity." Alex Paton's never been to church. Put a gun to his head and ask him to quote the Bible, you've got brains all over the floor.'

Flett scoffed. 'Come on, Duncan. You said it yourself in your report. They set too much store by the testimony of the sister. That was a blind alley.'

'I said they gave it too much emphasis! I never said she made it all up! How did you see the report?'

278

Flett shook his head. He was fiddling with his shot glass, rolling it round on the rim of its base. 'You know Levein's retiring?' he said. 'End of the year.'

'I don't want it.' The words came out crisply, too loudly. 'I don't want your fucking job. That's the last thing I want.'

'Is that right? You're sure about that? I move upstairs, you write your own ticket, son, the man who caught the Quaker. I've already spoken to Cochrane and Levein. It's your name on the door, Dunc, if you want it. Head of the Flying Squad. Want to piss that away?'

'I want to do my job, sir. I want to catch the Quaker.'

'Aye? I thought you wanted McGlashan. You'd a hard-on for Glash, all these years. That not right? You're head of the Flying Squad, Duncan, you can steam right ahead. Throw everything you want at the prick. You can take McGlashan. Leave this Quaker shite be, move on to the stuff that matters. Do the real job. Remember?'

McCormack sipped his whisky, felt the lovely burn on his tongue. This was what you wanted. This was the prize for nailing the Quaker. Get a crack at McGlashan. He realized now that he could no longer picture McGlashan's face. A mugshot of McGlashan had been tacked up on the wall beside his Flying Squad desk for close on two years but now he couldn't summon the features. As though McGlashan was a former lover whose eyes you no longer recalled the colour of. His face had been displaced by the poster of the Quaker, the artist's impression, the man who was still out there in the disintegrating city, the man who wasn't Alex Paton.

'What if he does it again, sir?' McCormack drained his glass and set it down. 'You thought of that? We've got Paton inside and the Quaker does another. What happens then? You're playing golf in Maidens. We're still here.'

Flett stood abruptly and lifted the bottle, turned and stowed it in the cupboard, clanging the steel doors. He stacked one glass on top of the other and set them on the mantelpiece. He stayed standing.

'Are we finished here, Detective? Cos I'm done trying to talk you off the ledge. You want to undo all the good that you've done, far be it from me. But you're on your own. You get no help. You do it in your own time. Now. Can you fuck off out my road?'

In the flat that evening, McCormack looked across the city at the cranes' long necks dissolving in the bluing light. The living-room window threw back his ghost, the image of a man who might have been somebody else. DI Duncan McCormack, Head of the Flying Squad. He saw it all now. The corner office, his name in gold leaf on the ribbed glass, the view across to St Andrew's in the Square and the trees of Glasgow Green. And McGlashan running scared. The combined might of the CID and Flying Squad crashing down on John McGlashan, punching through his empire like a wrecking ball. He had a vision of the gangster, hands cuffed in front of him, being taken down from the High Court dock to start his sentence, the dark suit and the thick black hair disappearing down the trapdoor stairs like Faustus trudging down to hell. But there was another trial to take place sooner, the trial of a man who might be hanged on the gallows of Barlinnie Prison if McCormack couldn't catch the Quaker.

35

McCormack was in a tearoom on Sauchiehall Street, waiting for Nancy Scullion. It felt like an illicit thing, a secret assignation. He almost felt normal. An everyday adulterer. Somebody's fancy man. Except Nancy Scullion was already divorced. He stirred his tea and watched his ghost in the window bring the cup to its lips.

After his argument with Flett, McCormack had lain awake. Now he had Flett's reluctant blessing. But where did he go with that? Back to the start, obviously. First principles. Do the basics. What were the basics again?

What should he do? You couldn't go back through the witness statements, even if you had time, and that was the wrong tack anyway. It wasn't about working back through the case, looking for the uncrossed Ts. They had ransacked the city like a tenement flat. They had torn it to pieces, searched it inch by inch, sounded the drawers for false bottoms, run knitting needles down the bedposts and table-legs, shaken out every book, taken up the floorboards, slashed all the cushions, the linings of chairs.

None of it worked. None of it yielded a plausible lead. A fresh start was needed.

And when he thought about fresh starts his mind kept going back to Nancy Scullion. For fuck sake, why? Nancy Scullion was the whole problem. It was setting so much store by Scullion that kept the squad bogged down in pointless details. The whole inquiry had been like putting together an identikit. Let's get the individual details right and see if we can conjure up a face. Life didn't work like that. They'd been through all the details, everything Nancy Scullion could recall about the Quaker. The hair, the overlapping teeth, the brand of cigarettes, the hole in one, the regimental tie, the biblical quotations, the slim build, the cut of his suit, the desert boots, the 'good' Glasgow accent, the broad striped watch-strap. Every element of the description had been probed, poked, tested, scoured, stamped on, pulled apart. They had chased each of these details across the city, come up with nothing.

So the description was wrong? No, but the description was worked out, dead, a waste of further time and effort. So what else could Nancy Scullion tell him? What fresh angle could she bring? Not what the Quaker looked like, maybe, but what he did, how he acted. How the Quaker carried himself.

Carried himself. McCormack snorted into his tea. He was Mertens the paragnost now. What mystical bullshit was this?

So now he waited in a tearoom on Sauchiehall Street for the woman who'd stymied the whole investigation. At first she'd been reluctant. When he phoned her at home she spoke very carefully and slowly, like someone reading from a script.

'But you've got him, haven't you? He's in Barlinnie. He's waiting trial.'

'It's not him.'

'The papers said it's him. They said the police are— Well, they're not looking for anyone else. In connection with the killings.'

'You know it's not him, Nancy, don't you? You've always known. It's why you couldn't pick him out in the parade.'

'It was a long time ago. I've seen a lot of faces. You've got to be sure.'

'Nancy.'

The bell clanged on the tearoom door and here came Nancy, peering round with a tragic, anxious manner till she spotted McCormack's half-raised hand. She half-smiled and put her head down and made her way towards his corner table. She ordered coffee when the waitress arrived and listened while McCormack tried to explain what he wanted. Not more details. Or at least, not the same details. More a sense of the Quaker as a man. In general. The *sense* of him. You might call it the overall impression. He could hear the conviction draining from his voice. He was floundering. He should stop talking. When he looked up Nancy Scullion was frowning. She wasn't trying to be difficult, she said, but she couldn't see what else she could tell him. She'd described the Quaker a hundred times, they had forced her to go back over every tiny detail. She was sick of telling it. Sick of her own voice. But his *manner*, McCormack insisted. Not what he looked like; what he was *like*.

'That too. I've been over all that. He stood up when you came back to the table. Pulled your chair out for you. He was polite. But cold, too. And smug, watching you from behind his eyes. He knew things that you didn't know. That's what his eyes said. Well, they were right, weren't they?'

In the end there was one thing, only one, that was new to McCormack, that he didn't recall from the witness statement.

The man had left them for a spell, Nancy told him. Maybe ten minutes, maybe more. Longer than it took to use the toilet. The women joshed him when he returned – *Was there a queue at the gents? Now you know how we feel* – but he smiled his tight smile and said nothing.

'He'd been at the bar, maybe?'

'Nope, I don't think so. He came back empty-handed.'

Something stirred in the swaying weeds of McCormack's mind, some dark shard floating upwards but he lost it and it sank away.

'It's as if she's been murdered twice,' Nancy was saying. She was toying with her empty cup and speaking down towards the tabletop.

'What was that?'

'I'm saying it's as if it happened twice.' Nancy looked up at him, a bright sad smile. 'He killed her, the Quaker did. But then the papers, it was like the papers brought her back to life, her face was always there in the *Record*, smiling out at you. And all the facts and stories, the wee details of her life. But then it petered out. Youse didn't catch him and the papers stopped bothering. The stories stopped. And now it feels like she's gone again.'

McCormack nodded. The big dark grandfather clock filled the silence, a homely sound, a deep warm ticking, like the slap of two fingers on double-bass strings.

'But *he* isn't gone.' She held the sad smile. 'He's coming back, isn't he? He's coming for me.'

'Nancy, come on. What do you—'

She grabbed his wrist. ''Cause I'm the one who can get him. It's me that can identify him. He needs me gone.'

'Nancy, if he wanted you dead, you'd be dead already.'

He glanced quickly down at her hand on his wrist and she followed his gaze, grinning weakly as she released her grip and looked at her hand like it belonged to someone else.

He paid for their drinks and thanked Nancy Scullion for her time.

36

McCormack went down to the newsagent's on Dumbarton Road and bought some marker pens and a box of coloured drawing-pins. Back at the flat he rooted around in the hall cupboard and found an old roll of wallpaper. He laid the roll on the living-room table and took the scissors and cut a section maybe five feet long. He took three pictures down from the back wall of the living room and took the picture-hooks out with the end of a clawhammer. Then he found the bag of wallpaper paste and the old splayed paste brush in the hall cupboard. He mixed a little of the paste in a bucket in the sink and pasted the strip of wallpaper on to the living-room wall, longways and with the patterned side inmost. Then he cleared up and washed his hands and stood with his hands on his hips in front of the blank white strip.

He took one of the marker pens and wrote SAFE HOUSE at the left-hand side of the strip. He underlined the words. Then he wrote and underlined HELEN THANEY in the middle of the strip and MQS at the right-hand side. Under SAFE HOUSE he pinned up a cutting from the *Record*'s report ('Lair of the Quaker') showing the interior of the flat where Paton had holed up. He also wrote the names that Billy Thomson had finally come through with, the supposed names of the Glendinnings string: Stephen Dalziel, Robert Stokes, Brian Cursiter. By rights he should have fed these names to Adam Halliday, who was heading up the Glendinnings investigation, but he was holding off for the time being, waiting to use them on Paton. Beneath HELEN THANEY he pinned a newspaper head-shot of a laughing Helen Thaney and an illicitly photocopied image of Helen Thaney on the floor of the ground-floor flat at Queen Mary Street. The ink in this image had been blurred and smudged by the copier and Helen Thaney's face was mostly black. Under MQS he pinned up the purple dust jacket of Antonia Fraser's *Mary Queen of Scots*.

There was a street map of the city in the bureau beside the window and McCormack took this and pinned it up next to the strip of wallpaper. He placed four drawing-pins on the map at Carmichael Lane, Mackeith Street, Earl Street and Queen Mary Street. He placed a different coloured drawing-pin at Bath Street to mark the site of Glendinnings Auction House.

He was still contemplating his handiwork when the telephone rang.

'Detective Inspector. Is this a good time?'

The voice was sly, hearty, full of bogus mateyness. McCormack glanced at the clock on the mantelpiece, as if the question had been literal.

'Who is this?' he said.

'I wanted to congratulate you, Duncan. Personally. You've done a great thing, Detective.'

There was something in the laughing timbre of the voice that McCormack recognized, and as he dropped into the wooden-backed chair and reached his cigarettes from the table it came to him: Levein. But why was the chief calling him at home? They worked in the same building. If he'd wanted to see him, why not walk down the stairs, or else summon McCormack to his office?

'Thank you, sir,' he managed, warily. 'I appreciate it.'

'Thank *you*, Detective. We appreciate *you*. I've spoken to DCI Flett. The Police Board too. Flett's moving upstairs when I leave. There'll be a new name on his door. Yours.'

McCormack looked out of the window. The black clouds above the river had finally burst and big cheerful raindrops were landing on the pane. He watched one dribble down the window – now slow, now fast – before spreading into nothing on the sill.

'That's if you want it,' Levein was saying.

Did he want it? Did he want to pretend that Alex Paton was the Quaker and that everything had turned out fine? Part of him did. Part of him did want that. But not the cop part.

'I've got some things to take care of, sir,' he said. 'Maybe it's not my time.'

The silence from Levein stretched out until it filled the room, the flat, the whole city. He could feel Levein's hostility seeping down the phone line and trickling into his ear.

'Well, I can't say he didn't warn me,' Levein said finally. 'Flett warned me about this. Pig-headed, was his phrase. Doesn't take hints. Needs things spelled out for him. Words of one syllable. You listening then, Detective Inspector? This thing is done. Finished. We caught him. He'll be tried, he'll go to jail. You're worried about *tim*ing?' Levein's voice rose tautly on the word. 'What *would* be bad timing, son, is queering this Quaker result in time for my retirement. That *would* be bad timing. You've given me the gold watch. Don't fucking try and take it back.'

37

They were playing a game called 'Unless'. McCormack was playing the game. Goldie didn't know he was playing. Goldie didn't know the game existed.

'But are they framing Paton?' Goldie said. 'Or is Paton just the guy in the frame?'

It was too late in the day for riddles. McCormack drummed his feet on the wooden boards, clapped his arms around his torso to keep warm.

'You want to translate that?'

'I mean is it personal to Paton? Is it specific to him or is Paton the convenient – what would you call it? Fall guy. Patsy.'

They thought about this. Music was playing tinnily through a loudspeaker system, Desmond Dekker and the Aces. It seemed too sunny and upbeat amid all this ice.

'How long's he been gone?' Goldie asked.

'You're right. It's ten years.'

'That's a long time to bear a grudge.'

'It's too long. You're right. It can't be personal. Paton's just in the wrong place. Is that your daughter?'

Goldie frowned. 'The blonde one? No. She's over there.' His

finger tracked a girl in a red coat, cinched at the waist, and a white woollen hat with hanging pom-poms. She saw Goldie pointing and raised a mittened hand as she glided past. They both waved back.

'But why now?' McCormack dragged on his Regal. You couldn't tell what was smoke and what was your own breath. 'He's happy to take the credit for the first three. Wants to frame someone for the fourth. Makes no sense.'

'Unless. . .' *and Goldie opens the scoring*, thought McCormack; 'unless he's finished. He's drawing a line. Plus, if it's finished, then it's not random. It's a series. A sequence.'

'The Four Maries,' McCormack said. 'But if it's a sequence, if it means something, he's going to want to claim the credit, isn't he? That's the whole point. Defeats the whole purpose if someone else gets the glory. What is she, fourteen?'

'Twelve. Unless . . .' *two-nil to the big man*; 'maybe it's not a multiple at all. I mean, this last one. Helen Thaney.'

'You think it's a copycat?'

'Well, it wouldn't be hard, would it?' Goldie's breath came out in billowing clouds. 'Cochrane was always too tight with those *Tribune* pricks. All the details were in the papers.'

'Were they, though? What would you have known from the papers?'

'You'd know the whole m.o., wouldn't you? He picks them up at the Barrowland, kills them within a hundred yards of their homes. Fucks them, chokes them with their tights, doesn't try to conceal the bodies.'

Goldie was still watching his daughter but his expression changed as he spoke. McCormack felt the old despair seeping in. Goldie was enjoying some time with his daughter and here you came to trample over it, polluting the ice-rink with the smell of death.

'So what wouldn't you know? What did we keep back? The

sanitary towels on the bodies, all the victims are menstruating? That was never in the papers, was it?'

'And the escalating violence,' said Goldie. 'The beatings getting worse with each one. But fuck – the Marine leaks like a bastard, always has. How many cops worked the inquiry?'

'I know. How many wives and girlfriends did they blab to?'

McCormack thought about the secret details spreading by word of mouth, the crowds of people who might know. The whirling skaters seemed like a visual illustration of his thought.

'Still, though. If the killer for number four is different, it could be someone who knows a cop.'

'Could be a cop.'

They thought about this.

'Except it's not number four, is it? It's number one. It's just been made to look like number four.'

'So what was the big breakthrough with the Mary Queen of Scots stuff?'

'I think it was rubbish, Derek. Wishful thinking. Whoever did number four had spotted a link: Battlefield; Bridgeton; Earl Street. But it wasn't a link at all. It was just coincidence. It was only number four – Queen Mary Street, the blindfold, the planted locket – that made it hang together.'

They sat in silence, watching the skaters. McCormack followed the red coat of Goldie's daughter for a while and then lost it among the crowd and just watched the moving bodies. It was hard to equate Goldie the CID detective with the anorak-clad dad who sat in the spectators' gallery waiting for his daughter. McCormack hadn't known much – or anything really – about Goldie's family. Had he known that Goldie had a daughter? Had he even bothered to ask?

Speed skaters were cutting through the crowd, teenage boys

jack-knifing forward with their hands behind their backs, their long legs slashing out to the sides. McCormack had visions of people slipping, bumping down on their backsides and putting a hand out instinctively to steady themselves as a speed skater sliced past. He saw the fingers rolling like sausages and the blood staining the ice, percolating down through the crystals.

Goldie's daughter skated over just then, shushing to a halt with a neat little twist of her hips. The ice from her blades spattered the barrier. She stepped through a gap between the boards and stilted across in her skates, the blades knocking hollow on the planks. Goldie introduced her as Debbie and told her McCormack was a colleague from work and she plucked off her right mitten and shook McCormack's hand. Her hand was warmer than he'd expected.

She started tugging at her laces. 'I'm going up to the café, Dad. Claire and Julie are there. Can you watch my skates?'

She took a pair of black pumps from the pockets of her coat, stepped into them and hooked them on with a curled forefinger.

'I'll be up in ten minutes, love. You need any money?'

'I'm fine, Dad. See you, Mr McCormack. Nice meeting you.'

They watched her go. How much did you miss? How much of your own life passed by as you worked for the dead, performing these pointless fairytale labours, spinning a roomful of straw into gold or shifting by teaspoon a mountain of sand? McCormack looked at the skates where Debbie had left them, canted on their sides on the black plastic mat. At least he had no kids to neglect, no one to fail on that front.

'What you working anyway? Anything good?'

'Me? Nah, nothing.' Goldie shook his head. 'Stabbing in Partick. Break-ins up in Hyndland. Rubbish. I'll tell you another thing, though.' He was fitting the black plastic blade-covers on to his daughter's skates. 'If Paton's been framed then one of the string's involved, the Glendinnings crew. Has to be.'

'I know that.'

'Aye, but does *he*?'

McCormack shrugged. 'Paton's thrawn. He won't give them up, Derek. That's his bottom line. It's this code of silence shite.'

'Then it's a short walk to the long drop, isn't it? You need to make him see that, Duncan. He doesn't give them up, you cannae save him. Nobody can.'

The skaters carried on in their ragged ring, round the icy oval. The rink was marked for curling, four red-and-blue targets at either end like the RAF roundels the Mods stitched on the backs of their parkas.

'Unless he knows something we don't,' McCormack said. 'Unless he's got friends higher up.'

Driving home across the city, McCormack put himself in the shoes of Helen Thaney's killer. If you make this killing look like the Quaker, and you frame Paton for it, then everything's finished. Tied up with a bow. Paton's the Quaker, all the murders are solved, and no one looks too closely at number four. No one sees that number four's different. No one pays any attention to Helen Thaney. She's another random victim, a woman who chose the wrong night to go dancing. You're home and dry. But if number four was different, then Helen Thaney's the key. Helen Thaney was murdered because she was Helen Thaney. Number four was personal.

So what now? Dropping down the gears to tackle the slope of Gardner Street, McCormack set out his immediate tasks. He needed to prove that number four was a standalone, that it wasn't the work of the Quaker. He needed to find out more about Helen Thaney. And he needed the name of whoever arranged Paton's safe house. This was progress, McCormack reflected, as the Velox laboured up the hill. Then it struck him. Now it wasn't one killer he was looking for but two: the Quaker and whoever murdered Helen Thaney. One step forward, two steps back.

38

'They got them, by the way. For the auctioneer's thing.'

Flett bumped his tray down on the table beside McCormack. He made a point of eating with his men, sharing the perils of the canteen food.

'Who got them?' McCormack was still addressing himself to a banknote-thin fillet of breaded fish, it took him a moment. 'Glendinnings? You mean Central got them?'

'Bertie King's boys,' Flett said. 'The potting shed plods. Wonders never cease.'

McCormack pictured the wooden police hut in Hutchesonstown. Single step up to the bare wooden door. The windowless gables, smell of creosote. It looked like someone had hung a POLICE sign on their garden shed. It was a joke posting, the place you did penance when you'd fucked something up.

'Halliday still heading it up, sir?'

'Adam Halliday? I would think so. Bertie King's golden boy. Bronze.'

McCormack phoned him that afternoon.

'Adam? It's Duncan McCormack.'

'The Tartan Pimpernel. I wondered when we'd be hearing from you.'

'You've got them then? Flett was telling me.'

'The Glendinnings thing? Yeah, we got them.' A little edge to the voice, as if to say *why would you doubt us?*

'That's a result, mate. Brand new. So what happened?'

'They rented a holiday cottage up Loch Lomond way. Landlord saw them shooting up bottles in the woods. Supposed to be hikers but, you know; guns, city shoes. When the news came out he phoned it in.'

'He ID them all?'

'We got Stokes and Cursiter straight off from his description. Cursiter gave up the others. His love interest included.'

'The insider. What about Paton?'

A bark of laughter. 'The man of the moment. Gets around, that boy. Anything else we can hang on him? Four murders. An armed robbery. What about cars? No stolen cars out your way? Domestics?'

So Halliday felt it too. Everyone did. Too easy all round. Something not right.

'That's what worries me,' McCormack said.

'Well.' You could hear the suspicion in Halliday's voice. 'There's worries and worries. You got his dabs, didn't you? Place him at the scene. It'll stand up.'

'On the door frame,' McCormack said. 'We got his dabs on the door frame. Not the room. And a bootprint, if you believe that. A bloody bootprint. It's *Send for Paul Temple*, for Christ's sake.'

Halliday cleared his throat, said nothing.

'Stokes?' McCormack was thinking aloud. Billy Thomson had been right. 'That's Bobby Stokes, Maryhill? He's McGlashan, isn't he? What was the other name?'

'Cursiter. Brian Cursiter. Big fucker. Muscle. And Stephen

296

Dalziel. And a young boy called Campbell. Aye, they're with McGlashan. Footsoldiers, but yeah.'

Flett came into the squad room, eyes flicking, someone was about to get a bollocking. McCormack hunched over the handset, dropped an octave. 'You ask them about it? Paton? The Quaker?'

'You mean, did they know? No. They didn't. I mean they can't believe it's true – they think we're trying to put something over on them. But, no, they had no idea. Listen, you said a bootprint?'

'That's right.'

'You busy right now?'

'You got something I should see?'

'I was you, I'd get round here. Sharpish.'

Hutchesonstown Police Station was a five-minute drive. In the squad room Halliday picked a chunky A5 booklet off his desk and tossed it to McCormack. The booklet was soft with multiple creasings, its cover worked to the thinness of silk. Each page was divided into three sections horizontally. Different handwritings listed items, units and prices: ball-peen hammers, galvanized buckets, protective goggles, garden shears.

'What is this?'

'Receipt book. Southside Hardware. It's an entry for July tenth you'll want to look at.'

McCormack riffled the pages, found June. Flicked forward, back. He found the entry. Items, sizes, prices, totals. A James Diamond had purchased five boiler suits. five donkey jackets. Six pairs of Irish Setter boots. A canvas holdall. Heavy-duty torch. Paid in cash.

'It's the Glendinnings string.'

'It's better than that. I spoke to the clerk. He remembers the buyer.'

'Dazzle?'

'Stokes. I took down some photos. He picked Bobby Stokes out straight off.'

McCormack studied the columns, the handwriting in small, blockish capitals, the innocent blue biro. 'Six pairs of boots?'

'I know. And look at the sizes.'

Various sizes, but two the same: two nine and a halfs.

'Where is Stokes? The Bar-L?'

'Naw. They split them up. Stokes is through in Saughton.'

'I owe you, Adam. Can I take this with me?'

'Long as you bring it back.'

McCormack took the new motorway through to Edinburgh, reached Saughton at noon. He was shown into an interview cell. Ten minutes later Bobby Stokes was brought in. Stokes sat down at the table in the red-and-white striped shirt of the remand prisoner.

An empty chair stood on the near side of the table. McCormack unbuttoned his jacket. He didn't sit down.

'Why'd you buy six pairs of boots, Bobby?'

Stokes had shaved that morning and he looked oddly innocent. His hair was neatly parted and he sat there in his starched shirt with his hands before him on the wooden table, fingers loosely knitted. He glanced up neutrally as if McCormack was a pigeon on a windowsill or a cat that had crossed his path and went back to looking at nothing in particular.

McCormack took the receipt book and slammed it down on the table, open at the page.

'We've got the receipt, Bobby.'

Stokes didn't look at the entry. He looked away at the clock on the far wall and spoke in a soft, bored sigh. 'Got the cheque too, have you? The one with my name on it? My address on the back?'

McCormack walked away to the far side of the room. When he came back he lifted the receipt book and slipped it back in his pocket. 'You paid in cash, Bobby. You're saying it wasn't you? Paton's already told us, we know it was you.' That was a lie, but what did Stokes know? 'What I can't work out, though? You bought five boiler suits. Five donkey jackets. But you bought six pairs of boots. What is it, boots were on special that week?'

Stokes's cheek bunched in what might have been a smile. How easy it would be to hit him, bring your fist crashing into the side of his head. Take his hair in both hands, slam his punchable face straight into the table. Watch the blood pooling on the wood.

McCormack walked to the far side of the room again, walked back. 'Who got the boots, Bobby? Who got the extra pair?'

'Never bought any boots.'

'Was it Maitland, Bobby? Did you get the boots for Walter Maitland?'

Stokes kept staring ahead, like the name of McGlashan's enforcer meant nothing to him.

'There was a sixth member of the string, Bobby. Who was it? Who got the boots? Was it McGlashan?'

'Never bought any boots.'

'Or was there no sixth man at all, Bobby? Eh? Was there some other reason for the extra pair? Now what could that be?' McCormack tapped the table. 'Two pairs of nine and a halfs, Bobby? What size do you suppose Alex Paton takes? Any idea?'

'Never bought any boots.'

McCormack had walked behind Stokes and now he stopped. He looked at Stokes's forearms on the yellow table, the neatly folded cuffs of the shirt. You could tell from the back of Stokes's head that he wasn't worried. He could sit here all day giving the same answer, keeping his temper, watching the clock on the wall. Stokes wasn't a hard man but he knew the score. This was a robbery. No one got hurt. Stokes was the driver, he didn't even enter the building. With only one prior – a juvenile housebreaking in '58 – he'd get five years max. He'd do three minus his time on remand. Be back on the streets in a couple of years, his rep enhanced, guy who did his bird, big man in the Royal Oak and the Saracen's Head.

McCormack took out his cigarettes. He sparked the match right behind Stokes's head and watched the flinch, the little blackbird swivel of the head. He leaned down close to Stokes's ear. 'You scared, Bobby?' McCormack could smell carbolic soap. He hoped his own sweat would be in Stokes's nose, his own rank scent. 'Cause you should be. But it's me you should be scared of. Not the guy who got the boots. Me, Bobby. Know why? Because I don't care where the money is, Bobby. I don't give a fuck about the Glendinnings job. But this other thing? This is the Quaker. And if the guy who got the boots turns out to be the Quaker, then you're an accomplice.'

McCormack moved back into view. Stokes was watching him now, the black eyes tracking him as if he was a dog that might turn dangerous. McCormack stood on the other side of the table, behind the empty chair. He leaned across, his knuckles on the wood.

'Accomplice to a sex killer. How do you like that? You can do three for robbery. Nae bother to the big man. Can you do ten, son? Twelve? Can you do a twelve-stretch as a nonce, with the heavy mob up in Peterheid? Think about that, son.'

McCormack straightened up. He crushed his ciggie in the ashtray and crossed to the cell door, slapped it with his palm.

The screw's head appeared in the Judas hole and the bolts slid back. Glancing back as the door swung closed, McCormack saw Stokes lean forward to snatch the smouldering cigarette-end and bring it to his lips.

39

Saturday morning. McCormack stepped out on Caird Drive, heading east. A figure on the opposite side of the street slipped out of a closemouth, moving fast, a man in a brownish suit, who modulated smartly to a normal walk, failing all the while to cast the smallest glance at McCormack.

McCormack slowed his pace. It was just before ten and the street was quiet. He listened for the footsteps of the man in the brown suit and caught them falling between his own, faint, jazzy, a distant syncopation.

At the corner with Hyndland Street McCormack stopped to light a cigarette and as he shook the match out he saw from the corner of his eye the man cross the street at an angle, swiftly, as if dodging an oncoming vehicle.

The sun was strong. McCormack closed his eyes for a few steps as he walked down Hyndland Street, feeling the heat on his eyelids. How far could you go without opening your eyes? Could you make it right down to Dumbarton Road? But straight away his sole slurred on the sloping pavement and he snapped his eyes open, crossing the street to the shady side.

It was a hazard of the job. Sometimes you saw a man coming

towards you in the street or climbing up the subway stairs and you flinched, your fists clenched at your sides, till the man had passed. You had put away so many, over the years. There was always the thought that one of them had clocked you and was coming for revenge. This could be one of those. Some housebreaker or peterman, fresh out of Barlinnie. Some rancorous lag who'd got hold of your address.

A late breakfast in one of the cafes on Dumbarton Road had been McCormack's plan, but now he stepped smartly round an elderly woman weighed down with shopping bags and skipped up the steps of St Peter's Church.

The cool air was pleasant after the heat of the street. Early Mass was over and the pews were all but deserted: a handful of figures dotted here and there on the right-hand side of the aisle. McCormack walked to the left-hand aisle and made his way down to the front.

As he dropped on one knee to genuflect, McCormack glanced back beneath his elbow to see the double doors open. The man in the brown suit took a seat at the back of the church.

McCormack sat with his forearms resting on the back of the pew in front. He glanced to his left. He was sitting underneath the fifth station. Simon of Cyrene, in a blue-green tunic and a hat shaped like an Air Raid Warden's helmet, was helping Jesus with the cross. Simon had on these ankle boots – like the Quaker, McCormack thought – and was caressing the long wooden shaft of the cross like he was cradling a baby. He didn't seem to be taking that much of the weight. Jesus still had the beam across his shoulder and was bowed down under it, while Simon of Cyrene was prancing along on the balls of his feet.

McCormack closed his eyes. The words of the Hail Mary started up in his head, repeating on a loop like piped Muzak while his mind drifted off to other things – the extra boots that Stokes had bought, the checked jacket on the back of Helen

Thaney's chair. Also, there was the good news from Goldie. After their talk at the ice-rink, Goldie had paid a visit to Barlinnie where he sat down with Alex Paton for half an hour, trying to bring home to him the gravity of his situation and how it might be in his favour to tell them who set up the safe house. He showed Paton a list of the Glendinnings string and asked him to point at the name. Eventually Paton placed his index finger on Bobby Stokes's name. No words spoken.

Now and at the hour of our death. Amen. After five minutes McCormack shuffled along to the pew's other end and set off up the central aisle, walking slowly. He was aware of the man in the brown suit jerking himself upright in his pew and then deliberately settling himself, dipping his head in a pastiche of prayer.

McCormack held his stately pace as he drew level with the man. Then he suddenly lunged, his two fists clamping on the man's lapels, and hauled him kicking from the pew, the brown arms flailing, and powered him through the double doors and down the church steps, the man's arms still rowing as though he were falling from a building, and threw him down against the wall with the spiked railings on top.

The man made to scramble up but then slumped back against the wall, his legs straight out in front of him. McCormack stood over him, worried a little that the man was badly hurt, he was grimacing in pain, but no, it was a smile, the man was smiling broadly, and now the head tipped back and a laugh came pealing out, a laugh like the cry of a jungle bird, that brought heads snapping round from the passers-by on Hyndland Street.

McCormack stood over him, fists flashing open and closed, hissing at him to shut the fuck up.

'I'm sorry', the man said. He held up a hand. The laughter came again and a crackle of snot burst from his nose. The man drew the sleeve of his jacket across his face and started to subside, shoulders heaving.

'The fuck are you laughing at?'

'I'm sorry. It's you. Jesus Christ. You look so . . . in charge.' The man shook his head. 'You've no idea, do you. I could finish you with two words.'

The man held up two fingers to match his words, smirking, holding McCormack's gaze.

McCormack felt the flood of rage. He drew back his foot but stilled it in time. 'You think you know me? Fuckface. You know who I am?' His hand was fumbling in his jacket pocket and he yanked it out, the warrant card, flipped it open and thrust it at the man's face.

The man didn't give it a glance. 'You're a polis,' he said. 'An upholder of the law. Were you upholding the law in the Queen's Park last Tuesday night, Detective? Do you uphold the law on Glasgow Green?'

McCormack felt the world buckle, the red tenements opposite seemed to nod down towards him and then right themselves. He staggered back from where the skinny man sprawled in triumph, back into the shade of St Peter's. The arm with the warrant card dropped to his side.

The man was grinning. He sat up, tugged on the lapels of his jacket. 'Maybe we should go someplace to talk.'

He reached up a hand. McCormack almost stooped to take it but checked himself, turned on his heel and waited at the bottom of the steps. In his own sweet time the man picked himself up. 'There's a café down the road,' McCormack said, walking off.

'You don't remember me?' The man was stirring his tea, a wicked shine in his bloodshot eyes. 'Oh Jesus, relax! It's not that. But we have met before.'

McCormack's coffee lay untouched on the waxy tablecloth. He was having trouble focusing on the man's words. This was the end. It was the end of the Quaker business. It was the end of his life as a cop. He saw it all, the whole dreary process unfolding. The man across from him giving his statement. McCormack's colleagues seeking corroboration from men they picked up in Queen's Park, Glasgow Green. The formality of the disciplinary hearing. He'd be thrown out. Probably prosecuted. Made an example of. The talk of the Park Bar, the Highlanders Institute, every living room and street corner in Ballachulish.

What did the man want? Was he asking for money? But money would just prolong it. A City of Glasgow detective getting blackmailed by some Partick ned. Better to end it now. There was a nugget of ice in McCormack's stomach but already it was being buoyed up, swamped, dissolved in a rushing flood of relief. He could stop pretending. He could stop kidding on he was one of the lads. But the man was still talking. Didn't he remember him? How would he remember him?

'In the Criterion Bar,' the man was saying. The zinc counter of the café was behind the man's shoulder and something flared in McCormack's memory. 'You and your mate. The fat one. The nasty fucker.'

The man's eyes slid to the side then, as the bell chimed on the café door. He rubbed his nose with two fingers and, in that gesture, it came back to McCormack: the steel urinal, the man's scared face and shifty eyes. It was the nonce they'd huckled in Shettleston.

The thin man saw the recognition in McCormack's eyes. 'That's right. You lifted me. You and the fat cunt. I thought I knew your face, when you huckled me in that pub. Thought I'd maybe seen you on the Green. But I couldn't be sure. And then I saw you last week in Queen's Park, got a good look at your face. And then I knew. Kilgour's the name.'

That was it. Kilgour. One of the deviants rousted by Goldie during that terrible late shift.

'You were wrong, though, eh? About the Quaker. It wasnae me.'

'You think you can blackmail me? Is this your angle? You want money?'

'Oh, no. It wasnae me,' Kilgour went on, as if he hadn't heard. 'Thing is, it's not him either. The guy you've got, the peterman. This boy Paton. He's not the Quaker.'

McCormack's voice tightened. 'What makes you say that?'

'And you fucking know it, don't you? Look at you. You know it's not him.'

'What makes you say that?'

Kilgour was turning the salt-cellar over in his hands, dribbling the grains on to the tabletop. He drew a cross in the spilled salt with his fingertip and looked up into McCormack's eyes.

'Because I've seen him.' Kilgour nodded. 'I've seen the Quaker.'

McCormack took the salt-cellar out of Kilgour's hand, set it down beside the pepper and the vinegar in its little wire tray.

'What do you mean you've seen him? Seen him when?'

'The night I got done for attacking that lassie. It was him that did it. The Quaker.' Kilgour grimaced. 'I told youse all this at the time. I was walking home and I saw this couple. On the waste ground by the empty flats. Shagging. Or I thought they were shagging. But you could see it wasn't right, she was struggling, her legs kicking out from under the bloke. I shouted something and started to cross. The bloke stood up, fastening himself. He looked round at me and got off his mark, away down Madras Street.'

Kilgour paused, his eyes tracking back and forth, replaying the scene. 'The lassie was hurt. She was spluttering, retching for air. He'd been choking her with her tights, they were still tied round her throat. I was stood there waiting to help. Then somebody jumped me and the squad car screamed up and the polis piled out. I tried to tell them. I thought she would set them right but she was half-dead, she was all fucked up. She didn't know if it was New Year or New York.'

'And the guy,' McCormack said. 'The guy who attacked her.'

'Big.' Kilgour spread his arms. 'A back like a sideboard. Big meaty bloke. And dark. His hair was black as molasses. It's not the guy you've got.'

McCormack felt the thrill of vindication. He'd been right. Even if nothing came of it, even if Paton was wrongly convicted and the Quaker stayed at large: he'd been right. And Cochrane, Levein and the others were wrong.

'And you told all this at the time?' McCormack said.

'What do you think? Of course I did.'

'But they nailed you,' he said slowly, speaking almost to himself. 'You did time.'

'They said I'd been with her all night. I'd picked her up at the Barrowland. Some fucker testified he'd seen me at the dance hall.'

'Did you not have an alibi? Where had you been?'

Kilgour pursed his lips and looked sourly, steadily at him. McCormack thought back to the case. He'd read the man's file. The attack took place on a patch of waste ground near Mill Street in Bridgeton. Late at night. Mill Street. Two hundred yards from the Green.

'Where do you think I'd been?' Kilgour said softly. 'I'm like you, polis. I take my pleasures where I can.'

McCormack slumped back in his chair. His brain was spooling ahead, processing the new information. Paton wasn't the Quaker. We knew that anyway. Kilgour's black-haired bruiser was the Quaker: waste ground, Bridgeton, the ligature. But if the Quaker turned out to be a stocky man with blue-black hair, why had the witnesses pegged him as slim and fair? Was Nancy Scullion wrong? But then another question – more urgent than these – floated up to the top of his mind. He stared at Kilgour.

'So what do you want?' McCormack asked him.

'I want to get him,' Kilgour said simply. 'I want to nail the fucker. I want to help.'

40

'Oh for Jesus' sake.' McCormack stood in the bright reception hall of Saughton Prison. He turned his back on the screw behind the desk, turned to face him again. 'You mean he's been transferred to Barlinnie?'

He'd driven through that morning from Glasgow. Another night of sustained cogitation on the case had yielded nothing more inspiring in the way of practical gambits than giving Bobby Stokes another go. The key, McCormack had decided, after a fourth large Springbank, was to find out who arranged the safe house for Paton. Stokes was the go-between, but someone else had set it up. Whoever set up the house was responsible for framing Paton. It was time to put pressure on Stokes. If you couldn't get a nyaff like Bobby Stokes to knuckle under, it was time to book your ticket. So he'd signed out a Flying Squad Velox and motored through to Edinburgh. Only now, as the cheerful screw was happy to confirm, the journey had been wasted. Stokes was gone.

'No,' the screw said. 'I mean he's been released.'

'Like fuck he's been released. *Robert* Stokes, this is. Remand prisoner. The Glendinnings thing.'

'I know who Bobby Stokes is. We let him go this morning. Do you people not talk to each other?'

They were enjoying this, the East Coast screws, grinning at the floor-show, Angry Man from the West. He asked to see the governor.

'You think he's a wizard or something? Think he's gonnae magic him back?'

'Just get me to the fucking governor.'

A smirking screw walked him through the clicks and bangs, the clanging doors, the landings, the corridors. After the endless evil shine of cold white tiles, the governor's office was nicely subdued, lots of wood and dark green leather.

The governor was flustered, a small man in a greenish suit, rising from his chair with a swipe of his hand across an oily comb-over. 'I'm afraid you'll have to take that up with the relevant— I mean, we can't be held responsible if you can't get your . . . Anyway. Look: will you sit down, Inspector . . .?'

'McCormack. I'll stand. Who authorized the release?'

'Surely, if you've come from Glasgow . . .'

'Who signed the docket?'

The governor couldn't hold McCormack's stare. He sucked his cheeks and shook his head briskly. There was a sheaf of papers in his out-tray and he flicked through them viciously. He stopped with an index finger on one sheet and ran his tongue along his upper teeth. 'The authorizing officer was DCI Flett, but if you think—'

McCormack was off, clattering out of the office, striding down the corridor with the screw trotting at his heels.

All the way back to Glasgow McCormack kept the Velox at ninety, the tendons standing out in his forearms. He used the siren when he hit the Gallowgate. He nearly wrenched the handbrake off when he parked it in St Andrew's Street. Flett was out of his chair and halfway round the desk before McCormack had burst through his door.

'I know, I know!' Flett's hands were hoisted, stick-up style. 'I know what you're going to say. You're right. But, Jesus, you were out the door before I could stop you.'

'You signed the fucking docket! You let the bastard go!'

'Duncan! Duncan! Listen to me.'

'He's the key to the Quaker. He knows who set Paton up. The whole thing hinges on him. And you let him walk?'

'No option, Duncan. There's a bigger picture here. Sit down, son.'

'Bigger than the Quaker?'

'Sit down, McCormack. Sit the fuck down!'

McCormack pulled the plastic chair out from Flett's desk, smacked it down on its four legs, dropped into it, crossed his arms. Flett took small steps to the door and closed it very gently. He walked back round the desk and took his seat.

'It's a bastard, Duncan. I know. But this is out of my hands.' Flett dropped his voice. 'Stokes is working for someone. OK? They're putting something together. They're at a delicate stage, blah-di-blah. You've done it yourself, Dunc. You know how it goes.'

'He's somebody's tout?'

'He's somebody's tout.'

McCormack nodded, sucked in his bottom lip. 'Whose?'

'Duncan. Be your age. You know I can't—'

'What are they working on? Have they found the fucking Ripper? Have they solved the Appin Murder? Because this is the Quaker I'm working on.'

Flett gave a little pout, looked at the desk. 'There's a school of thought, DI McCormack. There's a school of thought that the Quaker case has already been solved.'

'Right. But not if you've got anything to do with it. Not

if it's up to you. On you go, McCormack. Solve this case. Bring it home. Except, see this guy over here? The guy who knows the one bit of information that could help you actually solve the fucking thing? Yeah, you cannae talk to him. But carry on.'

The phone rang on Flett's desk. He held McCormack's gaze while he dealt with the call – Yes; yes; fine – and dropped the handset on to the receiver.

'Well, it all looks pretty simple then. If you can't do it without Stokes you can't do it. You can get back to proper police work. Start pulling your weight around here for a change.'

'At least tell me what they're doing with Stokes. The Glendinnings thing's solved. Is it McGlashan? Are they going after McGlashan?' McCormack clapped his chest. 'Then bring me in. I can help.'

'Aye. You can help by leaving Stokes alone.'

'I know more about McGlashan than anyone. I'll help them nail him. I just need to talk to Stokes first. I bring him in for an hour, sir. Half an hour.'

The chair groaned as Flett shifted position. 'Jesus. Can I send you back to Cochrane already? Let him get his head nipped. Leave. Bobby. Stokes. The fuck. Alone. All right? Is that clear enough? Don't go near him. If you can finish this thing without him, do it. And do it fucking soon. If you can't, then for Christ sake let it lie.'

McCormack blew out some air, pushed a hand through his hair. 'Right. I'll leave Stokes be. I'll find a way.'

He stood up to go.

'You used to be one of the easy ones,' Flett said. 'Did your job. No drama. No hysterics. Remember that? Back in the glory days of, what, last month. The fuck happened?'

'The Quaker,' McCormack said. 'The Quaker happened.'

* * *

313

On the way home that evening McCormack was riding the subway, rattling back to Partick. The train was entering a station when a sour spoor of perfume snagged him. Something told him this scent was important; he knew it without knowing why. He turned to see a woman pushing through to the doors as the train slowed. He plunged after her, panicking, working his shoulders through the tuts and gasps in the close-packed carriage and made it on to the platform just in time to see her white woollen coat swaying up the stairwell into the gloom. He took the stairs three at a time until he was at her shoulder, breathing deeply, sucking down the bitter scent. At the subway entrance she cast a jerky sideward glance at him and scuttled off down Byres Road but by then he had it. He stood stock still on the Byres Road pavement and closed his eyes. He was back in the foyer of the Barrowland, listening to Barbara Bell, smelling her acrid perfume and watching, over her shoulder, the queue at the payphone.

The payphone.

He'd been out to use the phone. That's what he'd been doing, the Quaker, when he left the table at the Barrowland that night. He'd been phoning someone. And McCormack remembered now the manager's statement, the fracas that night at the payphone, a patron had kicked up a fuss when a caller wouldn't get off the phone. Who could he be phoning with such urgency? A cab? A wife or girlfriend waiting at home? An accomplice? And the broad back of a man he'd never seen, a man conjured up by the discredited statement of a convicted nonce, rose up in McCormack's mind. The black-haired, thick-set man from Robert Kilgour's story. And he knew now why they hadn't caught him. The Quaker wasn't one man but two. It was the fair-haired man who set them up; the black-haired man who killed them.

McCormack looked at his watch. It was after six. Nancy

Scullion would be home from work. He walked down to Tennent's Bar and ordered a Guinness. He took his change from the barman and carried his pint down to the end of the horseshoe-shaped bar, where the payphone was mounted to the wall. He dialled Nancy's number. There was an outsize whisky bottle on the bar beside the payphone, with a bronze-edged slot in the neck. The bottle was half-full of coins and banknotes. The label on the bottle said 'Deprived Children's Annual Day Out'.

Nancy was home. She agreed to meet McCormack in the tearoom at the top of Sauchiehall Street in half an hour. McCormack swirled the last of his Guinness, downed it. He signalled the barman for another.

'I don't know.' Nancy Scullion tilted her head, gazing into the middle distance. 'Maybe. I'm not sure. Is it important? It's important, isn't it?'

'He never mentioned a call? He never asked you for change?'

Nancy frowned. 'I remember him *count*ing his change at one point, I can picture him stood there by the table. But I don't know if it was then or later. Anyway, I just assumed he was going for cigarettes.'

The tearoom was quiet. The waitress was bearing down on their table to take their order.

'Two teas,' McCormack called, lifting a hand to ward her off. The waitress turned on her heel without a word. 'But he already had cigarettes. You said in your statement that he gave you a cigarette when you first sat down.'

'That's right.'

'Was it a full packet?'

'I don't – actually I think, yeah. It was. I remember I had to hold the packet with one hand and pull the cigarette loose.'

'So he could have been going for the phone.'

'I suppose.'

'What's funny?'

She was grinning, slyly. 'No, it's just. It's the way you say things. It's nice. *Could haff been.*'

McCormack smiled tightly. He thought once again how much easier this would be if he could play along, if he knew how to flirt.

'So you get in the taxi with him at the end of the night. But this is the thing: did he know beforehand where you lived? Did he know that Marion lived in Earl Street? Had you talked about it earlier in the evening?'

She gave McCormack a look of theatrical sincerity. 'Look, I wish I could help you, Duncan. I really do. But I just don't know. I don't think we spoke about it but I don't remember. And maybe Marion told him, when they were dancing. I'm sorry. I know it's important.'

McCormack nodded. She looked as if she might be about to reach out and clasp his wrist. He leaned back to let the waitress put down the teas. 'You've been a great help,' he said, and the waitress looked at him sharply.

Robert Kilgour was replacing the nameplate on his front door when McCormack stepped out of the lift. Kilgour straightened up, a screwdriver dangling from his left hand. He looked at McCormack and he looked at the lift.

'Jesus Christ,' he said. 'Maybe a pipe band would be better next time. A bit more subtle. Or a big neon sign: *Tout Lives Here.*'

'Tout's the least of your worries,' McCormack said. 'Be a step up for you, getting known as a tout.'

McCormack explained the task. Paton had named the man who set him up with the house in Queen Mary Street as Bobby Stokes, petty thief and bit player in the McGlashan outfit. Until two days ago, Stokes had been in Saughton, awaiting trial for the Glendinnings heist, but the charges against him had been suddenly, stupidly dropped. Someone had sprung him. McCormack had been warned off by the higher-ups: Stokes was someone's tout, leave him alone. Kilgour's job was to tail Stokes, dog him at all hours, find out who he's touting for.

'Set a tout to catch a tout,' Kilgour said.

'Set a tout to catch a cop,' McCormack said. 'I need to know who's handling Stokes.'

'This boy Stokes. You think his handler's the key?'

'At this stage just finding the lock would be good. I think whoever Stokes is helping is the man who set up Paton. And the man who set up Paton is the Quaker or maybe he's working for the Quaker. He's the man we need to find.'

41

Not everything's a chess problem, son. Cochrane's words came back to McCormack as he stared at the ceiling, waiting for the alarm to go off. It was a chess problem now. He'd made sure of that. Chess problem? It was a quadratic fucking equation. The whole force had been searching for a single killer; McCormack alone was now hunting three men: the two Quakers and whoever killed Helen Thaney.

The permutations seemed to swirl around the tiny bedroom, the manifold leads and clues, the scraps of data. He felt as though the room itself was spinning, as though he needed to grip the sides of the mattress to anchor himself to the earth.

The alarm clock's heavy seconds thudded in his ear as he talked himself through it, setting out what he knew, paying out the cards. Helen Thaney, he told himself. OK then. Start with Helen Thaney.

That's easy. Helen Thaney had been made to look like number four. She wasn't. She was out on her own, a different thing altogether.

Meaning what, smartarse?

Meaning her killer wasn't the Quaker.

But her killer had inside knowledge of the inquiry.

Which means maybe he's a cop.

You'd like that, wouldn't you? Ratting on cops. That's up your street, isn't it? What else?

It means Thaney isn't random. She's not another woman who danced with the wrong man. It's personal. The key to Helen Thaney is Helen Thaney.

Oh, that's good. And what about the Quaker? Remember him?

Which one?

Right. Of course. The Quaker's two men now, isn't he? The killer, the actual raper and strangler, is Kilgour's Bridgeton hoodlum: big, bluff, stocky, shock of black hair. He depends on his fair-haired sidekick to set him up with women.

He does. But you've missed the key question: why can't he do this himself?

Fuck knows. Too ugly? He's disfigured, maybe.

But Kilgour didn't mention a disfigurement.

He'd have noticed, would he, in the dark?

He got a good look.

If not a disfigurement, then what?

Maybe he's famous. Or at least he's someone who might be recognized.

Now that *is* a thought. What were the possibilities?

Footballer. Pop singer. Actor, politician. TV newsreader.

He was bulky, though, remember? Kilgour called him an ape, a real bruiser.

Not a winger, then. Probably not a pop star.

So what is he?

He could be a cop.

Oh give it a fucking rest, would you?

He *could* be a cop.

And the blond one, the fair-haired sidekick the whole city's been looking for. How come he wasn't picked up?

Maybe he was. Maybe he was being protected, maybe he was issued with one of the CC's magic cards: *The bearer is certified as not being the Quaker.*

He's a cop, too, is he? They're all cops.

Well, he's not a bricklayer. He's not a navvy. Soft hands. Well spoken. Good standard of education, in all likelihood. Boss manner: accustomed to getting his way, giving orders. Acts like a gentleman.

But he picks up women at the Barrowland, the roughest hall in the city.

Ah, but does he? If he picked up women at the Barrowland he'd be a regular, he'd be hanging around, somebody would know him. He *takes* them to the Barrowland, but that's like the final stage in the ritual. He's gotten to know them elsewhere, long before he takes them up the Gallowgate to the shooting stars on the big neon sign.

So Cochrane was wrong?

Cochrane *was* wrong. There *is* something the victims have in common, beyond the obvious.

Yeah, Mary Queen of Scots, bright boy. They've got that in common, remember? How's that stroke of genius playing out?

The alarm went off then, a heart-stopping clamour. McCormack's arm flailed out to quash it and he swung out of bed, tugging the T-shirt away from his clammy chest, adjusting his balls in his boxers.

He filled a glass with water at the kitchen sink. He stood in front of the street map on his living-room wall, sipping the water, eyes tracking between the push-pins. They'd been through it all a thousand times. The Quaker's victims came from opposite ends of the city: East End, West End, South Side. There was nothing to tie them together. They didn't go to the same church: Jacqui Keevins was Catholic; Ann Ogilvie and Marion Mercer Protestant. None of them belonged to a political party. They had no hobbies in common, no sports or pastimes. They didn't use the same hairdressers or the same doctor's surgery. They didn't swim at the same pool or take their washing to the same launderette. The thing that seemed to tie Keevins and Mercer together – both of them had married servicemen – was nothing more than a coincidence. And yet McCormack was certain that all three women had met the fair-haired man long before he squired them on to the Barrowland dance floor.

McCormack drained his glass of water and set it on the draining board in the kitchen. He lit the ring under the frying pan and tipped in some cooking oil. He rooted in the fridge for the package of greaseproof paper and peeled off three rashers in turn and dropped them in the pan. The fat flared up with a sound like rushing water. He cracked two eggs on the edge of the pan and watched the albumen whiten, tossing the shells in the sink and wiping eggy fingers down the front of his T-shirt.

Three women. Three women with jobs and kids who had somehow found time to start a relationship with the fair-haired, well-spoken man. And they'd kept it secret. None of the statements from the victims' friends or relatives mentioned a boyfriend. McCormack pushed the food around with a spatula, keeping his distance from the spitting fat. But he'd known them somehow, the fair-haired man. He'd known them well enough to ask them to the dancing. To escort them home. To bring them into the path of the Quaker.

The food was ready. McCormack turned off the gas and shook the fry-up on to a plate. Milky cup of tea, two sugars.

321

Pan bread, four slices, margarined. Brown sauce. He looked at the clock. Still an hour before the day shift came on at St Andrew's Street. He shuffled his chair closer in to the table, splintered a rasher of bacon with a stab of his fork.

42

On the bus into town, McCormack had to stop himself from scoping the passing cars: white Ford Consul 375, dark Morris 1000 Traveller. It was a sickness, the Quaker obsession. You shared that space with these men for too long, you were bound to catch the virus.

He forced his gaze from the window. In front of him a wee boy, wedged between two talking women, was kneeling up, peering at McCormack over the back of the seat. McCormack lifted his hat from the seat beside him and settled it over his eyes as if he was taking a nap. Then he tipped his head right back and squinted at the boy from under the brim. The boy laughed.

'Jamie, stop bothering the man.'

'He's no bother.'

McCormack took his hat off and placed it on the boy's head, tilted back so the boy could see. The boy reached up with two hands and took the hat from his head and looked at the inside and put it back on so that it dropped down and covered his eyes. He laughed delightedly.

'Jamie! Give the man his hat back.'

The woman on the window side of the boy snatched the hat off his head and passed it back to McCormack, frowning.

'And sit properly! Face the front, Jamie.'

McCormack winked and the boy scrambled round, his blond head disappearing below the seat-back.

The two women were talking about waiting lists. The one on McCormack's left – the boy's mother, evidently – had an appointment at Clive House, where the Corporation housing office was based.

'It's who you know, though, isn't it?' the other woman was saying. 'Her through the wall, she got a three-bed semi in Knightswood. Her man works for the Cleansing Department, surprise surprise.'

'Backhanders,' the boy's mother said. 'That's what it comes down to. That's what you hear. Fifty pounds in a brown envelope and you take your pick.'

'Sicken ye. Who's got that kind of money?'

'Give one of these wee Hitlers a clipboard and a pen and they think they're God Almighty. Jamie, sit at peace.'

'Where you trying for?'

'Well, I wouldn't turn down Knightswood. Anywhere really. I'm not bothered. Anywhere nice.'

The bus slowed for the construction works at Charing Cross, followed the detour into Garnethill.

'You going to the Willow Tea Rooms after?'

'Aye, maybe. We'll see. If His Lordship behaves himself. Come on, you.'

The women rose to go, the wee boy looking shyly back at McCormack as his mother yanked him forward. They were stepping down from the bus when it struck McCormack like a push in the chest, a little jump in the blood. He was grinning like a wide-eyed madman, face pressed to the window, as the bus drew away. The two women on the pavement frowned fiercely up, the boy returning McCormack's silly grin. The boy's hand floated up in a tentative wave and McCormack saluted with a dramatic flourish and slapped the chrome bar on the seat in front of him four or five times. He almost punched the air. At Glasgow Cross he swung down from the bus and sprinted down the Saltmarket to St Andrew's Street.

In the office he phoned Tobago Street. DS Goldie was on night shift, the desk clerk told him; he wouldn't be on until eleven that night. McCormack said he would try him at home.

Goldie picked up on the seventh ring, a rumbling growl. 'Aye.'

'Get out your stinking kip, man!'

'McCormack? Holy Christ.' Goldie's voice was in his boots. He cleared his throat. 'It's two in the afternoon. Did they not tell you I'm on nights?'

'They told me, aye.'

'Oh really? Better be fucking good, then.'

'I know who he is.'

'Who?'

'At least I know where he works. I know what he does.'

'The Quaker?'

'The fair-haired one. The accomplice.'

'Go on, then.'

'Not over the phone. Meet me at Mitchell's. Half an hour.'

Goldie was tearing into an iced bun as McCormack stirred cream into his coffee. Goldie slurped a big mouthful of tea, chewed down a hunk of dough.

'A *housing* officer?'

'Think about it.' McCormack set his teaspoon down on his saucer. 'What do they all have in common? They're looking for a house. Jacquilyn Keevins was looking for a house. She was living with her parents in a two-bed flat. Ann Ogilvie had a daughter and two sons in a single end in Bridgeton. Marion Mercer lived in a damp flat in Scotstoun.'

'So how does he set them up?'

'It's perfect. He knows where they live, marital status, number of kids. He knows everything about them.'

'They're gonnae shag this guy to get a hoose?'

'Derek. What's the most valuable commodity in this city? It's not hoors or whisky. It's a Corporation house in a decent district. This is the guy who gets to say yes or no. He's god, basically, if you want a house.'

'The boss manner,' Goldie said. 'The arrogant air.'

'Plus it's easy to keep it secret. His wee affairs. If the women grass him up, he loses his job.'

'And then they lose their chance of a house.'

'Exactly. You're going to keep shtum, aren't you?'

Goldie chewed down the last of his bun, wiped the raspberry icing from his chin.

'We going over there now? Clive House?'

'Not yet.' McCormack looked at his watch. 'I phoned the Director earlier. Asked him for a list of male employees, physical descriptions. Height, weight, hair-colour. Age. Distinguishing marks. Should be on my desk tomorrow. We're getting there, Derek.'

Goldie was staring gloomily out of the window.

'What?'

'Naw, it's just—' Goldie shook his head. 'The hours we put in. Dentists, tailors, soldiers. Barber shops. Golf clubs. No one thought of the housing office.'

'Well. Let's not hoist the flag just yet. Might turn out to be nothing.'

But he knew that it wasn't. He knew in the bones of him that this was the breakthrough. This was the link that the others had missed.

43

McCormack studied the pictures on his living-room wall. The smiling face in one picture, the black smudge in the other. Helen Thaney. The glossy photo of her beaten, bloodied face reminded him of something. He closed his eyes but nothing came.

Helen Thaney. What did they know about Helen Thaney?

Almost nothing. Less than with any of the others. They had barely identified the Queen Mary Street corpse as Helen Thaney before forensics came back with a match for the prints and the hunt was on for Alex Paton. Helen Thaney – the woman with family and friends, a history, a job – got forgotten. Random victim. Background didn't matter.

And now that Helen Thaney's background did matter, they realized how little they knew.

They knew she'd had a boyfriend – at least that was what Denise Redburn, who worked beside Helen in the casino, had said. A secret boyfriend, whose name she never revealed, whose Prince of Wales checked jacket had hung on the back of a chair. They knew she'd had a troubled background, didn't like nuns. And they knew she'd dyed her hair, about a month before her murder.

He'd had her file copied and sent to him at St Andrew's Street and he looked at it now, on his own kitchen table, the meagre sheets. Helen Thaney was born in Waterford in the Irish Republic on 6 June 1940. Her only surviving kin appeared to be her father, William Thaney, deliveryman, who disclaimed all interest in his daughter when contacted by the City of Glasgow Police and point-blank refused to travel to Scotland to identify her body. When pressed further, he revealed that he had committed his daughter to some kind of church-run institution when she was fifteen years old and had not spoken to her since. Helen Thaney next turns up as an employee of the Singer sewing-machine factory in Clydebank in 1963, and, from 1966, a cocktail waitress at the Claremont casino. And that was it. There were copies of the statements given by witnesses who saw her dancing at the Barrowland, including the statement of Denise Redburn, and a brief, dispassionate note from the casino manager enclosing Helen's employment records.

McCormack closed the file and looked up once more at the pictures. The smiling face, the bloody mask. What made a father turn his back on his daughter, so that even when she came to this, when her happy face was smudged to pulp, he made her a stranger? What could so twist the course of his love? He thought of the reformatory or the convent school or whatever they called it. A pregnancy, of course. That would be the cause, the big disaster. Some flustered fumbling with a local boy, maybe an older man, and her father bundles her off to hide her shame. His own shame. And now we'd done the same, thought McCormack. None of us brave enough to look her in the face.

And it came to him now what the bloodied face recalled. It was the book he'd browsed last Saturday on the new arrivals table at John Smith's bookshop in St Vincent Street. A book about Iron Age bodies dug up out of Danish bogs, victims of sacrifice, miraculously preserved after two thousand years, their skin tanned to a peaty black, the ropework halters still knotted round their necks. She looked like one of the bog-bodies, did Helen Thaney, her visage black with bruises and blood, her nose and cheeks staved in, her eyelids closed as if in sleep, the ligature tight at her throat.

The author of the book – McCormack had skimmed the first chapter standing in the shop – speculated on why the victims died. He didn't seem to know if these were murders, executions, or ceremonial killings. McCormack wasn't much further forward with his own twentieth-century corpse. At least the author of the book had an excuse: his corpses were older than Jesus Christ.

It was time to put this right, time to find out more about the late Ms Thaney. McCormack slid the employment records from the file. He thumbed the lever of his ballpoint pen, circled Helen Thaney's home address.

44

'Knock knock.'

The next one poked his head round the door and McCormack waved him in. They were using the manager's office, McCormack and Goldie ensconced behind the desk, a bare plastic chair on the other side. McCormack did the talking.

'Shut the door, please, Mr . . . Bickett, is it? I'm Detective Inspector McCormack; this is Detective Sergeant Goldie.'

The man shook McCormack's hand; nodded at Goldie.

'How long have you worked with the Housing Department, Mr Bickett?'

'How long?' He fingered the knot of his tie. 'I'd say twelve years. Yeah. Twelve. Sheesh: it sounds a lot when you say it like that.'

'Straight from school then?'

'Pretty much. I had a couple of nothing jobs first. Barman. Worked in a garage for a bit.'

'Do you own a car, Mr Bickett?'

'Yes. Yes, I do.' Bickett was easing himself into the chair and he half smiled, his eyes flicking from McCormack to Goldie. 'Guilty as charged.'

'You do?' McCormack's raised eyebrows posed the question: How do you run a car on the salary of a Corporation housing officer?

'It's a bit of banger, really,' Bickett said, touching his goatee beard. 'Just a runaround.'

He was a slim man in a brown suit. White shirt. Paisley pattern tie. His hair was longish, fair, expensively cut. There was a little glinting pin on his lapel: silver, two curved intersecting lines: a stylized fish.

'What model?'

'The car? It's a Fiat 1300.'

'Nice car. Reliable?'

'It's not bad.'

'How long have you had it, sir? The Fiat?'

'Well now. I suppose. It must be . . .' Bickett crossed his legs and stared up at the ceiling. He seemed to be struggling with a tremendously complex calculation. 'A year?' he said finally. 'Something like that?' He flinched a bit and grimaced, like a quiz-show contestant waiting to hear if his answer was correct.

'And before that?' McCormack asked brightly.

'You mean . . .'

'I mean, what kind of car did you drive before the Fiat, Mr Bickett?'

'Oh. I see. It was, yeah, it was a Volvo.'

'Colour?'

'Red.'

'Do you recall the registration number?'

'The registration of the Volvo?'

'That's right.'

'No, Inspector. I'm afraid I don't. It's like old telephone numbers, eh?' Bickett's laugh was stillborn.

McCormack could reel off the telephone number of every place he'd lived, but he nodded politely. 'That's all right,' he said. 'A year's a long time. You've been very helpful, Mr Bickett. We may be back in touch. In fact, we probably will.'

McCormack started leafing through the papers on his desk.

'That's it?' Bickett had his hands on his thighs, ready to lever himself out of the chair.

McCormack watched the man's smile falter. He let the silence build. 'Why? Was there something in particular you wanted to tell us, Mr Bickett?'

'No. I just. I thought you might tell us, you know, what it's about. The, uh, case.'

'Murder.' Goldie leaned sharply forward at this point, glaring into Bickett's face. 'This is a murder inquiry, sir.'

'Right.' Bickett nodded uncertainly. Goldie's flat Glasgow voice sounded menacing after McCormack's soft Argyllshire.

'In fact it's three murders.' Goldie told them off, a thumb and two fingers: 'Jacquilyn Keevins. Ann Ogilvie. Marion Mercer. Three women.'

'Isn't that . . .?'

'The Quaker? Aye. It is.'

'But you've got him? Didn't you get him? The guy from down south? Whatsisname, Paton?'

McCormack put a hand on Goldie's arm and Goldie slumped back. 'We do have someone helping with inquiries, sir,' McCormack told Bickett. 'As you and others have been doing. The inquiry is ongoing.'

'And you think that someone in here . . .?'

'It's a line of inquiry, sir. Do you recall any of these names in your professional capacity? Maybe one of these women applied for a house?'

'No, I don't think so.' Bickett's eyes were flicking back and forth, his smile visibly sickening. 'I mean, maybe they did. I can't be sure, but I don't remember them.'

'That's all right, sir. As I say, we'll be back in touch. Thank you for your time, Mr Bickett.'

The chair scraped and Bickett hauled himself to his feet and waded blindly for the door.

'And Mr Bickett?' McCormack glanced up from his papers with a tight smile. 'Like they say in the movies: don't leave town.'

The door closed with the softest of clicks.

McCormack checked his watch; they had ten minutes till the next employee was due. He stretched noisily and stood, strolled over to lean his hands on the windowsill, forehead on the glass, watching the trucks and diggers down below, moving around at Charing Cross, working on the half-built motorway. People with a plan, people who knew what they were doing. He spoke with his back to Goldie.

'What's your thoughts, then?'

'Thoughts? Jesus Christ. It's the poster come to life. Man's a walking artist's impression.'

'There's a resemblance, certainly.'

'It's fucking him. Did you see the lapel badge? The wee fish? It's a Christian thing.'

'I know.' McCormack turned. 'We'll need more bodies – someone to go through the records here, looking for the women. I'll see Flett about it. When we finish up here, you get on to the DVLC, get details of his previous cars, back to '67.'

'You know it's him, don't you?'

45

'*Boy*friends?'

She said the word as if checking that she'd heard it correctly, or as if her pronunciation might be at fault.

'*Boy*friends? She's twenty-nine years old. *Was* twenty-nine. I'm not their mother. I'm not their priest.'

'I understand that, Mrs Haddow. It's just that, you know, you own the building. You live in the building. Maybe you noticed if Helen Thaney had a regular visitor. What he looked like. Maybe you heard his voice. That's all. It's a simple question.'

She nodded, slowly, with her eyebrows raised and a tight appraising frown, to let him see how wrong he was. 'There are twenty people in this building,' she said. 'You think I keep track of their coming and goings? Their guests and their . . . what have you? You think that's simple? You think I log them in and out?'

'No, I don't think that,' McCormack said. They were in the sitting room of Mrs Haddow's ground-floor flat in a tenement block in Dennistoun. Polished brass fire-set. China dogs on the mantel. McCormack slapped his palms on his knees to get some kind of grip on the situation. 'I don't think that at all. I do think that you might start answering my questions, though. I think maybe that would be a good idea.'

'Why?' Mrs Haddow looked at him evenly. 'What good can it do? The woman's dead. The man who killed her's in jail, God rot him. Waiting for what's coming to him. What good can answering questions do? You want to dig dirt about *boy*friends? What's wrong with you? The woman's dead.'

The rasping sound was McCormack breathing out through his nose. He spread his hands and tried again. 'Mrs Haddow. Here's the thing. The man who did the others. We don't think he did – we don't think he murdered Helen.'

Mrs Haddow looked pityingly at him. 'She was strangled with her tights. Raped and murdered. Dumped in a derelict building.'

'Nevertheless.'

'You mean it's like a copycat?'

'Mrs Haddow.' McCormack stood up now, buttoning his jacket. 'How about we leave the questions to me? I'd like to see Helen's flat, please.'

'I suppose you've got a warrant?'

'Jesus Christ!' McCormack had his hat in his hand; he shook it at the woman. 'She's dead, for Christ's sake! Helen's dead! I'm trying to find the man who killed her. You don't want to help?'

Mrs Haddow's face was the face of a martyred saint. Wordlessly, she went to the sideboard, drew out a bunch of keys that she plunged into the pocket of her cardigan. She marched to the door and held it open.

He followed her indignant hams up the stone stairs to the landing on the first floor.

'Wait here, please!'

Mrs Haddow disappeared briefly into the flat, then the door opened again. 'You may come in. I've kept it as she left it. Please don't disturb her things.'

The room was reasonably disturbed already. Clothes were piled on an armchair in the corner, as though Helen had been trying on various outfits. There were shoes piled drunkenly on the floor of the open wardrobe. An electric bar-heater squatted awkwardly in the marble fireplace. On the mantelpiece was a photograph of a smiling, thirtyish woman with windblown hair and a floral dress. She was standing in front of a thatched holiday cottage with a baby in her arms.

Mrs Haddow came in and hovered beside the half-closed door. He noticed that, in addition to the Yale lock and the mortice, there was a shiny new bolt on the back of the door.

McCormack wandered over to the dresser and picked idly through the bottles and canisters clustered by the mirror. Hairspray, deodorant, little bottles of whisky-coloured perfume. There was a bottle of hair-dye, 'Diamond Blonde'. A pewter ring-tree with a dozen rings and silver chains hooked on its branches.

He pulled open the drawers. Underwear. Tights. A box of pads. There was a chequebook in the top drawer. Clydesdale Bank. McCormack noted down the address of the branch.

A black lacquer drinks cabinet stood beside the television set. The double bed had a headboard of white padded leather, fussy ruffled pillows and a frilly valance. The sheets were silk, peach-coloured. A black silk bolster at the foot of the bed.

McCormack dropped to his knees. He swept a hand under the valance and his knuckles bumped on something hard. Chamber pot? No: his spidering fingers settled on a tacky dimpled surface and what he drew out was a slender ball-peen hammer. He thought of the hammer he'd wielded as he charged into Paton's safe house. Why would Helen Thaney need a hammer? He looked again at the door, the thick cylinder of the bolt, the chunky bracket winking in the sunlight.

He brandished the hammer at Mrs Haddow. 'Did you know about this? Did she think that someone . . . Did she know she was in danger?'

Mrs Haddow crossed to the sofa, wrapping her cardigan tightly around her. She sat with her knees pressed together and her arms folded under her breast, huddling against a cold only she could feel. She nodded tightly at the carpet. 'I think she did.'

McCormack waited.

'I think she knew. She asked me to watch out for people at the door. Visitors. There was a man, she said. Someone at work. He used to watch her.'

'Someone on the staff, did she mean? Or a customer?'

'Customer, I think. She was frightened of him. I asked her why she didn't just get him chucked out, but he never did anything wrong, she said. It was just the way he looked at her.'

'Did she describe the man? Was it someone she already knew?'

'I don't know. She didn't like to talk about it. A big man with black hair, she said. Thick moustache.'

'Age?'

'She didn't say. You think it's him who killed her?'

'Look, I don't know, Mrs Haddow. *Did* you keep an eye out for him?'

'I did. But I never saw anyone who looked like that. Maybe someone else saw him, one of the other tenants.'

McCormack's gaze took in the silk sheets, the lacquered drinks cabinet.

'About the tenants,' he said. 'Single women, are they?'

There was a pause before Mrs Haddow stepped heavily forwards, rubbing her palms down her hips. 'Now that's just about enough.' Her voice was shaky. 'We have families here. Nurses. Teachers. Where the hell d'you get off? Christian families. A po*lice*man, if it matters.'

'Really? Who's the cop?' McCormack turned, closing the doors of the drinks cabinet.

Mrs Haddow's face slackened. The wariness seeped back into her eyes. She was frightened she had said too much.

McCormack snorted. 'I can walk out there and read the nameplates, Mrs Haddow. The voter's roll. Who is the cop?'

'His name's Graeme Layburn,' she said resentfully. 'And he'll be hearing about this.'

'He certainly will.' McCormack clamped his hat on his head. 'Thank you very much, Mrs Haddow. Thank you for your time.'

Before he left he climbed to the third floor and worked his way down, knocking on all doors. It was six o'clock. Cooking smells hung in the stairwell. Men came to their doors shirtsleeved, chewing food, napkins dangling from their fingers. They rubbed their chins and nodded while McCormack spoke but nobody had anything useful to say. Almost nobody. A man on the second floor had seen Helen Thaney with a man he'd assumed was an older relative: late fifties, tallish, mid-brown hair.

No one answered at Graeme Layburn's flat.

Outside, the summer evening was exotically fine. People strolled – singly, in pairs – with no thoughts of murder. Or was that wrong? Maybe these idling, shirtsleeved men, these women in thin summer dresses, maybe they all had someone they wanted to kill.

The yeasty smell from the brewery was in McCormack's nose as he unlocked the car. Duke Street. High Street. The Saltmarket. He parked by the riverside, climbed the broad stone steps and nodded at the doorman. The weighted doors closed behind him with a satisfying whisper, sealing the high white lobby. He crossed the springy plush to the games room, where he wrote a cheque at the cashier's window and carried a short stack of chips to the blackjack tables.

The casino was quiet, some of the Garnethill Chinese at the baccarat table, a bald man in yellow tweeds glumly playing roulette. McCormack ordered a whisky and soda from a waitress in a white blouse with puffy sleeves, tight black pencil skirt. She was younger than Helen Thaney, mid-twenties at most. He tipped her with one of the chips.

The croupier was another young woman, dressed in a masculine white shirt and blazer, her hair tied tightly back. McCormack played a few hands, making modest bets, sticking on sixteen. At one point he looked up to see a short, stocky man in a tight dark suit standing by the fire escape. He nodded at McCormack and McCormack nodded back.

He was eight or nine quid up when he called it quits, leaving a chip for the croupier and another for the waitress. He drifted through to the restaurant. An elegant, ponytailed waiter with a Geordie accent took his order. McCormack was suddenly hungry when his steak and chips arrived. He cubed the pinkish meat, puddled the salty chips in the mix of blood and gravy, mopped it up with garlic bread. His carafe of red was almost gone when the man in the tight dark suit pulled out the chair opposite and sat down.

'Gerry.' McCormack finished dabbing his mouth, dropped the napkin on his plate. 'How's tricks?'

'Ach, struggling on, Duncan. This a professional visit? Or you just got some money you're needing to lose?'

McCormack laughed. 'I'm a few quid up, believe it or not. Drink?'

'Not on duty, thanks.'

'Right. I'll get to the point, Gerry. Helen Thaney,' McCormack said. 'How well did you know her?'

Gerry's head swivelled sharply on the short neck. 'You think I was fucking her? Who told you that?'

'Whoa, Gerry. Jesus! I just mean, did you know her well?'

Gerry was still frowning. He was a former cop – sergeant with the Fraud Squad – and you never lost the look. The truculent mouth. Smell of shit in the nostrils.

'What is it you're asking me, Dunc? Last I heard, you've got the guy in Barlinnie. What's the interest in Helen?'

McCormack shook his head. 'No particular reason. I'm just trying to get a sense of her frame of mind, before she died. I spoke to her colleague, Denise Redburn. She says Helen was nervous, the weeks before she died. Says she was acting like she knew she was in trouble.'

'Frame of mind?' Gerry said. 'Frame of mind? And Denise Redburn? She'd tell you the Pope's a Prod if there was something in it for her.'

'So she's just wrong then?'

Gerry rolled his shoulders. The fat bottom lip protruded. 'I don't know. Helen was Helen. She wasn't what you'd call the nervous type. She sometimes got a bit jumpy when her ex came in. But, fuck, I get a bit jumpy when her ex comes in. Everyone gets jumpy when her ex comes in.'

'Her ex?' McCormack failed to stop the tightening in his voice. He tried again, leaning back in his chair, casual, a man shooting the breeze with a former colleague. 'Who might her ex be, Gerry?'

The short man was grinning. Then he wasn't. 'Jesus Christ,

340

you're serious? You really don't know? McGlashan, Dunc. She was fucking John McGlashan. For about two fucking years. What, youse didn't think it was important? Youse didn't think to check the boyfriends?'

IV
THE DOOR WE NEVER OPENED

'Robes and furred gowns hide all.'

King Lear, 4.6.181

46

McCormack sat at his desk in the squad room. He had a photograph in front of him, a headshot of John McGlashan. This was the man Helen Thaney had been eager to avoid, the man she had her landlady looking out for, the big black-haired fucker with the bushy 'tache. John McGlashan. Her ex-boyfriend. The reason she feigned headaches, the reason she ducked out of work in the middle of a shift.

But why was she scared? McCormack flexed the photo. Maybe McGlashan was jealous. But Helen was his fancy piece, not his wife. And how had it ended? McGlashan, you had to assume, was the ditcher, not the ditchee – it was hard to envisage anyone mustering the chutzpah to give the city's top gangster his marching orders. But he could still be jealous. Probably he thought of Helen as belonging to him. He was angry at the new relationship. Maybe warned her to end it.

But would he kill her out of jealousy? It seemed thin. It seemed wild, way too wild and reckless, even for Glash. And anyway, wouldn't he lean on the boyfriend first? Threaten to have *his* legs broken. *Have* his legs broken. Unless the boyfriend was someone he couldn't touch? And he'd clearly been good to Helen, at least in some ways: the bank manager had got back to McCormack that morning to say there was upwards of two thousand pounds in Helen's account.

McCormack's train of thought was halted by the door smacking back against the wall as Goldie burst into the squad room, waving a sheet of paper.

'Volvo, says he. Volvo, my arse.' He parked his backside on McCormack's desk. The DVLC had phoned that morning: the previous vehicle registered to Ronald William Bickett was a 1963 Ford Consul 375. White. 'It's him. Has to be. Let's get him in.'

The following morning Nancy Scullion was standing at the window of her Scotstoun flat, waiting for a squad car to take her to St Andrew's Street for the identity parade.

She fiddled with the clasp on her handbag as she looked out on to the street. You could do three hundred parades and still have a knot in your stomach. At times like these she found herself talking to Marion. *Is my make-up all right, Em? You always used to tell me when I'd drawn the eyebrows too high. Maybe this is the one, Em. Maybe this time we'll get him.*

A car turned into the street and Nancy's hands bunched into fists, but it was a neutral blue Cortina and it sailed on up towards the junction. When the car passed she noticed a man standing across the street, smoking a cigarette. Something in his manner made her draw back a little from the window. He was a big man, burly, in a reefer jacket with the collar turned up. She could see the shine on his pointed shoes from where she stood. She watched him drop his cigarette to the pavement and put it out with a twist of his foot and the shiny shoe seemed to wink at her. The man plunged his hands in the pockets of his jacket and rolled his shoulders. She had the feeling that he was studiously avoiding looking her way.

She left her handbag on the windowsill and crossed to the

living-room press where she took down a bottle of vodka. She gulped two shaky capfuls. When she got back to the window a squad car was turning leisurely into the street and when it drew up in front of her building she raised her head and caught the eye of the man opposite. He was looking straight at her with a look of half-amused malevolence and as she turned away from the window she saw him start to cross the street.

Normally she would have clipped down the stairs to meet the squad car at the closemouth but today she stayed in her hallway with her eye to the front door's fisheye until one of the uniforms came stumping into view. As they crossed together to the squad car she raked the street with her eyes but the man in the reefer jacket was gone.

Twenty minutes later she was shown into an interview room at St Andrew's Street, where four men in blue suits and two in brown stood in a line with their hands behind their backs.

She started down the line of men with her handbag over her arm, like the queen inspecting the troops. She peered with hopeless intensity into each impassive face. She had been through this routine so often that she doubted her ability to recognize the Quaker. All the faces that weren't the Quaker's, all the nearly noses and not-quite-right eyes and the lips that were too full or not quite full enough and the teeth too straight or too crooked had overlain her memory of the face. Now when she thought of the Quaker it was the artist's impression she saw, the matinee-idol features, the smart side-parting, the curl of a smile on the lips. The original face had gone.

Except it hadn't. For here, as the fourth man straightened up at her approach, as his jaw clenched under her gaze – here, like a ghost stepping out from her dreams of that endless January night, as time slowed and the scarred walls seemed to dissolve away – here was the Quaker. Here was William from the dance hall. The hair was longer and the goatee beard was new, but the arrogant eyes were the same and the thin, pitiless lips, and just the build of the man, how he carried himself. She was smiling now, smiling in recognition, and the man's mouth flexed in a truculent frown. McCormack was at her elbow, breathless.

'Do you recognize this man? Is this the man you are pointing out?'

Nancy nodded. She never took her eyes from Bickett's face.

'Hello, William,' she said.

Flett was not impressed. 'When I said you could work on this in your own time, McCormack, I meant as in get it out of your system. Not rip up the whole fucking case. Take us back to square one.'

'Sir.' McCormack was out his seat, his hand held high like a preacher in a rapture. 'Sir, listen. You see this guy, you see his face just the once, you'll know. It's the face from the posters. Nancy Scullion's already ID'd him. This is the Quaker.'

Flett was scowling. 'First off, McCormack, sit down. Sit the fuck down!' McCormack sat, collapsed with a sigh, hands flopping between his knees. Flett rapped his knuckles on the desk. 'Now. What exactly is it you want, Detective?'

'Two bodies, sir. Not even Flying Squad. Uniforms. Two bodies to go through the Housing Office records for '67, '68. They'll tell us if the women had applied for a house. They'll tell us who was handling their applications. Then we'll know for sure.'

Flett tossed his glasses on the desk, drew his hands down his face, massaging his eyelids. He put his glasses back on and shook his head. 'Jesus Christ, McCormack. Levein's going to love this. It's his bloody retirement do next week.'

'Levein? The *Record*'ll love it, sir. The *Daily Express*. We

348

knew Paton wasn't the Quaker and we let him go down? Let him swing, maybe? Come off it, sir.'

'You've got Goldie on this with you?'

'Aye.'

'Fuck. Fine. I'll give you Walker and Kerr. Two shifts. Get the thing done.'

47

Bickett sat at the desk in the interview room, his hands pressed together between his knees. It had been five days since they quizzed him at Clive House. Not even a week, but he sat there in the cold light of the bare white room like a changeling. He'd taken sick leave from work. Face grey. The buoyant blond hair hung in waxy strands, darkened by grease. The tight goatee had blurred into the stubble of his unshaved cheeks. The smell that gusted from the neck of his grubby white polo-shirt, where a crucifix hung on a thin gold chain, was only partly the smell of unwashed skin. It was also the coppery rinse of despair, the smell of a life collapsing in on itself.

When Goldie asked him about the housing scam, Bickett seemed to slump with relief. He was grateful to be talking it out, putting the shape of a story to the chaos inside him. He confirmed the logistics of the thing, clawing all the while at a pink scurf of eczema in the crook of his elbow.

Walter Maitland was the go-between. People would approach Maitland to see if McGlashan could get them a house. Once they'd forked out their fifty quid, McGlashan would give the OK. Maitland would pass the name on to Bickett, who would bump them up the list, allocate them the next available house. Of the fifty quid, Maitland took ten; McGlashan and Bickett got twenty apiece. It had worked beautifully for the past three or four years. It got so that it didn't seem like a scam at all, Bickett said. It was more like the money was a professional fee for services rendered, or a bonus for improved work rate. Kind of like a tithe, Bickett said.

He stopped then and asked for a cigarette, but the desire to talk was still bright in his eyes, in the plump shine of his lower lip, slick with spittle. They both knew, McCormack and Goldie, without exchanging so much as a look, as they fumbled for the cigarettes and matches, they both knew that the trick now was not to spook him. Just let it come.

Goldie lit Bickett's cigarette with the solicitude of a lover and he waved the match out and set it gently in the ashtray and said softly, as if it was an afterthought, 'Tell us about the women, William.'

Bickett smiled shyly and glanced up from under his lids. Nodding, as if somehow this was a shrewd and penetrating question, not the only and obvious gambit. Goldie had been taking it all down in a notebook and Bickett waited until Goldie had turned a new page and nodded that he was ready.

It started by accident, Bickett said. He'd been showing a new flat to a prospective tenant, a pretty dark-haired woman in her late twenties, and her desire for the flat was so strong and so naked that it struck him, as a kind of neutral observation, that she would do almost anything to get it. He didn't even have to make much of a move. He just stood a little too close to her as she leaned into an airing cupboard and held his ground as she turned and put her startled palms on his chest and absorbed the heightened voltage of his gaze. Next thing they had collapsed like stepladders on to the bare mattress and were tugging at each other's clothes.

Bickett stopped again. He was fiddling with the gold chain round his neck, lifting and dropping the glinting crucifix.

He was still William Bickett, McCormack thought. He was still William Bickett at this stage in the story. But how did he become the Quaker, the face on the posters, the man we've been chasing for nearly two years?

'So this became a regular thing?' McCormack asked. 'With other clients as well?'

Bickett nodded. Someone stamped past in the corridor, whistling loudly and tunelessly. They waited for the footsteps to recede.

'But it didn't just keep going,' McCormack said, nodding. 'It turned into something else, William. How did that happen?'

They had heard back that morning from Walker and Kerr, the uniforms who'd been working through the Housing Department's records. Both Ann Ogilvie and Marion Mercer had been interviewed by William Bickett.

Bickett shrugged, balanced his goofy, stupid-me smile on his upturned palms. 'I told him.'

'You told who?' McCormack was practically whispering now. 'Who did you tell, William?'

'I told McGlashan. He was into it. Man, he kept asking for details. He wanted to come along. The next time I met one of the women.'.

McGlashan! McCormack tried to keep the excitement out of his voice. McGlashan was the killer. McGlashan was the Quaker. The real Quaker. The one who did the killing.

'What did you tell him, William?'

'I told him it was too risky. I told him I could lose my job.'

'But he kept on at you.'

'He said I could lose my job if I *didn't* let him come. He meant – well, the thing we had going with the housing allocations. He could tell my boss.'

352

McCormack nodded. Telling your boss would be the least of it. Once you'd been stupid enough to let McGlashan get something on you, it was over. He would squeeze you like a lemon, suck you dry, shuck the rind.

'So how did you do it?'

'He worked out this scheme. I would take them out for the evening and then take them home. I knew their addresses, of course – we had them on file. I would phone him at some point in the night and tip him off, so that he'd be waiting. Usually there was somewhere nearby – a derelict building, a patch of waste ground – where I could bring the women. Then – well, I'd pretty much leave him to it.'

And now Goldie and McCormack did share a look. Bickett caught it and held up his hands.

'But I didn't; it wasn't me who—'

His glance was bouncing between the two cops.

'You didn't know what would happen? To the women?'

'No! Nothing *did* happen to the women – not at first. I think he maybe gave them money. After he'd done his business.'

'After he'd raped them, you mean.'

'They were Magdalenes, officer. Women of low morals. They wouldn't have needed much persuasion. But, look: I didn't know he was going to start killing them. I had no idea that would happen. But when he killed the first one – well, I was an accomplice. I couldn't go to the polis now. I was as bad as he was.'

'You're talking to the polis now,' Goldie said mildly.

'Plus, once he'd killed the first one. I mean, if he killed the women, he would have no problem killing me. He'd have killed me if he had to. I'd have been next. You don't know what he was like. He wasn't right. In the head, I mean: he wasn't right.'

'You had no choice,' McCormack said. He spoke the words

353

in a flat tone, like a quotation, and they hung in the air for a moment.

'Tell us about the women,' Goldie said. 'What kind of women did you go for?'

'Good-looking women. He liked them dark. Youngish. Single mums, mostly. Needy.' He spread his hands. 'Desperate.'

'And bleeding.'

Bickett slumped a little. The tip of his tongue was wearing a groove in the centre of his bottom lip.

'How did that work, William?'

'I don't know. It was a thing. He had a thing about it. I told you: he wasn't right. He wanted me to wait until, you know. I mean I knew because I was . . . Well.'

'You were shagging them, William. Yes. We know.'

'So as soon as I found out it was time, it was their bad week, that's when he wanted me to set it up.'

'And why the Barrowland?'

Bickett straightened up. 'Easy. It was a place I never went. No one would recognize me. And after the first one, it was like, I don't know, a kind of superstition. We didn't get caught the first time. If I go to the same place, go through the same routine, maybe we won't get caught now.'

The slight curl of his thin upper lip was the poster come to life.

'And the earlier women. Where did you take them?'

'Different places. Wherever they fancied.'

'And you were never called in?' Goldie was shaking his head. 'You were never questioned till now?'

'No, no. I *was* questioned. When the artist's impression came out. I mean, it was pretty obvious it looked like me. People were pointing me out in the street, staring at me on buses. Two policemen came to my door one night. I told them I'd never been in the Barrowland in my life. Nothing else happened. I got a card – you know, from the Chief Constable.'

'Oh, I know,' McCormack said. '*The holder is certified as not being the Quaker*. Who got you that?'

'I don't know. McGlashan organized it, I think.'

Of course he did, thought McCormack. McGlashan's handler would have taken care of everything.

'How would McGlashan do a thing like that?' McCormack asked quietly, as though wondering to himself. 'He must know someone in the police. What was the name of the policeman?'

Bickett glanced up sharply, as though he'd said too much. 'I wouldn't know about that,' he said. 'I didn't have anything to do with that.'

Goldie looked up from his writing. 'So why did he stop?'

'Sorry?'

'McGlashan. If Marion Mercer was the last one, that's nearly nine months. How come he stopped?'

Bickett looked from one to the other. 'Well, I don't think he did. I mean, he stopped here. It was getting too risky. But he took a lot of trips. Down to London, mainly, far as I know.'

McCormack nodded. McGlashan had contacts with some of the big London firms. That was well known. Now they would need to contact the Met, get them to look at unsolved rapes, murders. And look at their own unsolveds, from before Jacquilyn Keevins.

McCormack got to his feet, buttoning his jacket. They were finished here, for the time being at least. Goldie stowed the notebook in the inside pocket of his jacket.

'Will it go in my favour?' Bickett was saying. Goldie and McCormack were at the door now and they both turned, looking down at the grey face with its eyebrows hitched in anticipation, a tragic half-smile on the sinuous lips. 'I mean, that I told you all this.'

McCormack walked back the four or five yards, leaned down over Bickett. 'You set up three women to get killed, William. You're an accomplice in three— Jesus Christ, man. *Will it go in my favour?*'

He spun on his heel and joined Goldie in the corridor. They walked down the hallway in silence.

48

McCormack stood at the mirror, looking at his shoulders in the dark blue suit, at the knot of his Paisley pattern tie, at the cleft in his freshly shaved chin. The face in the mirror stared back. He looked like death. He looked scarcely less dead than the faces on his living room wall. He tugged his lower eyelids down, exposing the livid red flesh, stuck out his green-coated tongue. He lifted a bottle of mouthwash and unscrewed the cap and tipped it back to gargle.

It was Peter Levein's big night, the evening of his retirement do. The whole Flying Squad was invited, along with most of the city's CID. A dinner dance in the ballroom of the Albany Hotel. Live band. Fifteen tables. A seating plan.

McCormack's date for the night was Nancy Scullion. She was picking him up in a taxi. His buzzer rang and he frowned – *Jesus, she's early* – but when he lifted the handset it was Robert Kilgour.

'I'm going out,' McCormack told him. 'I'm on my way out the door.'

'You'll want to see this,' Kilgour said. 'Trust me.'

McCormack pressed the button.

Kilgour had an envelope of photographs, processed by a mate in the Partick Camera Club. Photographs that featured Bobby Stokes.

'Yeah?' McCormack felt his mouth drying up, lips sticking to his gums.

'He's meeting his handler,' Kilgour said. 'At least, I'm assuming it's his handler. You'll know better than I would.'

Kilgour took three glossies out of the envelope and set them down on the coffee table.

'Hotel out past Newton Mearns. They met there last night. I got my mate to print these today.'

The photos showed two men coming out of a doorway on to what looked like a gravel drive. The doorway had a little upturned V of slated roof, like a church porch, and some kind of pot-plant to one side. The men were walking one behind the other, each holding a set of car keys. The one in front – slight and dark – was Bobby Stokes. Behind him, with his head down in the first photo and raised in the other two, where he seemed to stare straight at the camera, bouncing his keys, was Peter Levein.

'You recognize him?' Kilgour asked. 'Do you know the guy?'

'I think so.' McCormack shuffled the photos together and thrust them back into the envelope.

Jesus Christ. Levein. Holy fucking Christ.

'Did I come good then? Did I do well?'

'What? Yeah, that's brilliant, Robert. Here.' McCormack dug his wallet out of his hip pocket, took out a ten.

'Away ye go!' Kilgour had his hands up. 'I'm doing this for the pure love of it. The fucking hate of it. I want this bastard caught.'

McCormack shook the note. 'Don't be daft, Kilgour. You've earned it.'

Kilgour clicked his tongue; his fist closed round the money.

Kilgour was long gone when the taxi arrived. McCormack heard its horn in the street and clattered down the stairs with his raincoat over his arm.

Nancy's head was poking out of the taxi's side window, all teeth and eyelashes. She was still excited about Bickett. All the way into town she talked it out, how she couldn't believe it was him, how she never thought she'd see him again, or recognize him if she did.

At the hotel they were shown straight to one of the big round tables, where dinner – oxtail soup, then a choice of chicken or steak – was about to be served. When the pudding plates were cleared away (Black Forest gateau or sherry trifle), the dance band struck up, a twelve-piece with a slim, dapper bandleader called Harry Margolis who leaned in to croon a few lines now and then before spinning back to conduct the band with great fluid swipes of his arms. McCormack danced a couple of numbers with Nancy and then headed for the bar to refresh their drinks.

Most of the men had gathered by the bar. They looked ill at ease with their wives and girlfriends present. They looked *ashamed*, was what they looked. Ashamed and resentful, as if the women in the room could read their collective thoughts, know how they were when they all got together. They kept their noses in their drinks, spoke out of the sides of their mouths. Nobody knew where Levein was. The guest of honour was making them wait.

McCormack spoke briefly with some guys he used to know in the C Div days. Then he just stood, happy enough, leaning on the bar, drinking whisky. Nancy was dancing with George Cochrane.

'There he is.' McCormack recognized the deep, indulgent tones. He took a gulp of his whisky and turned.

Peter Levein was holding his hand out, stiff-armed, for McCormack to shake. But McCormack wasn't looking at the hand. He was staring at the pattern on Levein's jacket sleeve, the intersecting black-and-white staves that seemed to buzz and throb, that seemed to stand somehow clear of their backdrop, floating free on a plane of their own.

Prince of Wales check.

McCormack limply gripped the chief's hand as a chain of little explosions went off in his head.

The jacket on the chair-back in Helen Thaney's living-room was Levein's.

Levein was Helen Thaney's lover.

McGlashan was Helen Thaney's ex, so Levein was connected to Glash.

Levein was Glash's handler.

The indigo passport that Denise Redburn saw was a warrant card, not a passport.

He raised blank eyes to Levein's grinning face.

'You still with us, Detective?' Levein snapped his fingers before McCormack's face. 'You're miles away, son. I thought you teuchters could handle the drink. Away home and have a rest. You've earned it. We all have.'

The whisky sloshed in McCormack's glass as Levein clapped his shoulder. Then the big man was moving away, torso flexing under the jacket, the black-and-white parallels stirring like snakes.

McCormack subsided against the wall for a minute. Then he set his glass down on a nearby table and staggered out.

49

Things were slipping away. You reached this stage in a case sometimes, when all the strands and ramifications got on top of you and what you needed to do, above all, was just act. Do something. Make an intervention and see what happened.

McCormack had gone to Flett and told him what he knew. Not about Levein – he still didn't know if he trusted Flett that far – but about Bickett and Nancy Scullion and Helen Thaney and McGlashan. Flett had agreed to a raid, signed out revolvers for Goldie and McCormack.

McCormack also told Goldie. He told Goldie everything. Levein and Helen Thaney. Levein and McGlashan.

So now McCormack was crossing the river in the purple pre-dawn in the back of a Black Maria with Goldie at his side and four uniforms on the bench-seat opposite, the faint buttery glow from the streetlights sliding across the buttons of the tunics, the barrels of the Webley 38s. Flett had tried to get them the old Enfield 303s but the brass had demurred at the notion of rifles. This wasn't a national emergency: it was an alarm call for a hoodlum.

The van turned into St Andrew's Drive, heading west. They could see almost nothing from the back of the van but McCormack pictured the castles of the wealthy sliding past in the darkness, the blond sandstone cliffs, the chequerboards of massive ashlar blocks, the crow-stepped gables, the turrets and spires.

They were in McGlashan's street now, purring along under the big black silhouettes of trees, low branches scraping the roof. Then the van stopped with a jerk. Muffled curses up front, McCormack and the others craning to see through the mesh to the front windscreen. Something wrong here. What was happening?

The uniforms raised their pistols. The driver leaned back to hiss at them through the mesh. What was he saying?

'It's a squad car. There's a bloody squad car in the driveway.'

They pulled into the driveway anyway, piled out of the back, boots mashing on the gravel. Then they stood around looking at each other. They knew to the split second what they should have been doing, but now the plan had changed and they were all at sea. McCormack stamped up the path to the front door, cursing under his breath. Some arsehole had jumped the gun, some uniformed dickhead had queered the whole pitch. A uniform was coming down the drive towards him and McCormack's rage was so high that it took him some time to register the stiff awkwardness of the man's movements, the catch in his voice.

'This your doing, Constable? Who the fuck authorized this?' McCormack had his card out, shoving it in the uniform's face.

'Authorized what, sir? A man's been shot. It came over the radio. We just got here ten minutes ago.'

'Shot?' McCormack's anger was ebbing, but not quickly enough to catch up with his voice. 'What you on about, man? Who's been shot?'

'He's inside, sir. In a kind of study. Like a library. Ambulance is on its way, but I don't think . . . I mean, it looks like he's gone.'

There was the tell-tale smell in the hallway, the peppery whiff of cordite. McCormack followed the constable through to the back of the house. A dog was whining behind one of the doors, a high keening note.

'A neighbour heard shots, called it in. It's in here, sir.' The constable led him into a large, book-lined room where another uniform was leaning over a body sprawled in front of the fireplace. The uniforms stepped back to give McCormack room.

It was McGlashan all right. Even with his left cheek blown off and his eye-socket shattered, there was no mistaking the down-turned mouth and the blue-black hair. This was the face that had stared down at McCormack from the pinboard at St Andrew's Street.

He had fallen backwards and looked to have swept an arm along the mantelpiece as he fell. A couple of framed photos were lying face down beside the body and an elaborate porcelain beer-stein lay smashed in the fireplace, its pewter handle still fixed to the lid.

He was wearing pleated trousers in a rich blue mohair, a dull sheen on the nap; a creamy white shirt, sleeves folded to the elbow; tasselled black loafers in high-gloss patent-leather. There was a gold bracelet on the right wrist. The left hand was missing two fingers – he must have raised his hand to shield his face when the gun was raised.

Two whisky glasses were sitting on a coffee-table, one almost full, the other nearly empty. On a shelf above an L-shaped bar in the corner of the room stood a dozen or so bottles of whisky: Glenfiddich, Glen Grant, the cream-and-gold badge of a Macallan.

'What about family?' McCormack asked the nearest uniform. 'Is there nobody else in the house?'

'It's empty, sir. We've been through the rooms.'

The ambulance arrived while McCormack was standing over the body. Two lumbering paramedics in clumpy boots and overalls. The older one blew a tired raspberry. 'Jesus. No point even checking a pulse. This one's for the Fiscal.'

They clumped back out. McCormack heard the ambulance reversing on the gravel, pulling away. It sounded as though the van was following it.

The low whistle at his elbow was Goldie. 'I sent the soldiers away,' he said. 'Told them we'd get a lift in the squad car. Fucking hell.' He shook his head. 'Should have come for him sooner, shouldn't we? Soon as Bickett named him.'

'Well. We're here now.'

Goldie drew him aside, away from the uniformed constables. 'It's not a "gangland slaying", as the *Record* would have it. Is it?'

'Unless you treat your rival gangster to a crystal goblet of single malt before he plugs you then, no, I think we can discount that possibility.'

The two uniforms went out to the squad car to use the radio, report back to base. D Div, McCormack thought neutrally; Shawbridge Street.

'You think it's him?' Goldie was standing at the window, his back to the mess beside the fireplace.

'Of course it's him. He's cleaning things up. Putting his house in order.'

McCormack went over and joined him at the window. Daylight was breaking over Rutherglen, the streetlights flickering off. This was how it ended. No fanfare or great celebration. Just the city rousing itself to another day, going about its business. The Procurator Fiscal would be on his way. The pathologist too. There would be back-slapping in the police offices of the city when the news filtered through. But there would be no trial, no showpiece conviction. The Quaker was dead. But the man who'd killed him was very much alive.

50

The knock came when McCormack was fixing himself a drink, so he wasn't fully sure that he had heard it. He stopped stock still in the little kitchen, holding up the square whisky bottle like a man in an advertisement. His building had a door-entry system, so either this was a neighbour, or someone who'd gotten into the building as one of the residents was leaving. Someone from Levein? Was it Levein himself? Was McCormack next on his list?

The knock came again – light but sharp and clear, a measured double tap. McCormack put the bottle down.

The spyhole framed a red-haired woman in a light-coloured raincoat. When he opened the door he saw that she was carrying a small suitcase and that the shoulders of her raincoat were spotted with rain.

'Are you McCormack?' she asked him. Her face looked pinched and pale. 'Are you Inspector Duncan McCormack?'

She glanced down at the nameplate, which he had never bothered to change. Though he owned the flat now, his mail still came 'c/o Beggs'.

'I'm McCormack.'

'I need to see you. I need to talk.'

He stepped aside to let her through and followed her hips and spiked heels.

'Can I get you a drink?' McCormack said. He felt himself at a disadvantage, in his undershirt, suit trousers and stocking feet before this woman in heels and a belted raincoat.

'You can,' she said. 'If it's not just for decoration, I'll have a spot of that.' She nodded at the whisky bottle that McCormack had left on the coffee table when he answered the door.

He fixed two large whiskies and she took hers in both hands and gulped the first third of it down.

'Excuse me just a moment.' McCormack went through to his bedroom to put on a shirt and step into his slip-ons. When he came back she had taken off her raincoat. She was wearing an emerald silk blouse and a straight black skirt. Her drink was finished.

McCormack tipped some more whisky into her glass and sat down across from her.

The woman was thirtyish. A hard face, sharp-featured. Curtain of blond hair shading one eye. Good-looking, he supposed, in a carefully made-up way. She was gripping her glass as if she was trying to crush it, and breathing through her nose, but something close to mischief fizzed in her eyes.

Her face looked familiar but it was the voice – light, with an almost Highland softness – that made him wonder if she was from home, the younger sister of one of his old Balla schoolmates, maybe, seeking out a hometown polis in her hour of big city trouble.

'Do we know each other?' he asked her, crossing his legs. 'You look familiar. Where do you live?'

'I don't,' she said, and the sparkle was back in her eyes as she watched him over the rim of her glass.

The accent wasn't Highland, not exactly.

'You mean you've just moved to the city?' He glanced at the suitcase, tucked neatly into the side of the sofa. 'You haven't found somewhere to stay yet?'

'No.' She set her glass neatly down on the coffee table. 'I mean that I'm dead.'

McCormack nodded. It was a mark of how unflustered he was that his first response was to think, *Not Highland: Irish.*

He sipped his whisky.

'You don't look too bad,' he said. 'All things considered.'

'Thank you. I don't feel too bad. Of course, I've been in excellent hands. You yourself investigated my murder.' She craned round in her seat. 'I wouldn't be surprised to see my picture up there. On your wee wallchart.'

She turned back to face him. Above her head, on the strip of wallpaper pasted inside out on the living-room wall, was her name, like a caption.

McCormack sipped his drink.

'You knew all along,' she said. 'Didn't you?'

'I had an idea,' he said. 'When the PM report showed track marks on one arm. Plus the dyed hair. And what he did to the face.'

'Don't talk about it.'

'Who was she, Helen?'

Helen Thaney looked away towards the window. 'I don't know her name,' she said. 'She was a prostitute. She worked in a brothel in Dennistoun. Peter always said we could have passed for sisters. That's what gave him the idea.'

For the next hour he listened to Helen Thaney's story, filling her glass when it emptied, lighting her cigarettes. She'd come over from Ireland, she said, in '63, glad to see the back of it. Her mother had died when she was eleven and her father couldn't cope. He spent all his nights in the pub, left Helen to see to the wee ones. When she was fifteen she got pregnant by a neighbour's son. Her father sent her away to the nuns, to a laundry run by the Good Shepherd Sisters, a kind of slave-camp for wayward girls. She bought her way out in '63, took the boat for Glasgow.

It was when she started working at the casino that she met McGlashan. He took her out a couple of times, bought her Oysters at Rogano's. He set her up in a flat in a terrace on Great Western Road, overlooking the Botanic Gardens. He would come by to see her two or three times a week.

'And did you know?' McCormack asked her.

'You mean did I know he was killing women? No. I knew he was bad news. I knew he was a selfish arrogant prick. I knew he was a gangster. But that's all.'

It lasted for two years. When McGlashan finished it he undertook to cover the rent for another six months. But by that time Helen had hooked up with Peter Levein.

She knew Levein from the casino, where he lost middling sums at baccarat with good-natured regularity. Also, the Claremont had private rooms and McGlashan would some-times meet Levein in one of those.

'And how did Glash take it? I mean when you started seeing Levein?'

'Was he jealous, you mean? I think he was relieved, if anything. Glad to get me off his hands.'

'Had McGlashan told you about Levein? What the relation-ship was?'

It seemed important to McCormack that he gave Helen Thaney no pointers here, that she describe the arrangement just as she understood it.

'John told me nothing. About anything. Ever. Peter was different.'

'How was he different?'

She swept the hair from her eyes. 'John was just looking for

369

someone to fuck. Peter, God help him – Peter was in love. He wanted to trust me, he said. Confide in me. He told me things about John. I think he wanted to put me off. If I ever thought about going back.'

Go back? Why would you go near McGlashan in the first place? McCormack wanted to ask. He nodded, motioned for her to go on.

'He told me how it worked,' she said. 'John provided intel on other gangsters, other crews around the city, the fringe players in his own outfit. He had contacts all over the city, he had guys in all the pubs – South Side, East End, out west – that would tell him stuff. John would feed all this to the CID. In return, he got free rein on the Northside. The cops let him do what he liked.'

'They let him kill women. Did Levein tell you McGlashan was the Quaker?'

She looked at him through her hair. 'No,' she said. 'Not exactly. He came to see me one night. Late. One in the morning, maybe two. I was living in Dennistoun by then. I'd never seen him in such a state. He was shaking, freaking out. I poured him a whisky and he could hardly hold the glass. He kept pacing about, babbling about McGlashan. I put him to bed. Of course the next day I saw the papers.'

'Jacquilyn Keevins?'

She was nodding. 'Jacquilyn Keevins. And he was so full of remorse. It was "poor woman" this and "if I'd only done that". But of course there was nothing to be done. He was in so thick with McGlashan that he couldn't do anything. He'd taken McGlashan's money. He'd used McGlashan's hoors. God knows what else. So Peter just had to live with his conscience. Until he reconciled himself. Which never took long.'

Her eyes were wet with hatred. A sharp burst of rain drilled the window and her shoulder jumped spasmodically.

'So what went wrong?' McCormack asked.

'McGlashan started getting ideas. He got it into his head that I knew.'

'That you knew he was the Quaker?'

She nodded. She tried to take a drink but her glass was empty. McCormack was frowning.

'But how did you know?' he asked.

'That McGlashan was the Quaker? I've already told—'

'No. That he knew you knew.'

'He told Peter.' She shrugged. 'He wanted Peter to— Well. He wanted Peter to take care of it.'

'He told Peter to kill you?'

'Otherwise he would do it himself.'

Another gust of rain spattered the window.

'And that's when you got the idea.'

'It was Peter's idea.'

McCormack rolled his whisky round the glass. 'And that night at the Barrowland. The different men. The fight on the dance floor.'

'Yeah. That was Peter's idea. He wanted me to make sure I was noticed. Make sure people remembered me. That way there'd be less chance of questions.'

'When the body was found. And you went along with it.'

'I didn't have any choice. Don't you see? It was the only way I could be safe.'

McCormack nodded. The suitcase was poking out from beside the sofa.

'How safe do you feel now?'

She had her forehead in her palm at this point and she kept it there, shaking her head, saying nothing.

'So what are you doing now?' McCormack shifted in his chair. 'Why are you telling me this?'

'I think he's going to kill me,' she said simply, looking

371

up. 'Peter. He's getting rid of everyone who knows what happened. Everyone who knows the truth. He killed John, didn't he? I'm dead already, remember; no one's about to miss me.'

'Will you testify?' McCormack said. It was the question they both knew was coming.

'I'll have to,' she said. 'I'll have to, won't I? If I want help. Look: can I use your bathroom?'

'Surely.' McCormack set his glass down. 'I'll show you where it is.'

They both stood up. They were stranded in the middle of McCormack's living-room floor when the buzzer went, a harsh, peremptory, scraping sound that drilled through everything and held them where they stood.

'It's them.' Helen clutched at McCormack's forearms. 'They must have followed me.'

'You've been here for over an hour. If they'd followed you, they'd have been here by now. We just ignore it.'

They stood and waited. The buzzer came again, a long, rude, jeering ring. They clung to each other in the middle of the room, as if the sound was a strong wind. The ringing seemed to rise and fall in growling heaves, like a revving engine. When it finally stopped, McCormack found he could still hear it. But what he took to be the echo was the faint, hollow drill of the other buzzers being sounded in turn.

The click of the door-release echoed up the stairwell.

'Get through there.' He pushed her towards the bedroom, tossing her raincoat in after her. 'I'll get rid of them.'

He carried Helen's glass through to the kitchen, left it in the sink. At the last minute he remembered the suitcase at the side of the sofa and kicked it into a closet.

It was only one set of footsteps, so far as he could tell, coming up the stone stairs. He waited at the door, squinting through the spyhole. When the man came into view it was no one he recognized; big-shouldered, jowly, a ginger moustache. He rapped on McCormack's door and then shot a glance over his shoulder at the stairway.

'Were you on the job, for Christ's sake. You didn't hear your buzzer?'

'Who the fuck are you?' McCormack's hand came up to rest on the doorjamb, barring the way.

'Joe Cathro.' He held up his warrant card. 'Merrylee. You gonnae let me in?'

'Merrylee? You're far from home, Joe. Did you cross a big bridge and couldnae find your way back? What the hell do you want?'

'I'd sooner tell you inside.'

His head was bobbing around, trying to peer over McCormack's shoulder.

'I'd sooner you told me here.'

Joe Cathro touched a finger to his moustache, nodded. 'You're not making it easy, Detective.'

McCormack stepped back and went to close the door. 'You gonnae say your piece or what?'

Cathro looked behind him again. 'There's a girl,' he said. 'A woman. We think she might come round here. She's a bit unhinged. Making accusations. Just so you know.'

'Come round here? Why would she come round here? Accusations about what?'

'The Quaker stuff.' Cathro waved a vague hand in the air. 'She's got some wrong ideas. We're a bit concerned.'

'"We"? Who the fuck's "we"? I'm not "we" now?'

'Look.' Cathro shuffled his feet and set himself more squarely. 'Calm down. This is just a friendly chat.'

'Oh, I see that.' McCormack frowned. 'This is Nancy Scullion we're talking about?'

'No. Somebody else. A nutcase. She's claiming to be someone she's not. So, you know. Word to the wise.'

'You're not making much sense, Detective.'

Cathro looked at the floor, shaking his head. He rubbed a thumb along his bottom lip. Then he reached out with both hands and grabbed two fistfuls of McCormack's shirt.

'Leave it the fuck alone, McCormack. That's from right up there—' he jerked his head towards the ceiling. 'Let it fucking lie.'

Then he was off, clattering down the stairwell and McCormack closed the door and leaned against it for a moment. This place wasn't safe. It might not be safe for him but it sure as hell wasn't safe for her. Nor was Derek Goldie's. He flicked through the possibilities. Gregor Hislop? But Hislop had worked with Levein at C Div back in the day; who knew how tight they still were? In the end he settled on Kilgour. He would take Helen Thaney to Robert Kilgour's. She'd be safer in the care of a convicted sex offender who kept being forced out of his home than she would be with a CID Inspector.

51

The next morning, McCormack climbed the St Andrew's Street stairs in a mood that was oddly buoyant, even euphoric. He was doing this thing. Regardless of how it turned out, he was seeing it through. He wasn't sure what exactly he expected Levein to do, or how he himself would play it, but it felt like he was holding most of the cards and he would take it from there. There was an element of fear, of course, but what was Levein going to do – shoot him with his service revolver on the third floor of Force HQ?

Levein's secretary showed McCormack through; he'd phoned that morning to make an appointment.

'What brings you this high up, Detective?'

Levein was squeezed behind a chipped Formica desk on which a typewriter sat with its cover still on. A black Bakelite telephone at his elbow. The Prince of Wales jacket and a navy fedora were hanging on a hat-rack in the corner behind him. It was a small office, bare and shabby. The only other furniture comprised a filing cabinet, a wastepaper bucket and a moulded plastic chair on the near side of the desk. McCormack sat in it without waiting to be asked.

'Your wee message-boy came to see me last night. Joe Cathro. I thought I better check in with head office.'

Levein smiled warmly. 'Bit of a blunt instrument is our Joe. Means well, though. Do you want a cup of tea, McCormack? Coffee?'

'I'm fine, sir.'

Levein nodded, hands on the desk in front of him, fingers laced. Now that he was here, McCormack found it hard to get started. How did you tell your boss's boss, the head of the City of Glasgow CID, that you knew he was a murderer? That he'd shielded the Quaker?

'I had another visitor,' he said eventually. 'Last night.'

'You're a popular guy.'

'Not especially. This one was interesting, though. Given that I'd read about her funeral in the *Tribune*.'

Levein glanced at the door. You could see the blurred outline of his secretary through the ribbed glass, sitting at her desk in the outer office. He lowered his voice. 'You're so sure she is who she says she is?'

'Oh come on, sir.' McCormack scoffed. 'I need to pull her colleagues in from the casino to identify her?'

'Pull them in where?' Levein said quickly.

'Oh, no. There's been enough of that. She's safe, let's put it that way. And she's frightened. Frightened enough to talk. About how you knew McGlashan was the Quaker. How you let him kill those women because you were in too deep with him.'

Levein leaned back, his hands behind his head. His lips split in a gap-toothed grin. 'This is your star witness, Detective? A proven liar. Ex-hooker. A casino waitress. A woman from nowhere, no family, no history.'

'I think she's pretty credible, sir. I think her recent history's pretty interesting. And William Bickett. He's not a casino waitress or ex-hooker, from what I remember. You remember William Bickett? You got him a card from Lennox, one of these Quaker passes: *The bearer of this card is certified* etc. Remember him?'

'You can't prove that.'

'*I* can't. Not yet. But maybe someone else can. And then there's this other bloke. What's his name? Bobby something. Help me out here, sir. Bobby Stokes?'

'Robert Stokes is a police informant,' Levein said in an officious monotone. 'Anything he says is automatically suspect.'

'Really? I've got two people at least will swear he was part of the Glendinnings job. Two members of the string. You think Bobby Stokes will sit tight when he sees how things're going? When he's charged as an accessory to Queen Mary Street? When we tell him why he bought the extra boots, so you could use them to set up Paton? He'll give you up as quick as look at you. Face it, sir. This is finished.'

Levein was nodding, his bottom lip thrust out, deep creases either side of his nose. 'Fair play, McCormack. Fair play. Right enough. I shouldn't be surprised; they told me you were the business.' He cocked his head. 'I had you going, though, didn't I? For a while there. I had you going, give me that.'

'The Queen Mary stuff? You did. Where did that come from?'

Levein shrugged. 'I saw the opportunity. I noticed the date for the first one. And then the places. I'm in a local history group, McCormack. It's a bit of a hobby. I knew Queen Mary had stopped in Bridgeton. And Carmichael Lane and Earl Street fit right in. All it took was another royal reference with this last one to bait the hook, make it look like part of a series. Not everyone would have got it, though.' Levein pursed his lips and nodded. 'Not everyone would have seen it even then.'

Did he know how insulting he was being? Did he even know what he was saying? 'Seeing *through* it was the thing, sir. Not seeing it.'

'Right. Right. So what now? Let's say you're right, son. What happens now? I'm gone in a few weeks. I'm out of here anyway. What do you expect me to do?'

'I don't expect you to do anything, sir. I expect you to go to jail.'

Levein made a show of looking around him. 'I don't see the cavalry, McCormack. Where's the officers to take me down? Where's Gus Flett, at least? You haven't told anyone yet, have you?'

'I wanted to give you a chance to explain. I wanted to hear you out.'

'Is that right?' Levein held a finger up, pointed it across the desk. 'I don't think you did, though, son. I think you wanted to know what else I knew. You wanted to make sure.'

'Make sure of what?'

Levein tugged on one of the desk-drawers. For a second McCormack thought he was going to produce a gun but what landed on the desk was a flat brown oblong. Levein rested his fingertips on the envelope and slid it across the desk.

'Go ahead, son. That's yours.'

McCormack frowned. A bribe seemed beneath Levein, somehow; a foolish gesture, a misstep. They had gone beyond the stage of bribes. He lifted the card-backed envelope, let it wag between his finger and thumb to test the weight. He ran a forefinger under the lightly gummed flap and winkled his hand into the gap and felt his fingers connect with the cold, slippy surface. Were these the photos from earlier? How had he got his hands on Kilgour's photos? And then he knew. And slowly, slowly, he drew them out, glossy six-by-eights, black and white, and leafed through them, a dozen exposures, himself, more than one partner, more than one act. There was a wastepaper basket on the floor beneath Levein's desk and McCormack drew it to him and vomited smartly into it.

Levein waited for McCormack to finish wiping his mouth with a handkerchief.

'There was probably an easier way to do this. I'm sorry to be so, well, graphic. But I imagine I've made my point. I would observe, too, that regardless of the law down south, there is no Pansies' Charter in Scotland. These photographs are evidence of a criminal act. Acts. We're talking jail, Detective, basically. That's the size of it. And though you might put your evident talents to good use in that context, you wouldn't, I think, find it a very congenial experience.'

McCormack was loosening his tie, he was finding it hard to get a breath. 'How long?' he said. 'How long have you known?'

'About two years,' Levein said mildly. 'Something like that.'

'But you didn't act?'

'I'm acting now, Detective.' He waved a hand at the pictures on the desk. 'Let's say I had an inkling. I had an idea these snaps would come in handy.'

'So you knew when I got the Quaker gig? It was you who chose me, wasn't it? Flett didn't recommend me at all.'

Levein spread his hands. 'I made a suggestion.'

'And if I found anything, if I got to the truth . . .'

'But you *did* get the truth, McCormack. And you got what you wanted. You wanted John McGlashan? McGlashan's dead. The Quaker's dead. Bickett's going to jail for a very long time. So's our friend Paton, though not for as long as he thought.'

'And Helen Thaney?'

'Helen's going away. That didn't work out the way I'd hoped. But, hey, that's how it falls sometimes. I'll get over it.' He smiled his doorman's smile.

'And the woman? I don't even know her name. Do you even know her name?'

Levein nodded sympathetically. 'Mmm. And the Black Babies, McCormack – what about them? And the starving millions in Biafra? And the poor fried gooks in Vietnam. What's your point?'

There was a knock on the door and Levein's secretary poked her head in.

'That's Ken McCabe here to see you, sir.'

'Fine, Lizzie. We're just about done here.'

The door closed and Levein slid the envelope over to McCormack's side of the desk. 'You're welcome to take these away with you. I have the negatives. As you'd expect.'

'And that's it?' McCormack got slowly to his feet, he felt about a hundred years old. 'You just sail off into the sunset?'

Levein sat back in his chair, linked his hands across his belly. 'Don't get carried away, son. Look on the bright side. You get to keep your job. You get to stay out of jail. That's a pretty fair day's work, all things considered. Why don't you leave it at that?'

52

You could do what everyone else did. You could put in your shift, catch the subway home and take a shower. Hang up your suit and hat, ball your shirt and toss it in the laundry. The psst! of a tin of Export; canned laughter, stocking soles. You could divorce yourself from the human dimension, the way doctors are supposed to. Stay detached, unmoved, professional. Keep reminding yourself that your business is not with a human being but a case, a thing of fibres and footprints, timeframes and motives. A puzzle to be solved. You could draw your wages and two-putt the short fourteenth and study the luminous lime-green filaments on the dial of your alarm clock in the watches of the night. You could play the game.

A chime sounded and the No-Smoking sign and the Fasten Seatbelt sign clicked off together. McCormack flipped the lid of the ashtray in the armrest and lit a cigarette. The plane banked sharply to the left and a man in the row in front got up to use the toilet.

You could do all that. Or else you could get involved, you could let yourself feel. You could think about the families, the orphaned kids, the cold stiff sheets of municipal institutions.

You could reconstruct things from the victim's perspective. You could make up little scenarios involving the women who died, and write them down for your own edification. You could take it personally, treat it as a priesthood, treat it as a calling, not just a job.

Either way, it came down to the same thing. You failed. You let the women down. You let the men with the power do what they liked. You let the world go on in its crooked way.

The stewardess came down the aisle with her clanking trolley and everyone in front of McCormack straightened in their seats.

Or you could put it right. In your own small way, for once in your life. Give yourself something to celebrate.

McCormack ordered a large whisky. The stewardess set a paper doily on his tray, a cloudy plastic glass with two clunky ice-cubes. She put down two miniature whisky bottles, finger-thick, the square bottles with the slanted label. He cracked the seals, tipped them in with the delicacy of a Jekyll mixing his potion. The ice-cube numbed his top lip as the lovely burn slipped down.

Glasgow was slipping away, out the little elliptical window, down beyond the wing's tilting flap. A peripheral housing scheme, like rows and rows of dominoes; a patch of scrubby country. Already the wisps of white were overlying the view and now the fuselage was absorbed into the lovely cottony cloudstuff and McCormack pressed the button to tilt the seat and let his head fall back on the headrest. Behind his closed eyes he replayed it all, the last long reel of his life in Scotland.

After meeting with Levein, McCormack had gone home to Partick and crawled into bed. Levein's words had made him ill, had lain him out like flu. He put a bucket beside the bed in case he was sick again. Images flashed through his brain at

382

random: Kilgour sitting in the trough urinal; the overcoat on the stairs at the Bridgeton flat; the three-coloured sweat-stained headband of his CID fedora; Nancy Scullion's laughing face; two shinty sticks clacking together and the ball soaring high in a clear blue sky.

But the images that he tried and failed to hold at bay, the images that flared and pulsed on his bedroom ceiling, on his curtains, behind his flickering lids, were the images that had lain on Levein's desk. White flesh against foliage. A knot of limbs, a straining neck. He was fevered, he was sweating and cold, a prey to hallucinations, but one thing was clear. It was over. McCormack was over, his life as a polisman was over. Too many people knew. Kilgour, Levein, whoever Levein had told. A thing like this gets out; there's no way to keep it dark.

But if the job was finished, where was the threat? *You get to keep your job, son.* Fuck the job. *You get to stay out of jail.* Really? What about you? Do you anticipate enjoying the same privilege?

After four hours' fitful sleep he had phoned Greg Hislop. His father's old mate. The man from Balla. Greg to the rescue, good old Greg Hislop, who had slit a priest's throat – or maybe stabbed him in the heart – on his journey down occupied France.

Greg Hislop heard him out, sitting on McCormack's sofa while McCormack paced the room in bare feet and dress trousers. He asked four or five questions and listened frowningly to the answers. Then he made a phone call.

Half an hour later MacInnes arrived. James MacInnes, Levein's number two in the City of Glasgow CID, a Dunbeg boy with a long blue lugubrious chin, a doctor's manner, a dark kirk-elder's suit with the dusty gloss of a blackboard. McCormack told it again and MacInnes nodded, glancing now and then at Hislop. Then another call was made and they drove in MacInnes's car, north, to the Bearsden villa of Chief Constable Arthur Lennox.

There were things to be settled. Lennox was less surprised than McCormack expected. He was all business – *if this happens then that follows; and how do we deal with this?* – so that the central determination (a serving senior officer was to be charged with murder and accessory to murder) was rather buried in practicalities. At one point they left McCormack in the study and removed to a kind of billiard room next door. McCormack could hear them conferring in low expository tones, like the members of an appointment panel. They came back into the room wearing the same tight smile. He had got the job.

There were conditions, however. He would give a statement to MacInnes at St Andrew's Street and pass on all relevant paperwork. He would put them in touch with Helen Thaney and ensure her willingness to testify. He himself wouldn't have to testify. But he *would* have to leave. The City of Glasgow Police, naturally. But also the city. In fact, best to leave Scotland altogether. Start afresh someplace else. Maybe the Met could be an option.

McCormack shook the hands of all three men. MacInnes drove him back to Partick.

The next day, Levein was arrested. Somebody tipped off the papers and a photograph of the ex-Head of Glasgow CID with a uniformed officer gripping his bicep as he walked him to a squad car featured in the *Evening Times*.

With Levein in Barlinnie Prison, everything else would fall into place. Flett would move up to Levein's old job and somebody other than McCormack would now get the corner office at St Andrew's Street. William Bickett would go down for a long, long time and Nancy Scullion and all the other relatives would feel the better for it. Paton would be charged with the Glendinnings job and nothing else. Helen Thaney would emigrate. For Robert Kilgour there would be no retrial, no exoneration. But he would at least have a comforting thought. Of the bastards who cost him four years of his life, one was in hell and the other in purgatory.

And Derek Goldie? The buzzer rang in McCormack's flat, the night before he left. He had the suitcase open on the bed, filling its silk innards with the remnants of his Glasgow life: two suits; a handful of shirts; some underwear and paperback books. His refugee possessions.

'It's me,' the voice said.

'Hello me. Come on up.'

There was nothing to offer him, McCormack realized, but Goldie came up the stairs toting an off-licence carrier bag: a half-bottle of Bells and four cans of Export. They sat at McCormack's table and drank.

'How are they taking it then?' McCormack asked. He'd been off the grid for the past three days.

'Levein? No one's shedding too many tears, Duncan. They're containing their grief.'

'It'll stick, though, you reckon? He's down the road?'

'Oh, he's finished, Dunc. Bobby Stokes has done a deal. He'll do eighteen months in Low Moss or somewhere after he's ratted out Levein. But Levein's doing serious time.'

McCormack raised his tinnie and clacked it against Goldie's. 'And McGlashan's shitty wee empire? That'll go to the dogs now. Fun and games never stops.'

'It might do.' Goldie nodded. 'There again. I hear Maitland's taking over.'

'Maitland?' McCormack paused the tinnie at his lips. 'Walter Maitland'll never hack it. A jumped-up bouncer.'

'You think?' Goldie was half smiling. 'I spoke to Forensics.

They matched the whisky in the glass at McGlashan's. Matched it to one of the bottles.'

McCormack's eyes narrowed. His mind went back to the big room at McGlashan's house and then to a dresser in a shabby kitchen in Cranhill. He drew his head back, half turning from Goldie. 'Glen Grant?'

'The very same.'

'Levein sent Walter Maitland to kill McGlashan?'

'Well, who knows, Duncan? There were no dabs on the glass. But who better to send?'

'The last man Glash would suspect.'

'McGlashan gone. Levein gone. Who's still standing?'

'Right.' McCormack held up his hands. 'The jumped-up bouncer.'

Goldie drained his second tinnie. McCormack waggled the half-bottle, still two-thirds full.

Nah.' Goldie scraped to his feet. 'Thanks anyway. Early start and all that. Better be getting back.'

McCormack rose too. They stood beside their chairs, shifting their feet. Goldie's hand kneaded the air as he fumbled for the words.

'I wanted to tell you,' he said finally. 'It never made any difference to me. It never changed how I felt. I wanted to say.'

'You mean you hated me just the same. Boy genius of the Flying Squad. Meddlesome prick.'

Goldie laughed. 'Something like that.' He gestured round the room. 'So what'll you do with this?'

'Rent it out,' McCormack said. 'Furnished flat. Pack my clothes up and I'm done.'

'And MacInnes has fixed you up?'

'Aye. He sorted out the transfer. Start on Monday. The bloody Met.'

'Well. Meddlesome prick should do well down there.'

They embraced then, an awkward bumping of shoulders and clapping of backs, and Goldie was off down the stairs. McCormack finished packing.

And now the noise of the plane's engines was sending him to sleep. The engines and the whisky. McCormack opened his eyes. The empties were gone. Another two miniatures stood in their place. Fresh glass, fresh ice. McCormack filled the tumbler. A mid-flight lull had settled on the cabin. Through the cold little oval at his elbow he could see the cloud cover billowing off in soft cobbles, a red sun at the horizon flaring on the wingtip. He toasted his ghost in the window's reflection and tipped back the whisky and drank.

Acknowledgements

It's a privilege to work with Jim Gill and Yasmin McDonald at United Agents, and with Julia Wisdom and Finn Cotton at HarperCollins.

Anne O'Brien is the Lionel Messi of copy editors and sees things everyone else misses.

Bob Barrowman and Alastair Dinsmor shared their knowledge of police work in 1960s Glasgow. Allan Macinnes kept me right on the legend and lore of Ballachulish. Calum MacLeod corrected my Gaelic. For help and advice of various kinds, I want to thank: Angela Bartie, Liz Cameron, Gerry Carruthers, Wendy English, Colin Gavaghan, David Goldie, Paula Hasler, Carol Jess, Stephen Khan, Peter Kuch, David McIlvanney, Hugh McIlvanney, Siobhán McIlvanney, Aidan and Robert Norrie, Andrew Perchard, Alan Roddick, Sarah Sharp, Will and Joanna Storrar, Donna Young, the Caselberg Trust and the Stuart Residence Halls Council.

Valerie McIlvanney was there every step of the way: love, as ever, to her, Andrew, Caleb, Isaac and Diarmid.